CAPTIVATED

CAPTIVATED

BERTRICE SMALL

SUSAN JOHNSON

THEA DEVINE

ROBIN SCHONE

KENSINGTON BOOKS
http://www.kensingtonbooks.com

KENSINGTON BOOKS are published by

Kensington Publishing Corp.
850 Third Avenue
New York, NY 10022

ISBN 1-57566-450-X

First Printing: September, 1999
10 9 8 7 6

Printed in the United States of America

Contents

Ecstasy

by Bertrice Small

Prologue

The tall, veiled woman in the voluminous, brocaded blue robes scanned the platform carefully. Her dark eyes moved slowly and calculatingly over each of the naked men, discarding, then flicking on to the next. Finally, she raised a gold-braceleted arm, and a fat, white beringed finger pointed. *"That one,"* she said.

"The gods! The gods!" the slave merchant half moaned beneath his breath, but then he brightened a bit. This woman was the one buyer who just might find suitable the most difficult and dangerous slave who ever had passed through his establishment. He fixed the creature with a stern look. "Step forward," he commanded. "You are to be examined."

The man looked down from his great height at the short, plump worm attempting to order him about, and considered his usual form of rebellion, which consisted of shouting and swearing in his natural tongue and intimidating those attempting to enslave him with bared teeth and fierce looks until they finally sent him back to his cell. Then, for some reason, he looked directly at the tall woman in blue. He could see nothing of her but her fine dark eyes. They were dancing with amusement, as if she could read his thoughts. He stepped forward silently, frankly intrigued. After all, he reasoned to himself, he couldn't spend the rest of his days in that stinking prison.

"What is his history?" the woman asked. Her voice was deep and very smoky. "From where did you obtain him?"

"A caravan brought him in from the west several weeks ago," the slave merchant said. "He is a barbarian, and while he speaks our tongue, I can learn nothing from him of his past, great lady.

But he is strong, as you can see, and would be suitable for your mines, or your fields."

The woman emitted a sharp bark of laughter. "Indeed," she said dryly, her gaze lingering on the slave's large genitalia, and then, "Help me onto the platform, Master Ashur, so I may better see this possible purchase."

The slave merchant signaled to his assistants, and they aided the woman in blue to climb the steps.

"Elevate him so I may see him better," the woman instructed, and a smaller platform was immediately brought for the man to mount. Now his prospective buyer began to slowly circle him, touching him here and there. The skin was healthy and fine. She ran sure hands over his well-muscled calves, feeling him start just slightly. The hands moved to his buttocks, squeezing gently, pulling the cheeks apart to determine if he was a lover of women, or a sodomite. Satisfied he preferred female flesh, she said, "Step down," facing him again, and he obeyed her. "Open your mouth for me," she instructed him quietly, and, to her surprise, he did. She peered into his facial cavity, seeing rows of white teeth. "You have all your teeth," she noted approvingly, "and they are strong and healthy. That is good." He closed his mouth, and she looked directly into his eyes. They were very blue, rimmed in thick dark lashes, and the whites about them were quite clear. "Step back up again," she said, and moved back so she might view him fully.

He was a very tall man with broad shoulders and chest. His frame was large, yet delicate. His hair was black as a raven's wing, long, but tied back. The rest of his body was fair and smooth but for the bushy thatch of midnight-dark curls between his thighs. She noted that both his hands and his feet were well shaped and elegant. His face was long, with a long, refined nose, high cheekbones and forehead, and a big, narrow mouth. A tangle of dark eyebrows rose over his oval-shaped eyes. The jaw was determined, and his square chin had a dimple in its very center. He was neither a peasant nor slave-born, the woman decided. She could scarcely believe her good fortune, but hid her delight beneath her veiled face.

Stepping directly in front of him once more, she pushed his thighs apart with a firm fist, and, reaching up, cupped his balls in her palm. She felt the faint quiver run through him, but, looking up, she saw his handsome face was totally impassive. She fondled him, mentally weighing his sex in her hand. It was heavy and well made. Releasing the pouch with their twin jewels, she took his penis in her hand, and began to work it. She had previously noted its unusually large size. Now she wanted to see exactly how large he would become, and how quickly he could be aroused.

Unable to help himself, the man's cheeks flushed to be so publicly used, but, helpless to the wickedly skillful fingers caressing him, his eyes closed and he let himself enjoy the sensations of pleasure now beginning to sweep over him. The gods! How long had it been since he had possessed a woman? He had almost thought that part of himself dead and gone, but this odd female swathed in her blue shrouding was proving otherwise. At the same time he felt ashamed at what was happening to him, and struggled to hold back, but the woman would not allow it.

"I would see the copiousness of your juices," she said softly. "Release them for me now." And then she stepped away from him.

The sultry sound of her voice was mesmerizing. He could not have helped himself if he tried. With a groan he discharged the hot seminal fluids, spattering their creaminess onto the platform below him. When the last drop had been jolted from him, the blue eyes opened. "Have I passed your trial, lady?" he murmured low and defiant.

Looking directly at him, she nodded imperceptibly, then turned to the slave merchant. "He will do, Master Ashur. What price do you put on him? Remembering that I am probably the only buyer you will find for this great barbaric beast."

The merchant swallowed hard, but common sense overcame greed. "If he were less difficult I should ask ten gold latkas, great lady, but, under the circumstances, I think five will suffice."

"Four," she replied, handing him a silken bag.

The slave merchant's fingers slowly closed about the pouch. Then he took it from her. "Going once!" he cried in a loud voice. "Going twice! *Sold to the High Procuress of Kava!*"

Chapter 1

Dagon, Prince of Aramas, watched as the blue-robed woman murmured her instructions to the slave master. Then, without a backward glance at him, she moved away. The sale was over for the day, and the slave merchant turned to Dagon.

"Do you know how fortunate you are, barbarian? That was the lady Zenaida of Kava. If you can manage to keep that vicious temper of yours under control, you will live a life of luxury servicing the women of Kava. That equipment of yours looks as if it will give a lot of pleasure." He snickered. "You are to be bathed now, and then sent to the lady's encampment. They depart tomorrow for Kava."

Dagon remained silent, and followed the merchant's assistants to the public baths, where they announced to all who would listen that the barbarian had been purchased by the High Procuress of Kava. A murmur of excitement rippled through the steamy baths as he was put into the hands of the head bath master. His companions sat down to wait for him.

"What is this place? Kava?" he asked the bath master.

"It is the fabled city of women," came the reply. "Have you never before heard of Kava? No one is certain where it is, for those who have attempted to follow the Kavan caravans claim those very caravans disappear right before their eyes, leaving not even a trace upon the sands of the desert road. Once a year their High Procuress comes to Ramaskhan looking for male slaves. *They only buy males.*

"Kava is ruled by women. It is said their wealth is endless, and their land fabulously rich and beautiful. Great shipments of gold and precious gemstones from their mines pass through our land regularly. Silk from Kavan looms is famous and greatly sought after, as is the fine light wool cloth they produce."

"How do you know it is a city of women?" Dagon asked. He wanted as much information as he could gather about these women who thought they now owned him.

"Once, a very, very long time ago," the bath master confided, "a slave escaped from Kava. He finally reached Ramaskhan. It was a long and dangerous trek. He lived but a short time afterward. Before he died, he told of the city of Kava where men serve the women inhabitants but are not permitted in the city after dark except on rare occasions. He told of a place where the male children are taken from their mothers when they reach the age of eight years. Then those boys spend the next eight years being trained as warriors. It must be true, for that is another of Kava's exports. They sell cohorts of fighting men. The absolute best mercenaries to be had."

"If no one knows where the city is," Dagon said, "how is this all accomplished?"

"At the time of the winter solstice," the bath master replied, "Kava's female warriors bring the cohorts for sale that year to the winter festival, which is held outside the gates of this city. They never have enough cohorts, of course. The demand for Kavan cohorts far outweighs the supply. Some years they bring but a single cohort, in other years, perhaps two or three. Once in my memory, they did not come to the festival at all. . . . Now, will you seat yourself, please. I wish to wash your hair, and I must pare your nails." The bath master busied himself as he continued to speak. "You are a fine figure of a man, and will undoubtedly sire many sons on the beautiful women of Kava."

Dagon said nothing more. He had learned enough. He would never see Kava, but it would make an interesting tale to tell when he escaped back to Aramas. Once home, he would slay his traitorous twin brother, Nogad, who was even now usurping his rightful place as first heir to the King of Aramas. He would use the Kavan caravan to leave Ramaskhan, and two or three days into the journey, he would disappear into the desert to make his way back home. He had two deserts, and three seas to cross, but he would regain what was rightfully his. Nogad would regret the day he crossed his elder sibling.

When Dagon had been bathed, and a fresh length of clean linen cloth had been wrapped about his loins, he was taken to the encampment of the lady Zenaida. A leather-clad woman warrior took charge of him at the camp's perimeters as the slave merchant's assistants bid him farewell, but not before making a few snide remarks regarding his amatory future. The leather-clad warrior looked scornfully at the pair. Without a word, she motioned to Dagon to follow her, leading him to the largest tent set directly in the center of the camp. She pulled back the entry flap.

"Go in, barbarian. The High Procuress awaits you," she said.

He moved slowly through the entrance. Inside, the tent was luxuriously furnished, and the blue-garbed woman, now veilless, was seated upon a small dais. She was quite beautiful despite her girth. Her skin was the color of the white jasmine flower, and looked to be as soft as silk. She had an elegant nose, and a small rosebud of a mouth.

"Come in! Come in!" The plump hand motioned him forward, the black eyes sparkled. "Sit down opposite me. Are you hungry? Of course you are," she answered her own question before he might. "I doubt the fare in Master Ashur's slave pens is either tasty or even palatable."

Half a dozen young women were setting down platters and bowls from which tasty odors were emanating. The gold goblet near his hand was filled with a fruity red wine. His nostrils visibly twitched.

"First tell me your name, and then you may eat," the lady Zenaida said. "I'm sure you already know who I am. Ramaskhan is a city of gossips," she chuckled.

"I am Dagon, Prince of Aramas," he said without hesitation, and then reached for the goblet.

"And just how did you come to be in Ramaskhan's slave markets, Dagon, Prince of Aramas?" she asked him, reaching for the bread.

"I was betrayed by my twin brother, who desired to have our

father's throne," Dagon said. He pulled a small chicken apart, and began to eat hungrily.

"You were the elder," Zenaida said.

Dagon nodded, swallowing. "By about a minute or two, lady. They say when I was born, Nogad's hand was fastened about my ankle as if he were trying to prevent me from coming into the world before he did."

"A formidable opponent," Zenaida observed. "Eat now, and then we will talk more," she told him.

He ate slowly, carefully, not allowing himself to be fully satisfied lest he make himself sick. It had been several months since he had had a decent meal. He finished the chicken, a loaf of bread, and then swallowed down a dozen oysters, liberally quaffing the red wine so that his cup was refilled twice. When a platter of fruit was offered to him, he took a peach, splitting it with his two thumbs, and eating it with a grin of delight even as the juice ran down his chin. Finally, licking his fingers clean of the peach juice, he looked directly at her. "Do you always feed your slaves so well, lady?"

"No one goes hungry in Kava," she said quietly. "It is not our way to mistreat people. *We are not men.*"

"But you need men," he remarked softly.

"They toil in the mines, in the fields, and in other capacities," she replied.

"Where will I labor?" he probed.

"You are intelligent," Zenaida answered, ignoring his innuendo. "I believe you when you tell me you are a king's son, for you have not the look or the bearing of a peasant. After I purchased you today, your ears were undoubtedly filled with all manner of salacious gossip, and some of it is true. Men are subservient in Kava, but why is that so different from other cities where women are subservient?"

"Men are superior to women," he said quickly. "We are stronger, bigger, wiser."

"Stronger and bigger in many cases I will allow, but *wiser?* No, Dagon. Men are not wiser than women, and women are the superior sex, because it is through them that the gods have chosen to reproduce our kind. Before you protest that your seed is necessary to that task, let me remind you that it is the only thing required. Your seed is useless without a woman to nurture the new life, to bring it to fruition, and to finally birth it. And when it is birthed, we nourish it with the milk from our breasts. Men have nothing with which to nourish a newborn. Without the fertile field of our bodies, your seed is worthless, Dagon. That is why women are superior.

"What do men do in this world? They start wars which kill innocents, and ruin both agriculture and commerce. And why? For more land? More wealth? To do what with? Bah! That is why Kava exists, and is ruled by women. We use men's strength, and we use their seed, both of which are positive things. Men, however, are but an auxiliary to women, and must be kept servile. That is our way. We do not cause, or go to war. We are wealthy beyond your wildest imagination because we spend our energies in making things grow by our toil. You will soon see." She smiled at him, and then took a long draught of her wine before continuing.

"In Kava we are governed by a queen. When our queen falls in love and mates, a new queen is chosen. Kalida, the queen who now rules us, has never fallen in love. She has ruled longer than any of our queens, and while she has offered to step aside so a new queen can be chosen, we cannot allow it, for it breaks with our custom. She must fall in love, and take her mate. Or she must remain queen."

"And you think I am that mate?" he said.

"Possibly," Zenaida told him. "Understand, the queen must love you, not just make love to you. Few Kavan women under the age of fifteen are virgins. We celebrate life, our bodies, and all that it entails. Kalida has an insatiable appetite for making love, but, sadly, no man has ever captured her heart. If you can do that, my handsome princeling, your fate will be golden. You will live in the Outer Palace of the Consorts, and nothing, even other women, will ever be denied to you."

"But my sons, if the gossips of Ramaskhan are to be believed, will be removed from their mother's home at the age of eight, and trained as warriors to be sent off at sixteen, and never seen again," he said.

"But is that not what men love to do best, Dagon? Fight. We simply teach our sons how to fight, and how to survive in a man's world. Kavan cohorts are extremely valuable, and greatly sought after. We turn your male vice into a commercial asset," she chuckled. Then she reached over, and patted his hand. "You will not be forbidden from seeing your sons. Their barracks are quite near the Outer Palace. You will probably see more of them there than when they live within the city proper. Besides, your life will not be that of a love slave. You will have other duties that will keep you quite busy, I promise. Certainly a young man trained to be a king has other talents than a large penis.

"Now, however, you will want a woman to satisfy those pent-up lusts of yours. How long has it been since you have had a woman?"

He flushed at the directness of her query. "Months," he admitted.

Zenaida smiled, showing a row of strong, even white teeth. It was not a smile of amusement, but rather one of understanding. "My poor princeling," she consoled him. Then she turned to the young women serving them. "Well, which one of you wants him tonight? Do not quarrel among yourselves, for you will all have your turn."

"We already decided amongst ourselves, great lady," a yellow-haired girl said, stepping forward. "We drew lots, and I have won him for this sleep time."

"They are so practical, eh, Dagon, but, as you can see, there has been no quarreling about the pleasure of your company. Would men be so pragmatic regarding a beautiful woman?" Zenaida chuckled. "I think not. There would be some sort of argument, and then the poor girl would end up having to entertain a dozen randy cocks. Her name is Doré, by the way. Go along now, and enjoy each other's company," the older woman said.

Doré took Dagon by the hand, pulling him up from the cushions and leading him off through a red silk curtain into a small sleeping space. The curtain fell with a soft sound, shielding them from the rest of the tent. He looked about. The space was empty but for a large mattress set upon a wooden dais.

"On your knees, slave!" Doré commanded. "You must be

taught that women are your betters." She pushed him gently, but firmly.

His first instinct was outrage, but then, catching himself, he obeyed her. Escape meant gaining the trust of these women.

Doré slid out of her simple gown, revealing her nakedness to him. "You will place your hands behind your head, slave. You will not be permitted to touch me with your hands unless I give you permission to do so. Do you understand me?"

He nodded, saying softly as he did so, "Yes, mistress."

"Oh, that is very good!" Doré told him, sounding quite pleased. "I shall reward you, slave. You may lick my slit, but you will not push between my nether lips until I allow it." She positioned herself so that her lover's mount was directly before him.

His tongue slipped from between his lips, and with its very tip, he began to stroke the dark pink slash that ran down her plump lover's mount. Her lush body smelled of flowers, but her feminine musk was very exciting. He longed to touch her more intimately, but he did not.

Doré reached down with her hands suddenly, and pulled her nether lips open, revealing her treasures to him. "Pleasure me, slave," she said softly, "but remember, you must keep your hands behind your head unless I tell you otherwise."

His tongue immediately found her pleasure point, and he began to lick at it; softly at first, and then with vigor. She tasted like wild honey, and he watched, fascinated, as the sweetly tortured tip of her sex began to grow deep pink and swell with her rising excitement.

She moaned with her enjoyment, and then shuddered violently with delight as she reached the apex of her satisfaction. Her hands fell away, and she sighed gustily. "That was quite wonderful," she told him, her voice still a little breathless. "I shall be certain to tell the others of how clever a tongue you have, slave. Stand up now, and I shall return the favor." He rose to his feet, and carefully she unwrapped the length of linen about his loins. Then she fell to her knees, catching his hand up and beginning to suck his finger while her other hand fondled him. "Ummmmm," she murmured. "Your skin is so soft for a man." The hand caressed his buttocks while she continued to suck each finger in turn.

He stood quietly looking down at her. She was a pretty girl with nice big round breasts he would enjoy. "The gods!" He groaned aloud as she suddenly took him into her mouth. His fingers had obviously been but an appetizer to the main course. She pushed back his foreskin, and her tongue teased about the head of his cock, and then she began to suck him, drawing his length deep into her throat, pulling on him so strongly that he grew quickly hard. He was so swollen that he was amazed her seemingly dainty mouth could contain him. He groaned again, and, unable to help himself, loosed his juices down her throat. "Ahhhhhhhh!" Still, she suckled him forcefully, making certain she drew every drop he had to give. His legs almost buckled beneath him.

Then, as quickly as she had begun her sweet torture, Doré rose to her feet, her little tongue swiping about her mouth. "There!" she said. "The edge is off your lust now, and we can enjoy ourselves. Do not, however, loose your juices in the future until you are given permission. You are now permitted to touch me. Come. Lie with me, Dagon." She pulled him toward the large sleeping mat.

"You are experienced," he managed to say weakly as they lay down.

"I should hope so," Doré said with a toss of her yellow head. "I am seventeen, and have had at least a dozen lovers since my first man. He was my mother's body servant, and I gave him to myself on my fourteenth birthday. We lay beneath a full summer's moon. When my mother found us, he was atop me plunging mightily. My mother was furious."

"Because you stole her lover?" Dagon asked. His fingers began to worry at one of her nipples.

"Oh, no! She had long ago discarded Brann as a lover. He was merely her servant. She was angry because he was atop me, and I knew better than to allow a man the dominant position. So did Brann. She whipped him herself, and gave him for common pleasures for a whole day." Doré giggled. "The women so exhausted him that he could hardly walk when his punishment time was completed." Doré giggled with the memory.

"What are 'common pleasures?' " he asked her, curious, taking the nipple into his mouth to play with it.

"Ohhh, that's nice," Doré said, purring. "When a slave is disobedient in Kava, his mistress may take him to the main square of the city where he is spread-eagled upon a platform, and any woman who wants to, may use him as she sees fit. The platform can be rotated, and so the man may be taken in the proper position, whipped upon his buttocks, or taken in an unproper manner. Most women only punish their slaves for a few hours at the most, but even if I hadn't known better, Brann did, which is why my mother gave him to the city for a whole day. He was not a particularly good lover I have since learned. On your back now, slave! I want to sheath you."

And before he might protest that he wasn't ready for her yet, Doré reached down, pushing a hand beneath his balls, and with a single finger found a spot so ultrasensitive that he gasped aloud. "The gods!" He watched with amazement as she pressed against his hidden flesh several times, and his cock was immediately aroused, thrusting itself skyward.

Doré was immediately upon him, kissing the head of his penis, and then mounting him, sheathing him slowly, slowly, leaning back to balance herself upon her hands, her gray eyes closing. "*Ohh, that is nice,*" she murmured. "I have never before entertained a cock so large."

Reaching up, he grasped her two round breasts in his hands, and began to knead them as the girl atop him rode them both to the most incredible enjoyment he had ever known.

Were all the women of Kava this lustful? he wondered the following morning when he was awakened. Four times she had aroused him, and mounted him, and given them satisfaction. The answer to his question was yes as he learned over the next few weeks. The women of Kava were uninhibited, and totally free of any sexual restraints. Zenaida's serving women used him almost every night.

"You must be ready to service the queen, for after the size of your cock, your performance must be flawless. That will gain her attention, my princeling," the High Procuress told him. "Then you will teach her about love. You know love, don't you, Dagon?"

He nodded. "I was in love with Aurea, the daughter of a neighboring king. We were to marry, and the two kingdoms would one day be joined, for Aurea was King Arlen's only heir. Now my brother will have her to wife, may the gods have mercy upon Aurea. She never liked Nogad, but he wanted her anyway because she was to be mine. Nogad always wanted what was mine."

"Again the greed and ambition of men," Zenaida reminded him softly.

There was no escape from his captivity, Dagon quickly learned. During the day, a slave collar was placed about his neck. He was attached both in front and behind by a length of chain to another male slave. His ankles were also shackled. He marched in step with his companions. The situation was impossible. At night he lay with the serving women, and one night after the girl with him had fallen into a deep sleep, he arose, intending to slip from the tent, for night was the only time he was unshackled. He could not go out the entry because it was guarded, but, creeping across the floor, he lifted the fabric of the tent only to discover that he was in a cage with iron bars. Desperately he moved quickly to the entry of the sleep space, and drew the curtain aside to be met with more bars. He was amazed that he had not heard a gate being closed on him, but he had to admit he had not. There was no help for it. He would simply have to escape from Kava itself. It was not impossible, just unusual.

They traveled the main caravan route for a week, moving across the desert until one morning they turned north onto a smaller track toward the snowcapped mountains in the distance. After another week, they found themselves in the foothills wending their way along seemingly nonexistent paths deeper and deeper into what appeared to be a total wilderness. The canyons grew narrower, the stone walls higher, leaving but a strip of bright blue sky above them. Yet each night they camped at perfectly suitable sites near running streams. It was obvious that this was a familiar passage for the Kavans.

Once they had reached the foothills, each of the male slaves being transported was given a pair of sturdy leather sandals to protect their feet from the rough terrain. And to Dagon's amazement the men were not forbidden from communicating. He fell into the habit of speaking with the men behind and before him. Both knew of Kava prior to their enslavement, and were delighted to have been chosen by the High Procuress to become new members of the women's community.

"She is a former queen herself, old Zenaida," one of the men, called Wit, said one day as they walked and spoke of the future.

"How do you know that?" Dagon was surprised.

"One of the women warriors told me," Wit said with a chuckle. "She favors me, and has made our trip quite pleasant. Tell me, why are you kept in the High Procuress's tent each night? Does she favor you, Dagon of Aramas?"

Now it was Dagon's turn to laugh. "Nay," he answered, "but she means to give me as a gift to their current queen."

"Ahhh," murmured the other companion, Ziv, "to have a cock twice the size of mortal men, and half again as big as a god's!"

"Their women are wearing me out," Dagon complained. "I never knew such lustful creatures. Women should not be so forward. It is unnatural. They treat me like some toy with which they gratify their own desires and passions. I am nothing more to them than a plaything!"

"I can't complain about such treatment," Wit said seriously. "It is every man's dream, my friend. A lustful woman upon whom one can pleasure himself, and yet have absolutely no responsibility to that woman. I shall be very content in Kava."

The caravan climbed higher now, moving into the mountains. Soft, light wool cloaks were issued the slaves, for, despite the sun, the days were cooler, and the winds sharper.

One evening Zenaida announced to Dagon that they were but three days from the city of Kava, but on the morrow they would enter into its kingdom.

"Your mighty cock is well primed after all these weeks of travel," she told him. "My girls cannot say enough in praise of you, my princeling. Until we reach the city, you must rest that magnificent organ so the queen may know its full power the first time you couple with her. Tonight I shall tell you of Kalida."

They sat opposite each other, a charcoal brazier between them heating the tent. They had eaten a fine repast of roasted gazelle, a freshly caught fish that had been grilled with steamed greens and served with a bowl of groats, and a large bunch of green grapes. He was warm, and the wine was mellowing him.

"Is she beautiful?" he asked, curiously.

Zenaida nodded. "The goddess has more than favored her, and in more ways than just her beauty. Kalida's grandmother was a queen of Kava. She is a very proud woman, and a very intelligent one as well. This has perhaps contributed to her inability to fall in love. I do not think she believes she can give herself to anyone who is not her equal. Many men have been brought to Kava, both noble and peasant alike, but never have I found a king's son, a future king, among my slaves. I believe the goddess has sent you to be Kalida's mate, Dagon."

"And yet it was my great penis that attracted you first, lady," he teased her gently.

Zenaida chuckled. "Aye," she agreed, "it was, but was that also not a ploy of the goddess to bring you to my attention?"

He laughed with her. He liked this big kind woman who had more the qualities of a good mother, it seemed to him, than a queen or a dignitary. "Tell me what Kalida looks like," he said. "You say she is beautiful, and the goddess has favored her, but how beautiful?"

"She is tall for a woman. Her head will come to your shoulder. She is slender, yet her form is most womanly. Her breasts are like high cones of snow topped with rosy tips like a pale sunrise just touching the mountain's peak. Her face is shaped like a heart, her forehead smooth, high and unmarked. Her eyes are oval in shape, and the green of an emerald. Her nose is slim, and in perfect proportion with her face. Her mouth is large for a woman, and very, very sensual. Her hair is the color of gilt, the palest gold touched with silver. You have never seen hair this color before, I promise you."

"She sounds most fair," Dagon said softly.

"If you are to win her, you must tread a very fine line, my princeling," Zenaida cautioned him. "She must be treated like a queen at all times, but you must also make her feel like a woman. None have accomplished this feat before you. Do so, and your fortune is made."

"You are asking me to subvert my own nature to please your queen, Zenaida, and I do not know if I can," Dagon said honestly. "Your handmaids tell me each night as they mount me how inferior men are to women. Yet I believe the opposite. How am I to reconcile these two adverse reasonings then? And I must if I am to succeed in this endeavor."

"It is not unknown, although it is not spoken of aloud, for a man to hold a dominant position within his lover's bedchamber," Zenaida said quietly. "Although I shall deny it if asked, my size makes it far more comfortable for my mate, Durantis, to ride between my generous thighs than for me to mount his slimmer frame. I should crush the poor darling," she chuckled. "Once, however, I was as slender as our queen. Age has increased my girth, but even in our youth, Durantis and I sported in a variety of positions," she concluded. "You will have to have forbearance, Dagon, my handsome princeling. You must attract Kalida first with your great sexual prowess, and then with your intelligence and wit."

"How must I approach her?" he queried his mentor.

"First with respect, for she is a queen, though you are her equal. Still, make not the error one poor fool made several years ago when he decided that the queen was just a sweet little girl in need of a strong man's dominance. He was given that very night for public pleasures, and then sent to dig in our diamond mines where he still resides, greatly chastened, I am informed, and considered a fool by his companions. Kalida may try your patience at first, and even seem arrogant, but she knows of no other way, having been Queen of Kava since she was just fourteen. Once she believes your esteem for her is genuine, you may safely begin your campaign to win her heart. Every woman has a heart, even Kalida, the Queen of Kava."

"I shall try not to disappoint you, great lady," he told her. No. He would not disappoint her, for the only way he might escape Kava and return to Aramas would be to become the queen's mate. This would allow him to live in the Outer Palace of the Consorts, free of restraint. He had learned a great deal from Zenaida's handmaidens these past weeks. The consorts of the former queens were men who could be trusted. The women warriors who guarded Kava paid them little heed. He would indeed have to be patient, for it would take months to effect his plan of escape, but escape he would.

And one day he would return to Aramas. Nogad might have taken Aurea for a wife, and sired sons upon her, but he would nonetheless slay his traitorous sibling, and his spawn. If Aurea objected, he would slay her, too. He could not marry a woman defiled by his twin. And if their father still lived, he would applaud his eldest son's actions. His father was a man of honor. If his father, however, had gone to the gods, he would simply destroy Nogad and all that was his, and take his rightful place upon the throne of Aramas.

Halfway through the following day, the caravan stopped before the foot of a tall mountain whose top belched forth smoke. The High Procuress stood before a wall of flat, black rock at the mountain's base, and struck it three times with her staff of office, calling, "In the name of the goddess, Suneva, open to me!" With a rumble, an opening appeared in the rock, and the caravan passed through into a well-lit tunnel. Zenaida then turned, and, striking the earth with her staff, said, "In the name of the goddess, Suneva, close, and keep us safe!" The opening then disappeared even as it had earlier revealed itself.

They moved through the passage for several hours. It was very silent but for the sound of feet, both animal and human. The area was comfortably wide enough to accommodate the caravan, and very well lit. The air was still, and a trifle musty. Dagon had noted the smoking top of the mountain as they entered beneath it, but he saw no evidence of volcanic activity as they moved along. They stopped to rest and eat after an hour or more. A woman warrior came and unchained Dagon, reconnecting Wit to Ziv.

"The lady Zenaida wishes your company, barbarian," she said.

Reaching the High Procuress, he bowed deferentially to her.

She handed him a piece of flat bread to eat, and offered her flask of wine. "Walk by my side the rest of the way," she said.

"I thank you for your kindness," he answered.

"Nicely done," she remarked approvingly. "Polite, but not servile. I knew I might count upon your instincts, Dagon."

"Why does the mountaintop smoke?" he asked her. "This is no volcano, great lady."

"You are observant," she replied. "The top smokes because we make it smoke. People see it, and assume the mountain is dangerous. That, of course, suits our purposes as you will soon discover. It is so simple. The smoke comes from pitch burning in a kettle. The kettle sits atop a clay brazier so no flames from the fire can be seen." She held out a hand to him. Pulling her to her feet, he helped her into her cart, which was drawn by two sturdy white horses. "Another hour," Zenaida said, "and we shall exit this passage into the valley of Kava, my princeling. It will be another day and a half to the city from there."

It was late afternoon when they came forth from the tunnel. Immediately the sound of trumpets was heard echoing back and forth throughout the great valley with its rim of green hills. Dagon looked about him, and saw the fortifications at the tunnel's mouth. Upon the barricade walls stood well-armed women warriors, and a half a dozen trumpeters who were sounding both a welcome and a message to the forts farther on, and closer to the city itself. He was impressed in spite of himself.

They made their encampment that night by the tunnel fort. Looking out over the valley before the sun set, the Prince of Aramas thought he had never seen a more beautiful place. Their travels the following day confirmed his first impressions. Zenaida pointed out the road moving back into the mountains where the mines were located. They came down into an area of soft hills where sheep and cattle grazed. In the deeper valley there were orchards and vineyards. They passed through several small villages, the most interesting feature of which was the paucity of men, and older boys.

"Are there no men in these villages?" he asked.

"There are some graybeards, of course, whose good behavior over the years has earned them the privilege of remaining with their mates. Other men are allowed to come at planting and harvest times, and, of course, at festival times," Zenaida explained. "Each year on the great feast of Suneva the eight-year-old boys are gathered up throughout the land, and brought to the military barracks to begin their training."

"Have you ever had any sons?" he gently inquired.

"Durantis and I bred up three boys and four daughters," she replied matter-of-factly. "Our sons are long gone, and our daughters are a great comfort to us now. Sons leave their mothers when they take a wife anyway," Zenaida reasoned. "They would have gone sooner than later, my princeling."

It was midmorning of the next day that they saw the city for the first time. Dagon had to admit to himself that he had never before seen such a wonderful and fantastic place. It was all white marble. Golden domes and soaring silver-roofed towers that touched the sky, green hanging gardens, and glistening water courses all beckoned.

"There is the Outer Palace of the Consorts," Zenaida told him, pointing to a magnificent group of buildings as they passed it. "And there are the boys' barracks there."

He noted both were well outside the city's walls. He was surprised when the caravan turned off, but his mentor explained that the new male slaves would be bathed, evaluated, and then sent to their assignments. "What of me? Am I to go to the queen now?" he asked.

"No," she said. "You are my personal gift to the queen, Dagon. I did not purchase you with Kava's funds, but my own. You will come to my home to be bathed, fed, and rest. Tonight I shall offer you to Kalida with my compliments."

"I thought men were not allowed within the city walls at night," he replied.

She smiled at him. "They are not but for lovers, and rank has its privileges, my princeling, as you well know."

The palace of the High Procuress was a gracious structure of creamy marble. Entering into its courtyard, Dagon saw the great pillars holding up the porch were of red-veined marble capped in gold, and the courtyard was filled with flowers. By the time he was taken to the bath, Zenaida's handmaidens had already broadcast forth the details of his manhood, and he was surrounded by an extraordinary number of women.

"Get away from him, you lascivious little demons," the bath mistress scolded the murmuring, pointing females. "He is the great lady's gift to the queen this very night, and must not be worn out by your enthusiastic licentiousness. Go along with you now. Shoo!"

Disappointed, the women departed.

"I hope he displeases her, and gets sent to the square for common pleasures," one girl said. "Then I'll ride that big stallion to a froth, by Suneva, I swear it!"

"You never rode any man to a froth, Gaia," came a voice, and the other women erupted into laughter.

The old bath mistress cackled. "They will carry on at the sight of a bulging manhood," she said bluntly. She stripped the linen from his loins, and stared. "By Suneva, they have not lied! I've bathed many a man in my life, but never have I seen a manhood this big! It is at least thirteen marks in length. Can it be fully sheathed within a lover?"

"It can," he replied.

"Ahhhhhhh!" the bath mistress said wistfully. "To be young again, or perhaps not even so young." She fondled him, shaking her head and sighing. Then, catching herself, she took up the tools of her trade, and began to bathe him, calling to her assistants to come and help her, for there was much to do. Dagon must be fed, and rested, too, before the evening came.

He was taken naked from the bath, given a solid meal, and then washed lightly again before being taken to a bedspace to rest. He slept for several hours before being gently awakened. He was clothed in a length of snow-white linen which was artfully wrapped and draped about his loins, and a twisted golden torque was fitted about his thick neck. Gilded leather sandals were placed upon his big feet. Zenaida herself brushed his thick dark hair with sandalwood oil, and then tied his locks back with a thin gold cord. She ran her hands over his naked shoulders, turned him about, and ran them over his broad chest.

"You are beautiful," she told him with a sigh. "Keep your wits about you, my princeling, and remember all I have told you. Ah, to be thirty years younger!" Then she turned, and he followed her.

"We are walking?" he asked the High Procuress.

"The queen's palace is but across the square," she replied.

They were permitted to pass into the royal residence without challenge, as Zenaida was known by all. Zenaida moved swiftly for a woman of her girth. He moved after her. A beautiful young woman who looked familiar to Dagon greeted them at one point. She was garbed as an officer of the guard.

"Good evening, my lady," the officer said.

"Good evening, Captain," the High Procuress responded. She turned to Dagon. "This is my middle daughter, Berenike, who is captain of the queen's personal guard."

Dagon bowed. "I greet you, Captain Berenike."

"He is magnificent," Berenike said to her mother, barely acknowledging Dagon. "Do you believe he will be successful?"

"It is in the hands of the goddess, my daughter," Zenaida answered. "Is she waiting? What has she been told?"

"Only that you have a gift for her," was the reply. Then the captain let her gaze wander to Dagon's crotch. "Let me see, Mother!" she begged girlishly. *"Please!"*

Zenaida chuckled. "You are incorrigible as always, Berenike." Then she delicately lifted the draped linen up so her daughter might see.

"Ohhhhh," Berenike sighed wistfully. She reached out, and caressed the great length of flesh.

Zenaida slapped her daughter's eager hands away. "It is a most sensitive organ, and easily aroused. I will not have him spoiled for the queen, Berenike. Shame on you!"

"You never brought me a gift like that," the young woman complained.

"He is a king's son, and only fit for the queen," the High Procuress replied. "We must go now. Straighten your clothing, Dagon!" she scolded him, as if he were responsible for all that had just taken place. "Come along now! I can see if I do not get you off of my hands soon you may cause a riot within these walls."

She hurried down the wide hallway again, her captive in her wake. They stopped before a great bronze double door. The warriors on duty flung open the portals so they might pass through.

"I hope to always have your friendship, lady," Dagon murmured low.

She turned for but a brief moment, and smiled at him. Then she rotated herself ahead again, bowed low before the throne in front of them, and said, "Hail, Kalida, Queen of Kava!"

Dagon allowed his eyes to look directly upon the queen for but a quick blink of the eye, and, in doing so, his heart was lost forever. Zenaida had said Kalida was beautiful, but never before in his entire life had the Prince of Aramas seen such an exquisite creature. He knew in that moment that he would do whatever he had to do to win her heart.

Chapter 2

She wore a pleated, short-sleeved white gown with an open round neckline. Her pale golden hair with its silver lights was dressed in thick braids that were affixed atop her head like a crown. Her teardrop-shaped eyes were the color of emeralds, and matched the necklace of large stones about her slender neck. Her arms were filled with slim, bejeweled gold bangles, and on her feet were gold sandals.

"Is this the gift you have brought me, Zenaida?" she purred in a husky voice. "It lacks originality, I fear."

The High Procuress chuckled. "Nay, Majesty, I would not bring you *just* a man," she said. "This is Dagon, Prince of Aramas, his father's heir until he was betrayed by his twin brother, who, though the younger, always coveted the elder's place. I bought him for you with my own gold in the slave markets of Ramaskhan. He is unique. Remove your wrap, Dagon, and show the queen your assets," Zenaida concluded.

Standing unbowed, Dagon's fingers undid the linen cloth covering his loins, dropping it gracefully to the floor. Head up, he looked directly into Kalida's eyes, and almost jumped as the silent lightning passed between them. Then, clearly hearing her voiceless command, he unfocused his own eyes, but his head remained unbowed. He was, after all, a king's son.

Kalida swallowed back the gasp of surprise welling in her throat. She was the Queen of Kava, not some virgin gazing upon a manhood for the very first time. The truth, however, was that she had never seen anything like the penis now displayed before her. It was enormous; long and thick as it lay at ease upon its ebony bed of tightly bunched curls. About her, the women warriors who guarded her were just as openmouthed with their own amazement, and not just a little envious.

"Can something of that size actually function properly?" Kalida asked Zenaida. "We must have a demonstration here and now!"

"Trust me, Majesty, it is a very serviceable weapon that Dagon wields. My serving women will attest to it. They have spent the nights of our return journey, but for the last three, training this handsome young barbarian for your pleasure. Now he is yours, with my compliments."

"Berenike!" the queen called, and the captain of her guard stepped forward.

"Yes, Majesty?"

"You are the largest woman in the room. Arouse him, and let us see what this prince is made of before I take him into my household," the queen commanded.

He was astounded by Kalida's order. Had she no heart? he wondered to himself. Then he realized that this was precisely the problem Zenaida had spoken about. Kalida was beautiful, and, he suspected, passionate, but she was quite without feelings. *"My queen!"* The sound of his deep, musical, and very masculine voice startled them all. "Will you not let me speak, oh beauteous Queen of Kava?"

"It would appear that you are speaking," Kalida said dryly, but then she waved her hand at him, assenting to his request.

"For three nights I have rested from love's labors, oh Queen. The desire and the passion that have been building within me are for you, *and you alone.* I am a king's son. My love should be only for a queen. *For Kalida, Queen of Kava."* Stepping forward, Dagon knelt, and, taking the hem of her gown between his fingers, he kissed it.

"Would you disobey me then, *slave?*" she demanded of him imperiously.

"Nay, oh Queen. Whatever you so wish, I will obey, but fine wine should not be wasted. Captain Berenike is most lovely, and it would be an honor to be mounted by such a one, but if you truly favor me, oh Queen, you will keep me for yourself as the gracious lady Zenaida hoped you would. I am born a king's son, but to be your slave will be an honor."

"His tongue is quick," Kalida noted, half amused, half intrigued. She looked curiously at the man kneeling before her. She had never known a slave with such charm, or such boldness. Men arriving in Kava were either defiant or foolish. "I am sorry, Berenike, but perhaps I shall give him to you after he no longer amuses me. Take him to my private quarters. Later I shall see if he is indeed worth my trouble." She nudged Dagon with the tip of her sandal. "If you are not, *slave,* you will find yourself given over for common pleasures by the morrow."

"It will be a just punishment then," he responded seriously.

Kalida laughed. "I must teach you to speak only when spoken to, *slave.* Do not allow your boldness to overcome your obvious allure," she warned him. Then she turned to Zenaida. "I may thank you in the morning."

"Indeed, my queen, you will," Zenaida said with a smile, and then bowed herself from the royal presence even as Dagon was being escorted from the chamber. "Do not tamper with him," Zenaida warned her daughter when they were out of the queen's hearing. "I cannot have your lust destroying my plans. You are too much like your father."

Berenike laughed. "You do not object to his lust, Mother," she teased her parent. Then she grew serious. "I know how important this is to Kava. I will not play the spoiler."

"Very good," Zenaida replied. Then she turned to Dagon. "Your deference toward the queen was perhaps a trifle heavy-handed. Kalida is not a simpleton, as I have already warned you."

"I am rebuked," he said, a twinkle in his blue eyes.

"Do not outsmart yourself, Dagon of Aramas," she advised him. "I can be the best friend you have ever had, but do not be fooled. I could also be your deadliest enemy should you fail me.

Power is corrupting when held for too long a time. Kava needs a new queen, but we cannot go against our traditions lest the goddess punish us."

"Perhaps the goddess has meant for Kalida to rule as long as she has," he countered.

"Mayhap," Zenaida answered him with a small smile, "but now you are here. You are clever, and you are handsome. How can she not fall in love with you? Do your best, and keep me informed of your progress. Berenike will carry your messages to me. Commit nothing to writing."

"What is it you are not telling me?" he asked her.

"I am suspicious of the queen's household," Zenaida replied. "It is possible that they are encouraging the queen to her single state. You will learn if that is true or not. Trust no one, not even Kalida herself, my princeling. Now, go with Berenike." The High Procuress turned away from him, and hurried off down the corridor.

"It is beginning to appear that your mother has given me a harder task than I anticipated," Dagon said quietly.

"My mother is a patriot, and great believer in tradition. I agree with her. Kava has always prospered because it has followed the rules set down by the goddess herself in a time lost to our memories but clearly written down in our holy books," Berenike told him. "My mother does what is best for Kava. She has the backing of the Queen's Council, or she would not do so, you may be certain."

"Who heads the queen's household?" Dagon inquired.

"His name is Zeras, and he has been with Kalida since she was a child. Some say he is her sire, but no one is certain. Kalida's mother died when she was born. She was raised by her mother's two sisters."

"A man heads the royal household?" Dagon was surprised.

"Of course," Berenike said. "Many of our servants are male slaves. Women have far more important things to do than to be bothered with household tasks."

"But your mother had serving women," he said, puzzled.

"We do not allow our male slaves to leave Kava," Berenike explained. "The young women who served my mother on her trip to Ramaskhan are learning the business of trade. Buying and selling slaves comes under that heading, Dagon. Ahh, the queen's apartments. Be on your guard now."

The bronze doors to the queen's private apartments were swung open by the two female warriors at their entry. Inside the colonnaded anteroom the torches flared with golden light, the air was lightly perfumed, and all was calm. A man hurried across the black-and-white marble squares of the floor. He was of medium height, and slender in his white robes. There was a bejeweled gold collar about his neck. His face was both angular and severe.

"Greetings, Zeras," Berenike said. "I have brought you the queen's new toy. He is now in your charge." The captain then turned, and without another word departed.

"What is your name, slave?" Zeras asked.

"I am Dagon, Prince of Aramas."

"Indeed," Zeras remarked impassively. "And just how did such a fine royal fellow as yourself end up a slave?"

"Through treachery," Dagon said briefly. "I have learned since to be wiser."

"Well," Zeras said quietly, glancing down briefly, "I can see your obvious attractions. Perhaps you can keep the queen amused for a time or two, but be advised, Dagon of Aramas: no man remains long in her bed. Kalida has no heart. You will probably end up in the mines eventually, unless, of course, you have a talent for agrarian pursuits. Do not make yourself too comfortable within these walls. You will not be here for very long."

"We shall see, Zeras," Dagon answered him.

"You dare to speak back to me, *slave?*" Zeras angrily inquired.

"You are a slave, too, if I am not mistaken," Dagon replied. "If you were not born a king's heir, then your original station in life was inferior to mine. Now, however, we are both slaves within the city of Kava, and therefore equals. Unless I am told otherwise by our mistress, the queen, I shall speak to you as an equal."

"Welllll! Well, well, well, *well!*" Another voice chimed in, and its tone was decidedly mischievous. A small, plump man came into view. "It would seem, my dear Zeras, that the queen's new toy is not to be cowed by your usual pomposity." The gray-blue eyes suddenly bulged as they looked upon Dagon's manhood. "Suneva preserve us! Why was I not born a woman? I have certainly *never* seen anything like *that* in all my born days! It is surely enough for two men." He sighed dramatically, and then was all business again. "I am Vernus, dear boy. It is my duty to take care of the queen's playthings. Follow me, please. You must be prepared for her bed as soon as possible. Oh, do stop scowling, Zeras! It adds years to your face, which is not a particularly pretty one to begin with. According to my informants, Dagon is exactly who he says he is, *and* he is going to make Kalida very, *very* happy."

With just the barest nod to Zeras, Dagon followed after Vernus, who led him to a tiled bath.

"I was bathed earlier," the prince told Vernus.

"Just a quick wash then, and I shall see to it myself," Vernus replied. "Empty your bladder there first." He pointed to an open drain that was constantly being flushed with water. When his charge had obeyed, Vernus matter-of-factly grasped Dagon's penis, and pushed the foreskin back as far as it would go. "They always need washing no matter how careful you are," he said. Then, taking up a soft cloth, he carefully, and most thoroughly, cleaned the organ in his hand. "There, now, that's better. Raise your arms." Vernus smeared a thick whitish paste in the hollow of Dagon's armpits. Then, kneeling, he did the same to his legs. "She dislikes too much fur," he explained. "Your nether curls set off that magnificent cock, so I will not remove them unless instructed to do so. As for your chest, it is perfect, dear boy. Smooth, and soft, *and so well muscled.*" He sighed again. "I suppose you only enjoy women."

Dagon swallowed back his chuckle. Vernus was quite harmless, he could easily see. "Yes," he said.

"Pity," Vernus murmured. "If you should ever change your mind, dear boy, we could become *very* good friends." He scraped the hair from Dagon's body.

"I hope we can be *just* good friends," Dagon replied with a small smile in Vernus's direction.

"You are not offended then?" Vernus said. Usually these beefy fellows were very protective of their masculinity.

"Why? Because you find me attractive?" The prince laughed. "No, I am not offended at all. If I prefer women as lovers, that is my choice. You have obviously made different choices, but they certainly do not offend me. I see no reason why we cannot be friends simply because our sexual tastes are dissimilar."

Now it was Vernus's turn to chuckle. "Zeras will have a most formidable opponent in you, I think. Not that I mind," he finished with a purr. "Come, now, and let me rinse you with some perfumed water and get you dried. *She* has a large appetite for pleasure. I assume they have told you that. *She* is also very impatient, and having seen that formidable lance of yours will be eager to try it out."

"Have you been with her long?" Dagon made conversation as Vernus toweled him.

"My brother and I were brought here together years ago," was the reply. "His name is Durantis, and he is the mate of Zenaida." Vernus smiled knowingly at the startled look on Dagon's face. "Oh, I know what Zenaida hopes to accomplish. Though I dare not voice my approval"—and now he lowered his tone—"it is time for Kalida to fall in love, and take a mate. Zeras, of course, does not want that to happen. He has a passion for power. If Kalida is replaced, his power is gone. He is your enemy, and right now he has her complete trust."

"They say," Dagon answered in equally low tones, "that Zeras is her father. Is it true?"

Vernus nodded. "He is, and she is aware of it. Her mother died when she was born, and she was raised by her aunts, who put her in Zeras's care. They are both merchants of great importance, and had no time for a baby. Zeras found it was to his advantage to teach Kalida as a Kavan mother would have; but, unlike a Kavan woman, he taught her to scorn men. While the women here believe they are superior to the male of the species, they nonetheless enjoy their company, and their sexuality. Kalida, however, has been schooled by Zeras to deny her emotions. She sates her body with the pleasure a man can give her, but has been educated to feel no affection for any other living thing. Even Zeras."

Dagon nodded. "This is an impossible task Zenaida has set for me to complete."

"Nay," Vernus replied. "Of late Kalida has been restless and unhappy. Something within her that she does not understand yearns to be loved, not just with a strong, skilled body, but with a full heart. Zeras was foolish to believe he might keep her free of all emotion. He cannot. Even he once loved. It was the death of Kalida's mother that turned him to ice. He did not want to see his daughter die as the mother had, in childbed. It would have been easier for him if Kalida had not become queen, but she did.

"Then Zeras began to enjoy the power that came with being the queen's confidant. Now that power consumes him. He does not think of Kalida's happiness. Only of his own lust for domination. He will be a dangerous opponent, Dagon. Be careful . . . There! You are ready for the queen, the lucky bitch!"

Dagon laughed. "You are a most irreverent fellow," he said as he followed Vernus from the bath, down a corridor, and through gold-leafed double doors into the queen's bedchamber. His eyes widened at his first sight of Kalida's bed. It was a great square dais upon which was set a huge mattress covered in coral-colored silk. Above the bed hung sheer turquoise-and-gold draperies from a gold ring suspended from the painted ceiling. Dagon gasped softly, surprised, for upon the ceiling were the figures of men and women sporting themselves in all manner of sexual positions. By the bed was a woven basket of gold wire within which he could see a variety of lotions, and exotic toys. There was little else in the square room, whose creamy marble walls were veined in gold. The floor beneath his feet was also marble, squares of gold and cream.

"You are permitted to await her upon the bed," Vernus said. "You must drape yourself artfully among the pillows. Ahhh, yes," he approved as Dagon lay himself down. "Most charming. She will come when she comes. Whatever you do, don't fall asleep. You'll be punished if you do. She expects you eager for her arrival."

"How fortunate I napped earlier," Dagon said wryly.

Vernus chuckled. "Suneva help you," he remarked as he hurried from the chamber.

Dagon's mind was awhirl assimilating all the information the gossipy Vernus had imparted to him. How in the name of all the gods was he to breach the icy stone walls Kalida had allowed to be set up around her heart? Especially in a situation where the beauteous young queen believed herself superior to all men, and did not know how to yield herself to a lover's passion. He shook his head wearily. He was already half under her spell with just one look at her. She was much too lovely to be allowed to go through life without knowing love. He had to succeed!

"You are thinking," she said. She was standing by the bed stark naked. "Of what do you think? Your past life? Another woman?"

He had not even heard her enter the room. He tried to keep himself from gaping at her beauty. She had a body such as he had never seen. It was utterly flawless. Small, but perfect cone-shaped breasts crested by dainty pink buds. Her torso was in proportion; her belly flat; her limbs rounded and long. Her hair was now unbound, and hung about her like a shimmering curtain of pale silvered gold.

"I was thinking of you," he responded frankly. "Of how I could win your heart, my queen."

"How amusing you are," Kalida replied, slithering onto the large bed, and reaching out to caress his penis. "It is magnificent," she said softly. "I can barely contain my desire to sheath you!"

He caught up her hand, and, turning it over, placed a kiss upon the palm. "Pleasure," he said, "is best enjoyed when the anticipation and the appetite for it is whetted slowly. You are, I am advised, impatient. Let me teach you to be more composed with passion." He slipped one of her fingers into his mouth, and began to suck upon it, his deep blue eyes meeting her emerald-green ones.

"You are bold," Kalida murmured, fascinated in spite of her-self, "and you speak to me as if we were equals. I am the Queen of Kava. You are naught but my slave." She could feel her heart hammering erratically within her chest. "I will overlook your behavior this one time, for you have just come to Kava, and have not yet had time to learn our ways. You must obey me, Dagon, for I am your mistress. I am not above beating my slaves when they are disobedient. You are very beautiful, but you must be docile. I do not yet want to send you to the fields, or to the mines."

"I speak to you as I do, my queen, because of all the men you have ever met, I am your equal," Dagon replied softly. "They say you have no heart, but I do not believe it. How can someone so beautiful, so wise a ruler, be heartless? I am already half in love with you!"

Then before she might remonstrate with him, he pinioned her beneath him, and his lips met hers in a deep, passionate kiss. Kalida's head spun wildly. The mouth against her mouth was firm and warm. A tiny tingle of pleasure raced through her body before he lifted his head but briefly, and then again began to kiss her. His lips played along hers, touching at the corners, brushing over her eyelids.

"The gods!" he whispered. "You are so damnably sweet, my queen!"

Kalida attempted to regain her mastery over this unruly slave Zenaida had given her. "You do not have my permission to kiss me," she scolded him. "I will whip you if you do not behave! You must be trained to respect the superiority of the female, Dagon! Cease, or I will punish you!"

Releasing her, he leapt from the bed, and, looking into the basket by the bed, drew forth a small leather whip. "Punish me then, my queen," he said, "for I will not come to heel like the others who have peopled your bed. Passion is to be shared equally by the man and the woman, not just taken to be enjoyed by only one alone."

His kisses had rendered her almost drunk, but she was a queen, and not to be bullied or disobeyed. Taking the whip from his hand, she arose from the bed. "Stand upon the floor, and bend, bracing yourself with your hands upon the bed," she commanded him.

The gods! Would she really do it? he wondered, then winced as the fingers of the leather whip bit into his buttocks. Dagon grit his teeth. She would raise no cry from him, but to his surprise she struck him only three times before ceasing. His flesh was burning nonetheless, and there was a tingle in his manhood.

"You may reenter my bed," she said loftily. "Are you now chastised, and comprehending of my authority over you?"

He lay gingerly upon his back. "You are utterly beautiful when you are so masterful, my queen," he told her.

Her exquisite features darkened with her displeasure. "Must I give you over for common pleasures then, Dagon?" she demanded of him.

"Why are you angry with me because I find you beautiful?" he countered. "You have hair like thistledown." He took up a strand between his fingers, rubbing it, and then bringing it to his lips to kiss.

Kalida felt a catch in her throat. This man was confusing her. She was used to abject obedience, utter devotion, a quick, pleasant sheathing, and then she would send the slave away. Men did not speak as this man was speaking to her. Men were rough, crude creatures whose baser nature must be kept under strict control.

His hand wrapped about a length of her long hair, and he drew her down so that their faces were but inches apart. "You have always held the upper hand, my queen," he whispered so only she might hear him. "Have you never wondered what it would be like to give yourself over totally to your lover's care? It takes a *very* brave woman to do such a thing, but I believe that you are as brave as a woman comes. *Are you, Kalida? Are you?*" He drew her closer, his lips brushing hers softly. "My queen. My beautiful queen," he murmured low.

"Stop it!" she cried. "You are confusing me. Lay back so I may rouse, and sheath you. You talk too much, Dagon of Aramas!"

"By the gods!" he swore softly. *"You are afraid!"*

"I am not!" Her cheeks were pink with the denial.

"Then trust me, Kalida," he coaxed her.

"I did not give you permission to address me by my name," she scolded him nervously.

"Give yourself to me," he gently pressed. His lips brushed her brow.

"It is forbidden," she protested.

"Is not forbidden fruit the sweetest?" he countered teasingly, kissing the tip of her nose.

"I am the queen!" she cried. "You must let me have my own way! I shall send you to the mines if you do not!"

"I will be a king one day, and must have *my* way," he teased her mischievously. "And if you send me to the mines, you will never know the sweetness that only I can give you, Kalida, my fairest queen." He wrapped his arms about her, and pulled her against his chest. *"I want you."* But then he saw the real fear in her eyes, and quickly released her, reaching into the basket and drawing forth a crystal vial of pale-pink lotion. "I will massage you, with your permission, my queen."

"Yes," she answered him, and her voice was shaking.

She rolled onto her stomach, and he began to smooth the liquid cream onto her long back. It smelled of apricots. His hands moved rhythmically and soothingly. Dagon felt her begin to relax beneath his firm touch. Without realizing it, Kalida had given him the key to her conquest. He would stake his life on the fact that she had never felt real passion, and was possibly even afraid of it. The first man to bring true joy to her would be the man with whom she would fall in love and take for her mate. But cajoling her into giving herself over to him would not be a simple or an easy task. Still, it must be done tonight lest Zeras, who had obviously taught Kalida to stifle her emotions, intervene to prevent the queen from favoring him.

Dagon leaned over as he worked. Pushing aside her lovely hair, he bent to kiss the nape of her neck. It was soft, and delicately perfumed. His fingers dug gently but with strength into her shoulders. She murmured contentedly beneath his touch. His cupped hand took a dollop of the apricot lotion and smoothed it over first one buttock, and then the other. He kneaded the rounded halves of her tempting bottom firmly, his finger running teasingly down the shadowed groove separating the twin parts. Now he was spreading her thighs, his lotioned fingers sliding along the satiny flesh, caressing them, brushing gently.

Kalida was purring with contentment. She had certainly not expected an evening such as this one was turning out to be. Usually her male slaves were brought to her like a plate of pretty sweetmeats, all oiled and muscled, and she would choose one to favor that night. She roused him, sometimes allowing him to kiss, or even caress her. Then she sheathed him, and when he had released his tribute to Her Majesty she would send him from her bed. They rarely spoke to her, although some would murmur inane things. Only the boldest would reach out to fondle her breasts as she rode them. They certainly did not suggest the forbidden as Dagon had done; or massage her with such expertise as he had. Kalida had always wondered why other women made such a fuss about lovemaking. The queen took lovers because it was expected of her, but she frankly found it boring. None of the men she took to her bed had ever touched her emotions in any way. Tonight, however, was different. She was beginning to feel strangely. While she was a little fearful, it was nonetheless quite exciting, and she was enjoying herself very much. How far would he press her? Would she allow him to do so? *She was not afraid! She was a queen.*

He rolled her over gently, and seated himself upon her thighs. The hard flesh of his rump against her soft skin was strangely stimulating. Kalida could not see it, although Dagon could, but her cheeks were flushed pink with her arousal. Sapphire eyes met emerald eyes. He smiled faintly, knowingly. Then he poured a stream of lotion directly from the crystal vial onto her belly, and began to rub it into her skin, with light, delicate strokes. Kalida sighed with delight. This was absolutely wonderful! Her masseuse in the bath did not make her feel so delicious and tingly all over. "*Ohhhhhh!*" The sound was drawn forth from her as he began to cream her breasts. She watched his big hands, mesmerized, bronze against ivory; the delicate feathery touch as his fingers brushed across her flesh, teasing and gently pinching the little nipples. Her eyes closed with pure enjoyment. His fingers pressed against her mouth. Unable to help herself, Kalida kissed them. They were quickly gone, caressing her face gently, tracing her features tenderly.

"You are so beautiful," he said softly, "but you know it, my queen. How could you gaze into your mirror, and not see how very, very lovely you are, Kalida, my precious love." Lowering his dark head, he took a nipple into his mouth.

The warm wetness startled her, and her eyes flew open. Then he tugged upon the nipple sharply. Another small cry escaped her. Other men had fondled her breasts, but none had ever worshiped them as he was now doing. He continued to suckle strongly upon her. She sensed a hot thrill in the hidden place between her nether lips, and shivered with budding wonder, for she had never before felt such a sensation, and she liked it. She moaned low.

He raised his head briefly only to renew his attentions to her breasts when he had ascertained she was enjoying them. This time he sought out her other nipple, which he licked and encircled with his tongue until she began to squirm beneath him, unable to help herself.

He leaned forward, kissing her deeply, coaxing her lips apart, his tongue dancing about hers until finally she engaged him in battle. Now, he thought coolly, the time for the real seduction had come. He nibbled upon her mouth like a bee taking honey from a flower. She murmured, moving gently beneath him. Then he was gone from her lips; his body moving down her torso, slowly, seductively, placing a trail of fiery little kisses upon her quivering flesh.

"Wh-what are you doing to me?" Kalida's voice was tremulous.

He raised his dark head from her perfumed skin, and looked directly at her. "Will you trust me not to harm you, my queen? If you do, I shall give you a new pleasure such as you have never known." Because she had posed the question, he realized, amazed, that never before had any man ventured to really make love to Kalida.

"Y-yes," she whispered to him, wondering even as she said the word if she was mad to allow him to continue, but she simply could not help herself. Her body was filled with a powerful languor such as she had never before felt. She was astounded by her newly discovered ignorance and wanted to know more. While Zeras had always warned her about allowing her body to overrule her head, did even he know all she had learned this night? And if he did, why had he forbidden her to avoid such sweetness? Zeras had much to answer for, but for now she wanted to know more!

Dagon gave Kalida a moment to reconsider her decision, and then he proceeded forward. He had hoped that once he began to make passionate love to her, her natural curiosity would encourage her onward. He had been right. He nuzzled at the soft inner flesh of her closed thighs, gently nudging them apart, placing a warm kiss upon her lover's mount. Her legs fell open as if to offer him everything she had. He ran the very tip of his tongue up from the bottom of her moist cleft to its top. Kalida shivered. Tenderly

Dagon drew her swollen nether lips apart, and again using the tip of his tongue, delicately touched her pleasure point. She shivered a second time. He could hear her breathing growing harsh and strained with her rising lust.

What was he doing? In the name of Suneva, what was he doing to her? His tongue flicked relentlessly back and forth over that place Zeras had taught her to deny even existed. She should make him stop, but she could not muster the strength to forbid him. There was a hot sweetness flowing through her. Kalida, always honest with herself, knew that she didn't want her lover to cease this glorious torture.

"*Ohhhhhh, yes!*" she moaned eagerly. "I command you to continue!" But even as she said the words, something new was happening. She could feel the burning, tingling tension building and building within her. Then, like a wave crashing onto the shore, it burst inside her and slowly drained away, even as she strongly protested its loss.

Dagon rolled away from her and onto his back. Reaching out, he lifted her above his loins, lowering her slowly as he said hungrily to her, "*Now, my queen!* Mount me, and take your pleasure of me!"

Breathlessly, she slowly, carefully, absorbed his great length into her hot, wet sheath. She wasn't certain if she could consume all of the great penis, but she could feel the walls of her sheath opening to accept him, then closing about the hard length of him. He fit her perfectly as no man before him ever had. Amazed, she rode him furiously until, finally exhausted, she half sobbed, "Why will you not give me your tribute, Dagon?"

He had closed his eyes with relish as he had felt her taking him in, using him until he thought he would perish with delight. His eyes flew open at her poignant cry. Her beautiful face was a mask of striving, *but not attaining.* Shocked, he realized in that blinding moment that Kalida had never in her entire life reached the zenith of love. She believed that a man's release was all there was to a coupling.

In a single motion he rolled her beneath him, saying, "If I die for it, Kalida, you shall have this night the full pleasure every woman deserves! Wrap your legs about me, my queen!" To his delight she did, offering no resistance. He began to slowly delve into her hot, throbbing sex, each thrust taking him deeper and deeper. He was drowning in pleasure, but he wanted her to have an equal share of passion.

It was forbidden! But who had forbidden it? Kalida wondered. It was glorious, and splendid! She did not feel at all intimidated by the fact he was so lustily riding her. Indeed, her very bones were melting. Behind her closed eyes golden starburst followed golden starburst until she seemed to soar into the night skies. She was acutely aware of the powerful thrusts of his great, hard manhood as it plumbed into her very depths. She could feel herself trembling wildly, utterly consumed by a fierce heat; and then a wild abandon devoured her, her very innards convulsing as his tribute thundered into her secret garden.

Kalida cried out, startled to realize that until this very moment, she had never really known pleasure between a man and a woman. Her eyes opened, and she saw him smiling, not with any sense of triumph, but with the joy they had just shared.

"I did not know," she said simply, feeling like a virgin taken for the first time.

He wrapped her in his warm embrace. "Then I am forgiven for tempting you to the forbidden, my queen," he murmured against her ear.

She laughed softly. "You are forgiven, Dagon of Aramas," she said. She snuggled deeper into his arms, rubbing her cheek against his smooth, damp chest. "Will you tempt me again?"

"If you wish it, my queen," he returned. "There is so much I can share with you that I suspect you have never shared with any man." Then his voice grew more serious. "Tell me, Kalida, did you never until this night know real pleasure? How can this be, my love? You are so warm and eager for passion."

"Perhaps the goddess did not mean me to know passion until you came into my bed, Dagon," she answered him, equally serious. "Zeras has always warned me not to allow my emotions to over-rule my intellect. Zeras says a queen must be clear-headed, focused and free of foolish sentiments. In Kava our queens only rule till they fall in love. I like being a queen, but how could Zeras have kept this magnificence from me? I shall scold him quite harshly for it in the morning!"

"Do not, my love," Dagon cautioned. "You are the queen, but Zeras has raised you, and he is devoted to you. Perhaps he did not tell you of the sweetness of passion because he feared to lose you to another man when you took a mate, Kalida. That is the way with fathers. It is hard for them to give their daughters to another man. Besides, my beautiful queen, I have but offered you a glimpse of passion. You enjoyed it, but there is more to true love than passion. If you vent your anger at Zeras, he could prove difficult."

"It is said that Zeras sired me, but he is a slave. He had not the right to keep this wonderfulness from me. I will punish him, Dagon!" Her look was resolute.

"If you do, Kalida, he will find a way to make certain I die for my daring, or disappear from your life. You may not realize it, but Zeras holds a certain power within your palace, slave though he be. It is that way with upper servants of his class the world over. Tell him not of what you have learned this night, and do not punish him. Behave with him as you always have done. Let us have *our* little secret, which we will keep from Zeras. He need not know the delights we share. If it is your will to eventually make me your favorite, he may be irritated, but you are the queen. It is your will that shall prevail, not his. He has already told me you will quickly become bored with me, and discard me. Allow him to continue to believe that, my love, I beg you.

"When my eyes first beheld you, my queen, I began to fall in love with you. Sharing passion with you has but deepened that love. May the goddess turn your heart to me, Kalida. Even if Zenaida had not brought me here in chains, had I come to you of my own accord, I should have fallen in love with you, my queen. I shall never again desire any woman but you, for you are perfection, and having tasted of your sweetness, all else is ashes in my mouth."

"Why is it that other men have never spoken to me as you do, Dagon?" she asked wonderingly.

"Because they are fools, Kalida. They sought only but to slake their own lusts upon your beautiful body. I want your heart as well as your body, my queen."

"Zeras says a queen can have no heart, Dagon," she replied.

"You are a woman first, Kalida, and all women have hearts," he answered her, kissing the top of her golden head.

She laughed softly once again. "You are a very wicked man, Dagon. I should take my whip to you again for your irreverence, but instead I want you to fill me once more with that glorious manhood of yours!"

Now it was his turn to laugh. "I have unleashed a shameless monster," he teased her. "Do not be in such a great hurry, my queen. Passion shared must be gently cajoled to flame. There is pleasure in anticipation, Kalida. Let us rest for a short time, and then we will make love to one another once again."

"I am in your hands, Dagon of Aramas," she replied. "I have never before trusted a man, except for Zeras, but I will trust you, for you have shown me pleasure such as I have never known."

"You will not regret your decision, my queen," he told her, his heart soaring with excitement at her words. He really was already half in love with this exquisite woman. He desperately wanted her to fall in love with him, to take him as her mate. If he continued to please her, he believed he would attain that goal. "Sleep now, my love," he encouraged her.

Chapter 3

"Shall I send him to the mines, or to the fields, my queen?" Zeras asked his mistress the following morning.

"Neither," Kalida said. Then she laughed. "He amuses me, Zeras. Besides, it would be rude to dispose of the lady Zenaida's gift so hastily. I shall keep him by my side for a short time. Now, fetch me a bejeweled gold collar and a length of gold chain. After Vernus has bathed him, put the collar on him. And keep him naked. I want all the women of Kava to see his impressive and sumptuous assets. Let them have their dreams of the time when I shall send him for common pleasures prior to dismissing him." She slid off her bed and stretched lazily. Then, reaching out, she took up the small leather whip. "Buttocks up, Dagon!" she ordered him harshly.

"As my queen commands," Dagon replied, rolling over and rising onto his hands and knees.

Kalida laughed again. "Is he not amusing, Zeras? Watch!" She laid the whip with its half dozen knotted leather fingers across her lover's hard, rounded rump several times. "On your back, slave!"

He immediately obeyed, and Kalida slid the whip beneath his penis, raising it slightly so that it was draped over the whip's handle, a wicked smile upon her beautiful face.

"See, Zeras!" she said excitedly. "The whip begins to arouse my beautiful prince. Ten strokes, and he is ready to be mounted. I swear it! I have never had such an eager lover. I must keep him for a while longer. This Dagon is most entertaining. Now, I will go and bathe, Zeras. Carry out my orders immediately."

She ran off to her bath while Zeras glowered, irritated at Dagon. "Well, that cock of yours is more talented than I gave it credit for, oh prince," he said sourly. "Come along to Vernus while I find a suitable dog collar so your mistress may lead you about."

"Tell me absolutely everything!" Vernus said when Dagon arrived at the baths. His gray eyes were dancing with curiosity. "Did she mount you? Did you please her? Are you to remain in the palace? Dear boy, I simply must know!"

"I believe I pleased the queen," Dagon said carefully, remembering Zenaida's warning to trust no one.

The gray eyes rolled with their exasperation. "Suneva help us. A discreet lover! My brother, Durantis, has been here twice this morning attempting to ascertain your status, and all you can say is you believe you pleased Kalida! Surely there is a tiny bit more?"

"She has not dismissed me," Dagon replied. "And she asked Zeras to fetch a collar and chain for me so I may accompany her today. Beyond that, I can tell you nothing, Vernus, because I know nothing."

"This is good," Vernus noted. "This is good! She has never before kept a male slave so close. The lady Zenaida will be well pleased. She wants to see you, but if you are to remain by the queen, I do not know when such a thing will be possible. I shall send word, and leave her to solve the problem. Women are so much better than we men in solving problems like this." He picked up a soap-filled sponge, and began to wash his charge vigorously, all the while humming merrily beneath his breath.

Dagon was bathed. Massaged with a sweet oil that left his body shiny, his muscles well defined. Vernus brushed his dark hair with musk oil, tying it back with a length of gilded leather. He took the collar from Zeras, who joined them, examining it to be certain that it was lined with silk and lamb's wool to prevent chafing. The gold circle was an inch in width, and heavily bejeweled in emeralds, rubies, sapphires, and diamonds. Vernus removed Dagon's golden torque, and fastened the collar about his thick neck. It rested perfectly upon his collarbone.

With a barely disguised sneer, Zeras snapped the golden chain to the collar. "Come, slave," he said. "Your mistress awaits you."

"Do not yank upon the chain so!" Vernus scolded Zeras. "If you bruise him, I shall report you to the queen!"

Zeras brought Dagon to the queen's dining chamber, where Kalida was already seated. He handed the chain to the young queen.

Kalida gently tugged upon the chain. "You may kneel by my chair, Dagon," she told him, and when he had obeyed her, she smiled. "Good prince," she approved. "Now, open your mouth, and I will give you something to eat. You are to keep your mouth wide except when you are chewing your food."

About them, the servants moved silently, bringing the food, pouring liquid refreshment for the queen, who ate alone. Now and again she would pop food into his mouth. Bread, meat, fruit, and cheese. He played her game, nuzzling at her hand, licking her fingers mischievously. All the while Zeras remained standing at the opposite end of the table from where the queen was seated. He could see nothing of their byplay, which suited Dagon well, for every now and then he would lean down and nip at Kalida's thigh playfully.

"I think I shall walk through the city this morning," Kalida said when she had finished her meal. She bathed her hands in a basin held by an attractive young blond man, and dried them on the linen towel draped over his sinewy arm. "Have an escort fetched for me," she said to Zeras.

"Shall I also accompany you, my queen?" he asked her.

"No, I think not," Kalida said. "You would only stand behind me, and hiss at me about keeping my dignity. I want to show off my gift to my people. They will be admiring, and want to touch him, and perhaps I shall allow it. If you were with me, Zeras, you would scowl, and remind me that a queen is above the common people. But there are no commoners in Kava. You still hold with the values of your world, despite the fact you have been in Kava for twenty-five years. Now, go and do my bidding." She arose from the table. "Come, my prince," she murmured, pulling gently on his leash.

They left Zeras behind, and went out into the city with four women warriors escorting them. The guard was a sop to the royal presence, and entirely unnecessary. Almost immediately, the women in the streets began to point and call out at the sight of Kalida and Dagon.

"Ahh, to be Queen of Kava!" said one, giving Dagon's penis a friendly tweak.

"Does your stallion ride well, oh Queen?" called another. "He looks a right lusty mount!" The woman patted his bottom.

"He is," Kalida replied, laughing. *"Very lusty!"*

Dagon said nothing, but he was taken aback by Kalida's behavior of this morning. Gone was the warm, passionate woman he had loved last night. In her place was an imperious creature, but, remembering the Kalida of the previous evening, he held his peace. Tonight would surely reveal the truth of the matter to him. They entered into a square.

"This is the place of common pleasures," she told him. "It is here recalcitrant slaves are brought to be whipped. The Public Punisher administers the discipline so the slave's anger is not directed toward his mistress. Sometimes a slave is spread-eagled upon the block, and given over to any woman's pleasure. When that happens, the square is full to overflowing, particularly if the slave is handsome." She turned, and ran a seductive finger up and down his jawline. "I shall never allow another woman to mount you, Dagon, my prince. You are mine, and mine alone."

Her tone was tender, and for a brief moment, her eyes soft with her passion. Then suddenly she was the Queen of Kava once more. She led him off back to the palace where he knelt next to her as she completed the administrative tasks scheduled for this day, Zeras once again by her side, advising, murmuring in her ear. Dagon began to feel a gnawing of jealousy toward the older man. When the evening came, and she again sat alone at her meal, Dagon realized how isolated Kalida was, for other than their short excursion into the city streets that day, she had had no contact with anyone but Zeras and her servants. There was, it seemed, no court; no friends. Just Zeras. *And now Dagon.*

Halfway through the evening meal she dismissed Zeras and the rest of her servants. "I wish to be alone," she said, and not even Zeras would dare to argue with her. She ate silently, absently feeding him bits of food. Finally, when several minutes had passed, and she appeared to have forgotten him, the leash slipping from her hand, Dagon slid beneath the table. Positioning himself before Kalida, he began to slowly push her gown up, kissing her feet, her ankles, her knees as the fabric slithered higher and higher until it reached the tops of her thighs. Wordlessly she opened her legs to him, and he licked the soft, warm flesh of her inner thighs. Then his dark head dove deep, his fingers peeling back her already moist pouting nether lips as he sought her pleasure point. His tongue flicked back and forth over the pinkish flesh. He saw her excitement build as the softness grew darker, the nub swelling and stiffening.

Kalida's breath was coming in short, hard gasps. Her slender white fingers kneaded his dark head, encouraging him to continue. The tightness built, and she struggled to hold on to the delicious feeling, but she could not. The hot sweetness broke, filling her with pleasure, even as he drew away from her. "That was wonderful!" she told him enthusiastically. "I shall end my meal each night that way from now on, Dagon!" She managed to stand up, albeit shakily. "Let us seek my bedchamber. You have but whetted my appetite for passion."

Once within the privacy of her chamber, Kalida tore off her gown and unfastened Dagon's collar. "There!" she said. "We are now once again equals. Were you angry at me for my behavior today? I believe Zeras does not suspect a thing, my prince. I was very bad, though. Will you punish me, Dagon?"

"It is not a slave's place to punish his mistress," Dagon said. He reached out to take her in his arms, but Kalida spun away from his grasp.

"I was very bad," she repeated. "I should be spanked, Dagon."

"Spanked? You want to be spanked, my queen?"

"Yes!" she said. "I command you to spank me!"

He was astounded by her request. "Have you ever been spanked?" he asked her. "What do you know of spanking?"

"Zeras spanked me when I was a little girl," Kalida told him. "Of course my aunts made him stop, and sent him for common pleasures to punish him for behaving so crudely toward a female. He would have stopped anyhow, though," she giggled.

"Why?" Dagon demanded.

"He discovered that I liked it," Kalida replied with complete candor. "When I told my aunts, they said I was an unnatural child. That I must never relinquish myself to another's power, particularly a man's. I have not been spanked in many years, but when I saw how your glorious manhood reacted to my whip today, I remembered being spanked, and the childish pleasure it gave me. You have opened my world to pleasure once more, Dagon, and I have given you my trust. I would be spanked by you."

"What if someone should hear you cry out, my queen. Your guards would rush to your aid, and seeing me apparently abusing you, they would slay me where I stood," he protested.

She pushed him into a seated position upon the bed. Then she stood between his long legs. "Once we draw the draperies about the bed, Dagon, no one can hear us. All Kavan women have draperies of this sort. They look as if they have been spun by spiders, but drawn, no sound penetrates them. It is a magic known only to Kava." Reaching for the drawstring to the curtains, she drew them so that they encircled the bed. Then she called out in a loud voice, *"Guards! To the queen!"*

To his great amazement, no one came.

Kalida looked down into his handsome face. "Spank me," she purred at him, and lay herself facedown across his broad lap.

Dagon looked down at the split peach of her deliciously round and tempting bottom. "Your behavior in dragging me about the city this morning was rather unforgivable," he reasoned. His big hand smoothed in a circular motion over her skin. She wiggled against his lap in a most provocative fashion. Raising his hand, he brought it down hard.

"Whoooooo!" she squealed, wriggling more, and the hand punishing her came down again, and again and again until her backside was stinging and she could feel the heat of it. There was also a distinct tingling in her nether regions that was very familiar, and felt quite good. "More!" she demanded of him.

"No," he said quietly, "but you shall learn something else new, my sweet, naughty queen." His hand again smoothed over the very pink, warm flesh. Then his finger found its way between the twin moons of her bottom to rub suggestively against the tight, puckered orifice.

Her breath caught in her throat, and for a moment she could not breathe. Finally, she said, "I had heard it could be done there, but I never have. None before you even hinted at it."

His finger pressed firmly against the aperture. "Only if you desire it, and not tonight, my queen," he told her. "We but explore the possibilities now." He felt the vent yielding to the pressure of his finger, and then it slipped in to the first joint.

"Ooooooooo!" Kalida hissed breathlessly.

The finger pushed deeper, first to his knuckle, and then its entire length where he kept it, allowing her body to adjust to this new invasion. After a short while, he began to move his finger rhythmically within the narrow channel. His other hand slipped beneath her lover's mount, cupping it, a single finger seeking and finding her pleasure place, teasing it until his hand was sticky with her love juices that his dual actions had convinced her to release in a shuddering zenith of pleasure.

She slid off his lap. Kneeling between his legs, she took his already aroused manhood into her mouth. Her pointed little tongue encircled the ruby head of it, teasing, taunting. He was astounded, and utterly gratified, when she took him completely into her mouth, her throat relaxing as she half swallowed him. He groaned with delight, his eyes closing as he allowed the pleasure to sweep over him. But he wanted to release himself within her body, and so he finally pulled her away, lifting her up to sheath him as she sat upon his lap.

Kalida sighed with enjoyment as she felt him pushing into her. She surrounded him with a hot throbbing that roused his lust even higher. Dagon took her face between his two big hands and kissed her deeply, passionately, his sensuous mouth ravishing her with pleasure. Their bodies moved together in a hot, furious rhythm.

"It is too much! Too sweet!" Kalida cried as their crisis approached. Then she collapsed against his shoulder, drained and replete with pleasure.

His cock shuddered within her as she squeezed the last drop of his tribute from him. "Ah, the gods! If I were yet my father's heir, I should take you for my queen, Kalida. I love you. There is no other woman for me!"

Now it was she who took his face between her hands, and looking directly into his eyes, Kalida said, "You are he for whom I have been waiting all these years. *You are my mate!* I would have your daughters."

"My love," he said, as they lay back among the pillows of the bed, "you honor your slave, but I would have you be certain."

"I am certain," Kalida said. "You are the only mate for me, Dagon. Do you not want to be my mate?"

"*I do!*" he cried, "but allow me a small trial. Tomorrow night, invite both me and another of your choosing into your bed together. If when the dawn arrives, you are still certain that I am your mate, then so be it, my lovely queen. You are the only woman I have ever truly loved, but I love you enough that I would be certain that you will be content and happy with me. For to take me as your mate means that you must give up the rule of Kava, and turn it over to another. Are you certain you are ready to do that?"

"Yes," Kalida answered him without hesitation. "Being a queen is a lonely pursuit. I shall allow you your test of my love,

Dagon. You shall see that you are the only mate who can make me happy."

In the morning, Zeras again wished to know if Kalida would send Dagon away.

"No," she answered him. "Have I not said this slave amuses me? What is it that you do not comprehend, Zeras? When I wish to be rid of Zenaida's gift, I will tell you. Do not keep asking me each dawn. I find you irritating beyond all." She turned her back on him, saying to Dagon, "Go to Vernus to be bathed, my pet. Then rejoin me, and we will break our fast."

Dagon bowed deferentially. "As my queen commands," he replied.

"I do not like that fellow," Zeras said when the prince had gone. "Why do you bother with him? You are a great queen. You do not need such a creature about you defiling you with his big hands, and his muscled body. If it is that monstrous dangling penis of his that keeps you entertained I will have it cast in plaster. We shall make a most realistic dildo in any variety of materials for you. Then we may be quit of this Dagon of Aramas."

"You overstep your boundaries, Zeras," Kalida said coldly. "Do you think because you are my body slave, and have been since my birth, that you have the right to speak to me as you have just done? You do not. You are nothing more than a slave, as Dagon is a slave."

"I am your father, and as such am entitled to your respect," Zeras said pompously.

"You are not my sire," Kalida told him. "My mother mounted you once, twice, no more. My mother had dark hair as do you. If you were my sire, how could you have made such as fair a child as me? My sire was golden-haired. His name was Valcon. I'm certain that you remember him. He loved my mother with all his heart. When she died giving birth to his child, he killed himself. I'm sure you remember that, too.

"It suited my aunts to convince you that I was your child. That way, you would care for me with devotion. They had, as you well know, neither the time nor the inclination to raise an infant. They were actually sorry I was not a boy that they might have rid themselves of me when I reached age eight," Kalida said. "You have served me well, Zeras, and certainly with devotion, but you are a man. In this world men do not have the right to criticize women. You are inferior, as all men are. You hold your little position because I allow you to hold it. Do not overstep your boundaries, Zeras. I have raised you high as I was raised high. I can easily cast you down," Kalida warned him.

"You are a queen because I made you a queen!" he countered angrily. "Do you think the goddess's dove alighted on your shoulder by chance, foolish woman? It was I who sewed grain into the neckline of your gown, thereby guaranteeing that the dove would choose you from all the maidens gathered in the arena that day. *I did it! I, Zeras!*"

"I never before realized what a schemer you are, Zeras," Kalida told him. "You have kept me isolated and imprisoned in this palace as Kava's queen far longer than I ought to have reigned. You think you exploited my choosing, but you did not, and you shall no longer keep me from the fate the goddess means me to have. I believe you when you say you sewed grain into my gown that day so long ago; but grain or no, I was chosen by the goddess, even if you choose to believe otherwise, Zeras.

"Do you think the messenger of the goddess would be tempted by a little grain in a gown? I have been Queen of Kava not because of what you tried to do, but because it was the will of the goddess, *not the will of Zeras,* a mere man. Go from me now. I am very angry at you, but I will not cast you aside as I should do. Your loyalty to me must count for something."

"Are you preparing to take him for your mate?" Zeras demanded boldly.

"I have not decided yet," Kalida lied smoothly. She would tell Zeras nothing lest he attempt to spoil her happiness. "When I do take a mate, the announcement will be made as tradition demands."

"How do you know Valcon was your sire?" he asked her. He had often wondered how he, Zeras, had made such a beautiful golden child.

"When I became queen, my aunts told me the truth," Kalida replied. "They feared your influence over me."

"Will you make public the truth?" he persisted.

"The truth of what?" she asked him.

"Your parentage," he answered.

"What difference does it make?" she wondered aloud, and then she smiled slyly. "Ahhh, I see, old schemer, what you are about. You have traded upon the rumors that you were my sire to gain your small foothold. Now you fear to lose your prestige." Kalida laughed. "If you do not annoy me further, I shall say nothing. Why would I? It matters not who my sire was. Not in Kava. Go now, or I shall send you from my service forever, Zeras." She watched him leave her presence, his shoulders drooping just slightly, but she noticed as he exited the bedchamber, he made an effort to straighten himself up. Kalida smiled, then turned, and hurried off to her own bath, her thoughts turning to Dagon as she went.

Dagon, meanwhile, had gone to seek out Vernus. To his surprise he found the High Procuress awaiting him in his bathing room. He bowed low to her, then stood awaiting her pleasure.

"What news do you have for me, my prince?" she asked him.

"It goes well, my lady Zenaida," he said, his eyes going to Vernus, who stood with another man.

"You may speak before Durantis, my mate, and his brother, Vernus, my prince," Zenaida said.

"You were right, my lady," Dagon began. "Zeras exercised great control over the queen. He taught her from childhood not to give in to her emotions. So it was that she had never tasted real pleasure until two nights ago when I brought her the gift of joy. Indeed, our bodies fit so perfectly together, it is as if the goddess had fashioned us for one another, as I believe she did. She desires to take me as her mate, but I have demurred, for while I love Kalida, I want her totally happy. Tonight she will invite me and one other man to her bed so she may be certain it is not just lust she feels for me. On the morrow she will, I believe, take me for her true mate. Kava may then choose a new queen."

"Are you certain that this is a wise thing to do?" Zenaida asked him. "If she is content to have you for her mate, then so be it, Dagon. Why must you tempt her with another man?"

"Kalida has been Queen of Kava longer than anyone else, my

lady. You said it yourself. No man has ever really pleasured her until me. By taking another man into her bed tonight, she will learn with certainty that I am the only man who can pleasure her. She will then feel no reluctance in relinquishing her power over Kava; and nothing Zeras says to her will change her mind. His influence will be ended, and Kava will have another queen. You must trust me, my lady Zenaida. For Kalida's sake, this is the best way to proceed."

"You are a clever man, my prince," the High Procuress noted. "I am not certain that you are also a dangerous man as well."

"I am but a man in love, my lady," he answered her smoothly.

Zenaida laughed, genuinely amused. "Very well then, if you are certain Kalida will not be distracted by another lover and decide not to take you for her mate, then I must be content with your plan."

"I am the only man for the queen," Dagon replied with certainty.

When Zenaida and Durantis had left, Vernus said, "You do realize, dear boy, that women tend to be fickle. Having opened the gates of passion to our beloved queen, how can you be so certain that another man will not now be able to stoke her fires?"

"Because, my friend," the prince replied, "I know something about Kalida that no one else does. When I told Zenaida that our bodies were well matched, I did not lie. I have never been able to fit my manhood entirely into any woman until I met Kalida. Her sheath is longer than any I have ever known. She devoured my entire length easily. Part of the problem was that no man had ever been able to fill her. Is there another man here in Kava who can match the size of my penis? If not, then there is no man who will offer the queen the pleasure I can; and only the man who can please her will mate her."

Vernus was almost faint with this revelation. "Ohhh, the lucky girl," he murmured, "to have such ecstasy for eternity!"

Dagon laughed. "A year ago, if I had been told I would be betrayed by my brother, sold into slavery, and become the mate of a beautiful queen, called Kalida, I should not have believed it," he said.

"Then you are content," Vernus said.

"*For now,*" Dagon, Prince of Aramas answered him.

Chapter 4

Kalida had chosen a handsome young slave named Adon to join them in her bed that night. He was of medium height with curly blond hair and melting brown eyes. His body was stocky, but well muscled, and his penis was thick, at least eight inches in length. Vernus washed him vigorously, strangely silent.

"You have cared for her other favorites," Adon said nervously. "What is she like? Will I please her? What has happened to the slave with the enormous penis? Did she tire of him that quickly?"

"He will be with you," Vernus said. "He has pleased her greatly. It was his suggestion to her that she might perhaps enjoy having two men to play with rather than just one. You must be at your best, Adon."

"Two men at once," the young man said wonderingly. "The queen's appetite must be a great one indeed, Vernus."

"Oh, it is," he agreed. "I don't envy you, Adon. Women are so demanding, aren't they?" He smiled at the boy.

"What is the other slave's name?" Adon asked.

"Dagon. He is a prince," Vernus replied. The queen, clever creature she was, had chosen a baby, he considered. Obviously she had made her decision, but to please Dagon, was going along with his test of her affections, Vernus thought. Adon was a pretty lad. He hoped they would not devour him whole. "I shall be here in the morning to take care of you, dear boy," he murmured, patting the young man's rosy buttock. Adon did not flinch. "Come now, and I shall turn you over to Zeras, who will take you to the queen's bedchamber," Vernus concluded with an encouraging smile.

"What in the name of Suneva is the matter with you?" Vernus asked Zeras as he delivered the young Adon up for the sacrifice.

Zeras shook his head wearily. "It is all over," he said despairingly. "There is simply no accounting for the vagaries of a woman. I thought I had kept her from her emotions. Now we are ruined, and all because of that man!"

"Nonsense!" Vernus retorted. "We will simply move from here to there. There will be much honor in her former position." Then he glanced meaningfully from Adon to Zeras.

"You are right," Zeras said. "In my disappointment I, who pride myself on my composure, have almost forgotten myself." His scornful glance went to the handsome young blond man. "Come," he told him frostily. "The queen awaits you." Then he ushered Adon to the doors that opened into the queen's bedchamber and pushed him through. He did not go in this time. He could not bear to see Kalida so suddenly and smugly content like some ordinary woman of the city.

Now that they were alone, Vernus said, "If she indeed chooses to take Dagon as her mate, it will be several weeks before a new queen is chosen, and we have to leave the palace. Her private residence has been ready for her for several years now in anticipation of her coming. We'll have a great deal to do, opening it up, furnishing it, preparing for her arrival. And, of course, Dagon's apartments at the Outer Palace of the Consorts must be done up as well. There will be absolutely no time for either of us, or the other servants, to brood, Zeras. It is past time the queen took a mate. Surely you know you held no real power here. *This is Kava.*"

"As long as she was queen, I held power, Vernus. Do not fool yourself. I have been a man of importance; an adviser to the queen."

"Well, it more than likely is over now. So best not to grieve but to move on, Zeras," Vernus said in practical tones.

The tall, lean man sighed deeply. "I suppose you are right," he admitted. "For all my years in Kava, I never have really gotten used to women controlling everything."

"Let them have the power, and the responsibility, my dear," Vernus said with a chuckle. "I enjoy being taken care of, and having no worries except whether I can obtain oil of gardenia for the queen's bath supplies." He took Zeras by the arm. "Let us go and have a goblet of wine, my dear. Everything always looks so much better after a small draught of the grape."

"Two men at once," Zeras despaired. "I have never known her to be so insatiable. You will not believe what she said to me today."

"Well, do come along and tell me," Vernus replied; but as they hurried off, he glanced at the closed doors of the queen's bedchamber. Poor little Adon. He did hope they would treat him kindly. *What on earth did a woman do with two men?*

The doors closed behind him, and Adon stood a moment, his eyes growing used to the dimness of the queen's bedchamber. The only light was that of flickering candles set about in gold and silver holders upon the marble floor and on the inlaid tables. The room was filled with the fragrance of wildflowers. The queen was sprawled naked upon the great bed, and the slave with the great penis lounged assuredly by her side. Adon stood frozen. They were the most beautiful couple he had ever seen. He felt a tingling in his manhood.

"Come and join us," the queen called silkily to him. "Do not be afraid, my pretty Adon. I shall not bite you . . . well, at least not yet." Then she laughed softly, her slender hand beckoning him forward.

Encouraged, he walked across the chamber until he reached them.

"Onto the bed, my pretty Adon," Kalida commanded gently. "I want to see more closely what you have for me." She caressed him as if she were patting a favored pet. "Ohh, how strong you seem." Her elegant fingers sleeked over his muscled arm. "What do you do?"

"I work in your gardens, my queen," Adon said.

"Do you like my gardens, pretty Adon?" she purred.

"Yes, my queen! I was a farmer's son before I came to Kava," he replied. "The caliph's tax collectors took me in exchange for the additional taxes they said my father owed them."

"And how old are you, little pet?" Kalida asked him.

"I am seventeen, my queen."

"You had no wife?" Kalida's hand brushed Adon's thigh.

"A betrothed. We were to be married in the full moon after

her first show of blood, but I am no virgin, my queen. I know what a man must do to please a woman."

"I am twenty-three," the queen told him, "and I have been pleasing myself with men since I was thirteen. Have you had a woman since you came to Kava?"

He blushed. "No, my queen. There are no women in your gardens, I fear. That is where I have been in the year since I arrived."

"Do you know how the women of Kava make love, little Adon?" The queen's green eyes narrowed as she spoke, assessing her new lover.

"I have heard rumors, my queen," he said, blushing further.

"You will do nothing without my permission, *or Dagon's,*" Kalida told him, the fingers of one hand now marching down his chest, across his taut belly toward his groin. "Dagon knows what pleasures me, and so I have given him permission to act for me when he divines I wish it. Do you understand, my pretty little Adon?" She took his penis in her hand and squeezed it lightly.

"Y-yes, my queen," he half gasped.

"Excellent," Kalida said, releasing her hold on him. Turning onto her back, she put her hands behind her head. "You may both now begin caressing me," she told them sweetly. She watched through slanted eyelids as their hands began to move over her body. Dagon's touch was sensuous and sure. Adon's was shy and hesitant. She could understand that he was not certain of himself. She took one of his hands and placed it upon her small, round breast, smiling into his startled face even as she did so. "Do not be afraid, pretty Adon," she purred.

He grew bolder with her encouragement, slapping her breast lightly, pinching the nipple gently. Then, seemingly unable to help himself, he bent, and began to kiss the plump little breast.

"Lick her," he heard Dagon say to him.

"Ohh, yes!" Kalida agreed as the two men began to stroke her with long, warm, wet sweeps of their tongues. They licked her lithe body from her neck all the way down to her toes. Then Dagon turned her over, and they began to tongue upward over her legs, her thighs, her buttocks, the length of her back, pushing aside her long hair to finish with the nape of her neck. She was again rolled over. Dagon, pillows propped behind his back, took Kalida between his open legs, his big hands wrapping themselves about her breasts. Kalida's legs fell open, revealing her bounteous treasures to the wide-eyed Adon.

"Go on," Dagon encouraged him. "You know what to do now, don't you? Her pretty cunt is as sweet as honey. Taste it!"

"Oooooo!" Kalida squirmed in Dagon's embrace as Adon's pointed tongue began to explore her most intimate places, hesitantly at first, then with bolder stabs, and caresses that set her aflame. It was absolutely delicious, she thought. While she wanted Dagon for her mate, she would certainly keep her facile-tongued little gardener about. His tongue plunged into her sheath, and she squealed again with delight. Having Dagon pinching her nipples and fondling her breasts while little Adon tongued her pleasure point was wonderful. Her hips wiggled furiously. Finally, when she could take no more of his incredibly sweet torture, she managed to gasp, "On your back, Adon! I want to mount you!"

Adon obeyed her, whimpering with his own delight as she swung over him, and encased his thick penis within her body. She rode him hard, but even as Dagon had predicted to Vernus, she could not gain the pleasure pinnacle. Finally, Adon could no longer sustain himself, and his juices burst forth as she dismounted him, the creamy substance spilling upon his taut belly. Ignoring him, Kalida was already upon Dagon, and, moments later, she cried out as body and mind touched the heavens.

"He is useless as all the others before you were," she murmured to Dagon as she lay sated within his arms. "Let us send him away."

"Not yet, my beautiful queen," Dagon advised. "Will you allow me to guide us through the rest of the evening's entertainment?"

"Agreed," Kalida said. "But first we must bathe." She arose from the bed. "Come," she beckoned to her two lovers, and they followed her to her private bath.

Immediately the two men quickly rinsed themselves free of sweat and love juices. Then they took up soap-filled sponges and began to wash Kalida. Next they rinsed her, and toweled her dry. Returning to Kalida's bedchamber, Dagon took up the little leather whip, and handed it to the queen.

"Adon's lack of control must be punished, my queen," he told her softly. "He allowed his love juices to flow without permission."

A slow smile lit Kalida's beautiful features. "You are right, of course, Dagon. Adon needs correction for his lack of self-control." She turned her green eyes onto the younger man. "Palms on the bed, Adon, and buttocks up!" she commanded. When he had obeyed, a fearful look in his brown eyes, Kalida brushed the whip lightly across Adon's back, its knotted leather fingers tickling his skin. "A slave never releases his love juices before his mistress gives him leave to do so. Are you not ashamed of yourself, Adon?"

"Yes, my queen." Adon's voice was low, a trifle frightened.

"And do you not deserve to be chastised for your naughtiness, Adon?" Kalida murmured, her tone sad.

"Yes, my queen," her victim replied nervously.

"So be it, Adon," Kalida said. "Be warned, however, for each time you cry out, I shall add another stroke." Then she brought her whip down hard across his buttocks. He winced visibly, but was silent. Kalida smiled, and began a rhythmic flogging of her young lover's bottom. Soon it was pink with her efforts, and Adon's penis was thrusting forth between his thighs. "Is it enough of a lesson?" she asked Dagon.

"I believe so, my queen," he answered. "Upon your hands and knees now, my beauty. It is time for Adon to put that fine weapon of his to good use. Come, Adon, and put yourself within the queen's mouth; but this time you will not release your juices until I give you the signal to do so. Is that understood?"

Adon nodded, his calloused hand reaching out to tilt Kalida's head up as with his other hand he pushed his thickened penis into her open mouth. He trembled as her tongue and lips began to work him.

Dagon hid a smile. Poor little Adon with his burning bottom was going to have a difficult time of it. Kalida had the most skillful tongue Dagon had ever known. Kneeling behind his beauteous lover, he whispered in her ear, "Which route shall I take, my queen? That of Suneva herself, or that of Sodom?" His hand caressed her twin moons, and, drawing them open, he pressed the tip of his penis to the rosy aperture. But seeing Kalida shake her head, he slid his great hard penis down, pushing forward to slide effortlessly into the throbbing wetness of her hot, humid sheath.

Kalida arched her back for him as his hand tightened about her hips. Her head was swimming with the sensuousness of it all: the thick cock in her greedy mouth, which she was now most vigorously sucking upon, Dagon's most magnificent length plunging in and out of her with an almost primitive cadence. Why was it, she wondered muzzily, that of all the men she had known, he was the only one to truly please her? Was it because Suneva had meant him for her mate? Was it like this with all women and their chosen mates?

Her crisis was approaching, and, sensing it, Dagon called out, "Now, Adon!" even as his own juices thundered from his strong body and into her exquisite one. He heard the young man almost howling with his own pleasure as Kalida skillfully milked his tender balls, fiercely drawing forth his juices and greedily swallowing them. Then they collapsed together into a heap upon the cool marble floor.

After a short time, Kalida and Dagon came to themselves, and helped Adon onto the bed with them so he might recover fully. The queen drew the curly-haired blond slave into the comfort of her arms and crooned softly to him, caressing him lightly. For a time he lay motionless, but then he began to respond, lowering his head and fastening on to one of her nipples to suckle upon it. She caressed him gently, smiling as Dagon took her other nipple into his mouth.

"Ummmmm. That is so nice, my darlings," she praised them. Her nipples were tingling with pleasure, and her small breasts were swollen with this fresh arousal. Finally, she pushed her younger lover away, saying, "Fetch a basin of perfumed water, Adon. You will bathe my sex first, then Dagon's, and then your own." Then she lay back with a sigh as Dagon began to kiss her with deep, passionate kisses, his tongue playing with hers; licking her face, running teasingly along her soft lips. "I adore you," she managed to say when he freed her lips briefly. "I have not changed my mind."

"I am yours, my queen, now and forever," he told her. Then he began to kiss her again, their lips pressing, releasing, pressing again. He nibbled her mouth, kissing its corners.

Kalida murmured her contentment. Adon was now bathing her sex, which was tender and very sensitive. His touch, though delicate, was extremely sensuous. When he had finished, he daringly bent down and kissed her lover's mount. When he had bathed Dagon's sex, and finally his own, he removed the basin before rejoining them upon the bed.

Dagon now reached into the golden basket by the bed and drew out a vial of pale-lavender lotion. "Shall we massage your skin with this lotion, my queen?" he asked her.

Kalida looked at the purple stone vial in his big hand. "No," she said. "Rather, Adon and I shall massage you."

He lay obediently upon his stomach while the two pairs of hands rubbed the spicy lotion over his back, his shoulders, his buttocks, his long legs. At one point the queen's little hand pushed between his legs to massage his balls.

"How cold they have grown," she noted. "Now, Dagon, my handsome one, roll onto your back."

He obeyed the command, and they continued to rub the pale-lavender lotion into his skin. Dagon suddenly realized that his body had become extremely sensitive, and when she drew back his foreskin to rub the head of his penis, the sentient organ felt as if it were going to explode. "What is it?" he asked her through gritted teeth.

"Just a little something to enhance your performance, my love," she told him. "Adon, seat yourself behind Dagon and hold his feet when he raises them up as he will now do. That's it. Ohhh, what a lovely view," she teased her princely lover. Then, kneeling before him, she leaned forward and began to lick at his balls, which were so well displayed for her. They hung heavy and pendulous, and they were downy to the touch as she teased at him with her facile tongue. Then she gently took them into her mouth, rolling them about as he groaned with the pleasure-pain she was so deliberately inflicting upon him. His penis felt as if it was going to burst and shatter into a thousand pieces. It was thrusting skyward, its ruby head almost glowing, and quite dark red.

Kalida released her hold upon his balls, and slipped back, saying as she did, "You may release his feet, Adon. You may lower your legs, Dagon," and when he did, she mounted him, slowly absorbing his throbbing length into her eager body. "You will never forget that I am your queen, my prince, will you?" she murmured as she rode him. Then she leaned forward, and kissed Adon.

"Witch!" he said low, so only she might hear him, and raised his head just high enough so he might nip at her breasts.

Kalida broke away from Adon, and laughing replied, *"Slave!"*

"My beautiful queen," Dagon replied, and pulled her down into his embrace to kiss her until she was quite breathless.

"Give me your tribute," she whispered, and sighed as he filled her again with his love juices. Finally, when she had recovered from her passion, Kalida ordered Adon to bring them wine. Then the trio sat together upon the bed sipping the sweet vintage. "You have pleased me, little Adon," Kalida said in kindly, approving tones, "but now you must return to your quarters. I will not forget your charm, your obedience, or your skillful mouth. You will always be my slave. When I return to my own home within the city, which even now awaits me, you shall be in charge of my gardens. Will that please you?" She gently ruffled his blond curls.

"Oh, yes, my queen," the younger man replied.

"Kiss me," the queen said, and he sweetly brushed her lips with his own. "Now, go," Kalida commanded, and she watched, smiling as Adon left her bedchamber. Now she turned to Dagon. "You are my mate," she said. "Tomorrow I shall announce it to the city, and the search for the new queen will begin. We will sleep for a while, my prince. Then I expect you to mount me, and ride me with your full vigor."

"It shall be as my queen commands," Dagon answered her.

They slept together, limbs entwined, for several hours. Kalida was awakened by the sensation of soft kisses upon her face. She sighed, stretching herself languidly like some exotic cat. He took her face in his hands, drawing her up, and kissed her deeply, his tongue running along her lips in a teasing manner. His fingers dug into her head, combing the gossamer strands of her gilt hair. Kalida slid her arms about his strong neck, pressing her breasts against his broad chest.

"You are my mate, Dagon of Aramas, and for you I will give up a kingdom," she murmured softly against his mouth. Then, moving her head slightly, she bit his earlobe gently.

"You could have me as your slave and still keep your kingdom," he tempted her, curious to see what she would say in reply.

"I could indeed," Kalida agreed, "but I could not have your children, and I want your daughters, Dagon." Her fingers kneaded the back of his neck gently. "Our daughter might one day be Queen of Kava."

He was silent. *Our daughter,* she had said. But what of their sons? *His sons,* who would be taken from her house at eight, and sent from Kava at sixteen. And this was why he would not remain in Kava, Dagon thought silently to himself. He would be Kalida's mate, and go to the Palace of the Consorts to live. There was time enough to plan his escape in the next year or two. He would take Kalida if she would come with him, *and their sons,* but he would not remain in Kava; nor would he allow his sons to be taken from him.

"What are you thinking?" she asked him. "Your face is so serious, my love. What troubles you, Dagon?"

"You are such a good queen, Kalida," he began. "Do I have the right to take you from your people?"

"A woman is meant to mate and have children. That is how we perpetuate our species, Dagon," she replied. "I thought that I should never fall in love, and I was saddened by it; but the goddess meant for me to wait for you. Now you are here, Suneva be praised, and I am happy. *Really happy!* It is time for Kava to have a new queen. I am more than glad to relinquish my power and my authority so I may be loved by you and bear your daughters."

"But what will you do?" he asked her. "Will you not be bored just being in your home?"

Kalida laughed. "I shall belong to the Council of Queens," she told him. "We are the judiciary here in Kava, and there is always someone in the courts testing our laws. I also own a third share in my aunts' trading company. I am not an absentee owner, Dagon. I have always been involved in their commerce. We own several mines yielding gemstones, and a silk factory. The women of Kava are never idle. Idleness is a form of death, and abhored by the goddess."

"You amaze me," he said, and he meant it. "I have never before known women to be so intelligent, and so industrious, Kalida. In Aramas women are owned by their fathers, their families, or their husbands. Their primary function is to give their husbands sons to carry on the family name. They live inside their homes most of their lives, rarely venturing out even to the market or shops, for their servants do that for them. The women of my class spend their lives beautifying themselves and making life pleasant for their men. Of course, among the poor it is a bit different. They must struggle so to survive. Tell me, how did Kava come into being, Kalida?"

She snuggled deep into his arms. "No one is truly certain, but the legend says that a group of women, captured in a war, were being transported across the desert to be sold into bondage. Among them was a beautiful girl, the only child of the murdered, vanquished king. Her name was Suneva. it was she who secretly rallied the women into refusing to accept their ignominious fate. During a terrible sandstorm she led them out of the victor's encampment. When the storm was over, they could no longer even see their enemies' camp, and they had no idea of where they were. The princess, however, was a strong leader. She led her little band of women into the mountains. They wandered for weeks, and during that time, Suneva taught them how to be independent of everyone except themselves, for they were very much like our women are today. She taught them to rely on each other to govern and defend themselves.

"Then one day they were attacked by bandits who sought to enslave them. Forced, despite their best efforts, into a canyon with but one entry, they believed all was lost. It was then that Suneva struck the face of the rock mountain, and a passage opened for them. The women escaped into the passage, Suneva ordering the rock to close behind them. Thus they once again outwitted the men who would seek to subjugate them. They followed the tunnel to its end, and into the valley of Kava.

"Under Suneva's direction they built the city, discovered the riches of the earth, and learned to be autonomous of men. But because we understood that males have value else the goddess would not have created them, we brought men into Kava as slaves to do the heavy work, and we needed them to immortalize our race. But we have never allowed them to have sovereignty over us, for men are a troublesome sex, Dagon. Look at your own condition. Had your brother not been greedy for all that was yours, you should yet be your father's heir."

"What happened to Suneva that you deified her?" Dagon asked, stroking Kalida's silky hair.

"Suneva never grew old as the others who had originally escaped with her eventually did. It was quickly realized that she was not like other women. One day she went into the temple to pray. She was never seen again in mortal form. The next day a great marble statue appeared in the exact place where she was last observed. None could explain where it had come from, or how it had been placed within the temple. The women knew then that Suneva had been possessed by the spirit of a goddess because she had been able to lead them so capably, for the princess they had known in their own land was certainly no stronger than they had been. Who this great and generous spirit was they did not know, so it was the Suneva that they had known all those years that they prayed to, and have prayed to over the centuries. She has never failed us, and I hope we have not failed her."

Her story was an amazing one. Dagon wondered how much of it was truth, and what the real truth was. They would never know, he suspected. Reaching down, he tipped her face up to his. "Will you permit me to make love to you, my queen?" he asked softly.

Kalida smiled into his face and nodded, her small hand cupping the back of his head and drawing it down to hers. Their kisses were heady, and like the finest vintage wine. They were quickly intoxicated with each other as their tongues intertwined in a sensuous dance, but suddenly she drew away from him, smiling at his puzzled look.

"Come with me," she said, rising from their bed and holding out her hand to him. She led him to the far side of the bedchamber through a colonnade of marble pillars, out into her private garden. The space was silvery with the light of the full moon. On the far side of the garden a second colonnade gave way to a view of the mountains beyond, its terrace falling steeply down a sheer, smooth rock incline. While Dagon could not identify the shadowy growth of bushes and flowers, he could smell both the sweet musk of roses and the heady, potent fragrance of lilies. "Can you swim?" Kalida asked him.

"Yes," he answered, puzzled, and then he saw the pool with its delicate marble shell fountains at either corner. The water glistened darkly in the moonlight.

Releasing his hand, Kalida moved down the marble steps of the pool, and began to swim away from him. Dagon watched her, fascinated. He had never known a woman who could swim. Her gilt hair spread out behind her like a spiderweb, half shielding her lithe body from his sight. She dove beneath the surface, and for a moment he was frightened. Then he laughed, seeing her shadow swimming toward him. He moved swiftly down the steps into the water and plunged beneath the surface, swimming to meet her, their lips touching first.

As they broke into the night air again it was Kalida who laughed aloud, and it was a most joyful sound to his ears. "How well you understand me, my beautiful Dagon. How can this be in so short a time?"

"We have been destined to be together since time began," he told her, smiling and drawing her into his arms again. "It is the will of a most generous Suneva, my queen."

Her hands cupped his buttocks, drawing him closer to her. She could feel his love lance stiffening as it made contact with the soft pillow of her mount. She stood on tiptoes and ran a taunting tongue over his lips. "Aye, the goddess is very kind," she purred at him. Then, turning, she threw herself back into the waters, but she was not quite quick enough.

Dagon had anticipated her teasing mood, and his fingers closed swiftly about one of her ankles. For a moment she struggled to free herself, then she relaxed, floating lightly upon her back in her captivity. He bent and, taking her foot in his grasp, licked it with broad strokes of his tongue, pushing it between each of her toes, and finally sucking them individually in turn. Releasing her foot, he took the other and rendered it the same homage before freeing it, too.

For a long moment she floated before him, eyes closed, her long, beautiful hair streaming out behind her like gold and silver threads of spider's silk. Then she opened her emerald eyes, and she could see his great penis thrusting up from the ebony thicket of his groin. The tip of her tongue slid swiftly over her lips as if she were anticipating a delectable meal. Seeing her slight action, he reached out, and, taking her in a gentle grip, first her ankles, then her calves, and finally her slender thighs, he drew her inexorably forward to slowly impale her.

Kalida sighed gustily as he entered her body. With a wicked skill she tightened the muscles of her sheath about him, holding him firmly, releasing him, again and again. Bracing her, his hands beneath her back, Dagon leaned carefully forward. His tongue slipped from between his lips, and he began to encircle the nipple of one breast with a teasingly delicate motion. He made no other move but to encircle the sensitive little nub over and over again, just occasionally flicking at it with the very tip of his tongue. Her eyes closed, and by watching her face, he could see her passions rising moment by moment.

Finally, he raised his head from the first breast, and moved to the second. This time, however, his actions were harsher. He suckled fiercely on the second nipple, his teeth sometimes biting down on the tender flesh, not so hard as to harm it, but hard enough to send a jolt of lightning through her. He could feel himself growing bigger and harder within her, if such a thing was even possible, but the hot, spongy morass of her depth was arousing him now as she had never before aroused him.

Kalida could feel him throbbing furiously within her. The frenzy and turbulence of their hungry coupling was madness. She gasped desperately for air as she reached her crescendo, half sobbing as her love juices sprinkled forth, liberally and generously moistening the blazing red crown of his penis, but not satisfying it in the least.

Raising her up, Dagon carried her to the steps of the pool, setting Kalida down on her hands and knees. She arched her back, raising her buttocks up, and uttered one word. *"Yes!"* Standing behind her, he pulled the twin halves of her peach apart, positioning himself before the rosy aperture. Carefully he pushed against it, gently, gently, then more insistently, more assertively. The flesh gave way, opening slowly, and then suddenly the tip of his love lance entered the hitherto unexplored orifice of her lush body. She gasped, more in surprise than pain, and he pressed onward, one hand holding her firmly.

She was so tight. He knew at once that it would take little effort for him to reach the pinnacle of his own passions. He was halfway inside her now. Unable to help himself, he thrust his full length. Kalida gasped again, but forbade him not. He withdrew slowly, and thrust again . . . and again . . . and again. To his great surprise her bottom began to wiggle itself and press hard into his belly. Leaning forward, he sought and found her pleasure point with his other hand. She was creamy with her juices. His finger teased at the swelling nub as he moved himself within her until finally they arrived at the meridian of their lustful satisfaction, his tribute thundering into her wasteland while she squealed with her pleasure, almost squirming away from the grip of his hand in her excitement, while the hand beneath her was soaked with another libation of delight.

Finally, he withdrew from her. Kalida slowly turned over onto the pool steps to view the state of his love lance. She smiled, pleased at the sight. He was more shriveled and smaller than she had ever seen him. "I have milked your balls quite well, Dagon," she said with a chuckle.

He laughed weakly, seating himself next to her, the warm water of the pool lapping at them. "Aye, my queen, you have," he agreed. "I never knew such frenetic, hot desire as we have just experienced, but we shall make no babies that way, Kalida." He took her hand in his, turning it about to kiss its palm.

She smiled wickedly. "I have never allowed a man to do what you just did. It was interesting, and very exciting, but I do not think I would do it often." She took the hand holding hers, and sucked her juices from his fingers. Her heart was only just beginning to slow its furious beat.

Above them the sky was beginning to show signs of lightening. There was the faintest smudge of pale lavender-gray above the purple mountains. It would soon be dawn, the beginning of a new day. The lovers rose from the water and returned to the bedchamber to sleep, for they were both fully exhausted, their labors of the night even now drawing to an end.

It was there Zeras found them several hours later, Kalida curled into the protective curve of Dagon's muscled arm, a small smile upon her face. Seeing them thus, Zeras knew Kalida's decision was made, and there was nothing he could do to prevent it.

"Oh, well," he said softly to himself, "I suppose it was time for us all to retire." Then he bent, and gently shook the lovers awake.

Chapter 5

It had been over ten years since the population of Kava had been called into the Arena of the Queens. The marble and colonnaded sphere had but one entry, through the great temple of Suneva itself, for its purpose was but twofold. The abdication of one queen, and the choosing of another. The large bronze doors opening into the arena were always kept closed but for those two special times, which were separated by three days' time.

Kalida had, upon awakening, bathed, dressed, and then gone directly to pay a visit upon Uphala, the High Priestess of Suneva. Uphala was a tall, statuesque woman with raven's black hair and silver-gray eyes. Ageless, she had been Suneva's High Priestess for most of Kalida's lifetime. She now came forth to greet the queen upon the front portico of the snow-white temple, bowing deferentially and saying, "Hail, Kalida, Queen of Kava! I bid you welcome to the temple of Suneva."

"I salute you, Uphala, High Priestess, and beloved of the goddess," the queen responded, and together the two women entered the temple proper.

When they were seated in Uphala's private chamber, wine was poured by a young novice, who, bowing, withdrew, leaving the queen and the High Priestess alone. Kalida arose, and going to a little altar, poured a small libation of her wine into the offering dish at the feet of a slender statue of the goddess.

"Power and position have not obviated your sense of respect for Suneva, I see," Uphala remarked, pleased.

"How can I deny Suneva when she has answered my prayers so admirably?" Kalida answered the High Priestess.

"Then the faint rumors I have but only heard recently are true?" Uphala said quietly.

"Yes. I have chosen my mate," Kalida replied.

"You are certain?" Uphala queried the younger woman. "I am given to understand that his attributes are greater than any ever before seen here in Kava. It is not just that, is it? After all, if it is, you do not need to mate with him to enjoy him."

"I know," Kalida told the High Priestess. "He, himself, asked me the same question, and made the same suggestion as you did, but the answer I gave him, I give you. I love him."

"So," Uphala noted. He was obviously clever this man, to have captured Kalida's icy heart so quickly.

"I have waited all my life for Dagon. I know now it was the will of the goddess that I not fall in love until she brought him to me. He is a man, and my inferior, it is true, but he loves me, he respects me, and in his own land would have been a king one day. He seems to know what I am thinking before I do. He makes me laugh, and he is frankly the most incredible lover I have ever had. He is the only man who has *ever* brought me to true joy. Is there a better reason for me to take him as my mate, Uphala? If so, tell me, I beg you!"

The High Priestess could see Kalida's sincerity. "No, your reasons are valid, my daughter," she told the queen. "I have never seen you so happy, or so content. It is truly Suneva's hand in this matter. I accept her will. The temple will this very day send out messengers to all the villages in Kava, calling upon our women to come to Suneva's temple in three days' time so you may

announce your decision. And three days after that, all thirteen-
and fourteen-year-old girls shall be gathered in the Arena of the
Queens that the messenger of the goddess may choose a new
queen from among them. Suneva be praised!" Uphala drained her
cup.

"Suneva be praised!" the queen echoed, draining her own.

The High Priestess rose. "Let us go into the temple, my queen,
and pray to the goddess for your happiness with your mate, Dagon
of Aramas. I shall look forward to meeting this man who has
secured your heart when so many others before him failed."

Together the two women knelt before the huge statue of
Suneva. It was most unique, made of flesh-colored marble, its
eyes two enormous blazing blue sapphires. Strands of gold and
silver were worked into the marble that covered its head and long
hair. The goddess stood straight, yet relaxed, one arm by her side,
the other with its hand raised in blessing. On her shoulder sat a
snow-white marble dove. She was naked but for a large wreath
of fresh flowers that was placed about her neck daily. Her whole
demeanor was one of benign love as she stood silent within the
flickering lights of the candles and torches of the temple's main
chamber.

Their prayers completed, the women stood, and the High
Priestess kissed the queen upon both cheeks. "I feel her blessing,"
Uphala said.

Kalida nodded. Then, turning, she departed the temple.

Those who saw her crossing the square back to the palace
longed to stop her and ask her if the murmurs and whisperings
were true. Kalida walked, a slight smile upon her face, and while
she had always been approachable, this time, despite their great
curiosity, no one asked her to halt and speak with them. There
was something about the queen today that made them hesitate,
and so she passed by unopposed.

Kalida called upon Zenaida next. "I owe you a great debt,"
she told the older woman. "He is magnificent."

"*And?*" Zenaida pressed the queen.

"You mean Vernus has not already dashed here to share the
gossip with his brother, Durantis? And Durantis with you?" Kalida teased.

The High Procuress shook her head. "We have not seen Vernus since yesterday, my queen," she answered honestly.

"So," Kalida remarked almost to herself, rather pleased to learn that Dagon could be so discreet.

"*What? What?*" Zenaida begged the queen.

Kalida smiled mischievously. "Perhaps I should say nothing yet until Uphala sends out her messengers."

"*My queen!*" Zenaida sounded exasperated, and Kalida laughed.

"Oh, very well, Zenaida. I shall repay my debt to you by telling you that I have decided to take Dagon as my mate; but you somehow knew I would when you purchased him in Ramaskhan, didn't you?"

"I did," Zenaida admitted. "Suneva be praised!"

"Yes," Kalida agreed, "it is all the doing of the goddess. I firmly believe it, Zenaida. *I do!*"

The two women embraced, and then the queen took her leave of the High Procuress, returning to her palace, where she called Zeras and Vernus to her privately.

"I have been to visit the High Priestess, Uphala, and the High Procuress, Zenaida, to tell them of my decision to take Dagon of Aramas as my mate. Now I tell you, because you are both my trusted servants. I ask that you allow my news to be nothing more than an open secret until the formal announcement. Neither confirm nor deny it."

"Yes, my queen," the two chorused.

"We go to the Arena of the Queens in three days' time, and three days after that, the messenger of the goddess will be set free to choose a new queen from among the young girls. You two have a great deal to do before then. I expect you to be so busy that you will not have the time to gossip. Now, find Dagon, and send him to me," Kalida instructed. She turned on her heel, and entered her bedchamber, closing the door behind her as she went.

"Well, there it is," Zeras said bitterly. "*It really is over.*"

"Oh, don't be so querulous," Vernus replied. "Have you any idea of how much must be done in less than a week's time? We have so many decisions to make, I don't know where to begin! What servants are we to take, and which will remain for the new queen? Has anyone bothered to see if the water pipes in Kalida's home are connected? And what in the name of Suneva are we to do about furnishings? And we have to obtain a decent apartment for Dagon in the Palace of the Consorts!"

"First I must fetch Dagon," Zeras grumbled. "Have you any idea of where he may have gotten to, Vernus?"

"He's steaming himself in the baths," Vernus replied. "It was obviously quite a night, dear boy. *Quite a night!*"

"The baths are part of your province," Zeras snapped. "You fetch him for the queen. I can barely stand to even look at the brute."

"I like looking at him," Vernus chuckled. "He really is gorgeous, with those big muscles, his ebony hair and blue eyes."

"And that obscene penis," Zeras said sourly.

"Why, Zeras, dear boy, I didn't think you had noticed that magnificent cock at all," Vernus murmured slyly. Then with a chortle he hurried off to find Dagon.

"Custom demands," Kalida told Dagon when he had been brought to her, "that now I have chosen you for my mate we be parted for the short time prior to my formal announcement. When I tell my people of my decision, it will be required that we mate publicly before them. I will mount you in the Arena of the Queens, and you must then show my people that you can give me pleasure as no other can. Only then will they accept my decision. You may have whatever women you require during the time of our separation, Dagon, or you may be celibate—as you choose."

"I want none but you," he said quietly, and she believed him.

"Vernus will see you are housed and cared for until we meet in the arena, my love," Kalida told him. Then she kissed him ardently, and his penis immediately rose up. Laughing, she allowed him to cup her buttocks, and raise her so she might wrap her legs about his waist as he plunged deep inside her. Backing her against the wall allowed him to hold her with one big hand, while two fingers from his other hand drove into her other orifice. Kalida squealed, wiggling herself as she tried to satisfy both the burning itches he had aroused.

"Oooooooo!" she murmured hotly in his ear, bending her head to sink her teeth into his shoulder as he doubly pistoned her.

"Bitch!" he groaned, feeling his crisis nearing. "I shall have a thin little silver dildo made to help me pleasure your outrageous desires. And three matching balls for your eager sheath," he told her.

"And I shall have a carved ivory ring made especially for your cock," she threatened him. "I shall keep you in a constant state of desire for me. Ahhhhh!" she cried out softly as they reached the top of the mountain together. Her head dropped onto his shoulder, and she sighed gustily with her deep satisfaction. Her legs dropped away, and he held her close so she would not fall, amazed he could stand himself.

Finally, Kalida pulled away from him. "Go now," she said, "and in three days' time you will show all of Kava how much you love me, my beautiful Dagon."

"It shall be as my queen wishes," he promised her, smiling, and he backed from the chamber.

When he was gone Kalida sighed. When he had promised her he wanted no other lovers to amuse him during their time apart, she had promised him no such thing. Still, she thought, no one had ever given her the pleasure Dagon had, and she expected that nothing had changed in that respect. Even sweet little Adon with his facile tongue would not make her happy. Like Dagon, she realized, she was doomed to three days of longing, and deepening desire. Somehow it didn't seem fair, but he was worth it!

The queen was not seen for three days as word of her impending abdication was broadcast throughout the land of Kava. It had been so long since a new queen had been chosen that there was great excitement and anticipation of the celebration to come. Every mother with a female child between the ages of thirteen and fourteen, who had had her first show of blood, imagined her daughter as the next queen. The record of each eligible girl was carefully checked, for there were those who were tempted to cheat the authorities with daughters who were yet twelve, or closer to fifteen, or had not yet become women.

The day of Kalida's abdication came. It was a beautiful day, clear, warm, and sunny. For two days, the city had been filling with those women from the farthest reaches of Kava's borders.

Now the flow of females of all ages surged up the temple steps, and out its rear bronze doors into the Arena of the Queens with its green-and-white pillars. In the center of the arena's sandy floor a large, flat marble altar had been set. The arches and balustrades of the arena were draped with colorful flowers of all kinds, and the air was heavy with fragrance.

The queen's box was on the west side of the arena. The female genitals, carved in gold, were proudly displayed on the box's front. An awning sewn from cloth-of-gold shaded the single throne, and marble benches about it. The cacophony of chatter died immediately as the queen, the High Priestess, and the High Procuress entered the royal enclosure. Then a mighty cheer went up as Kalida stepped forward and acknowledged her subjects. They grew silent again as she raised her hand in order that she might speak.

"Women of Kava! Ten years ago I was chosen by the goddess to rule over you. I have ruled longer than any queen in Kava's history. Until recently no man captured either my heart or my attention enough that I would give up the throne, and my crown, to mate with him. Recently, however, the goddess has brought to me a man for whom I am willing to do just that. Today I come to you to tell you that I have taken a mate, and will, in three days' time, give up my authority over you. Suneva has blessed me. I would that you, my beloved sisters, render me your blessing, too. Pray that the new queen will rule you as well as all those who have come before her have ruled you. We have thrived, and survived since the days of our earliest existence because of the peace and concord among us as women. We are not like men, who war and destroy. Suneva be praised!"

"Suneva be praised!" the entire arena of women cried out.

The High Priestess now came forward to stand by Kalida's side. "The time has come for the queen to mate," she said so that all might hear her. Once more the arena grew silent with anticipation.

Dagon was brought forth into the arena escorted by a group of beautiful young women who were clothed in nothing more than wreaths of flowers and their long hair. There were flowers on their ankles and wrists, and about their necks and in their flowing hair. The nipples of their breasts were stained a carmine red. Dancing and laughing, they surrounded the queen's mate.

He towered above them all. He had been bathed and primped by Vernus, who was almost beside himself with delight that Kalida had chosen Dagon for her mate. His dark hair shone with a blue-black sheen. It was tied with a gold-and-pearl ribbon, and topped with a floral wreath. He wore a simple linen wrap about his loins, and was barefooted. The muscles of his chest, his arms, and his legs were oiled to best show them off. He was bronzed and handsome, and the women leaned forward to obtain a better look at him, nodding appreciatively to one another.

They brought him before the royal box, and Kalida, walking slowly down the staircase, joined him, to stand by Dagon's side. Reaching out boldly, he took her hand in his, lifting it to his lips to kiss. She could not help but smile at him, and a murmur of pleasure rose from their audience. Then the High Priestess raised her hand, and all grew silent once again.

"Kalida, Queen of Kava," Uphala said, "is it your wish to take this man for your mate, knowing that by doing so you must renounce your queenship with all its power and authority?"

"It is my wish," Kalida replied.

"Do you comprehend that he is now your charge and responsibility and that you may not repudiate him slightly or in pique, but only if he becomes disobedient and cannot be corrected. Understanding this, Kalida, Queen of Kava, is it still your wish to have this man for your mate? Answer truly, for Suneva alone knows the secrets of your heart."

"It is my wish," Kalida repeated.

"You have heard the queen," Uphala said to the assembled. "Have you anything to say to her, oh women of Kava?"

"*Is this your wish, Kalida, Queen of Kava?*" the women cried.

"It is my wish," the queen said a third time.

"So be it," the High Priestess said. "Bring the mating cup."

Two young girls hurried forth from the space beneath the royal box. One carried a large double-handled gold cup, carved about with both male and female genitals. The other held a carafe. They came before Uphala, and bowed low.

"Pour the wine," she instructed them, and they hurried to obey her.

Then the girl with the carafe put it aside upon the ground, and helped her companion to hold the double-handled mating cup up for the High Priestess to bless, which she did. The cup was then brought to Kalida and Dagon, and they drank deeply from it.

The crowd cheered, and took up the chant: *"Mate him! Mate him! Mate him!"* This was, after all, what they had come to see. All mating ceremonies were alike, but this big man who had taught the queen how to love came with a reputation that was not to be believed. Still, they were anxious to see if those fabled attributes of his were real.

Dagon was once again surrounded by his escort of laughing girls. Dancing and singing in a tongue he could not comprehend, they led him to the marble altar in the center of the arena. Finally before it, they removed the wrap about his taut loins, revealing him to a thousand pairs of eyes as they turned him slowly about for all to see.

"Ahhhhhhhhh." The collective sigh went up. The rumor was truth. More than truth! The women turned to each other, chattering excitedly and pointing. Many were seen to rub themselves in lustful anticipation of the public mating to come.

Dagon's companions now set to work arousing him. A pot of pale-green cream was brought forth from behind the altar, and several pairs of hands began to massage him rapidly over his entire body. His legs were spread, and the cream lavishly laved on his genitals. One girl knelt before him, taking his penis in her mouth to suck vigorously upon it. Another slipped beneath him, and took his balls into her mouth, rolling them about, and tonguing them until he was groaning loudly with his rising lust. There wasn't a part of his body they left untouched, and where their hands moved, his skin became so sensitive that he was hard pressed not to scream with the acute sensuality that was rising up and threatening to smother him with his unfulfilled desire.

The girl entertaining his love lance could no longer contain it within her mouth. She fell back gasping for air. The girl with her teasing tongue also released him. His penis was enormous, and, seeing it, a shriek of excitement rose from the audience as they stood as one, pushing and shoving to better see this incredible man. The cup was put to his lips, and he was ordered to drink, which he gratefully did.

"He is ready now," he heard Kalida say.

His legs were near to buckling with the hunger racing through his entire body. The troupe of women brought him to the foot of the altar, and, laying him back, drew him up upon it. The audience was screaming with delight at the sight of his great love lance raised high to salute the queen. Dagon's head was swimming with a mixture of wine, and pure unfettered lust. He did not see them remove Kalida's simple white gown, but suddenly she was mounting him; slowly, and to his great relief, encasing him within her burning sheath. The sound of her voice calmed him.

"Do not release your juices until I give you leave, my love," she warned him. "If you shame me now, our mating cannot be completed."

Dagon drew in a deep, cleansing breath, and, reaching up, grasped her breasts in his hands. "Ride me, my queen," he said. "I will be strong as long as you are strong." Then he flashed a smile at her.

Kalida smiled back, and began to ride him; slowly at first, rising up, and then grinding herself back down into his groin. She went on like this for some minutes, then her tempo became faster and faster. The watching women caught quick glimpses of his great lance as it flashed back and forth within the queen, in and then out again. They screamed, maddened, and many tore their clothing, rubbing and playing with their own genitals until the entire arena of women burst with an orgasmic crowning of pleasure even as Kalida cried, *"Now!"* to her mate, and they together howled their satisfaction.

The arena was suddenly quiet, and then the women broke forth in a thunderous clapping of approval. *"They are well and truly mated!"* arose the collective blessing of the women of Kava. They stood, hands applauding the newly mated couple.

"I do not think I can get up," Dagon said, a twinkle in his blue eyes. "You have totally exhausted me, my queen."

Kalida dismounted her lover, springing lightly from the altar, and said, "Show the women how strong you are, my love, and tonight I will give you leave to do whatever you desire with me."

"Anything?" he said, cocking an eyebrow at her.

"Anything," she promised him, and he leapt up to stand by her side with a grin. Kalida laughed. "You are a villain," she said.

"You have promised," he reminded her, "and I promise you a night of such unbridled ecstasy, my queen, that you will not regret your decision to give up your throne."

Together they exited the Arena of the Queens through a passage beneath the royal box that took them back to the palace without having to appear again in public that day. When they had reached the queen's apartments, Dagon excused himself.

"I must see Vernus if I am to keep my promise to you, my queen," he told her. "In another place this would be our wedding night, and I would have it be a very special one for you, Kalida."

"I am in your hands," she told him happily.

Chapter 6

Vernus was more than delighted when Dagon came to him for his help. It was he who would be the most important member of the former queen's new household. Poor old Zeras would be relegated to managing Kalida's commercial interests, but he, Vernus, master of the queen's household, would reign supreme, and his mistress's consort was already paying him the deference due to his position. Vernus felt mellow, and overflowing with goodwill. He positively beamed at Dagon.

"How may I aid you?" he asked the prince. "I must say that your performance in the arena this afternoon was absolutely spectacular; if you will permit me to make the observation."

"I did not think men were allowed in the Arena of the Queens but for a consort," Dagon said, amused.

"I watched from the tunnel entrance," Vernus said, chuckling. "No one saw me, or I should be punished for my presumption.

These women are so proprietary about their little ceremonies. Such a fuss over very little, but, of course, in your case . . ." He chortled once again. "Now, dear boy, how may I help you?"

Dagon told him, and Vernus's gray eyes grew wide, but he nodded vigorously as the prince spoke quietly to him. "Can it be managed?" Dagon finished.

"Yes, of course it can," Vernus said, "but why there?"

"Kalida has given me permission to do whatever I desire with her tonight; a reward, if you will, for my pleasing behavior this afternoon in the arena. Since I intend introducing her to some rather unusual experiences, I should prefer we be in a more private setting than the queen's quarters here in the palace. A cry of passion might easily be mistaken by the queen's guard, who could come dashing in at exactly the wrong moment." He winked broadly at Vernus. "Now, I shall also need . . ." he said, lowering his voice.

Again Vernus's eyes grew wide, and he said admiringly, "Of course, dear boy, I can obtain everything you need. I can but imagine how delightfully inventive you will be. I shall personally see to everything for you, and the queen will be there at the appointed hour."

He hurried off, humming beneath his breath in anticipation. Dagon's plans were broad in scope, and he wondered if Kalida would really cooperate . . . but one could ask.

One hour after the sunset, Dagon crossed the deserted royal square, hurrying along the private street to Kalida's home where she would live after her abdication. He saw no one as he moved through the darkness, but he had practiced the route several times during the late afternoon, and knew the way well now. He could have traveled it sightless. Entering the unlit house, he made his way to Kalida's bedchamber. This room was lit by many candles and empty except for a mattress set upon a wooden dais. On the floor next to the dais was a large basket filled with the items he had requested, a carafe of wine, and several goblets.

Kalida, herself, was restrained, spread-eagled between two marble pillars. She was blindfolded with a strip of silk, and gagged.

And she was totally naked. Seated silently near her was the young blond slave, Adon, also naked. Dagon removed her gag.

"W-who is th-there?" Kalida half whispered.

"Be silent, wench," Dagon replied in a harsh voice. "You are here to give pleasure, and to be pleasured in return, not to ask foolish questions." He removed his loincloth, and peered into the basket. For a moment he considered the contents, and then he drew forth a long, stiff white feather with a tiny, well-honed point. Seating himself cross-legged on the floor before Kalida, he ran the feather slowly along her slit, and across her plump lover's mount.

She gasped, surprised, unable to decipher just exactly what he was doing to her, yet he certainly was not hurting her.

Dagon ran the feather back and forth over the tempting little crease for several minutes. Soon Kalida was squirming, and her nether lips were beginning to pout and grow puffy. He could see new moisture just behind the folds. He plied the feather a bit more deftly with quick strokes and small jabs until he was able to push through her defenses, seeking her pleasure point.

"Ooooooo!" Kalida shrilled as the feather's tip found its mark, and she began to squirm. Was it Dagon plying the feather? *It had to be Dagon.* She wasn't so certain now she should have offered him such freedom to act on his own, but she would look weak and frightened if she went back on her word now. "Daaagon!" she moaned, but he didn't answer, and the feather kept working itself over her pleasure point until suddenly it burst, and she sighed gustily at the release.

The feather brushed sensuously at the inside of her right thigh, and then was gone. "Whoooooo!" she shrieked as a tongue began to lap up her juices, setting her afire once again. The tongue moved relentlessly over her flesh, stroking at her pleasure point so hard that it hurt, but then the fire began to once again burn. She strained against her bonds.

Hands were fondling her, but as she couldn't see, she couldn't decide how many hands. They slid up her legs, stroking, caressing, pushing both into her sheath and her rear aperture, driving and thrusting inside her until her constrained body was twisting wildly. She realized she wasn't afraid at all, but was very excited as she struggled naked, blindfolded, and bound, totally at the mercy of who? Dagon? *But who else?*

The hands moved softly over her thighs and buttocks now. They slid across her belly, and up her back. A hand grasped her face, and turned her head to one side. Lips pressed down on hers, a tongue drove past her lips, and teeth into her mouth, sucking upon her tongue. Kalida's head whirled. Her breasts were being fondled, and kissed lightly. Another tongue began to lick at them, nuzzle between the twin mounds, lapping and encircling the nipples roughly. A mouth closed over a nipple, and sucked hard upon it, sending a streak of lightning from the nipple to her pleasure point. Teeth lightly scored the sensitive flesh, and she screamed softly with her pleasure.

Then she felt her limbs being quickly untied, and the blindfold was taken away. Kalida blinked several times as her eyes grew used to the light once again. Seeing her mate, she smiled tremulously at him, and then her eyes swung to Adon, widening with surprise and delight.

"You are so bad," Dagon said sadly. "We pleasure you, and you do not even thank us, Kalida. You must be taught to be mannerly." Reaching out, his fingers closed about her slender wrist, and he dragged her across the room to the bed upon the dais. Sitting, he pulled her over his knee, and his hand descended hard upon her pristine white bottom. "You are a very wicked girl, Kalida, aren't you?" The hand came down a second, and yet a third time. "Answer me, wench!" He smacked her again, and again, and yet again. "Have you nothing to say to me?" His hand came down upon her buttocks a seventh and eighth time as she began to squeal, and he noted that the previously snow-white bottom was beginning to grow pink with his attentions. "Tell me just how wicked you are, Kalida!"

"Very wicked!" she confessed, wiggling provocatively as she lay across his knees. "I need to be spanked! *I want to be spanked!*"

He obliged her until her tempting haunches were red and hot, and his hand had actually grown sore. He was quite surprised by her capacity for this kind of treatment. The hand that had spanked her was firmly in the arch of her back now; he slid his other hand beneath her mount, and was not in the least surprised to find her wet with her juices.

"You are shameless," he said, half laughing. "Adon, bring me the balls. Our fair queen needs to be punished for so enjoying her spanking." He turned Kalida over, and, cradling her in his arms, kissed her soundly. "You really are quite naughty," he told her, but his eyes were dancing with amusement.

"What are you going to do?" she asked him.

"Why, teach you to be even naughtier, my love," he told her.

Adon brought Dagon a small red silk box embroidered with dragons. The prince took the box, and, opening it as he balanced Kalida in his lap, he showed her the contents. Inside, set in silken niches, were three little balls, each slightly larger than the other. One was gold, one was silver, and one was carved of ivory. Inside the gold ball, which was the largest, were several metal tongues. Dagon inserted it deeply into Kalida's sheath first. Next came the silver ball, which held a drop of mercury, and lastly the ivory ball, which was hollow and empty. "I think you will be well punished by these," Dagon said mischievously, and then he tipped her from his lap. "Walk about the chamber, my beautiful queen, and when you have completed three full circuits, you will dance another three. Then you will bring Adon and me a goblet of wine. Such sweet torture is thirsty work."

Fascinated, Kalida began to walk about the room. She had taken only a few steps when she felt a curious sensation in her pelvis. By the time she had circled the chamber once, she realized she had never before known such pleasure-pain. He was watching her, and, gritting her teeth, she completed the next two circuits. Then she began to dance about the room. By the time she had finished, and brought them both a goblet of wine, she was half mad with the sensation blazing throughout her entire nether regions. "In the name of Suneva, take them out," she said through gritted teeth. She stood very still, desperately avoiding movement of any kind, for when she moved, and the wicked balls smacked against one another, it was torture. Delicious torture, but all she really wanted was Dagon's big cock piercing her.

Dagon put down his wine cup, and, pulling her into his lap, extracted the three balls from her sheath. Then he ordered her on her back, and she lay with excited anticipation upon the mattress. But he again surprised her. She could see that sweet Adon had seated himself at her head.

"Raise your legs," her mate ordered her, and she obeyed.

Adon then leaned forward slightly, taking Kalida by the ankles, and pulling her legs back so that her sex was now exposed completely to Dagon's view. He reached into the basket, and drew forth first a vial of lavender oil, followed by a thin silver dildo, which he dipped into the oil. Then, placing the vial upon the floor, he slowly, and most carefully, dipped his fingers into the oil, and lavishly anointed her fundament with it. Taking up the silver dildo, he pushed it into her aperture, working it slowly at first, and then more rapidly, his slick fingers grasping the dildo's handle. It was cool, and very hard.

Kalida moaned with her rising lust. He was clever, her mate. His own love lance was really too big to be comfortable, but this thin little dildo was perfect, and it was arousing her greatly. Then he sensed that she was close to breaking, and he ceased his actions. She protested fiercely, but he only laughed.

He took her legs, one at a time, and lowered them slightly, nodding to young Adon, who half rising, popped his penis into the queen's open mouth while Dagon slid between her legs and plunged into her burning sheath. Kalida's legs wrapped about his waist, and she closed her eyes with her pleasure as he pistoned her while she sucked vigorously upon Adon's thickening member. The sensation of being ravished in all three of her orifices was incredible. She had never known anything like it. When their passions burst simultaneously, she couldn't believe it. She seemed to fly before crashing into the blackness, so totally satisfied she almost wept with her delight.

The trio lay half conscious upon the bed for some time. Finally, Dagon pulled himself to his feet, saying to Adon, "The night is young. Let us bathe, and then continue our orgy of pleasure."

Adon struggled to his feet, and together they drew Kalida up with them. Her eyes were still glazed with her passion as they led her to the bath. Torches in silver holders lit the room, whose walls were painted with scenes of men and women engaged in erotic pursuits, the women having the dominant roles; riding their lovers, whipping them, entertaining them in groups.

She stood silent as they took up the soap-filled sponges, and gently bathed her. The scent of gardenias filled her nostrils, and she vaguely wondered where she was, for Vernus had not told her when he blindfolded her and brought her to this place. It was strangely familiar, and yet she could not quite place it. "Where are we?" She had finally managed to find her voice again.

"This is your house," Dagon told her. "The place you will live after your abdication, my love. I thought such an evening as ours would be better spent in a secret place, away from prying eyes." He slipped the sponge between her legs, and gently washed her sex.

She nodded.

"We have not frightened you, Kalida?" His voice was concerned.

"No," she said, "but I never imagined . . ." Her voice trailed off, but there was a small smile on her lips.

"Shall we continue, or shall I send Adon to his own bed, my beautiful queen?" he asked her. "This is for your pleasure, Kalida, but if it pleases you not, then it comes to an end now."

"Until you, Dagon," she said softly, "I did not know love, or even true passion. Since I was fourteen I have mounted any man who took my fancy, but my purpose was to dominate. I gained no joy, as you well know. You have shown me that passion and love must be found together. And you have exposed me to the forbidden, which I seem to find most delicious." Her emerald eyes laughed at him. "And how kind of you to include our sweet Adon. I am glad you are not jealous of him, for while he does not offer to me what you do, I still enjoy him." She drew the blond slave to her, and kissed him tenderly.

The boy blushed, and said boldly, "I am proud to be your slave, my queen. I will always serve you in any manner you desire."

"Come," Dagon said. "The queen is bathed as are we now, and Vernus has brought us a special jar of cream to massage into our skins. And I have a thirst for some wine."

They returned to the bedchamber, and Adon poured them all a draught of wine which Dagon knew had been doctored with special herbs that would stimulate their lusts further. They drank, and then using Vernus's special cream, began to rub each other's bodies, pressing against one another as their desires began to rise once more. The two men had Kalida between them. They fondled her breasts and her buttocks. Finally, the trio fell upon the bed, each of the males on either side of the queen.

Dagon faced his mate. His mouth fused against her in a deep kiss, his hands going about her to caress her rounded and taut buttocks; while Adon, behind her, reached around to play with her swollen and aching breasts, pinching her nipples to arouse her further. The only sound in the chamber was the harsh panting of the combatants.

"Put your legs about me, my love," Dagon instructed his mate, "and remain on your side."

Kalida slid one leg over him, and another beneath his body so that she might embrace him with her limbs if she desired, but that was not, she quickly discovered, her mate's intent. Instead, Dagon quickly thrust his great penis into her eager sheath, impaling her fiercely. She sighed with pleasure, and then gave a little shriek as behind her Adon pulled the twin moons of her bottom apart, and slowly, slowly insinuated his own hard lance into her temple of Sodom. Kalida gasped for air. The sensation was overwhelming. The dildo had hardly prepared her for Adon's thick and very lustful penis.

"There's a rhythm to it, my love," Dagon murmured in her ear. He pulled her forward so that she was pressed tightly against him, and the pressure in her rear lessened somewhat. Then her other lover drew her back, and she found her bottom pushing at his belly. Back and forth. Back and forth. Back and forth. "You see," he encouraged her.

Kalida's head was swimming with her hot desire. Arms about Dagon's neck, she pressed her breasts and belly against him; then propelled her rounded hips back against Adon. The young man was moaning with his boiling lusts, and he boldly bit the soft nape of her neck in his passion. Unable to help himself, and sobbing, Adon released his juices in hard spurts until he was totally and completely drained. Then he rolled away from the queen, curling himself into a ball, exhausted with his efforts.

Dagon turned Kalida onto her back, pushing her legs back so he might delve into her more deeply than he ever had. The sensual pleasure-pain of his driving penis loosed the tigress in her. She clawed wildly at him. She sunk her little white teeth into his muscled shoulder, drawing blood which she licked away with her tongue.

"*Bitch!*" he growled into her ear, nipping at the lobe.

"*Don't stop! Don't stop!*" she panted hungrily. "Ahhhh, Suneva! It is finally enough!" she cried, her passions exploding but a moment ahead of his. She strained, her sheath becoming a greedy mouth that sucked him dry, contracting and expanding about his love lance to squeeze every possible drop of the tribute that he had to offer her. Then Kalida fainted, unable to bear any more of their combined lusts.

When Dagon had recovered his strength, he said to the blond Adon, "Go now, and remember your promise to Vernus to tell no one of this night. You will be well rewarded, not simply by the queen, but by me as well. You have done us a great service, Adon."

Adon rose from the bed, and re-dressed himself in the short tunic he had laid aside upon entering the room earlier. "I shall speak to no one of this," he said. His eyes strayed to the exhausted woman. "I would not hurt her, Dagon. I adore her. I know you are her chosen mate now, yet I cannot help but love her, too."

"I understand," Dagon told the younger man. "If she desires you, I cannot forbid it, although I do not promise I can contain my jealousy," he finished with a wry smile.

Adon nodded, and then departed.

When Kalida awoke several hours later, she found only Dagon by her side. Bending, she brushed her lips lightly against his, and his blue eyes opened. "Thank you," she said to him. "It was wonderful!"

"I hope you do not expect all of our nights to be so exciting," he said, smiling lovingly at her. "I think I have depleted my font of originality." He wrapped his arms about her. "How I love you, my beautiful Queen of Kava."

"A queen no more in two days' time," she told him.

"It will not matter, Kalida. I shall always love you even when you are old and wizened," he replied.

"In Kava, women do not become wizened," she replied.

He laughed. "I shall love you no matter," he promised.

"Let us remain here together until the time comes for the choosing," Kalida said. "Vernus can bring us food, and we have each other. It is enough for me, my handsome prince. Can it be enough for you as well?"

"I could remain here in this room with you forever!" he said.

"Then I command it, my prince!" she agreed.

So while Zeras fussed and fumed at the queen's unexplained absence, Vernus enjoyed his part in the conspiracy with the lovers.

"She has duties to perform," Zeras complained.

"Not until the morning of the choosing," Vernus replied, "and she will be there to complete her reign. When have you ever known Kalida to shirk in her duties, Zeras? You raised her to be better than that."

So Zeras was forced to wait until the morning of the third day since Kalida's official mating, when she appeared from her bedchamber as if she had been there all along. She was radiant, and seemed full of energy. Zeras scowled seeing Dagon by her side, but then he sighed. The beast was her mate, and he must live with it.

The queen was dressed in a simple sleeveless gown; but this day, rather than the white she usually favored, Kalida's gown was cloth-of-gold, fashioned into tiny, narrow pleats that ran from waist to hem. She wore a rope of enormous emeralds that lay upon the smooth, fitted bodice of her chest. Gold-and-emerald armbands had been clasped about her slim upper arms. The only other ornament she wore was her ring of office, which she would today pass on to the new young queen. Her hair hung loose, contained only by the narrow, filigreed crown of gold and silver, which was studded in emeralds. Dagon wore a simple pleated white linen wrap about his loins, and his gold torque about his neck. His was, after all, the lesser role.

"Have the maidens been gathered?" Kalida asked Zeras.

"Aye, my queen, it but awaits your coming," Zeras replied sadly.

Kalida nodded. "Then it is time," she said. Then she turned to Dagon. "You will walk just behind me a pace or two," she explained. "Today, however, you may enter the royal box and stand just to my right. Zeras. Vernus. If you should like to see the ceremony, I will permit you to watch from the tunnel entry," Kalida told them generously.

"Thank you, my queen," Vernus bubbled, delighted to be included.

"No," said Zeras. "I hid in that place the day you were chosen to be Kava's queen, but I cannot be there today when another is picked to stand in your place. It is too much to ask of me!" His voice broke.

Compassion lit Kalida's beautiful features. She reached out a hand, and touched Zeras's shoulder gently. "You do not have to come if it would make you unhappy, Zeras," she told him. Then she turned again, and was gone, followed by Dagon and Vernus.

A mighty cheer rose from the assembled women as the queen and her mate entered the royal box. Vernus tucked himself into the shadows below the stairs, but he had an excellent view. Uphala and Zenaida had been awaiting the queen. Below in the arena there were slightly over a hundred young girls between the ages of thirteen and fourteen standing nervously and talking in whispers. They grew silent as Kalida arrived.

When the cheering had died, the queen stepped forward. "Today we choose a new queen," she began. "I am proud to have ruled Kava these past ten years. My reign has seen our prosperity grow to its greatest levels. May it continue to grow under your new queen, and may Suneva guide her as well as she has guided me," Kalida finished, stepping back to take Dagon's hand in hers. He squeezed it encouragingly.

The High Priestess now took the forefront. "It is time," she said. "Remember that she whom the goddess chooses will bear a great burden. I advise the new queen, even before she is chosen, to remember from whence her blessings come. They come from Suneva who guards and guides us all. Suneva be praised!"

"Suneva be praised!" came the echoing cry from the benches in the arena, and from the girls below the royal box.

A temple novice stepped forward and handed the High Priestess a small box. As Uphala lifted its lid, a snow-white dove flew forth and circled the arena three times. The crowd held its collective breath, gasping in total shock when the bird alighted upon the dark head of Kalida's handsome mate, and there it sat preening itself before the stunned women.

Uphala snatched up the dove, and flung it into the air once more. Again the bird circled the arena thrice, alighting a second time upon Dagon's head. There were cries of "Sacrilege!" but Uphala held up her hand to silence them.

"Go," she instructed Dagon quietly, "and stand in the entry to the tunnel below the royal box." Then she took the bird from his head once more.

He did not argue, realizing this was a difficult situation, and he could easily find himself dead if it pleased these women.

"What is going on?" Vernus asked Dagon as the prince came down the stairs and stepped into the tunnel entrance.

"The messenger of the goddess has twice lit upon my head, instead of choosing one of the maidens gathered before us," Dagon said.

Vernus's eyes widened with surprise. "What can it mean?"

"That the bird is stupid," Dagon said softly. "Now that I am hidden, it will alight upon one of the proper candidates."

The messenger of the goddess, released a third time, however, flew aimlessly round and round the arena, refusing to alight on any of the maidens. The crowd began to murmur nervously.

"What is happening?" Kalida asked the High Priestess.

Uphala did not answer her. Going instead to the edge of the royal box she called down, "Dagon of Aramas, conceal yourself among the maidens for me," and when he had, the dove flew immediately to him, lighting upon his head with a triumphant little cry.

The Prince of Aramas walked through the group of wide-eyed and silent maidens, back up the staircase to the royal box, the dove perched atop his head. Uphala took the messenger of the goddess and returned it to its case, handing it to the stunned novice. Then she stepped forward to address the women.

"It is prophesied in the Holy Book of Suneva," she began, "that there will come a time when a queen will rule longest of any before her; and when she finally falls in love, and takes her mate, it is *he* who will be chosen by the goddess as a sign that the queen, and her daughters, and her daughters' daughters are to rule in Kava in perpetuity. Because Kalida had ruled for so long, I remembered the prophesy, and consulted our holy book for its accuracy. It is there for any and all to see, and none can doubt it. I proclaim Kalida, Queen of Kava, and her mate, Dagon of Aramas, the very consort that Suneva prophesied of back in the dawn of our history. Are there any among you who do not believe or would question the will of the goddess?" Uphala challenged them.

The arena was very silent.

"Then, all hail to Kalida, Queen of Kava, and to her consort, Dagon," Uphala cried loudly, and a thunderous cheering rose from the assembled.

"All hail to Kalida, Queen of Kava, and to her consort, Dagon!" the women cried loudly.

"I am to remain queen?" Kalida asked the High Priestess, as surprised at what had transpired as any of the other women.

"You will become Kalida the First of Kava," Uphala said, "and Dagon will remain by your side, your equal in all but the government of this land, although his voice will be respectfully heard should he raise it, and his words considered. Your eldest daughter will be our next queen. This is written."

"But how can a queen rule well when her mind and heart will surely be torn in all directions? Kava's queens have succeeded because they had but one goal. *To rule Kava,*" Kalida said.

"We cannot deny what has happened here today, Kalida," the High Priestess replied. "I can imagine your confusion. You have ruled Kava well, and believed, according to custom, that you could lay aside your heavy duties to live peacefully with your mate and bear your children. But the goddess has decided otherwise."

"I never wanted to be queen," Kalida said softly.

"And perhaps," Uphala answered her, "that is precisely why you were singled out for this great honor. For you, ruling has been a duty. You have never been overwhelmed by any sense of power or authority. Be content with this, my daughter. Come into the temple now with me. We will pray for guidance. I will show you the prophecy in the Holy Book of Suneva. I will help you to come to terms with this." Uphala led the queen away. As they passed through the group of half-relieved, half-disappointed young girls, she gave them her blessing, and the queen reached out to sympathetically touch as many of the maidens as she could. They had no idea how fortunate they were not to be in her sandals.

When they had gone, Dagon turned to Zenaida. "Did you know of this prophecy when you purchased me in the slave markets of Ramaskhan?" he asked her. Then he sat next to her on the marble bench.

She shook her head, and her fine dark eyes looked directly at him. "No, I did not know. I was as surprised as anyone else here today by what has happened."

"There will come a day, Zenaida, when I shall want to take my sons and escape Kava," Dagon said quietly. "I cannot allow the fruits of my loins to be sold away to die on battlefields fighting for nameless kings and warlords. I am the rightful heir to the King of Aramas, and my brother shall not usurp my place, nor that of my sons."

"You cannot go back," Zenaida said to him.

"I must claim my inheritance," Dagon insisted.

"You cannot," Zenaida told him. "Hear me, Dagon, and hear me well. For each year that passes in Kava, twenty-five years pass in the world beyond ours. That is one of the reasons we have been able to keep our kingdom safe from outsiders and marauders, who if they found us would plunder our riches and enslave us because we are women. We are more legend than fact to the people beyond our valley. We sell our cohorts who have been given a potion so they may leave Kava, and exist in the outside world. We sell our silks, our wools, and our gemstones there. We come and go so quickly none get to know us. We know the secret of controlling time. When we enter their world, we exist in their time, but when we return home to Kava, it is only as if a few days have passed. You were not born in Kava. If you leave, you will become the age you should be in your own world. Time has slowed for you here.

"When I brought you to Kava, how long had it been since you had seen your own land? A year? And if you reentered your world, and actually managed to reach Aramas, it should be another year. And the few weeks while you have been here in Kava over six years have passed. Six years, Dagon! Can you imagine what has happened in that time? You have told me that your father was frail, which is probably why your brother acted to rid himself of you when he did. Undoubtedly he rules in Aramas, Aurea by his side, their children about them. You would bring civil war to your land if you returned now.

"Remain here in Kava by Kalida's side, for you love her, I can see. Look what has happened today. A queen who was expected to step aside and enter retirement has been told she will rule until her death, and that her female descendants will follow her. This will be a great change for Kava. Who is to say there cannot be other changes? If a queen can rule forever, cannot her sons be put to better use than being sent away to fight other men's wars?"

"Do you think such a thing is really possible?" he asked.

"Change comes slowly, Dagon," Zenaida replied, "but *anything* is possible. I am not the only mother who wept secretly to see her sons sent away. It is true that men are an inferior sex with their penchant for violence, cruelty, and greed, but why can that not be changed as well? If you leave Kava, who will engineer that change? I believe the goddess brought you here not just for Kalida's benefit, but because she knew there would come a time when the women of Kava must begin to learn to live with their men in a more equitable, objective, and unbiased manner. You are the key to that change."

"There is much wisdom in what you say," he told her thoughtfully.

"Stay with us," she said softly.

"It is an enormous undertaking," he answered her.

"I know," she replied, "but I chose you not simply for the hugeness of your penis, but because I believed your intellect was as immense as well."

He laughed aloud, and, taking up her hand, kissed it. "You must have been a very wicked young woman," he told her.

"I am still very wicked," she answered him with a chuckle.

"My lord Dagon, Consort of Kava," he heard Kalida call.

Turning his head, he saw her standing in the center of the now empty area, for while he and Zenaida had spoken, the amphitheater had emptied.

"My lord, come and escort me home," the queen said. "We must talk on what has happened this day, *and* you have your marital duties to perform if we are to give Kava a new ruler one day."

"You are insatiable, my queen. I can but hear and obey," he called back to her, rising from his place by Zenaida's side.

"Then you will remain?" the High Procuress said softly to him.

Dagon's blue eyes were fastened on Kalida. Kalida, his beautiful mate, his queen, his lover. He had never known anyone quite like her. Strong, brave, intelligent, yet vulnerable. She needed him. *He needed her!* "I will stay," he said to Zenaida, and then hurried down the steps from the royal box, running across the arena to catch Kalida up in a passionate embrace. Then, together, a smiling queen and her happy consort departed the arena.

"Well, well, my dear," Vernus said to his sister-in-law, "what a day this has been, has it not? And what will happen next, I wonder?"

Zenaida tucked her arm into his. "We are witnessing the beginning of a new era, Vernus. Suneva only knows what will happen."

"Indeed," Vernus said dryly. "You are asking me to supper, my dear, aren't you? If you do, I shall tell you, and Durantis, *but of course it is for your ears alone,* the delicious naughtiness the queen and Dagon have been up to these past few days. They brought that charming young blond gardener, Adon is his name, my dear, into their midst to partake in the royal orgy, and he told me . . ." Vernus dropped his voice as they exited the royal box and walked across the arena.

"No!" Zenaida was heard to exclaim at one point, but she sounded more titillated than shocked by what she was being told. *"Are you sure?"*

"Adon, the dear boy, relies on me," Vernus said smugly. "Now come along, sister. My brother, Durantis, will want to hear it all."

And arm in arm they walked together through the temple proper, and out into the main square of Kava, where the celebrations were already beginning to usher in this new will of the goddess that would change their lives, and certainly the destiny of Kava, forever.

BOUND AND DETERMINED

by Susan Johnson

Chapter 1

"I'm leaving town today."

"And brave your sister's wrath?" Lord Akers glanced across the billiard table, his skeptical gaze taking in the Marquis of Crewe's lounging form. "You're supposed to be hosting your niece's coming out ball tonight."

Hugh Dalsany shrugged one shoulder negligently before lifting his glass of cognac to his mouth. "Fanny won't care if I'm there or not so long as I pay for it."

"Your legion of lovers will despair at your absence," his friend drolly noted. "Don't you service two or three a night?"

"Precisely why I'm not going." The young marquis grimaced before draining his glass, the last few days of carouse enervating. "I'm sick of them all," he murmured, leaning forward in a ripple of honed muscle, reaching for the liquor decanter. "I'm done fucking."

Charles Lytton's cue scratched down the green felt, missing the ball completely. "Are you on your deathbed?" he sardonically inquired, tossing aside the cue and standing upright. "Or just out to win this game?"

"Neither. I'm just bored to death. How many years have I been fucking?" The marquis slid lower in his chair and contemplated the liquor in his glass. "Too damned many," he said, half to himself, and, lifting the glass to his lips, he washed the taste of surfeit from his mouth.

"You're just grim about having to play the gentleman for your niece this Season. The debs will put any man out of sorts. Spend a week or so with Lavinia and you'll change your mind."

"Lord no, she's talking marriage. I'm serious, Charlie, I'm done with cunt. I must have fucked a thousand women in the last decade. That's enough for any man. I'm going up to Woodhill and settle into farming."

"You won't last a fortnight." Walking around the end of the billiard table, Lord Akers dropped into an adjoining chair. The game room was deserted, the men's disheveled evening attire from the previous night not untypical for the more libertine club members. "Besides, we promised the Bellemy sisters we'd entertain them after your niece's soiree."

"You'll have to do it alone. I'm having my driver pick me up in a few minutes." The marquis smiled. "I'm sure you'll manage without me."

"Five thousand says you won't remain celibate for—what . . . a month?" Charlie's brows lifted in ironic query. "Or are you having all your house and dairy maids sent into purdah?"

"You'll lose your five thousand, and the maids will be perfectly safe." Save for his heavy-lidded gaze, the marquis's handsome face bore no marks of dissipation regardless the relentless debauch of the last few days. "You don't realize the extent of my ennui, Charlie."

"Nor would anyone watching you the week past."

The marquis shrugged again, any attempt at explanation beyond Charlie's understanding. "Give my regards to my sister Fanny if you see her tonight. I've sent her a note, but she's bound to have questions."

"Not that I could answer them. Good God, Crewe, this will astound everyone. They're going to say you're raving mad."

"If I was concerned with people's opinions," the marquis lazily drawled, "I'd have led a very different life, now, wouldn't I?"

"Can't argue with you there." Charlie and the marquis had been the bellwether for scandal since adolescence.

"Come up for fishing when you have your fill of London," the marquis offered, setting his glass aside and rising from the chair. "And I'll show you the improvements on the estate."

"Are you sick, Hugh?" Charlie's voice had gone soft, genuine concern and bafflement in his eyes.

"Don't worry, Charlie. I haven't been brought low by Venus's revenge. I've just decided to find something else to do besides fuck."

"You've never talked like this before."

Crewe's tone was tolerant. "Don't worry, Charlie. It's not contagious." He glanced at the clock on the wall. "Pierce is waiting. I'll see you when next you come to Woodhill." And with a wave, he walked from the room.

"Where's Pierce?" Standing on the curb outside Brookes, the marquis surveyed the unknown driver seated where his head groom should have been.

"He was taken sick, my lord."

"And Oates?"

"Driving Lady Castleton and Lady Jane, my lord."

"I hope you know the way to Woodhill," Hugh gruffly noted, disconcerted to find someone other than his personal driver at the reins. Pierce was more than a driver; he was privy to much of the marquis's personal life and held the enviable position of confidant.

"Yes, sir, I know the way, sir. No question o' that."

"Then get me there post haste. I'm weary to death of London," Crewe added, moving toward the carriage door held open by a small page he didn't recognize. "Are you from Dalsany House?" he inquired, placing his foot on the step, his weight putting a strain on the carriage springs. His second step put him inside the carriage, and the boy's response went unnoticed, for he found himself with company as the door shut and the carriage pulled away from the curb.

Female company.

"Who the hell are you?" the marquis curtly inquired, dropping into the opposite seat, a faint frown marring the perfection of his forehead.

"I apologize for taking Pierce from you."

"Taking him where?" Leaning back against the green leather squabs, he crossed his legs and scrutinized the woman seated across from him. She was fashionably dressed in primrose China silk patterned with blue flowers, the sumptuous summer gown, feminine, beribboned, and flounced, lush foil to her heavy auburn hair and porcelain skin. His gaze slowly traveled down her body, long-held habit still operating despite his new venture into celibacy. Her opulent bosom, slender waist, the curve of her hips garnered his approval if no longer his interest.

"Pierce's destination isn't important right now," she said, her posture unlike his, stiffly upright, her gloved hands folded in her lap. "He's perfectly fine. You needn't be concerned."

"Pierce can take care of himself, I'm sure," the marquis softly murmured, taking measure of the woman's unease. "You, however, have two minutes to explain your presence before I put you out."

"I'll be brief then." An underlying sultriness colored her voice; he took immediate note of it. "I have a proposal I'd like to make you." She hesitated briefly, and when his brows rose in silent query, she said in a rush, "I need a child."

He didn't pretend not to know what she meant. "Why come to me?"

"Because you have the reputation for being"—a blush colored her cheeks—"accommodating to women."

"Sorry. You're a day too late."

"I wouldn't be here unless my situation were critical."

"Look," the marquis gently said, "it's nothing personal. I've just decided to rusticate for a time. But there's any number of men who would be more than pleased to help you."

"Unfortunately, my husband chose you."

His lounging form stiffened at her words. "Chose me?" he murmured, his voice chill. "Who are you?"

"I'm not at liberty to say, but your reputation brought you to my husband's attention. While rumors of your most recent child by the Countess of Lismore last month apparently determined his final decision. I'm sorry."

"This is preposterous, of course." He'd relaxed again, the woman's story beyond the limits of possibility. He was wealthy, well connected; his ducal father was powerful, a personal intimate of the queen. This woman's proposal—or her husband's proposal—was ludicrous. And he said as much again.

"Perhaps it won't take too long," she only said, and added again, "I'm sorry to involve you."

"You haven't," he snapped, reaching up to rap on the front panel, a signal for the driver to stop.

But rather than stop, the carriage picked up speed.

"Someone's going to pay for this," he muttered, his hand on the door latch.

A second later, in response to his glare, she calmly said, "It's locked from the outside."

Flinging himself back onto the seat, he swore in a lengthy stream of invectives before settling into a moody silence, the streets of London flashing by in rapid succession. The irony of his position had not escaped his notice and he contemplated briefly whether some mysterious vengeance was being exacted for his past sins. He further considered who might be behind this grotesque form of retaliation, but the list of disgruntled husbands, fathers, brothers was too lengthy to contemplate with any certainty. The lady's faint accent wasn't English—although his amorous activities hadn't been confined to England so that only narrowed the possibilities marginally.

Surveying her from under his long lashes, he tried to recall whether they'd met before, and while the blur of women in his life was a constant, her dramatic beauty would have made her memorable. She was the kind of woman he and Charles would have rated in their green youth as worth a week of their time. Even now, in their jaded manhood, she would have been unforgettable. And if he'd not reached the ultimate point of female saturation *and* had she not forced herself on him, and further had he not been a *damned prisoner* in his own carriage, she might have piqued his interest.

But in his current hot-tempered misogyny, she was anathema.

Surveying the passing landscape as they moved into the countryside outside London, he considered the possibility of kicking the door out and jumping from the fast-moving carriage, but outriders flanked the conveyance front and back, he discovered, the large troop conspicuously Slav, their flat-boned cheeks and dark coloring, the medieval character of their armament giving evidence of their Balkan heritage. A practical man, he realized how ineffectual any attempt at escape would be and came to understand as well that the lady in his carriage or her husband at least had roots in the area east of the Adriatic.

Although at closer inspection, the lady, opulently titian-haired, white-skinned, and emerald-eyed, had none of the look of the East. Richly dressed, her sapphire jewelry first-rate gems, her mildly imperious air all bespoke a patrician world, but her eyes, brilliant green even in the shadowed interior, had none of the *jeunesse dorée* languor habitual to the beau monde. They shimmered with a barely restrained heat, like the husky contralto of her voice and the flaunting voluptuousness of her form would have lured a monk from his vows.

And now apparently he'd been selected to satisfy her husband's impulse for an heir. "Is your husband old?" he asked, curious.

"Yes."

"I see."

"No, you don't. He prefers young men; he's always preferred young men, but in his position a wife is required. As is a child eventually."

"Are you a virgin then?"

"Do I look like a virgin?" she coolly replied, blunt like he.

"You look like you probably seduced your first tutor."

"Or he me," she said in that same neutral voice. "Was it a housemaid for you—your first time?" she blandly inquired. "I expect your looks had them all giddy to sleep with the duke's son."

"And you wouldn't be giddy."

"I haven't been giddy for a very long time, my Lord Crewe."

"Your husband's going to have to find someone else. You know that, of course."

"You don't know my husband. He won't be finding anyone else."

"He can't force me."

"Actually, that's my job."

"You're wasting your time."

"We'll see about that, I suppose. A note has been sent to your family so no one will expect you in your usual haunts the next month. My husband is very thorough, you see . . . and very determined."

"Fuck you," the marquis brusquely said.

"Now there's a sensible young man," she purred.

In a very short time, they turned off the main road onto a country lane, and moments later, the vehicle passed through an imposing gateway that offered a splendid view of a Capability Brown landscape, manicured to perfection so it had the look of a Lorrain painting.

Why didn't he recognize the estate? he wondered; there were only so many gardens by the Brown dynasty in England. This one had apparently escaped his notice.

"The Spanish royal family originally owned this," she said, perhaps interpreting his reflective look or perhaps simply being courteous. "A cadet branch, I believe. It passed to the Hapsburgs in one of the royal marriages. I think you'll find the stables excellent."

"Will we be riding?"

"Of course. You're my husband's guest."

"He's here?" Was the man a voyeur, too.

"Of course not. He has no interest in me—in this . . . other than the end result."

"There won't be any end result. Let me make that perfectly clear. I insist on sending your husband a strongly worded protest. And once he understands how useless his ploy, I'll bid you *adieu* and hope our paths never meet again."

"I understand," she calmly said, as though consoling a recalcitrant child. "It's all quite barbaric. I suggested he adopt one of his nephews. His sisters breed like rabbits, but he insists on the fiction this child is his. I'm so very sorry," she added in a dulcet murmur. "But please, feel free to send your objections to him."

The country home had been begun in Elizabethan times, the old redbrick and Gothic-arched windows covered with ancient ivies. As each successive generation added to the original structure, one architectural style overlay another, but the sprawling whole still looked as though it were wedded to the land, the grand scope of English history written on its exterior. They entered by the most recent Gothic-revival portico into a small secondary entrance hall gleaming with hand-rubbed paneling and massive silver pieces from India. No servants appeared, their escort two of the quasi-military troop that had flanked the carriage from London. Hugh was shown into a large bedroom suite on the main floor, the view of the rolling lawns falling away to a sylvan lake put there by Capability Brown like a perfect jewel in the green countryside.

"Pierce will be up shortly," the lady said, standing in the doorway.

Hugh swung around from the windows. "You've thought of everything," he drawled. "My compliments to your husband's thoroughness."

"Since Pierce served as your batman in India, my husband considered him appropriate for valeting you in this rather rustic abode. The staff is minimal for obvious reasons."

"While the mounted troop is large."

"Exactly. We dress for dinner despite the rural setting. You'll find your clothes in the dressing room." Although the marquis's brows rose at her last statement, she went on as though she were hostess under ordinary circumstances. "We keep country hours here; dinner is at eight." Moving back into the hall, she allowed the guard to swing the door shut.

It was locked, of course, but he had to check, and returning to the windows overlooking the lake, the Marquis of Crewe surveyed the countryside and pondered the startling circumstances of his captivity.

Pierce arrived shortly with servants carrying water for a bath, and once the staff were dismissed, the two men exchanged stories of their abductions. Pierce had been stopped in the mews behind Dalsany House, where the lane was narrow and out of sight of traffic. Both the tiger and groom had been taken as well. "I don't know for certain where they are, but I was most kindly treated considering. Why are we here?"

"Apparently I'm to stand stud to this nameless lady."

"A command performance," Pierce said with a sly smile. "You should manage."

"I dislike being coerced."

"If it's the lady I seen in the corridor with red hair and a right comely shape, sair, she'll make the coercion sweet enough I don't doubt."

"Her husband's a brute."

"Not likely that should matter none. Seems lots o' ladies you bed have husbands like that. They like you the better for it."

"Don't be so bloody reasonable, Pierce. This is fucking irritating to have some Balkan satrap decide I'm to produce his heir. Damn his impertinence. I'll bed whom I please."

"If'n it's just the coercion, sair, hell, there's men who pay for that in them fine brothels."

"I'm not one of them."

"I know, but she's a fine piece for all your temper. How can it matter—a night or two with this'un after all the years of fucking, sair."

Another logical insight, Hugh thought with disgust, and had he not been glutted and weary of the concept, he could have been logical, too. "How many guards do they have?"

"It looks like forty or so; only a small troop followed you here. The rest were in place when I arrived. It won't be easy if'n you're thinking of escape." The small, wiry, sandy-haired man had served in Hugh's regiment in India and decided he preferred the position of batman to the marquis than the brutal life in the Army. He knew combat firsthand and was the very best man to have beside you in a tough fight.

"Are you allowed any freedom of movement?"

"Not without a guard at my side, sair. It's a right tight camp they've set up here."

"Do what you can in tracking their schedule. I don't intend to stay any longer than necessary."

"I'll try, sair, but I'm not allowed much movement. See what the lady has to say at dinner. If she doesn't wish to be here, either, she might be able to help. She goes about without a guard."

When Crewe entered the dining room at eight, his escort fell back, and with the silence that seemed habitual with them, they shut the doors behind him. The marquis stood motionless, taking in the large dimensions of the dining room, his gaze sweeping over the allegorical mural of Apollo driving his sun chariot above his head, coming to rest on his hostess yards away down the length of a mahogany table. She looked very small in the cavernous room.

"Do you have a name?" he asked, strolling toward her, his evening shoes sinking into the plush nap of a Tabriz carpet custommade for the chamber.

"Call me Juliana."

"You don't have a name then. Why don't I call you Delilah?"

"It would be very much easier for us both if you simply did what you apparently do so well," she replied, ignoring his discourtesy. "The record of your female conquests is formidable. What do they call you—The Rajah?—for the number of women in your personal harem. Do they take a number? How do you arrange to satisfy them all?"

"I see I was vetted."

"Most carefully. My husband has memorized the *Almanach de Gotha;* your bloodlines are pure enough even for a descendant of Charlemagne. Do sit down. You'll find the menu to your liking."

"Your husband's spies are competent," he noted, taking his seat at the place setting beside her. "You have my favorite champagne."

"My husband's security system is extensive. And more than competent. Keep it in mind, my lord," she gently said, nodding minutely in the direction of the large standing portrait of a Hapsburg in Elizabethan hunting dress. At which point, a procession of serving men flowed through a hidden door in the linen-fold paneling, carrying an array of silver platters and dishes filled with the marquis's preferred foods. Each roast and fish, soup and vegetable, dainty and sweet were arranged French style down the long table, and as silently as the servants had appeared, they disappeared through the concealed door.

"I thought we might have an informal dinner tonight—without staff. I hope you don't mind."

"And if I did?" he softly inquired, pouring his champagne goblet full, his sidelong glance sardonic.

"I told the prince you'd be difficult."

"Impossible, actually. Tell him that."

"I wish it were so simple, my lord. Marko unfortunately has no understanding of dissent." She rose from her chair, her pearl-embroidered gold net gown rustling faintly as she moved toward the splendid display of food. "Please help yourself," she remarked, as if immune to her companion's umbrage, spooning a serving of trout and morels on her plate. "You must be hungry after your recent days of debauch."

Surprise registered for a flashing moment in his eyes.

"One of the women was in my husband's employ," she explained, looking up from a decorative lobster aspic, the spoon in her hand suspended above the elaborate jellied mold, her breasts mounded high above her low decolletage equally lush. "Clarissa gave you high marks," she added, a faint smile lifting the corners of her mouth.

"This isn't going anywhere," the marquis curtly said, resisting the magnificent display of feminine pulchritude, lifting his glass to his mouth and emptying it down his throat. "No matter how damned urbane you are." He reached for the bottle again, refilled his glass, and, raising it to his lips, glared at her over the rim. "I wouldn't fuck you if you were the last woman on the face of the earth." After which pithy statement, he drained the glass, pushed his chair away from the table and rose to his full commanding height.

He was outrageously beautiful, she thought, all bristling resentment and affront, tall, powerful, dark as sin—the contrast to her despised husband so striking, she almost felt compelled to thank Marko for his good judgment. Although certainly, if her husband had any expertise, it was in the appraisal of young, good-looking men.

Turning from the table, the marquis stalked toward the door through which he'd entered only to be stopped midway by the appearance of four guardsmen stepping from behind a large ivory screen shielded by the ubiquitous palms, which were de rigueur in every Edwardian interior.

They stood directly in his path, men as tall as he, armored in crimson leather jacks like some Byzantine praetorian guard, their swords drawn.

"They have orders to only detain you so you needn't fear the sharp blades," the lady remarked. "If you're sensible, you'll rejoin me for dinner. They have instructions to tie you in your chair and feed you if necessary. Not my orders," she calmly added, cutting her fish. "And if it were possible to apologize enough for this distasteful situation, I would—most profusely. But I learned long ago not to ignore my husband's commands and I suggest you do the same. There are a dozen more guards in the adjoining room."

Hot-tempered or not, he couldn't take on sixteen men. And, cursing, he turned to retrace his steps.

"For your information," she quietly said as he sat down again, "the estate is well secured, too. Or did Pierce tell you?"

"And how are *you* guarded?"

She seemed to stiffen slightly, but her smile when she spoke was so genial, he questioned his observation. However, her reply was pitched low, her words barely audible. "I'm guarded—always. Please, have something to eat, my lord," she went on in a normal tone. "You'll enjoy the roast beef."

And dinner proceeded as if they were actors on a stage. He ate in a minimal way, drank two bottles, responded to the lady's conversational gambits in a desultory fashion, and, in general, planned revenge on his unknown adversary. The marquis had been born and bred a golden child, gifted with all of nature's bounty: beauty of face and form; wealth beyond measure; the bluest of blood and lineage; intelligence rarely found in those of his class; the enterprise to work as hard as he played. And he intended to find his way out of this snare, no matter how many guards were in place.

But he didn't understand the price of failure when the despotic Prince Marko of Badia was displeased. Men died at his orders, the bastinado his discipline of choice—his principality remote from the civilized world when it suited him.

Both his wife and guards understood they must heed his commands.

So once the marquis had been returned to his suite after dinner, the lady entered his bedchamber a brief time later, elegantly robed in green cut velvet against the cool evening. A fire had been lit in the grate, and the marquis, still dressed, stood at the window, a bottle in his hand, drinking away his discontent. He didn't turn at the sound of her voice nor when she came up behind him and, reaching up, touched his shoulder.

"Go away," he said, lifting the cognac bottle to his mouth.

"I can't. No more than you can."

"If he's not here, you can do anything you damned well please. I'm not fucking you. How many times do I have to say it?" The stars shouldn't be shining so brilliantly tonight, he sullenly thought, when he was so afflicted—his sense of injustice keen, the idea of captivity galling.

"You have to."

He swung around so violently, startled, she jumped back. "No," he whispered, unbridled rage vibrating in his voice. "I don't."

He took a threatening step forward, but she stood her ground. She'd learned long ago to never show fear.

He carefully set the bottle down as if to restrain his more brutish urges and, towering over her, quietly said, "Get out of this room."

She raised her hand the merest distance from her side, a gesture so small it would have gone unnoticed had she not been closely watched.

The dressing-room door opened and his four warders from dinner strode into the room, their faces impassive.

"Tie the marquis to the bed," the Princess Marko softly said.

He didn't succumb passively, and during the struggle, additional guards were called in, several of them bearing damage from the marquis's powerful fists before they were able to subdue him sufficiently to tie his wrists and feet. He was carried to the bed and placed on his back on the crimson brocade coverlet, four guards firmly holding him down while four others untied his feet and, slipping his shoes off, secured his ankles to the bed posts with thick, braided silk cord. Restrained by the weight of four guardsmen, his wrists were then untied and, after forcing his arms above his head, he was bound to the headboard with knots pulled so tight, there was no question of him gaining his freedom.

One of the guardsmen spoke to the princess in an unfamiliar language, his phrases in the nature of a question. She shook her head slightly, replied in a few brief words and waved them out. Without even a glance at the bed, she turned away from the door, walked to a chair by the fire, sat down and, resting her head against the pillowed chair back, gazed into the flickering flame. The heavy genoa velvet of her gown spread in folds at her feet, the opulent fabric lush, touchable, like her pale skin and silken hair. The delicacy of her features, the tumble of her loosened hair on her shoulders, gave her a look of innocence at odds with the depraved circumstances.

The silence was a balm to her agitated senses, the dancing flame mesmerizing, and she wished for a moment she could sit here forever in this suspended moment of time. But she couldn't, she knew, reality too intense and demanding, the requirements of her hermitage in the country exacting. She was to conceive an heir to Marko's title. Like the marquis, she was a prisoner . . . worse—his durance vile would end in a month and hers would not.

The lady before the fire evinced such melancholy, even in his vengeful mood, the marquis was struck by her sadness. And her words from dinner reminded him she was no more free than he. "Come and talk to me," he neutrally said, surveying the room, wondering where the peepholes and listening posts were.

She looked up, but neither moved nor replied.

"I'm not asking to be untied. You're safe enough."

"A relative term."

"Come closer," he cajoled, his understanding of women acute after years of sharing their beds. She might be as interested in her freedom as he was in his. "Tell me exactly what's expected of me," he added, wanting to coax her near so they could talk with less fear of being overheard.

"Nothing out of the ordinary for you, if gossip is true."

"I can't hear you," he murmured, arching a brow toward the dressing-room door, where the guards apparently had set up their watch.

She seemed to understand, for she rose and walked toward him.

"Sit down," he suggested when she stood indecisive at the foot of the bed. "Tell me your name."

She sat a circumspect distance away, and when she said, "Sofia" in little more than a whisper, he felt a curious provocation quite distinct from logic. Maybe it was the sultry undertones of her voice or the wafting sweet scent of her hair; maybe it was because he'd loved a Sofie once who'd died when they were both very young and he'd never loved anyone again.

This Sofia's lashes were sooty dark as if they'd been kohled although they hadn't, and her eyes were like tamped green flame. And her flamboyant auburn-haired beauty wasn't like his Sofie at all, who had been very blond and childlike and much too young to die. But provocation and beauty aside, he had no intention of fathering a child on this unknown woman. "Is there any way you can get us out of here?" he murmured. "I'll protect you from your husband."

Instant fear shown in her eyes.

"Bend down and kiss me," he whispered, "so we can talk."

She hesitated, skittish under the surveillance.

"I could say seduce me if you can," he murmured, challenge in his dark gaze, his mouth quirked in a smile.

"I wouldn't have to kiss you for that." How curious that he could almost make her smile when so much in her life was cheerless.

"You might enjoy it."

"And so might you."

"Not likely," he said in truth and also to nettle, wanting her to move nearer.

Both considered themselves jaded, worldly, immune to trembling anticipation, but when she accepted his challenge or his offer to talk and moved closer, gracefully leaned forward— when her silken hair brushed his face and her perfume pervaded his nostrils, when she stroked her palms lightly down his temples and held his finely modeled face between her hands, they both felt an irrepressible impatience, a restless enticement quite distinct from previous amorous encounters. "I think I hear choirs of angels," he lightly breathed.

"No—cherubim," she whispered, her voice as teasing.

Then their lips touched and pure lust dissipated more temperate images of heavenly bliss. His body instantly responded, the shock of desire so intense he wondered if he'd been drugged at dinner. She pulled away as if burned and sat trembling beside him.

"Untie me," he whispered.

She seemed to come back from some inner world and, appalled at her response, at what she perceived as the disreputable marquis's expertise and cunning, she said, cool and brisk, "Let's keep this impersonal."

"It's too late."

"You're wrong."

"I can make you hear those cherubim anytime you want." Seduction was so familiar to him, even he didn't know whether it was emotion or necessity driving him. But this woman was the only way to freedom.

That he knew.

"Untie me. It's safe enough with all the guards. And if we must do—this . . . baby making," he gently said, his gaze guileless, "why not make it more pleasant?"

Debating his sincerity, she gazed at him, his power undiminished despite his bondage. He stretched the length of the large bed, his powerful musculature evident beneath the fine wool of his evening clothes, his thighs and biceps straining the fabric. And then her glance slipped downward and his arousal brought a heated blush to her face.

"There are enough guards to protect you," he quietly reminded her and, taking note of her gaze, insolently added, "Do you like it?"

"Whether I do or not doesn't matter." Her eyes turned cool.

"I can make it matter if you'd let me," he lazily drawled.

"Maybe I'm offended by such libertine charm."

"Really. You don't look as though pleasure offends you."

"This isn't pleasure, Crewe—not by the farthest stretch of the imagination."

"Untie me and I'll change your mind."

His voice was like velvet, his husky promise tantalizing even while she resisted the urge to believe him.

"How can it hurt? We're both here as captives, and if we must perform, why not at least attempt some semblance of politesse. I'd prefer holding you."

She softly sighed. "Can I trust you?"

"Hardly a word for you to use with me," he lightly remarked, lifting his arm the marginal distance allowed by his tight bond.

"Touché," she softly murmured.

"Would it be too much to ask you to cover the peepholes?" he queried, his brows lifted faintly.

"No, and I apologize once more for"—she lifted her hand in a gesture of futility—"for everything . . ."

"We can argue degrees of blame later," he pleasantly said. "Right now I'd prefer not having an audience."

He watched her cover the surveillance points, four in all, pulling drapes over two, sliding a picture into place over another, hanging a pillow sham over one beneath a hook on the door. And when she returned to the bed, she said, very low, "This is very difficult."

"Just untie one of my hands and I'll do the rest. You can shut your eyes and pretend you're somewhere else."

"Wouldn't that be nice," she sardonically murmured, reaching for the knot at his wrist. She struggled with the tie while he lay quiescent, trying to appear calm when his mind was racing with the options available to him once he was freed. "There," she said, the knot loosening, and she unwound the braided cord on his wrist.

Half sitting up, he smiled at her and reached for the bonds on his left wrist. Swiftly he released the tie and then those on his ankles in quick succession. One floor to drop, he thought, the landscape outside his windows etched on his brain. Springing from the bed, he sprinted toward the windows. Reaching them, he lifted a heavy upholstered chair as though it were weightless and heaved it through the leaded glass. Following his juggernaut through the large opening in the glass, he leapt to the ground below.

Of course he would have tried to escape, Sofia reflected, picking her way through the shattered glass on the carpet, moving to draw the drapes over the broken window. Next time, she sensibly decided, tugging on the crimson velvet, the sounds of a skirmish coming out of the darkness before she shut out the cool night breeze and the strident accents, she'd be sure to leave him tied.

The guards under the windows should soon have him in custody once again.

Chapter 2

When they next met a brief time later, the marquis was captive again, bound to the bed in another room. Nude.

"I'll kill your husband for this," he snarled.

"I hope you weren't hurt." It took effort to keep her voice temperate. He was magnificent—his musculature tautly defined, the sense of rampant power only barely leashed, riveting. The width of his shoulders was startling, the ridged muscles of his lean torso classically sculptured, the strength in his thighs evidence of years in the saddle. How could fashionable evening clothes have disguised such brute strength?

Such striking virility. Even in repose, the length of his penis was formidable. Aroused, he would be—a tiny flutter raced up her spine—monstrous. His legendary reputation was well deserved.

"You're all fucking crazy," he growled. "And yes, jumping fifteen feet to the ground leaves a bruise or two, not to mention your guards who are none too gentle."

"Why not agree to my proposal and be done with this?" She gestured at his bindings.

"Because I'm not inclined to suffer capture docilely. Your deranged husband will rue the day he chose me as stud for his dynasty."

"Then we might as well get on with this," she said with a repressed sigh.

"You forget there are some things your husband can't control," he snapped. "I'm not in the mood for sex."

"Then shut your eyes and pretend you're somewhere else,"

she noted, in parody of his earlier remark. "I'll take care of every-thing else."

"Good luck," he curtly said.

But when she unclasped the jeweled closures of her robe and slipped it from her shoulders, he found himself drawn to the glorious sight despite his raging anger, regardless of the bindings cutting into his wrists and ankles. Her husband must have had her vetted before marriage, he thought, for her sumptuous body was perfection—every depiction of Venus from antiquity to the present outdone by the flaunting pride of womanhood before him.

He swore under his breath, the term "compromising position" advancing front and center in his mind, and he wondered how long he'd be able to control himself. It would take an impotent saint to withstand such blatant sexuality. And sainthood had always eluded him.

"I have instructions to see that you come in me twice a day during this month-long hermitage," she murmured, walking toward the bed. "I hope it won't be too arduous for you," she went on, a half-smile forming on her mouth as his erection came to life. "Apparently not," she sardonically noted.

Her demented husband understood lust at least, even though his other sensibilities were suspect, Hugh thought. He knew his nude wife would be irresistible. Now what the hell was he going to do?

As if logic and reason had a chance against rapacious desire. As if deductive analysis would serve as a reliable restraint in the next few minutes.

Squaring her resolve, the princess knew she must do what she must do. In sending her to England, her husband had taken added measures to see that she obeyed him; her mother was hostage at her husband's court. She must submit to his commands. "I'm as resentful as you," she said, moving onto the bed, kneeling beside him. "Neither of us wish to be here . . . so this should be"—she exhaled softly—"interesting."

"Do you play the whore for him often?" the marquis mali-ciously drawled.

She slapped him so hard, her fingers left red welts on his face.

"Touchy, are we?" he sarcastically murmured, the taste of blood in his mouth.

"You don't know anything, Crewe, about man's inhumanity to man. And until you do, I'd suggest you reserve judgment on others. Now I'm going to have intercourse with you and I expect you'll enjoy it whether you want to or not. Consider this your first lesson in the realities of life."

Having spent three years in India, he'd seen misery on a grand scale, but he supposed the princess wasn't in the mood to compare life experiences. "Perhaps someday, I'll be able to return the favor," he coolly said, "in terms of showing you the realities of life."

"I doubt that. At the end of a month, we'll never see each other again."

"Don't count on it," he brusquely muttered, vengeance burning through his brain. "I don't plan on walking away from this, no matter what you and your crazy husband want. This won't be over in a month."

"I'm not here to argue with you."

"No, you're here to fuck whomever your husband tells you to fuck," he viciously replied.

"You don't understand."

"A slut is a slut."

"While your libertine ways are—what—masculine prerogatives? Why don't we see how virtuous you can be, how righteous and unsullied," she murmured, leaning forward to trace a gentle finger down his chest. "Will you resist temptation? Can the profligate Marquis of Crewe say no?"

He twisted in his bonds, trying to avoid her touch, but her hands lay warm on his flesh, her plump breasts quivered before his eyes and when she purred, "Gossip says a night with you ruins women for other men. Why not show me that splendid . . . expertise?" she dulcetly breathed. Bending low, her breasts brushed his arm, seared his senses, the silken pressure of her pliant flesh reminding him that she was pliant . . . everywhere, and if not exactly willing, receptive. "You can refuse me, of course," she whispered, lightly cupping his testicles with one hand, the fingers of her other hand closing around his penis.

He tried to recall every repugnant image, every gruesome picture in his memory, he tried counting in German, mentally recited the alphabet in Greek. But the pressure and rhythm of her fingers slowly increased, her scent accosted his senses, her warm body half covered his, and in brief moments, he was in heated rut, his erection rock hard, lust pulsing through every nerve and muscle in his body.

"I don't suppose you're saying no . . . with this," she whispered, tracing a delicate path around the swollen crimson crest of his penis. "You must set records."

"Like you," he rudely retorted. "Have you found stripping naked has predictable results?"

"It depends on the man," she flippantly replied. "Or do you prefer a single style of woman?" She knew better; the only thing Crewe preferred in a female was availability.

"I'd prefer to be untied," he ground out.

"But then I'm not witless. The only freedom you're allowed is with this deliciously rampant penis. Do you think you might be interested in putting this"—she lightly squeezed the pulsing tip—"inside me?"

"No," he said through clenched teeth, his refusal taking every shred of willpower at his command.

"You *seem* interested," she murmured, dipping her head to brush a flickering caress over the distended head.

He groaned, every muscle taut with restraint.

"Such self-control, Crewe. Your vicar would be proud. Perhaps I'll have to exert myself more. Can you feel this?" Her closed fingers slid downward again, her grip tightening, the pulsing veins of his erection graphic in high relief as his penis reared higher. His breath caught in his throat and he arched his back against the exquisite sensation. "Damn you," he grunted.

"And damn you, Lord Crewe. But then, this isn't an amorous interlude," she murmured, her fingers sliding up his erection, "so we needn't like each other at all—only procreate. Something you're very good at." She watched his arousal swell larger, disturbed by her own flaring desires, irritated that she could be aroused, that the throbbing between her legs was immune to his venom.

She should thank him, she supposed, for making it so easy, for being so virile and male, for exciting some sordidly voracious need she didn't realize existed. Such pulsing anticipation was reminiscent of her youth when the first, tremulous stirrings of carnal urgency, inexplicable and illicit, had overwhelmed her senses. She hadn't felt like that for a very long time, the men in her life no more than idle distractions.

"When this is over, I'm going to find you both," he panted. "Keep that in mind." Anger pulsed through him with as much vehemence as the lust bombarding his senses, revenge a powerful craving.

"If a child comes of this," she said, suddenly wanting to expedite the proceedings, uncomfortable with her feelings, with feeling anything at all in this hideous drama, "it won't matter what you do. Because it'll be too late," she grimly added, moving to straddle his thighs.

"I'll take the child away," he brusquely muttered, his pulse pounding in his ears.

"Why?" Shocked, she sat motionless on his hard thighs, her green gaze on him. "You never have before."

"Who knows if any of the children are mine with married women?"

"How is this different?"

"You said yourself your husband wasn't interested in women."

She shrugged. "I have many lovers. Does that put your mind at ease?"

He struggled against his bonds, his frustration monumental. "Fuck you," he whispered, his body twisting against the silken cords.

"At last we agree," she murmured, rising on her knees enough to position the crest of his erection on her throbbing labia. "Tell me how this feels," she insolently murmured, taking note his breathing had stopped, her own breath momentarily in abeyance, the exquisite wash of pleasure rippling up her vagina so intoxicating, a moment of pure personal pleasure overrode the repellent coercion.

He suddenly heaved his hips upward and drove into her, his body's responses automatic, necessity, blind instinct operating.

She cried out as he rammed into her, stretched her, thrust so deeply inside, it felt as though he were in her throat. "Oh, God," she breathed, impaled, his enormous erection buried to the hilt, her tissue taut, pulsing, a dizzying delirium burning through her brain.

"And now I'm going to fuck you," he growled, embittered, an unreasoning need for retaliation driving his lower body deeper and deeper, the drumming urgency of both vengeance and orgasmic release a heedless tumult in his brain, the powerful rhythm of his carnal lust forcing her wider and wider until she was gasping, panting, hysterical, frenzied, meeting each surging thrust with a passion as rapacious as his.

It was a mating, pure and simple.

When she first climaxed, he swore, and when she climaxed again he called her whore, slut, wanton, but he lived in a world of double standards, and when his orgasm came rushing down, filling her sleek interior with a white-hot river of semen, he forgot deviations of morality, overlooked impropriety and self-denial and ejaculated the blue-blooded sperm so coveted by the lady's husband.

The Marquis of Crewe had performed as required.

But then, Prince Marko had counted on the young lord's well-developed sexual drive.

When it was over, he called her every vile name in his extensive repertoire, and after extricating herself from his still-rigid erection, she coolly said, "Your cooperation was greatly appreciated." Then she leaned forward and carved a bloody path down his cheek with the nail of her forefinger. "I understand retaliation, too, my lord," she murmured. "And if cursing would help, I'd add mine to yours." Sliding from the bed, she picked up her robe and slipped it on. "Your next scheduled orgasm is after breakfast," she remarked. "Pleasant dreams."

She disappeared through the door into an adjoining room, and, minutes later, Pierce entered through a door on the opposite wall. "Were you a spectator, too?" the marquis heatedly inquired.

"Not likely, sair. Such piquant sights are raffled off in the barracks. There's only so many observation points and the lady closed most o' them."

"Like slaves in a breeding shed," Hugh disgustedly spat, although he'd performed for spectators in the occasional orgy common to young, hot-blooded London bucks. "Get these bindings off so I can punch a hole in the wall."

"I wouldn't recommend it, sir," his batman gently responded. "Seein' as how you might need that there hand"—his voice lowered to a whisper—"for riding or shooting later, if you know what I mean."

At which point, the men's conversation continued in tones pitched too low for those listening outside the room.

The Princess Sofia dismissed her maids immediately as she entered her rooms and, lying on her bed, mentally checked off the first of sixty required encounters with the Marquis of Crewe. There was no point in bursting into tears, although she was very close to losing her composure. But her family depended on her, her mother in the most dire peril at the moment under her husband's guard, so she must see that this month with the marquis ended successfully.

Conception was a requirement. Once it was certain, her mother would be freed, and after that, there was always the hope in the following eight months she herself might find a way to escape. She had no intention of leaving a child under Marko's supervision, and she desperately hoped the world was large enough for refuge once that time came.

Morning arrived too early; she begrudged the sun shining into her room, and no matter the glory of the spring day, her mood was dismal. She slowly dressed herself, unable to face the necessity of talking to the servants. And she wondered what would happen if she didn't appear in the breakfast room as scheduled. But her mother was a pawn in this dangerous game, so she did what was expected of her.

The marquis was in a glowering mood, the wound on his face prominent even against his tanned skin.

"You'd think in this pile of rooms, we wouldn't be required to eat together," he growled as she entered the sunny chamber.

"Take your complaints up with my husband. He has a droll sense of humor."

"He's a sadist, you mean."

"How astute, my lord. You noticed. Although I see, your sullen mood hasn't affected your appetite," she insolently added. His plate was piled high with bacon, kippers, ham, eggs scrambled with mushrooms and tomato. He was buttering a croissant, not his first apparently from the debris of crumbs at his plate.

He looked up from his buttering, his mouth set in a grimace. "Let's hope you start puking soon and this charade can come to an end."

"One can but hope," she sardonically replied, the sight of food curiously unpalatable. It was impossible, of course, that she could be pregnant after a single encounter with the marquis, but when the first sip of her morning coffee turned her nauseous, she wondered if all his rumored bastards were indeed the result of a remarkable virility. They ate together in silence, or rather he ate and she picked at a piece of dried toast, her lack of appetite eventually coming to his attention.

"If you don't eat," he nastily said, "you'll faint when next you climax."

"I may not," she coolly replied.

His brow lifted in loathsome irony. "Faint?"

Her own brows delicately rose. "Does it bother you if I have an orgasm?"

He debated his answer for a moment, not sure why he was offended beyond his captive status. "Yes. Don't ask me why," he honestly added.

"It seems to me I should get some pleasure from this ordeal."

"Ordeal?" he skeptically repeated. "You could have fooled me."

"Would you like me to compliment you on your physical prowess? I didn't realize you were so vain."

He wasn't, and another niggling second passed while he wondered at his indignant response to the princess's passion. "How many lovers have you had?" The impulsive question surprised him, but he didn't retract it.

"Not as many as you. There are records and there are records," she gently noted. "I'm very much outclassed by your repute."

"And you've never become pregnant?"

"I wouldn't have dared. Marko has very strong feelings about pure bloodlines."

"And yours are pure?"

"How rude you are."

"You're much too beautiful." It was his first civil remark.

"You mean only chorus girls and actresses look like this."

"Generally, yes."

"And you should know."

"And I should know."

"My family is Hungarian on my mother's side and noted for their favorable matches."

"If they all look like you, I can see why. So Marko has money."

"That's what favorable means, my lord. You know that better than most. My father's family is Venetian; they settled in Dalmatia long ago and gave numerous counts to the Hapsburg court as envoys to Venice. Does that suitably satisfy your standards?"

"I have no standards as you no doubt know," he replied, rude once again, his brief moment of compassion revoked by recall of the compulsion behind his visit to the country. "Although under other circumstances, you and I might have had a damned good tumble in the hay."

"Have you dispensed with your recent attempt at celibacy?"

"Temporarily, it seems. Will your husband's schedule permit another cup of coffee before the next fuck?" he insolently inquired.

"As long as you don't take too long," she replied, snide and oversweet.

When the guards came into the breakfast room shortly after, he stood and sketched her a brief bow. "Until we meet again, madame," he impudently murmured. "On stage."

It minutely salved his anger to see her furiously blush, a minor concession to his umbrage, but satisfying. And after he'd entered his bedroom, he held the guards at bay with an upturned palm, undressing himself this time. He preferred not being touched by other men, a fact he explained to them in fluent Italian. Since she was from Dalmatia, he assumed Italian would serve as a bridge between the guards' native tongue and English.

"We have our orders," their leader explained, his tone mildly apologetic.

"Everyone does, do they not with Prince Marko," he dryly retorted. "But tell him when next you see him that I'm coming to kill him once this is over." The marquis stood eye-to-eye with the tall guard, their gazes both unflinching.

"I'll tell him," the man replied, "in a month. Do you need to be tied?"

"If you want me to stay."

"I thought so." And the trooper nodded his head toward the bed.

The tying was swift and efficient, everyone civil, accomplished at their tasks, and then the marquis was left to wait for the prospective mother of his child. He shouldn't have been left alone so long, for the added interval gave him unwanted opportunities to recall their heated coupling of the previous night. The princess was flamboyantly sexual, hot-blooded, unbridled in her response. Irresistible to a man of libertine propensities. His thoughts fluctuated equivocally between provocative arousal and hot-tempered annoyance, but he was realistic enough to wonder how long his annoyance would last once she stood before him in all her naked glory.

When Sofia came into the room, a cool self-possession masked the tumult of her feelings. "I don't know if I can do this," she quietly said, standing just inside the door. Only the pressure of her mother's welfare had brought her back to this room.

"But they're watching."

"Perhaps."

"You don't strike me as naive," Hugh mocked. "Maybe we should just chat about the weather," he silkily went on, "and see how long it takes before someone comes in and forces us to copulate."

"Right now I dearly wish I were an orphan." She hadn't moved from the door, her hands pressed to the wood as if seeking strength from the sturdy oak. Her white dimity robe lent her an air of touching innocence, the blue ribbon in her tousled hair slightly askew, like that of a fey maiden.

How did she do it, he wondered—alter so completely from incarnate sexuality to this trembling, unsure adolescent with high color on her cheeks?

"How old are you?" His gruff voice sounded very loud in the silence.

She looked up, startled, seeming to forget where she was. "Today?" she queried as though getting her bearings. "Much too old," she added in a whisper.

"Tell me."

"A million years old," she simply said, her green gaze distant.

"I'm twenty-seven."

"I know. You were twenty-seven in March. I read the dossier."

"You're younger, aren't you?"

"No." Her brows tilted upward in whimsey. "But thank you."

"Should I guess?"

"No, it doesn't matter. Nothing matters," she breathed, her voice trailing away.

"Are you all right?" A modicum of concern infused his voice, but he caught himself in time, not about to allow himself sympathy, and as her eyes flared wide in astonishment at the compassion in his tone, he'd already lapsed into a moody scowl.

"You were almost human for a moment," she murmured. "Don't worry, I won't tell anyone."

"Are you going to stand there all morning?" he gruffly muttered, wanting her when he shouldn't. But he'd lived too long in the world of privilege to question what he wanted.

"Are you ready then?"

He couldn't help but smile at her naiveté, his teeth flashing white against his tanned skin. "Come and see," he whispered.

"Should I draw the drapes?"

His gaze flitted from them to her, and he shook his head. "Unless you want to," he hastily added—his first small courtesy.

"I'm sorry about the scratch," she offered in turn, her hand fluttering upward briefly toward his face.

"This is turning too civil," he teased.

"You prefer angry women?"

"I prefer seeing that robe on the floor."

"Please, don't be coy," she returned, smiling for the first time . . . in an age. "I can't untie you, can I?"

"Not really," he said with a boyish smile. "But you can kiss me if you like."

Such delicious charm, she thought, even in this extremity. How lethal his allure must be under more gracious circumstances. "What makes you think I want to kiss you?" she asked, the merest flirtation in her tone.

"I can tell," he said, his dark gaze amused.

"Because every woman wants to kiss you?"

"When I'm nice they do."

"Like now."

"You noticed."

How could she not. He exuded joy and warmth along with a tantalizing sexuality. Not to mention that he was the most beautiful man she'd ever seen. "Do women ever say no to you?"

"Only one," he said with a beguiling smile. "And I'm trying to coax her nearer right now."

"So your record won't be spoiled."

"So I can fuck her," he wickedly replied.

Irrepressible desire trembled through her body, memory a powerful impulse.

"If you sit on me," he murmured, "I'll let you come as many times as you like." His gaze flickered downward toward his swelling erection.

"I shouldn't want this," she whispered, transfixed by the riveting sight.

"And I shouldn't be here, but . . . since I am," he quietly noted, "and since you are"—his heated glance slowly traveled down her body—"why not make the best of it."

"I should refuse."

"I know. So should I. Tell me how strange this is."

"It's strange," she quietly agreed.

"Tell me about it at closer range," he softly suggested, his smile ravishing with promise.

Pushing away from the door, she responded to his heated smile, to his stark beauty, to the mesmerizing lure of his enormous erection. Her robe trailed across the pale Aubusson carpet as she moved from the door to the bed, a small, incipient joy beginning to warm her senses. "Tell me this is all right," she hesitantly murmured.

"This is very fine," he breathed. All the rest was hellish, he thought, but even thin-skinned and moody, he recognized the rarity of emotion drawing them together. "Come sit by me."

When she did, she placed her hand on his thigh as if she needed solid reassurance, as if his strength could sustain them both. "I don't want to take my robe off," she said, her voice low, strained.

"Then don't."

"I had to last night . . . because—"

"I know."

"They may be watching."

"What's the commanding guard's name?"

"Gregory."

"Gregory! Fucking shut the closures!" he shouted in Italian. "The lady would like some privacy!"

The scraping sound of closing apertures indicated assent, and Hugh pleasantly murmured, "Now we can get to know each other better."

"He must like you."

"Or dislike your husband. Which apparently isn't very hard from the sounds of it. Gregory and I have an understanding," he said with a mischievous wink.

"I still don't want to take my robe off."

"You don't trust them to shut all the peepholes?"

"One learns not to trust anyone."

"How long have you been married?"

"Fifteen years."

"Good God. You must have been a child. How frightening for you."

"The marriage settlement was considerable."

"I'm sure it was," he cynically murmured.

For a flashing moment, the pain shone in her eyes, but as quickly it was shuttered away. "He's often away."

"I could protect you from him."

She shook her head. "You don't understand."

"Show me the way out of here," he quickly said, "and I guarantee your safety."

"I can't. He has my mother."

His surprise showed. "As hostage?"

"Until I return pregnant."

"And then what?"

"He releases her."

His gaze narrowed. "Can you trust him to do that?"

She nodded again.

"Jesus," he muttered on a slow exhalation of breath.

"Does your life look more pleasant now?"

"Untie me," he abruptly ordered.

She withdrew her hand and marginally distanced herself from him, her fear apparent. "I don't dare after last night."

"I give you my word. I won't run."

She contemplated him for a lengthy moment, wanting to believe there were honorable people in the world. "Lord, Crewe . . . what if you're lying?"

"I wouldn't do that to you—to your mother," he softly added.

His quiet addendum convinced her, as did the tenderness in his eyes. "We both suffer if you renege," she quietly warned.

"Don't worry. I'll take care of you."

Her eyes glistened with tears. No one had taken care of her for a very long time. With the death of her father, her family had been left unprotected. "Thank you," she softly said. "But I'm not your responsibility."

"You are now," he brusquely answered. "Untie me."

But when she released him, he put his finger to his mouth, rose from the bed, and carefully surveyed the room to see if they were being observed.

Her heart beat wildly while he moved about the large chamber, not certain he would keep his word and stay, her thoughts in such chaos, she couldn't separate joy from fear, desire from anxiety. Nor understand why she was sitting, hands clasped tightly in her lap, shivering, trembling for him.

When he'd offered to care for her, she'd blindly wanted him to, like a heedless young maiden. But harsh reality wouldn't allow such fantasies for long—not with a husband like hers. And a wave of sadness washed over her, the emptiness of her future devastating to consider.

He was walking toward her, a calmness about him, an ease, warmth and kindness in his eyes. "It seems we're actually alone," he lightly noted. And then he saw her forlorn eyes "I said I wouldn't go."

"I wasn't sure." Her tears welled up, suddenly vulnerable to the cruel torture of hope.

"I can get us both out of here," he said, touching her clasped hands lightly, smoothing her fingers with his, warm comfort in his touch. Bending low, he kissed her lightly on the cheek, like one might a child in reassurance, and then, sitting beside her, he gently lifted her onto his lap. "Don't be sad," he murmured, holding her nestled against his warm, solid chest, his hand gently stroking the curve of her back.

Overwhelmed by his kindness, her tears spilled over.

"It's going to be fine," he soothed, thinking she was frightened and unsure. "We'll find a way." Tugging a portion of the sheet loose, he wiped away her tears.

"You . . . don't . . . know him," she hiccuped.

He brushed a finger over her cheek. "All you have to do is ride," he softly said. "I'll do the rest."

Wistful hope shone in her eyes. "You make it sound possible."

"We'll ride out later and survey the countryside."

"There's still my mother." Cold reality intervened.

"I have friends at the consulate in Trieste. They can help her to freedom."

Her spirits lifted again. "Do you answer everyone's prayers or only mine?" A new lightness infused her voice; he made the daunting odds seem feasible.

"Just yours, darling," he roguishly murmured. "Ask me for . . . anything."

Her mouth quirked in a faint smile. "Are you flirting with me?"

He grinned. "I didn't know I had to with your husband's schedule. You're available to me twice a day with or without seduction."

"How quickly you've changed your mind." Playful, arch, she gazed up at him with a mischievous light in her eyes.

"The incentive turned out to be—irresistible," he finished in a husky whisper.

"I return the compliment, but you already know that, don't you? Actually, I find myself extremely pleased," she went on in a lush contralto, "that my husband found you for me. Don't be alarmed," she hastily interjected, his sudden apprehension obvious. "I'm not interested in permanence any more than you."

Relief flickered across his face, although he was courteous enough to say, "I'm not alarmed."

"Just cautious," she sportively corrected, sliding her arms around his neck and smiling up at him. "I don't blame you. They all want to be married, don't they?"

"I never ask," he briefly replied, and then intent on changing the subject, he dropped back on the bed, pulling her with him. Rolling over her a flashing moment later, he said, hushed and low, "Does our morning schedule have a time limit or can I fuck you all day?"

"Just to reassure you, Crewe," she silkily murmured, aware of his evasion, "I'm only interested in your enormous cock; I don't need your title or money."

He softly chuckled. "A woman after my own heart."

"Do you have one?"

"On occasion."

"Does it permit you to indulge me now?" Her green gaze was bewitching. "You *did* promise me as many times as I want," she purred.

"At your service, Your Highness." He was already easing himself between her legs, nudging her thighs wider, pulling her dimity robe off so his heated flesh touched hers. "You're nicely wet for me," he murmured moments later, his fingers sliding over her pouty vulva.

"And you're always nicely hard, aren't you?" she pleasantly observed, his erection hot against her skin. "I'm so glad you came to visit me."

He laughed at his curious reversal of motive and impulse. "It turns out I am, too, with sweet, eager cunt like yours to enjoy."

"While I have a virtuoso rake to enjoy."

"We're here to please you, ma'am. Although you may have to beg me the first time as payback for last night," he teased, lightly brushing her sleek, pulsing labia with the swollen crest of his penis.

"Under the circumstances, I'm definitely not averse to begging," she breathed, needful, sensual urgency a constant with the Marquis of Crewe unclothed and aroused before her. She lifted her hips to more readily accommodate him.

"Tell me how much you want this," he murmured, inserting the tip of his penis the merest fraction, the pressure on her swollen tissue exquisite.

"I want you wildly, madly, feverishly," she whispered, moving her hips in a lush, sensuous undulation, enticing him in.

"Don't be shy," he sardonically murmured, smiling, and he guided himself into her drenched passage, his degree of lust as irrepressible. Adjusting her hips minutely, he penetrated slowly so they both felt the tremulous friction, the reluctant yielding as his huge cock stretched her, invaded her, forced her pulsing tissue wider.

All feeling was suddenly concentrated in the heated core of her body, the unspeakable flux and flow as he began moving a heady, breath-held delirium. There were degrees and more glorious degrees, she feverishly reflected, dissolving, dizzy with intoxicating pleasure.

How fuckable she was, he thought, plunging into her soft body, an intense, primordial satisfaction bombarding his senses—fathomless, inchoate, different. Unbridled in her desires, lushly demanding, she was as selfishly intemperate as he.

In a slow thrust and withdrawal, he plunged deeper and deeper in an unrestrained rhythm that only partially satisfied his inexplicable craving. And she met him in her own wild, carnal urgency. It seemed as though they were completely alone in this strange bedroom and manor house, in the world and universe, all else displaced by raw, turbulent desire. Crying out, she clutched at him, drawing him closer, deeper, greedy, wanton, and suddenly he found himself thinking that a woman of such flagrant appetites had men in her past. Brushing his hair back from his face, as though an unobstructed view were required, his gaze narrowed on the flushed, passionate woman beneath him. "You do like fucking, don't you," he murmured, harsh and low, images of a crowd of amorphous men invading his consciousness.

Whimpering, impaled, she couldn't respond, could barely think beyond the delirious echoing mantra equating the marquis's hard erection with paradise, waves of carnal heat pulsing and throbbing through her vagina in a mindless, frenzied rhythm, orgasm, seconds, moments, away.

Suddenly resentful of her fierce abandon, he withdrew marginally and, frantic, she cried out, grasped him more tightly.

"No," he roughly breathed, holding himself motionless in mid-passage, rankled, wondering how many other men had brought her to this point of sexual hysteria.

Her hips arched high to draw him in, her fingers bit into his lower back.

"Fucking *no*." Stung, maddened by an unnatural jealousy, he resisted her tenacious grip.

"Yes," she imperiously cried, panting, ravenous. The throbbing between her legs echoed in her brain and body, in every cell and tissue and coursing vein, her climax beginning to shudder on the fringes of her mind. "Damn you," she breathed, willful, commanding, the strength in her hands astonishing. "Give it to me."

She shouldn't have used those words.

They struck a perverse emotion, base prerogatives, untamed urges coming to the fore. "You want it?" he whispered, driven by powerful impulse. And teeth bared, vicious, he drove into her, unrestrained, merciless, giving her what she wanted—what he wanted—this hot, hot, burning hot princess who made him forget everything but lust and debauch and burying his cock hilt-deep inside her.

She was panting, her climax so close, the peaking pleasure had begun flowing, that first runnel of rapture racing, leaping, swelling an instant later, bearing her to an orgasm so torrid and blissful, her high-pitched scream brought the guards to attention.

The marquis's climax was only seconds behind, and as the last vestiges of her cry died away, he abruptly withdrew and came on her stomach.

"No . . . no," she panted, her gaze still half-lidded. "You can't . . ."

It was too late, and rolling away, he lay sprawled on his back, eyes shut, breathless, inexplicably angry.

She lunged at him. "You can't do this to me!" she screamed, pummeling him wildly.

His eyes snapped open at the first blow, and, catching her fists in a brutal grip, he shoved her away. "I'm not . . . a pawn in your game." His breathing was labored, his body sweat-sheened, his steely grasp hard like his eyes.

"This isn't a game," she said through clenched teeth, trying to shake his hands off. "It's not negotiable."

His hold only tightened. "I don't care what it is. Find some other man to"—he drew in a deep breath to stabilize his breathing and temper—"do what you want. I won't."

Poised on her knees beside him, prisoner in his grip, she raged, "You don't realize how necessary this is—for me. How can I make you understand?"

"You can't." All he could think of was her eager, untrammeled passion—of all the men who had been where he'd been, when it shouldn't matter, when it had never mattered before. "Are you always so fucking enthusiastic?" he growled.

She went motionless. "You are bothered by that?"

"Maybe I am."

"Maybe I don't care," she hotly replied, struggling to pull free of his grasp.

"Answer me." His fingers were crushing.

"What do you want me to say? No? No, then. I was a virgin when I met you. Like all the other women you fuck," she snapped, as temperamental as he, as moody, as sullen. As troubled by disquieting feelings. "That's your specialty, is it?" she sarcastically went on. "Fucking innocent maids. Strange. Rumor has it you like adultery best—all those society belles whose husbands don't satisfy them flock around you in droves. What's your record for a night? Eight?" she waspishly noted. "Or was it ten. I forget the dossier figures." Tantrumish, she glared at him. "So don't lecture me on morality," she said, testy and thin-skinned. "You don't qualify as a critic."

His rising temper was almost visible as her sarcasm escalated, and when she finished, he curtly said, "I prefer quiet women."

"Shall I tell you what kind of men I prefer?" she insolently returned. "We could compare the best of our repertoires. I've always found that men who—"

Her words were cut short by his fingers pressed hard against her mouth. "Why don't I tell you instead what I want from you," he said, rude and glowering. "Stop that or I'll break your wrist," he gruffly added, warding off her blow with his shoulder, his grip viselike on her other hand. "Maybe I'll tie *you* to the bed this time," he brusquely said, restive under incomprehensible emotion, unsated lust flaring at the sight of her still pinked with passion telling him of other men. What had they done to her and she to them? he wondered, his erection swelling. How often did she respond like she had with him? Why did he feel this overwhelming need to possess her?

There were no answers, nothing simplistic to explain the inexplicable. "You wanted numberless orgasms, didn't you?" he murmured, shifting into a seated position in a smooth flow of muscle, flipping her over on her stomach. "Let's see what we can do about that," he went on, moody, insult in his tone, raising her to her knees with effortless strength.

"Stay," he ordered as he would to a recalcitrant pet, slapping her bottom as she tried to escape, holding her securely around the waist while he moved into position behind her. His grip was pitiless, his fingers leaving marks on her pale skin. "You never even need stimulation, do you?" he silkily murmured. "How convenient," he sardonically went on, her dew-wet cleft tantalizingly available, the pink curve of her bottom provocatively raised to meet him. And, resentful of his stark craving for her, he thrust forward without preliminaries, gliding in too easily, he thought with chafing displeasure—her vagina slick again with the sweet liquid of desire.

She shouldn't respond to such brute disdain, she querulously reflected, and while her intellect understood the ruinous barbarism of his actions, a molten heat dissolved through her body, the feel of him—gloriously large, exquisite, the delectably forceful friction of his penetration sending fevered tremors coursing through her senses. She shivered at the heated rush, moved backward in greedy, shameless longing, slavish to the pleasure he provoked, an orgasmic flutter already pulsating deep inside her. She gasped, whimpered, the aching pressure flaring, quickly reaching tinder point as though he had to no more than enter her and she climaxed.

His savage rhythm continued unrestrained, each stroke driven by the entire force of his lower body throughout her orgasmic spasms and beyond, unrelenting, powerful, and within seconds she was crying out again in violent climax. Raw sensation tore through her mind and body and senses over and over again as the Marquis of Crewe gave vent to his moody need for submission. He rode her with a reckless disregard for everything but his own inexcusable need to assert himself, to master this woman who challenged his susceptibility to feeling.

"No more, no more . . ." she panted after numberless orgasms, her body oversensitized, ravished. "Please . . . no more . . ."

Her soft appeals finally pierced the mindless fury of his discontent and an enigmatic satisfaction pervaded his mind as he allowed himself his own climax outside her body, the soft curve of her lower back alternative to her fertile interior. Then his hands gentled on her, and he felt the silken texture of her skin as if for the first time and in a voice pitched low, filled with grace and charm, he whispered, "I'm sorry."

She twisted around so violently, he was taken by surprise. Swinging her arm back, she slapped him with such fury, she was shaking in the aftermath. "I wish I had a whip so I could thrash you bloody," she stormed, trembling, glaring at him.

Her capitulation full recompense for his resentments and, momentarily sated, he was in a mollifying humor. "Perhaps we can accommodate your fetish for flagellation later," he suavely said.

"Only if you die in the process."

"Then where would you be in your quest for an heir?" he pleasantly queried.

"No worse off than I am now in your uncooperative mood. At least I'd have the satisfaction of wiping that insolent smile from your face."

"Forgive me," he murmured, schooling his face into somberness, currently in harmony with the world. "I'm completely to blame."

"Damn right you are."

"Now, if there were only some way I could compensate you," he murmured.

"Don't toy with me, Crewe. I nearly expired with your particular brand of recompense and I'm no nearer pregnant than I was before."

His facile smile vanished and his extended sigh recognized the extent of their dilemma. There was no denying her sensual appeal, and whether he fucked her out of spite or desire wasn't particularly clear. "Is there no middle ground?" he queried.

"Not if I care to live. Or my mother."

"Don't say that."

"I wish I could sugarcoat the truth, Crewe, but there you have it. Look," she plainly said. "You know as well as I do—the whole world knows, you don't exactly use caution in the dispersal of your semen. So do me a favor. Think of me as one of your nameless London belles, many of whom offer your children to their husbands without a qualm. Disregard this quibble with coercion and be as obliging to me."

"But it *is* coercion."

"I can be as accommodating as Lady Lismore or Caroline Bennett or any number of others. Would it help if I saw that you had your freedom on the estate? Let me talk to Gregory."

His interest immediately piqued by her offer, he weighed the odds of her becoming pregnant before he could escape—before they both escaped if she wished to leave as well. An expert gambler, no one understood the laws of chance better than he. "How much freedom?" he bargained, an edgy excitement flaring through his brain.

"We'll talk to Gregory and see what's possible. I need a child, Crewe, and I'm willing to negotiate."

"Call him in."

Her brows rose. "Should we dress first?"

"You should, at least," he casually replied, familiar with the company of men.

But he pulled on a pair of riding pants while Sofia found her robe, and before long they were discussing the requirements of Gregory's role as warden on the terrace below, the east view from the house bucolic in the morning sun.

"The marquis would like some incentive to go along with my husband's plans," the princess explained.

The captain gazed across the marble table at the marquis, his gaze blank. "Why?"

"Don't be difficult, Gregory," she interposed. "I would prefer cooperation, if you must know."

His gaze softened as he looked at his mistress, which fact the marquis took note of. "Would you cooperate then?" the captain inquired, his oblique eyes flicking to Hugh, his glance suddenly piercing as though he could see into the marquis's mind.

"Yes," Hugh said, knowing what the quid pro quo would be, counting on the favorable percentages in terms of time. If he could escape in a day or so, a pregnancy might be averted. "How much freedom would you be willing to concede?"

"A hundred yards in the open. Your privacy in the house."

"Two hundred yards and freedom of movement in the house."

"Fine."

It was too easy. "Any guarantees?"

"Are you giving any?"

The perimeters of trust were clear. There were none.

Although the men might have been related in a more perfect world, their looks so similar. Only the subtle ethnic differences set them apart: their eyes, the marquis's slightly fuller mouth, the nuance of a curve in the marquis's nose where it had been broken in public school. But they were both dark, tall, powerfully built, and interested in the princess.

Perhaps that interest could be turned to his advantage, the marquis thought. "Why don't we ride out and see the estate," Hugh suggested, anxious to test the limits of his freedom. "Can my batman come along?"

"Certainly."

"Obliging," Hugh softly murmured, his dark eyes on the captain.

"As long as you're obliging to the princess, my lord, I'll continue to offer you every courtesy. Do we understand each other?"

"Perfectly. Let me get my boots and a shirt. How much time do you need?" he courteously inquired of Sofia.

"Ten minutes."

"A woman who can dress in under two hours. Where have you been all my life?" the marquis silkily intoned.

"We aren't all china dolls, my lord. Perhaps you've been associating with the wrong women."

"Obviously," he replied, his gaze amused. "Very obviously," he softly murmured, his glance altogether different.

She blushed.

The marquis smiled.

The captain did not.

"Well, then," Hugh pleasantly said, rising from his chair, the order of precedence having been nicely clarified, "why don't we meet at the stables in ten minutes."

The princess looked glorious in a form-fitting forest-green riding habit, the military cut accentuating her voluptuous femininity, her veiled hat seductive.

"You turn heads, my lady," Hugh graciously said as she approached. "Do I detect a Worth creation?"

"How perceptive, my lord. While you look like a red Indian in your buckskins."

"I dress for comfort," he replied, smiling, his fringed jacket and chamois riding pants consummate foil for his harsh masculinity.

"Have you been to the American West?" she inquired, moving toward a splendid Thoroughbred held by a groom.

"Several times. The hunting is superb."

"A change from your pursuit of females?"

"Females inhabit the West, my lady."

She cast him a sharp glance. "Of course. I should have known."

"Men must be a constant in your life as well." His tone had turned minutely chill. And he cautioned himself to restraint, every rational impulse reminding him to ignore the princess's amorous partners.

And for a flashing moment, he acceded to the persuasion of reason.

"Do you hunt or do they hunt you?" he abruptly inquired, following her, waving away the groom.

"I don't need your help," she murmured, gesturing the groom back.

The marquis said "Get away" in such a vicious tone, the man literally leapt aside. "There, now," Hugh softly murmured, cupping his hands to lift her up, "let me help you mount."

"A change for you," she tartly said, her smile brittle.

"And when it seemed as though you were enjoying yourself," he sardonically replied, watching her cheeks turn pink.

"Perhaps I can repay the favor someday," she brusquely declared, placing her booted foot in the scoop of his hands. An unwanted shiver ran down her spine as he smoothly lifted her weight and dropped her onto the saddle.

"I wait with bated breath, my lady," he murmured, adjusting her foot in the stirrup with an authority that triggered a rush of heated memory. His palm drifted up her leg, smoothed the folds of her skirt, stroked her knee curved over the pommel of the sidesaddle. "You look . . . ready," he whispered.

She shouldn't react to such insolence, she thought, nor respond to the carnal heat in his voice, but her body failed to understand degrees of pique and she felt a damp heat liquify between her legs. "You irritate me, Crewe," she curtly said, repressing her shameful carnal urges.

"That's not all I do to you, Princess," he quietly remarked, skilled at recognizing female arousal. "Should I see if you're wet for me?" he whispered with unctuous charm.

She brought her whip down on her mount's flanks in answer, and he quickly stepped back, his smile knowing. Striding to the mount prepared for him, he leapt into the saddle and threw a swift glance at Gregory and his troop, at Pierce. "Keep your distance," he ordered, and, whipping his black, he galloped after her.

Matching his mount's pace to hers, he maintained several yards between them, surveying the country through which they passed, taking note of landmarks, his eye on the sun, gauging their direction . . . until he spied a distinctive grotto on a distant hillside and, overtaking her, he forced her mount to turn.

She fought against the pressure of the large black he rode, the horses shoulder-to-shoulder in a hard gallop, the inexorable pressure of his larger mount bringing hers around. "I don't want to ride with you!" she shouted.

"Show me the view from there!" he shouted back, ignoring her words, pointing at the tumble of stone perched atop a wooded rise. And when she continued to oppose him, he leaned over, grabbed her reins, and pulled the horses to an easy lope. They slowed as the ascent became steeper, but he didn't release his grip on her reins and, pursed-lipped, she rode beside him.

"How much can Gregory be trusted?" he asked, glancing back to see their guards the required distance away. Pierce rode alone behind them. "Not talking, are we?" he noted a moment later, surveying her set face.

"What good would it do?"

"I thought you wanted to get away."

"I'm to trust you, you mean." Her tone was filled with disgust.

"I suppose you'd have to."

She snorted, her swift glance barbed. And they settled into silence the remainder of the way up the rise. The grotto turned out to be much larger at close quarters, the entrance two beautifully cast bronze doors worthy of at least a baptistery if not a cathedral, the pile of stones artfully arranged specimens of exquisite marbles and malachite in harmonious hues, a riot of vines, flowers, moss ornamenting the stone. "A very expensive alehouse," Hugh blandly remarked, sliding from his saddle, aware of the common entertainments for picturesque follies like this.

"Or a dolly house," Sofia flippantly noted, staying in her saddle, her reins still securely in the marquis's gloved hands.

"Is that why you didn't want to come here? You don't trust me?" the marquis impudently inquired, walking around to lift her from her mount. He put up his hands.

"Must I?" she coldly asked.

"Unless you think you can wrestle me to the ground and then ride away," he drolly returned.

"Lord, you're difficult."

"Down," he ordered, beckoning with his index finger.

"I could scream for help," she petulantly said.

"And that would get you a baby?" His smile was boyishly innocent.

"Damn you."

"But I'm a necessary evil," he softly replied. "Now, if you prefer, I can haul you from that saddle."

Abruptly pitching forward, she fell limp as a rag doll, and only his quick reflexes saved her. Grunting, he absorbed her sudden dead weight, steadied himself, and, scooping her up against his chest, hatless now since her fall, he lightly said, "Your husband might have good reason to be out of sorts with you. You're damnably headstrong and independent."

"Only men are supposed to be headstrong and independent?" she hotly contended.

"Of course. Haven't you read the rules?" His voice was teasing as he moved toward the small structure.

"Then it's time to change the rules."

"Good. You'll come away with me then," he advanced, looking down at her, his gaze suddenly grave.

"Maybe I will." But even as she spoke, caution warned her against believing a man she'd met a day ago, a man captive and intent on escape.

"You *can* be accommodating after all," he murmured, more inclined every moment she was in his arms to graciously acquiesce to his assigned role as stud. "And I did promise Gregory to honor my part of the bargain," he softly added.

"Will you now?" she queried, as aware as he of their closeness, her voice taking on a tantalizing nuance.

"The thought of coming in you is beginning to hold great appeal," he honestly replied.

"I'd be most grateful," she said with equal honesty. A pregnancy would put her beyond her husband's retribution and save her mother.

"A folly of another kind in this architectural one," he mockingly declared, bending slightly to turn the knob. "I hope we both know what we're doing." The door swung open on well-oiled hinges onto a sun-dappled chamber illuminated by latticework skylights. Cool marble covered the walls and floor, elaborately inlaid with gilt mosaic. Off to one side a small pool, moss-banked with a lightly flowing current reflected the sunlight in sparkling luminescence. The furnishings were faux rustic, primarily willow and bamboo chaises covered in colorful patterned silks. "Apparently vice was the entertainment of choice here," the marquis dryly noted, surveying the numerous chaises. "Shall we find the softest one?"

"I should be hostile and cross."

"Instead of hot and excited," he murmured, his gaze roguish. "I know."

She smiled. "It must be kismet."

"Nothing so romantical, darling," he lightly teased, his endearment a spontaneous utterance he considered with brief astonishment. But she *was* darling at the moment, he thought, and damned luscious. "Carnal urges, more likely," he added. "But if you want romance, I can do that, too," he offered, his generosity equally spontaneous.

"Are you sick, Crewe?" she teased, her grin infectious. "Such politesse."

"Sick with a sudden craving for your hot cunt," he murmured.

"How indecent of you," she whispered, his words triggering an unconscionable, shocking rush of pleasure deep inside her as though he'd entered her already.

"My specialty," he said, his voice low. "I've been in training."

"Lucky for me."

"I'm not so sure who's more lucky," he softly declared, a small heat in his dark gaze. "So tell me, what do you want to do first?"

"We could bathe," she murmured, gesturing toward the glistening pool.

"Wrong answer." He grinned. "Sorry. I'm currently in rut."

"How unusual for you."

"Or for you," he replied, his gaze returning from contemplation of the chaise nearest the door. His dark brows formed into a faint scowl. "Actually, I find myself offended by your lascivious passions. Don't ask me why," he gruffly added.

"Could you be . . ." She quirked her lacy brows. "Pardon me for using such an unpleasant word—jealous?"

"No." His scowl deepened.

"If it helps," she said, surveying the most sought-after lover in the western world, thinking herself grossly ingenuous to even consider honesty, "I've never physically responded to a man like I have to you."

"You're lying."

"I wish I were," she quietly said. "It would make everything so much easier."

"A fuck is a fuck, you mean."

"Something like that."

"And it isn't now, is it," he slowly said, the faintest frowns marring his brow.

"Not for me at least. I'm sorry," she said, watching his gaze shutter. "I should be more urbane. How tired you must be of women telling you they want you."

He walked the few feet to the nearest chaise and put her down before he spoke, and when he did his voice was well bred but circumspect. "We're both worldly people," he carefully said, standing a prudent distance away. "We both have other lives. I'm not sure what's happened here, but the usual rules don't seem to apply. You're not nameless or faceless in the customary way." He shrugged, the fringe on his jacket moving minutely. "You know what I mean." He looked at her as if needing affirmation, and she said, "Benign promiscuity. I know."

"All I want to do is fuck you," he murmured, the disbelief in his voice patent.

"And you want me to tell you that aberrant feeling will pass."

"It would be reassuring." His mouth twitched into a rueful smile.

Perhaps she'd had to make more compromises in her life or perhaps he'd never had to make any. "You won't remember me in a month," she pleasantly declared, when she wasn't sure she'd forget him in a dozen lifetimes.

"Really." A current of resentment underscored the word. "So a new man will be listening to your orgasmic screams."

"Look," she quietly said, "we both know this can't go anywhere. And no, there won't be another man. But this is jealousy, Crewe, in case you've never experienced it. Mark it on your calendar."

"I could take you with me." Single-minded, he wanted what he wanted.

"For how long? Be practical. You'd be looking for a way out within a fortnight. I won't go into a closet until you call for me or melt into the woodwork like some doxy thrilled you've looked her way. You'd have to see me across the dinner table and consider this, Crewe, when lust isn't doing your thinking for you—across the breakfast table as well. That should put the fear of God in you."

He smiled at her blunt depictions. "Is it really that bad?"

"Let's not talk about that."

"We should keep everything in the present tense?"

"Certainly a habit of long standing with you."

"So . . ." he murmured, his voice husky, a familiar touch of amusement vibrating in its depths, "are you interested in having my child?"

"You've returned, darling," she playfully replied. "I think we'll both be more comfortable with the normal, profligate Hugh Dalsany. And the answer is yes." She raised her arms to him in slow, deliberate invitation, and, leaning back on the golden silk, she purred, "Let me entertain you . . ."

She lay Venus-like on the willow chaise, all blooming flesh and curves, her narrow waist corseted to hand's-span width, the flowing riding skirt trailing on the floor, the braided frogs and closures on the jacket so overtly masculine, her voluptuous form seemed more perversely erotic in contrast. As though green serge and severe tailoring, all the accoutrements of military dress, could scarcely contain the lush fertility of her womanhood. And if he had any misgivings, the image before him would have tempted more virtuous men than he.

He was slipping the bone buttons of his fringed jacket free as he moved toward her.

He walked through the dappled light, his dark hair gleaming intermittently as sunshine and shadow bathed his form, the sculpted planes of his face cast and recast in flickering splendor. She wondered for a moment what parents begat such handsomeness, and a heatbeat later realized they might be parents someday to a similar young man.

Past and present images raced through her mind toward a staggering unknown, and for a transient moment the stark reality of parenthood overshadowed even her husband's lethal threats. But, as quickly, those reflections were suppressed by more powerful instincts of survival.

There were no choices in this obligatory country sojourn— neither for herself nor the marquis.

She watched him discard his fringed jacket in a pale, velvety heap on the marble floor, and when he tugged his shirt from his riding pants in one smooth pull, she found herself focusing on more immediate sensations.

Her nostrils flared as though primordial emotion responded to the Marquis of Crewe's audacious sexuality. He undressed casually as if he'd done this numberless times in similar situations, unconscious of the impact of his lean, powerful body. And fascinated by his virility and strength, she gazed, tempted like Eve herself in the presence of such flaunting masculinity. "You show well, my lord," she murmured, his conspicuous erection garnering her full attention.

"So I've been told," he unabashedly replied. "I expect you could silence a room without much effort. I won't ask if you have," he cheekily added.

"We don't have the same exhibitionist impulses," she softly said.

"Obviously you have some," he murmured, moving closer, "or you wouldn't offer yourself in such a seductive pose. How many men have seen you like that," he went on, sitting down beside her, "in that arms'-open welcome? How many have you offered to entertain in that lush, tantalizing purr?" He placed his hands lightly on her thrusting breasts, palms down, and, leaning forward, a sudden uncharitable light glittered in his eyes. "Tell me," he whispered, "how many?"

"We don't want to start comparing numbers, Crewe," she quietly replied. "Believe me."

His slender, tanned fingers tightened.

"Do you like violence with your sex?" Insolence colored her tone.

"Sometimes," he murmured, not sure himself why he couldn't overlook the men in her past. "Is your husband violent?"

"If you're talking about sex, I wouldn't know."

"The others then."

"How can it matter? This is only sex, not ownership. Or do you only like women who slavishly adore you?"

Her remark raised a smile, and, diverted from his inexplicable resentments, he said, "I particularly avoid women who adore me."

"Then we should get along famously, and if you'd ease your hold, I could take this very constricting riding habit off."

"Would you like help?" he lightly asked, sitting upright, his hands falling away, finding himself capable once again of depersonalizing his feelings.

"I'm here to accommodate you, my lord," she softly said. "You tell me."

"Such *carte blanche,* Princess. It almost makes one believe in heaven."

"A male heaven no doubt," she observed, one brow pertly arched.

"No doubt," he murmured, taking in the lush vision of paradise before him. "Undo those fastenings on your jacket."

His quiet voice of command made her shiver, the plain words, the authority, more seductive than a score of kisses. "And then what?"

"Then I'll tell you what I want next—and because you're here to accommodate me . . . you'll oblige, won't you?"

"Of course." She slipped the first silken frog free.

"And you'll like it, too, won't you?" he sardonically observed.

"You make it very pleasant." Her voice was bland.

"How tame you make it sound. Would you prefer we go riding instead?"

"I'd prefer riding that splendid cock of yours."

"That's what I thought," he gently said, "and as soon as you take all those clothes off, I'll let you climax once or twice."

"I should despise your arrogance."

"Do you actually like fawning men?" His mouth curved into

a wicked smile. "You seem as though you prefer something—different."

"Meaning you."

"Meaning me," he impudently replied. "Take your time, though; I can wait."

She paused in her unfastening. "Maybe I can, too."

"Suit yourself," he murmured, lightly grasping his erection, sliding his closed fingers downward so the full length reared upright, the swollen red crest gleaming. "I don't *have* to come in you."

"Yes, you do," she hotly whispered, and, swiftly moving upright from her lounging pose, she covered his clasped hand with hers and, leaning forward, lightly licked the full, stretched head. Looking up at him a second later, she murmured, "Now let's see who can wait." And opening her mouth, she drew the pulsing crest into her mouth.

His eyes shut, a soft groan punctuated the silence, and his free hand automatically moved to cradle her head. The dynamic suddenly shifted, levels of lust instantly equalized, and for a lengthy interval, the only sound in the grotto was the light ripple of moving water and a soft sucking sound.

When the princess raised her head sometime later and gazed at him, her lips, pinked and wet, he muttered, rampant and resentful, "You're much too accomplished."

"You didn't like it?" she dulcetly inquired. "When it seemed as though you were"—her eyes were amused—"responding . . ."

No longer interested in a skirmish of wills, interested only in possessing her completely, his hands clamped hard around her slender waist, and, swinging her upright in a blur of muscle and sinew, he set her on her feet facing him. "Lift up your skirt," he curtly ordered.

She instantly obeyed, as aroused as he, as selfish, not quibbling over motive with libidinous desire torrid in her blood. Urgent, lustful, he stripped her doeskin pantalettes down her hips with a brusque, wrenching jerk.

He swore under his breath at the delay while he unbuckled her boots and stripped them off so he could slide the sleek leather over her feet, his erection throbbing, aching, his need for this woman beyond any former concept of wanting.

She was panting at the last.

They were both trembling.

"Tell me there's a rational explanation for this," he muttered, lifting her again as though she were weightless, depositing her on the chaise, sliding between her welcoming thighs a second later with the ease of considerable practice.

She shook her head. "It's insanity," she whispered. "We're losing our minds . . ."

But her last words were lost in a muffled moan as he drove into her, plunging so deep, he bodily moved her up on the chaise, and intellect and reason instantly gave way to riveting sensation. She came in seconds, as if she'd waited for this man, this hysteria, this exquisite degree of bliss, her entire life.

And now she'd found the secret key.

He knew all the keys; they weren't secret to him but the result of years of amorous diversion, a discriminating eye and sensitized perception. And more importantly, perhaps, he had a genuine passion for women.

Another orgasm washed over her brief moments later and, crying out, she fiercely gripped his strong body, his erection pressed hard against the extreme limits of her honeyed passage. Intoxicating bliss, bewitchment, melted through her brain, pulsed through every nerve and cell, touched the depths of her soul— and miraculously entered her heart when she'd thought all feelings of love had died long ago.

And when he teasingly whispered, "There *is* a Cupid," she gazed up at him in wonder.

"You're feeling this too?"

His faint smile was close and hers, she thought with sudden revelation. "It's sorcery," he murmured.

"Pagan witchcraft," she agreed, reaching up to touch the curve of his mouth. "But don't break the spell."

"Never," he breathed, moving inside her, gliding against her slick, silken tissue, withdrawing just enough to make the resultant penetration more exquisite. The slow rhythm of his thrust and withdrawal overwhelmed their senses, the universe centered in their conjoined bodies, lust, wanton feeling, affection—a new, tremulous love singing in their blood.

Perhaps the planets were all perfectly aligned or sorcery indeed had taken a hand. Or maybe biology alone was the potent force. But they both understood the unprecedented wonder of the occasion.

"This baby is mine," he breathed, his orgasm beginning to rush downward.

"Ours," she whispered, clinging to him.

"Ours," he said, his eyes closing against the intensity of feeling inundating his body. And as the marquis poured into her, she met his heated climax, opened her heart and body to the awesome mystery and welcomed him with love.

Moments later, prostrate on the silken chaise, they lay panting, heated, touched by a rare sense of closeness.

"Now what are we going to do?" the marquis murmured, postcoital unease reassessing such injudicious feeling.

"I thought we might cool off in the pool if you'd help me take off these yards of serge."

His sigh of relief was audible. "You're damned adorable," he murmured, his smile dazzling.

"While you have a very winning charm, my lord," she lightly returned, extricating them both from the byzantine trap of too ardent feeling. "Are you as . . . resourceful in the water?"

"Let me know, Princess," he said with a teasing grin, rolling to his feet. Lifting her from the chaise, he carried her to the pool, stripped away her clothing with a deft expertise, eased them both into the cool water, and said, "Now I'll see if I can keep you warm."

He did.

With great skill.

And it wasn't until Gregory banged loudly on the door hours later that they noticed the day had vanished with the setting sun.

Twilight shadow filled the grotto with a suffused lavender ambiance, creeping darkness settling in the remoter corners of the chamber. "Do you want to stay or go?" he softly asked, kissing her gently as she lay on the mossy bank.

"You decide . . ." she whispered, blissful lethargy pervading her senses.

"Ten minutes!" Hugh shouted, but they found themselves reluctant to leave the enchanting grotto, and it was nearly an hour before they appeared outside in the falling dusk. He carried the princess cradled in his arms, her eyes shut like a drowsy child.

"She's tired," the marquis laconically announced, his gaze sweeping the mounted troop in mute challenge. "And we don't need company," he brusquely added, his glance settling on Gregory. "Two hundred yards," he reminded him.

On the ride back, the evening dusk seemed to enfold them in a gossamer warmth, the air velvet on their skin, the quiet of the night like the contentment of their souls, and when he whispered, "Thank you" in a husky murmur, she smiled up at him and softly breathed, "You bring me joy . . ."

It pleased him that he could bring her joy and he realized with a small exalting gladness that he adored her. And more, he knew, for love had crept in past the boundaries of his selfishness and avoidance in the hours past, or perhaps only the revelation. "Do you believe in fate?" he softly queried.

"Only if it's good." She didn't want to risk the bliss enfolding her. She wanted only agreeable speculations.

"Do you believe in love?"

She hesitated because before today, she hadn't and too, the marquis was hardly the kind of man susceptible to declarations of love. "Why do you ask?"

"So cautious," he said with a faint smile.

"I live my life with caution."

"Then I'll say it first. I love you, darling Sofia."

"Are you drunk, Crewe?" Playful and teasing, she couldn't afford for him to love her or she him.

"It wouldn't matter if I were. I love you drunk or sober, in the dark of night or in the morning light. I love you," he murmured, jubilation in the rich depth of his voice. "And you must love me back."

"I can't."

"But you do." He knew—perhaps that knowledge had

prompted his own gratifying realization. His dark gaze held hers in the gathering dusk. "You do."

Only the sound of frogs and crickets disturbed the silent evening for a lengthy interval.

"I do," she whispered, her eyes wet with tears.

They stayed together that night in the princess's room, making love in endless, leisured variety, both of them drowsy and oddly awake—elated, as though their minds were contending with their tumultuous feelings of love in alternate and parallel planes. And they made plans or Hugh made plans for their life together.

She awoke first at dawn's light and lay in blissful quiescence, understanding true happiness for the first time, her gaze traveling over the finely modeled features of the man who'd made her believe in love during the long hours past. He breathed quietly like a young child, his chest barely moving, his long lashes like black shadows on his cheeks, the curve of his mouth both sensual and tender like his kisses, his bronzed body half uncovered, as if he'd been too warm during the night. *That arm held me,* she thought, her gaze trailing down the tanned, muscled length, *and those fingers touched me,* the smallest quiver of excitement warming her senses at the memory of his skilled touch. And his long, powerful legs had twined around hers or served as firm support when she sat or lay on him. Her gaze traveled down the flawless perfection of his lean, rangy form and then back again to come to rest on his face. She liked his smile best, she reflected. When he smiled, he seemed to offer her boundless joy.

She'd miss that most.

For a few moments more, she memorized the sight of the man who had appropriated her heart and then she cautiously left the bed. She stood for a short interval more, wanting to remember every detail and minutiae, wanting to be able to bring the image of him into her mind with perfect clarity a thousand years from now.

But the clock in the hall softly chimed the hour, drawing her attention, and, with time so critical, she went to find Gregory.

"He wants me to leave with him tonight or tomorrow," she

said, seated across from her troop captain in the downstairs steward's office.

"And will you?"

"If I could persuade him to wait two days, could you telegraph Milosh and have him set the schedule ahead?"

"Everyone's been ready for six months, Your Highness. Only your scruples have curtailed our plans."

"And my mother? Can you guarantee me her safety?"

"Like I have a thousand times before. Katerina will take her out through the tunnel and back to Hungary. It won't be a problem."

"I should go myself and see her out."

"And risk your husband's insanity? I'll personally see that you don't." He leaned back in his chair and shut his eyes for a moment. "Forgive me. My words were uncalled for."

She twisted the brocaded ties of her robe, ran the silken fabric through her fingers, her agitation pronounced. "We're taking an enormous chance with everyone's lives."

"It's necessary. Everyone knows it. Everyone's known it for a long time. Leave it all to me. Stay with the marquis for a fortnight, a month if you like. By that time, all will be resolved and you can come home in triumph."

"I'm allowed this small bit of happiness?"

"You deserve more, and if it were in my power, I'd give you the world, you know that." His heart was in his eyes, but he spoke with a brusque authority.

"I know, Gregory. Thank you," she softly said, understanding how he felt about her. He was her rock and guardian, her protector. "Two days then before we ostensibly escape?"

"I'll see that Pierce has access to the stables two nights from now. I'll send a telegram once all is in place for your return."

"My return," she softly murmured.

"You'll rule with or without an heir. The stipulation requiring a child is in effect only so long as your husband remains on the throne."

She nodded and rose from her chair. "Godspeed," she murmured, "in this treacherous game of state."

Chapter 3

They fled the estate two nights later, Pierce having smuggled three mounts out of the stables. By morning they were halfway to London, and after stopping briefly at Dalsany House for fresh horses, clothes, and a quick luncheon, they continued north to the marquis's estate at Woodhill. It was dark by the time they arrived, but within minutes lights were blazing from every window, the entire staff bustling to see that the master and his guest were made comfortable.

The princess was introduced to Hugh's majordomo, his housekeeper, steward, and, at the last, his chaplain, John Wright, who said with a smile, "Hugh and I have been friends since boyhood. He's very generous with his tenants and the parish." By omission, the princess understood, the chaplain overlooked the less righteous qualities of his patron. And after a variety of orders had been transmitted by the marquis to his staff, he and the princess retired to his chambers.

"So this is where you were going to rusticate when I took you away," she said, gazing out on the moonlight lawns.

"This is where *we're* going to rusticate," he corrected, coming up behind her and enclosing her in his arms. "Just past those hills is the village. I'll take you there tomorrow and show you off."

"And no one will wonder who I am?"

"Let them wonder. A Princess Sofia is sharing my life. What else do they have to know. And if I love you, they will, too. Life is very simple here," he went on, filled with a rare contentment, the warmth of her body against his sufficient to make him believe in paradise.

"A simple life sounds very nice," she softly said, covering his hands with hers.

.

"We'll raise our child here. Our children. And if this is insanity," he said, a smile in his voice, "don't wake me up."

"Nor me," she murmured, tears welling in her eyes.

The days passed in such joyful pleasure, the marquis and princess found themselves feeling pity for the rest of the world. They spent every minute together in a kind of harmony poets portrayed in lyrical stanzas and sonnets and those less poetical condemned as fantasy. They lay abed some days and made endless love; on others, they rose at dawn and rode or walked the estate, the gardens, the village lanes. Everywhere they went, people turned to watch them, such happiness startling, awesome, as if bliss and exaltation had taken corporeal form.

And when, after a fortnight, the princess noticed her courses hadn't come and shyly told the marquis, he decided to call the entire household and village to a celebration feast. "I won't embarrass you," he said, grinning from ear to ear. "We'll call it some summer harvest festival or the name day of some saint; we'll think of something." But many a watchful eye that day and evening when the parish ate and drank and danced on the marquis's front lawn took note of the marquis's tender attention to his princess and a countdown of days began.

"He'll have to marry her now," the housekeeper stoutly said, tipsy after several glasses of the marquis's best wine, "or his heir won't come into the title right and tight."

"Can't if'n she's married already," the head groom noted, casting a cool gaze at the housekeeper.

"He'll have to buy her a divorce then," the majordomo solemnly maintained, his hauteur still intact despite numerous glasses of the aqua vitae he favored. "The House of Lords does it all for a tidy sum."

"Which himself can afford. Did you see the new diamonds he gave to the princess? She wore them to dinner last night."

"And also while swimming in the pool in the white garden this morning, I hear," the groom roguishly pronounced.

"You tell those nasty stable lads to mind their own business or I'll box their ears," the housekeeper hotly returned. "I declare, there's not a speck of manners between the lot of them."

And as the evening progressed, bets were made and taken on the arrival date of the marquis's new heir.

While the master and his guest enjoyed the festivities in their own private way.

At ten, they excused themselves to a roar of ribald cheers and comment and retired to a small guest cottage beyond the noise of the festivities on the manor lawn.

The small stone house was lit by candles, the golden glow warm and inviting, the scent of lilies and roses permeating the rooms. Vases of flowers stood on tables and consoles, a cold supper had been left in the small dining parlor, the bed had been turned down in the tiny bedroom tucked under the eaves.

"Do you like it?" Hugh asked, holding her hand in his as they stood on the threshold of the bedroom.

"It's like a doll house or a fairy tale cottage."

"And quiet."

"Yes. But everyone seemed to be enjoying themselves. You're much loved."

"John and my steward see to most of it. They're very competent."

"They couldn't do it without your approval." She knew first-hand how brutal and uncaring authority could be.

"My tenants might as well enjoy some of the benefits of my wealth, too. I'll show you my farms at Alderly tomorrow. We're trying out some new crops and machinery."

She smiled, thinking how different the country marquis from his libertine persona. "I'd like that," she said.

"Is there anything else you'd like?" he murmured, bending to nibble on her ear.

"Supper in bed?" she teased. "I'm famished all the time."

"And you should be. I want my baby well fed," he lightly declared. "Now, lie down and I'll bring up food and feed you."

"You *are* a darling."

"And you're the love of my life," he murmured, drawing her into his arms.

* * *

That night, after their supper and after they'd made love, much later when the moon was moving toward the horizon, he quietly said, holding her in his arms, "I want you to divorce your husband."

He felt her stiffen in his arms.

"I can have a divorce secured without fanfare. No one need know the details or circumstances. My lawyers will be discreet."

"My husband won't allow it."

"I'll see that he does." He spoke with an authority that had never been gainsaid.

"Let's talk about it in the morning. Would you mind?"

"No, of course not," he gently said. "I'll do whatever you wish. But you know I want this child to be legitimately mine."

"I know," she whispered, and, reaching up, she kissed him, tears welling in her eyes.

"Don't cry. I'll make everything right," he tenderly said, wiping her tears away with the back of his hand.

"I know you will." Her smile quivered for only a moment.

She was gone when he woke in the morning.

He tore the house apart, the village, the parish, searching for any clue to her whereabouts. He hired detectives from London, from Paris, but there was no Prince Marko and consort; he had every British consulate looking for her, too, without success. She'd disappeared, as if the earth had swallowed her up.

When he retired from the world shortly after, there was talk of various maladies and illnesses. Some said he'd turned hermit as penance for his numerous sins; those who knew him better saw his desperate pain and sorrow and worried for his sanity. But as the weeks turned into months, he came to accept Sofia's disappearance as inevitable and the rhythm of his life settled into a pattern measured only by the seasons of the field and farm. He kept to his estate at Woodhill, although his closest friends would come to visit. He traveled to London only rarely—for the marriage of his niece and later that of his friend Charles, or for business once or twice a year; he appeared at an occasional race meet when his stable was performing well, and his local hunt club enjoyed his presence regularly during the hunt season—although the level of risks he took at the jumps reached such proportions, wagers were made on whether he'd survive the sport.

Two years passed, with the young marquis living a life so antithetical to his former existence, all the ladies of his acquaintance despaired of ever experiencing the pleasure of his company again. More determined than most of the pursuing women, the lovely Countess Greyson once managed to infiltrate his household and appeared in his bed.

He took one look at her, she later related, calmly remarked, "I prefer sleeping alone," and left his bedchamber without a backward glance. After that episode, he gave new orders to his staff concerning his privacy, and no one breached the gates of Woodhill without his approval.

One August afternoon, several months later, he was going through his daily correspondence, the study doors open to the warm sun and summer breeze. What was she doing right now? he wondered as he often did when opening the latest letter from the detective firm in Paris he still kept on retainer. Expecting no more than the usual quarterly invoice without any new information, he unfolded a brief note and lifted out a newspage photo. "Is this the necklace?" his contact in Paris had written. Raising the scrap of paper closer, he gazed at the indistinct image. An arrow had been drawn on the newsprint, indicating a woman in the background at a soiree for the Austrian ambassador in Paris.

Her face rose out of the crowd and his heart seemed to stop.

Cautioning himself against rash hope, he quickly scrutinized the photograveur. The woman was blonde; the hair color changed Sofia's looks but the eyes were hers, and the perfect mouth. His gaze moved to the highlighted necklace, and his last present to Sofia glittered at her throat. Suddenly the blonde hair altered in his mind's eye to a rich, warm auburn and the woman in the background of the thronged soiree stepped from the page back into his life.

He left Woodhill within twenty minutes and was crossing the Channel five hours later. When the detective bureau opened in Paris the next morning, he was waiting at the door, having just arrived from the Gare du Nord, unshaven, disheveled, demanding immediate answers.

It took the remainder of the day to track down enough people in the photo to positively identify the woman with the diamond necklace.

She turned out to be Princess Mariana, regent of a small principality on the border of Dalmatia and Montenegro. Her son, for whom she ruled, was the young Prince Sava.

His journey took him from Paris to Salzberg to Zagreb. The train traveled through countryside dark with floods outside Zagreb before coming to the Adriatic, which looked that day like one of the bleak Scottish lochs. Sky, islands, and sea were all merged into the gray mist and sweeping rain. He took a steamer down the coast, past Korchula, Gruzh to Ragusa. There he hired a carriage and went inland.

The country through which he drove was so picturesque, it had the appearance of a stage set: high mountains, deep lakes, orchards and vineyards in the valleys, roses frothing over every wall and ledge. The woodlands were the clearest green laced with dark pines, the forest overseen by a majestic, snow-covered peak in the distance. He passed waterfalls that burst straight from the living rock, the limestone country cleft asunder as if by a giant's hand. Judas trees, fig trees, poplars, beech, wisteria vines were in wild abundance like an earthly paradise, and when he came at last to the small capital city he was reminded of a miniature Venice, all pale palaces and churches shimmering in the summer light.

The royal palace was constructed of gleaming white marble, its various levels and terraces spilling down a steep hillside amidst flowering shrubs and roses. But the marquis had no eye for the magnificent beauty of the setting or the splendor of the building.

All he could think of was seeing her again.

Guards stopped him at the entrance gates, but he insisted on seeing Gregory, speaking to the soldiers in a half dozen languages until they at last understood him and took him to a small sentry's lodge to wait.

When Gregory opened the door and saw him, he said, frowning, "I was hoping you'd forgotten her."

"But then, I was hoping she'd stay with me at Woodhill," the marquis replied, his voice chill. "So we were both wrong."

The captain came into the room enough to shut the door. "I can keep you away from her."

"Don't make this difficult," Hugh said, his gaze direct, challenging. "The British prime minister is more than willing to take a personal interest in my affairs."

Gregory minutely shifted his stance. "Why would he do that?"

"Because I'm his godson, which isn't so important," Hugh blandly remarked, "but he actually likes me as well and finds the old matter of my coercion intriguing." He tipped his head slightly toward the door. "So I suggest you tell the princess I'm here."

"What do you intend to do?"

The marquis held the captain's gaze for a long moment, a palpable tension in the air. "I'm not sure," he finally said.

She'd had time to compose herself after the initial shock of Gregory's announcement, and when she walked into the salon where the marquis waited, she was able to say, poised and unruffled, "You found me."

"Did you think I wouldn't?"

She shrugged, the flowered silk ruffle on her shoulder fluttering marginally. "It's been almost three years," she said, not mentioning his reputation for forgetting the females in his life.

"You're well hidden," he coolly replied.

"It was necessary." Only monumental self-control allowed her to speak as though he were a stranger when his presence filled the room, when his eyes burned with such fury, when she could still remember how it felt to be held in his arms.

"You didn't think I'd care that you kept my son from me?"

"Of course I did."

"But—?" he sardonically murmured.

"You're not that naive, Crewe."

"No, I suppose I'm not," he softly agreed, thinking of all the British consul in Ragusa had told him. "Your husband's dead, I hear."

"Yes." It took effort to withstand the scorn in his gaze.

"Did you kill him?"

She didn't answer immediately. "I suppose in a way I did," she finally said, lifting her chin a fraction as if to ward off his disdain. "Did you come all this way to revile me?" she coolly asked, not willing to take on the role of villainess regardless of his perceptions. "If you did, I'll bid you pleasant journey back to England."

"What color is real?" he brusquely asked, gesturing at her pale hair.

"Does it really matter?" Tart, acrid words.

"I remember you differently, that's all," he softly said, his tone suddenly altered—kind, warm again, the voice she remembered from the days and nights at Woodhill. "I saw you had my necklace on in Paris."

She forced herself to an exterior calmness she was far from feeling, the husky intimacy of his voice triggering a flood of memory she'd tried to lock away forever. "I wear it often," she replied. Every day, she reflected, although she didn't tell him that, his gift her sustaining talisman in a lonely world not of her making.

"You should have written. At least when our son was born."

"I wanted to; I wanted more than that, but"—she softly sighed—"circumstances wouldn't permit it. I don't have a personal life, Hugh. You must know that."

"Nor have I since you left. I've missed you," he softly murmured. He stood very still, tall, dark, sinfully handsome just as she remembered, his words the fantasy she'd dreamed and wished would come to life.

"I didn't dare miss you. I wasn't allowed," she said with the faintest of smiles, thinking perhaps prayers were answered after all.

"Gregory."

Her smile broadened minutely. "He bolsters my sense of duty."

"While I've missed my son's baby years."

"Forgive me for that. But my life had to be sacrificed for this . . ." She lifted her hand in a brief sweeping motion that took in the broad vista of the city outside the windows. "And I thought you'd soon find other entertainments anyway," she gently added.

"Did *you* find entertainments?" His voice took on a sudden harshness.

"I've been like a nun if you must know, while I expect you've been finding pleasure in your usual way." An unwished-for jealousy flared at the thought of his licentious prodigality. "Have you had any new children lately?" she murmured, the taint of insolence in her words.

The word *nun* had abruptly absolved the tumult of his bitterness and spleen. "What would you do if I said I'm staying?"

"Answer my question," she said.

"None. No children, not one," he carefully enunciated, understanding invidious suspicion and mistrust. "I haven't made love to a woman since you left."

"I've heard differently." Her green eyes sparked.

"Then Gregory is lying," he said with silky malice.

"It wasn't Gregory."

"One of the other advisers who control your life then."

"I chose to come back; no one controls me."

"Then free will isn't an issue," he brusquely noted. "Do you love me?" His voice shouldn't have been so chill, he realized. "Do you love me?" he repeated, a softer appeal in his tone this time.

She gazed into his beautiful dark eyes, then looked away, the crushing responsibilities of her life overwhelming.

"I'm not asking if you're allowed to love me," he gently said, "only if you do."

Her gaze swung back, and a lush warmth shone in her eyes. "You know the answer to that."

"I'm not as arrogant as I once was," he said with a rueful smile. "Tell me."

"I love you," she whispered, looking young and vulnerable in her summer frock. "I love you now, yesterday, a thousand years from this moment. I'll always love you."

"Three years is a very long time to live without you," he quietly said, holding his hands out to her. "There were times I thought I'd lose my mind."

When she still hesitated, he crossed the small distance between them and took her in his arms as though years and countries and politics didn't divide them. As though they were back at Woodhill and the sunshine of the world was shining on them alone. "I love you in every way a man can love a woman, and whatever you have to do, we'll do together," he murmured, holding her close.

"This is a dangerous part of the world," she softly warned.

"Then my son could use another guardian."

She gazed up at him. "You'd stay?"

"I'd do anything for you; you should have asked me three years ago."

"I didn't know. Forgive me . . . for everything—well, almost everything." Her smile lit up her face. "Sava looks just like you, you know; you couldn't deny paternity if you wished," she lightly asserted. "And he always wants his own way, too—like you," she went on with a grin. "Would you like to meet him?"

"I would have taken on Gregory and his entire troop to see my son." His mouth quirked into a half-smile. "Love is strange."

"And miserable at times."

"Not anymore," he cheerfully declared, lifting her off her feet and swinging her up into his arms. "From now on," he murmured, smiling down at her, "we're the luckiest people on earth."

When father and son met short moments later, Sava raised his pudgy hands to his father and repeated the word *Papa* his mother had used, his babyish smile open and warm.

His eyes glistening with emotion, Hugh glanced at the princess and whispered, "Thank you," before lifting the young toddler into his arms. He spoke to him in a low, gentle voice, telling him of his journey, of the trains and ships that would interest a young child, and before long, father and son were busily engrossed in the mechanics of a beautifully wrought model of a new steam-driven automobile.

They were like a matched pair, their features so pure and fine the princess marveled that the Crewe pedigree bred true to such a finite degree. Two dark, ruffled heads were bent over the delicate mechanism, identical black ochre eyes scrutinized the auto, and when they sent it racing down the nursery floor, they both laughed with the same abandon. Hugh Dalsany and Sava became fast friends that day, and in the years to come, the Marquis of Crewe reconciled to the role of legal guardian to the young prince. Guided him, nurtured him, loved him as a father.

The marquis and Mariana married when the prince was five, and three more children were born of the happy union. They stayed in the mountain kingdom far from the tumultuous events of Europe until the Treaty of Versailles rearranged the map of Europe once again, wiping away the last of the isolated Balkan principalities.

The duke took his family home to England then, to the estates he'd inherited on the death of his father years before. And the Duke and Duchess of Temerley, along with their children, lived a quiet, private life of great happiness.

Because of love.

And the rustication he'd once contemplated out of frustration and ennui became instead his blissful solace and content.

DARK DESIRES

by Thea Devine

Chapter 1

"If you force me to marry that man, I will never, *ever* let him touch me . . ."

She had said it; she had meant it. And now she stood beside Courtland Summerville, powerless, still as stone, hiding behind her veil, her pride, and her rock-ribbed determination to never ever submit to him.

He was not the man she was supposed to marry.

He was a monster, and her father had sacrificed her to him, and she couldn't look at him, or the crowded church, or at the minister without feeling like the whole thing was a nightmare.

She hated him. And she hated Gerard Lenoir, the man she loved, who had just stood by and *let* her father give her to Court. It was inexplicable, unforgivable, that he hadn't even fought for her, and she would never understand why.

She felt as if she were all alone in that church, that there was no one there for her, and that the man who had walked her down the aisle and handed her over to Court was a stranger.

She heard the words of the service; she heard Court's strong burnished voice reply to the time-honored questions of love, honor, and duty in the affirmative, and her heart started pounding painfully.

Had she truly thought he would say no, he wouldn't. Take her.

Oh, God, take her . . .

Or that Gerard would charge up the aisle at the last minute to save her?

Gerard was nothing less than a craven coward, brought to heel by the wealth and influence of Court's family, and the determination of her father, who so desired this marriage that he was willing to trample anyone who got in his way.

"Drue Caledon, do you take Courtland Summerville . . ."

She swayed slightly; she felt as if she were watching a play, and that someone else was responding to the minister's words.

That someone said, "I will," and heard the minister pronounce them husband and wife; *that* someone turned as he presented them to the assembled guests.

Someone else . . . who was she?

To his credit, Court didn't try to kiss her; his expression was impassive, forbidding. She couldn't imagine him ever touching her, even though the marriage contract between him and her father specified that he had every right to have her and that she would submit.

Written in stone. Her life, his to do with as he pleased . . .

Dear Lord—

It was unimaginable.

She placed her icy hand in the crook of his elbow and allowed him to lead her out of the church and into the blazing sun of a sultry Louisiana morning.

The heat hit her like a wall, suffocating, thick, imprisoning. And they still had to get through the reception; no matter what the reality, all the amenities had to be observed. They waited on the bottom step until the youngest daughters of the surrounding parish families came to the forefront to strew petals in their path as they led the way to the rear of the church.

Her father and Court—they did everything to a nicety . . . everything to circumvent gossip and make it look as if the marriage was real.

She kept her gaze down as they paced slowly behind the children and the fluttering rose petals, with the guests following in their wake.

. . . Gerard my love—

But it was a love not staunch enough or powerful enough to save her from this . . .

Behind the church, the servants of Wildwood had made a veritable wedding bower in the garden under the direction of the minister's wife.

I don't want this . . . I don't—

People she'd known all her life coming up to her, pleased for her, delighted for her, swelling with the summer-rich sense of the passion to come. Everyone loved a love story, but better than that, they adored an excellent dynastic match.

And of course that was part of Court's thinking when he'd agreed to her father's proposition.

I won't forget that. I'm a commodity, with a value set like a sack of rice or a bale of cotton. I am worth his paying off father's debt and accruing a half share in Oak Bluffs, and he gets a housekeeper, a manager, and an heir into the bargain.

What do I get?

Mauling by a man I despise. Marriage and status—and the loss of the true love . . .

How can I ever find forgiveness? How could he use my father like that?

Court was watching her; she felt those dark, unfathomable eyes grazing her as she moved amongst the guests accepting their good wishes.

She girded herself. She was neither hungry nor thirsty, and Court had provided enough food to feed the whole parish for a month. But that was the way. Every expectation must be met.

Except mine.

She accepted a cup of café au lait.

He had wanted a morning wedding, a breakfast reception. And then they would go to Wildwood where they would spend two weeks alone, with only a skeletal staff to serve them.

He had planned for everything.

She watched him as tightly as he watched her. There was no denying that Courtland Summerville had a commanding presence and an elegance that should have made him very pleasing to her. Certainly the unmarried ladies of the parish were gaping at him like lovesick girls, almost as if they didn't care that he had made his decision, and as if they harbored the unrealistic fantasy that things could change.

Forbidden thoughts.

Oh God . . . Gerard . . .

She felt the ache spiraling through her body. Never to have

Gerard, gentle, sweet, kind Gerard with his soft kisses and even softer hands. He knew how to coax, when to press, how to wait, when to beg.

He was not a brigand, like Court. He was a gentleman, and self-made.

And maybe that was part of what she loved about Gerard. That he had risen above his circumstances and earned his wealth, his reputation, his fame.

He took nothing for granted, Gerard, not even her. And he had been going to marry her; everything had been planned.

Don't even think about it.

"Drue?" Court, standing beside her, and she hadn't even noticed.

She summoned up a weak smile. "Court."

"I trust everything is as you would have wished."

"It's a lovely reception," she said, injecting some sincerity into her tone. It *was;* she didn't have to lie about that.

"Now, why don't you pretend that everything else is what you wish as well," he said harshly. "You look like you're lost at your own wedding, and that doesn't sit well with me."

Let the lies begin.

She stiffened her spine. She wasn't going to allow him to ride roughshod over her, even though he scared her to death.

"Surely you didn't expect me to pretend I'm in love with you," she hissed.

"You will be."

The arrogant ass. "I wild do my duty, nothing more, nothing less. It's an arranged marriage, and I don't see any reason to give any more than has been contracted for." She was shaking all over now. She'd never shown him any defiance, any emotion at all to define how ill-used she felt by her father and him.

"How interesting. The fawn has sharp little teeth."

"I bite, too," she said viciously.

"I hope so," he murmured.

"Don't you—"

"No!" He grasped her arm. "Don't *you.* You're mine now, little fawn. And as you say, you'll honor every single clause of that contract."

A feeling of dread washed over her. The hour was coming closer when they must leave, and she didn't know how to prevent it. "That's all I am to you—a piece of property to furrow and plant your seed."

"And a convenient way to extend my empire—don't forget that," he added venomously. "A half interest in Oak Bluffs—your father will never have to lift a finger again. And isn't that the point of the exercise?"

"Paying off his gambling debts was the point. And you knew exactly what you were doing when you loaned him the money and then squeezed him for payment. What else could he do?"

"It was his proposition," Court said flatly. "He wanted it."

"You took advantage of him."

"We've had this conversation, Drue. I've taken advantage of nothing. I have saved your father's reputation and his life."

"And filled your coffers, your bed, and your nursery besides."

"I call that smart business, Mrs. Summerville. You should be proud you have such an astute husband."

She felt the familiar fury envelop her. There was no arguing with him. He saw himself as their savior even though he was the man to whom her father was indebted. She would never understand such skewed thinking. It could only have been his plan from the first. And that meant he was a conniver and an opportunist.

"I'll never forgive you."

The light in his eyes flared dangerously.

"I don't care," he said heartlessly, and, always mindful that people were watching them, he smiled at her as if she had just told him she loved him, he dropped a brutal kiss on her mouth and callously walked away.

"My dear." Her father, with his palliating tones, his reasoned arguments. He looked as proud as if this wedding were real and Court her choice instead of his. "You are absolutely doing the right thing."

"For whom?" she asked bitterly, but she had always known she would do anything for him. And now she had: she had signed away her life to Court so that her father's life could continue on just as it always had, with the sole stipulation that he never gamble again.

What if he did? she wondered. What if her bluff, gladhanding father went to New Orleans and put a dollar down on the outcome of a horse race? And lost. What would happen then?

But she knew. Court had given her father an ultimatum, all of it spelled out in the contract. He would bail him out once out of duty; twice out of honor, and the third time, he would take the remaining half of Oak Bluffs and leave Victor with nothing.

And Victor was not a man who was used to *nothing*. The threat scared him. And the fact he had two chances to get it right was a speculator's dream. He had been very good, her father, in the past months since he had bartered her and half of Oak Bluffs away. He had stayed at the plantation, tending to business, salivating over the money that Court had deposited in his bank, even knowing that Court would demand an accounting of every penny spent.

That was how partners operated, Court said. Everything in writing. None of this trusting to the honor of the other business. That was how a man got trapped in a lie.

So how did it happen that she was ensnared in the biggest lie of all?

The cost was too great, she thought despairingly as her father dropped a light kiss on her cheek. Her body. Her loyalty. Her life.

She hadn't seen it in quite those terms in the light of her father's desperation. The moneylenders were after him, he'd told her. He'd lost three seasons' profits, and the money had to be paid. It was a simple business deal: an alignment of two of the parish's wealthiest, most distinguished families. No one would know the worst.

And she— Oh, here was the best part, her father said, she would be provided for—he would never have to worry about her again.

She remembered how she had gone still, her body frozen at the idea of being provided for. By Courtland Summerville. Her father's creditor. Her father's friend.

"You look beautiful," her father said, stroking her silk-shrouded arm.

But he'd said that earlier, after he had walked her down the aisle in her drift of virginal white, just before he relinquished her to Court's care.

"Thank you." What could you say to a father who thought that the sacrifice she had made for him was really a blessing for her?

"Soon you'll be in your new home, all snug and safe with your new husband," her father went on. "I can't tell you how happy that makes me."

I just bet it does.

Her thought shocked her. She had never, ever had any negative feelings about her father's situation.

But that was before she had actually promised to love, honor, and obey his worst enemy.

"Are you happy, Father?" she asked quietly.

"Aren't you?" he counterd, as if she had always seen the solution the same way as he.

She looked away from him. It was getting easier and easier to lie. Court could have taken everything in payment of the debt. But he had only demanded a partnership in Oak Bluffs—and *her.* She was only trading one satin cage for another. Except that one was occupied by a tiger.

"I am—content. This is the best solution."

"Let him take care of you, Drue. He's a good man, really."

He's a monster. "I'm sure we'll rub along just fine."

"There could be love, if you let it . . . He's a passionate man, as I'm sure you well know."

She shuddered. Her father was no romantic; he had lived his own life to the fullest while her mother was alive. And Mother had run Oak Bluffs and kept every feeling, every resentment, to herself till the day she died.

Passion had never entered into it—except where her father's gambling was concerned.

There was passion, larger and grander than any love story she could concoct. And it had seduced him, sucked him in, held him utterly in thrall. It was the love of a lifetime, and he wasn't over it yet; maybe he never would be.

Who would willingly submit to such ungovernable feelings?

You'd get towed under; you'd be rendered helpless, you would drown.

Not me.

Not me . . .

And then the thought came, unbidden, unwanted, never spoken: *There was only one way to get through it.*

. . . Like Mother. Just like Mother. Removed. Restrained. Resolved.

Respectable.

. . . now she understood . . .

That was all a woman could ever hope for . . . and nothing had changed in a thousand years.

She lifted her chin. "The whole of St. Faubonne Parish knows what a *vigorous* man Court is."

"Now, now, Drue. A lady never listens to gossip. And you are now his foremost advocate. Never forget, my dear. No matter what, he's your husband, right or wrong." Her father's gaze skewed to where Court was standing, talking business with the gentlemen of the parish.

My husband, oh, my God—my husband . . .

All wrong . . .

She wanted to run. Oh, God, she just wanted to drop everything and flee and let her father take responsibility for his own weakness, his own stupidity.

But there was no escaping Court. He was as inevitable as the sun, aware at every moment where she was, and—she thought, panicked—what she was thinking.

Don't move, his impassive gaze seemed to say. *Not a move without me. You're mine now to do with what I will.*

Her father moved toward Court, toward the knot of men who were the most influential in the parish, and she felt as if her anchor were gone. He just floated away from her, drawn by the business of men, drawn by Court, who was as magnetic as iron.

And just as hard. There was no mistaking that look. The minute her father joined the group, Court broke away and headed toward her.

And she—she just stood rooted to the spot, waiting for him.

Her husband . . . the word stuck on her tongue.

Her legs felt like jelly. She knew her face was pale and her hands were shaking.

"So beautiful, my love," Court murmured as he held out his hand.

She had no choice but to take it. He could take everything from her father in an instant. The least she could do was take his hand.

Together, they walked into the crowd as rose petals rained on them, the signal that it was time to go.

Oh, God—so soon . . . ?

Their carriage drew up in front of the church, driven by Isaac, who was dressed as formally as Court.

Her legs wobbled. *Time to go. Time to fulfill every promise. Time is up. Time, her enemy.*

Court helped her into the carriage and climbed in after her; Isaac snapped the reins and they were off, circling around the church drive, past the gardens and the trees in the distance.

She turned around to look at the receding crowd of well-wishers waving them home, and it was then she saw it—the figure moving restively in the shadow of the trees, recognizable by the bend of his body, the agitation of his movements.

Gerard had come; dear Lord, Gerard *had* come. He'd been with her from afar, suffering with her, for her, as helpless, as devastated, as she.

Oh, Gerard . . . my love—thank you, my love . . .

He'd come. He'd watched. He'd agonized. He hadn't let her go through it alone.

Chapter 2

So beautiful . . . so treacherous—

That bastard, skulking in the bushes . . . as if he could have missed it. As if Gerard Lenoir had wanted him to miss it—or Drue's reaction.

Tears.

Damn him. Goddamn tears . . .

He was seething as the carriage bowled onto the River Road toward Wildwood, cutting through heat as thick as cotton.

It wasn't worth it. Goddamn . . . he had made the biggest mistake of his life, saddling himself with a vice-ridden father-in-law, an encumbered plantation, and a woman who hated him.

Stupid—for the first time in his life, his greed and a moment of rare opportunity had gotten the better of his common sense.

Or had he ever had common sense where Oak Bluffs was concerned? He'd watched for years as Victor Caledon ran it into the ground while he pursued the passion and promise of the gaming wheels in New Orleans.

And Drue, standing by, defending him, watching her mother work herself to death, and knowing not the half of her father's corrupt nature.

Drue . . .

When had he first become really aware of Drue?

But he knew—when Gerard Lenoir had begun to pursue her— as the direct proportion of money her father owed him increased.

Drue was to have been Gerard's payoff. And Oak Bluffs was to have been his by virtue of his marrying Drue.

But Gerard had been too busy seducing Drue to be aware that Victor Caledon would never, ever sanction the union. Gerard Lenoir would never step foot on Oak Bluffs—even as a guest.

So Victor had come to him, and offered him Oak Bluffs— and Drue—in exchange for the partnership and a face-saving perversion of the truth: that Court was Victor's creditor, and that Drue and a stake in Oak Bluffs could satisfy every debt, every lien, every loan . . . every lie.

And Drue was never, never to know that Gerard was the one to whom her father had owed that vast sum of money.

And so a man got ensnared. Court had dearly wanted Oak Bluffs. And, shockingly, once he made the bargain, he found he wanted Drue as well. And that was something he hadn't planned on.

Or was she all the more desirable because she wanted another man?

Or was it because he didn't want Lenoir to have her?

He slanted a glance at her pensive profile under the parasol Isaac had provided her to ward off the sun.

She stared straight ahead, as if keeping her gaze rooted would repulse other things. Real things. Him.

She was so beautiful, with her long black hair that Edme had braided into a coronet to support her veil. She looked regal. She looked as if she were going to meet her fate.

She had lifted her chin, a defiant little gesture, to combat the luster of the tears drenching her blue eyes. She would not cry. She *wouldn't.*

She bit her lips, perfect soft lips; he wanted to kiss them right there, right then, to make up for the kisses he didn't bestow when he took her to be his wife.

But she wasn't thinking about Court Summerville. All of her energy, her desire was focused on Gerard Lenoir. Her tears were for Gerard, and her kisses. And her body, sacrificed on the altar of duty to *him,* would have been Lenoir's as well, if he hadn't poured a hundred thousand dollars into Lenoir's pocket to save Victor Caledon's reputation and prestige.

Court felt a tremor of pure fury. Drue was his now. He'd bought her, he'd laid out the terms so there would be no misunderstandings, and, by God, she'd agreed. She was *his,* all of her, her body, her mind, her soul, and she had no business pining for Gerard not a half hour after the wedding.

His jaw tightened. Before this night was out, he thought, he would hold her to the bargain. And he would do it without force and without recourse to the baser nature of man.

He was going to make her want him. He was going to arouse her to a fever pitch until she understood what it meant to be consumed by desire.

He had all the time in the world, he thought. It would be like taming a wild animal. You did it slowly, by increments, showing, playing, stroking, rewarding, until it trusted you.

And then—oh, and then . . . it would do anything you wanted. *Anything.*

His body quickened as he savored the thought.

Everything . . .

He thought of a hundred things in that instant that would encompass *everything* and his body responded accordingly, raw, hard, *there*.

Yes . . . he would subjugate the little fawn, and he wouldn't rest until he wiped Gerard Lenoir from her memory and made her beg for his lust, his sex, his love, him.

Wildwood!

The beautiful moss-draped, tree-lined drive at the end of which was the house, white columned, stately, four-square, and, as the carriage drew closer and closer, huge.

Nothing like the comfortable, manageable house at Oak Bluffs.

She could get lost there, swallowed up.

She felt as if Court had devoured her already.

She couldn't bear to look at him. Or to think what came next.

No, she knew what came next: the discharge of her father's debt, her body, her will, her future as the payoff.

She suppressed a shudder.

Gerard . . . oh, Gerard— The ache almost consumed her.

I can't think about Gerard . . . if I think about Gerard, I'll—I'll—never be able to . . .

. . . to—

—oh, my God . . . to . . .

Her body went cold. The carriage quivered to a stop in front of the broad front steps.

Immediately the butler emerged from the house through the etched glass double doors, followed by a half dozen servants who lined up on the veranda and down the steps in order of precedence.

Isaac came around and put a cushioned step under her foot, and Court gravely helped her down.

"This is Joseph," he said, indicating the butler. "Mary. Evie. Lucy. Charles. Louisa."

She nodded in turn to each of them, and then, lifting her skirts, she mounted the steps and he guided her into the reception hall.

Grand. Too grand for her. It was overwhelming, with ceilings that had to be fifteen feet high at least and a swooping staircase rising up to her right, all the way to heaven. There were sofas and console tables lining the walls and gilt-framed paintings that glowed in the soft light of the chandelier that was lit for the occasion.

She stepped hesitantly onto the first of three Oriental rugs that were scattered on the parquet floor, noting the beautifully molded arches that led off to the downstairs rooms, the doors of which were just tantalizingly ajar.

Home.

My home. Now.

. . . oh, God—

She was aware of everything: the weight of her dress as she walked farther into the hallway and it tailed out behind her. The silence. The scent. A different scent than at Oak Bluffs. The grandeur.

The sound of footsteps retreating to other parts of the house.

She felt the train being lifted off the floor. The thickness of the carpet beneath her feet. Court, beside her, watching her intensely.

It was all too much. And she couldn't love it. Dear God, she couldn't love anything except Gerard.

And she had better stop thinking about that . . . *about him—* or she would never be able to fulfill the bargain and Court would take Oak Bluffs away from her father as surely as he planned to take her.

Best to get it over with, she thought. Best to just let it happen, and then it would be done and maybe Court would just leave her alone.

Apart from the introductions, he hadn't said a word since they left the church. And neither had she.

He was struck by how much he wanted this moment to be more than it was. But then, he was not bringing to this house the woman he had chosen, the woman he loved.

Rather, she was the pawn in a game to enlarge his empire. And pawns didn't have feelings or preferences. They were just moved where they were the most expedient and, in the end, they were expendable.

But the fawn had feelings. The fawn could bite the hand that was about to shroud her in luxury the likes of which she had never seen at Oak Bluffs. The fawn could run away.

No! He made that decision instantly. However they had started in matrimony, she was still *his,* and he felt as possessive as if he had loved her all his life. The bargain, suddenly, did not enter into it.

He wanted Drue Caledon. Right then. Right there. Wanted to pull off her virginal gown, expose her naked body and sink himself deep inside her. Wanted, wanted, wanted . . .

The force of his arousal shocked him. He wanted . . . he conjured up a dozen things he wanted to do to her, all of which were as explosive as fire.

"Get her upstairs," he said roughly. He had to plan this. He couldn't just force her. He couldn't just take her. He clamped down on the heat that raced through his blood.

"Yessir."

Evie, behind her, helping with her train. "Missus . . ."

Drue reached blindly for the banister. *Oh, God, she was going to have to do this. She heard it in his voice.*

"Get her ready."

"Yessir." Evie, like a little shadow, trailing behind her as she climbed the steps. A mountain. A thousand steps to meet her fate. Why didn't he just attack her there? So much easier. Over quickly. She'd get an heir, and then it would be done.

"Evie!" His voice, ragged and raw. Evie halted, waiting until he took the steps two at a time to reach her and whisper something in her ear.

"Yessir." Evie shifted the heavy train. "Missus . . ."

She swallowed hard, blinking back her tears, and continued up the steps. And finally, the landing, decorated with the same rich furnishings as the hallway below. Muted light here, and a half dozen doors leading to the bedrooms.

"First door, missus, to your right."

"Of course," she murmured. That would be to the front of the house, the biggest, most luxurious rooms.

The door opened readily into a sumptuous room that was as large as the parlor at Oak Bluffs, and swathed in satin and lace.

"Master say undress you, missus, and make you comfortable."

"Yes," she whispered. "Yes." *Comfortable . . . that didn't nearly describe this beautiful room. And all for her.*

She stood still as a mannequin as Evie positioned her in front of the armoire mirror and pulled forward a cushioned stool.

"Missus is tall, pleasing to the master," she murmured as she stepped up and began pulling out the pins that held Drue's wedding veil. It fell in a drift of tulle onto the thick Persian carpet.

"We gonna fold him up and store him away, save him for missus's daughter someday," Evie said, as she retrieved the fragile material and laid it on the bed.

"You hold still now, missus. We gonna be real careful with this beautiful gown."

Drue could just see her over her shoulder in the mirror. *If I could just disappear into the mirror . . .* She watched in fascination as Evie carefully unfastened the intricate hooks and slipped the dress off her, inch by inch; first the shoulders, then the bodice, then down over the hooped petticoat until it lay in a puddle of ivory silk at her feet.

And like a little bird, Evie hopped down, lifted the dress up and draped it on the bed. "Louisa gonna take care of that for you, missus. Not to worry. Now, that old cage petticoat—" She untied the strings and it was gone. "And them drawers and stockings. And that corset. Should be burned, it so tight. You feel better when we get it off. Then we get you a nice bath and dinner, and you be ready for the master."

She was chattering, Drue thought, to keep *her* calm, and to keep her mind off what was to come. But she was thinking of nothing else, and when Evie helped her into a satin wrapper, she was terribly aware of the feel of the creamy material against her hot, bare skin.

"Come."

This was luxury: Evie led her to an alcove between the bedrooms, a bathing room with an iron tub set on a marble platform, which Charles was in the process of filling with steaming water. And Louisa waited, with a tray of soaps, oils, and towels.

"In you go, missus."

Drue sank into the heat like it was her lover's arms. *Gerard . . . NO!*

The water lapped against her skin, hot, welcome, reassuring. *Focus on Court. Think about Court. Let Court into your thoughts. Just tonight. Just once. Court's not an animal. Court won't hurt you.*

Soft . . everything soft . . .

She sank into the water, closing her eyes against reality as Louisa began washing her hair. This was the dream: a life of inutterable wealth as the wife of one of the most prominent men in the state.

What was a moment of surrender compared to that?

Soft . . . his hands would be soft, like Gerard when he petted her and coaxed her into giving him a kiss . . .

No!

She moved restively in the water, sending waves over the side of the tub.

"Shhh, missus, shhhh . . ." Louisa crooned as she poured a vial of oil into the bath water. "Master not gonna hurt you no how. Don't you worry none . . . shhhhh . . ."

How did she know? How did she know?

Drue leaned back into those gentle hands that were massaging her head so firmly, so competently, into the rich oily water that soaked into her skin.

"Shhh, missus, shhhh . . ." Louisa soaping her body, singing under her breath now, lulling, soothing, comforting.

She could stay there forever, she thought, just give herself over to Louisa's kind hands, and float away to oblivion.

"Missus . . ." Evie's voice intruding on the silence. "It's time."

Time? Time? The water was cold now, her hair drenched, her body dripping as she reluctantly took Louisa's hand and stepped out of the tub and into the towel Evie held out for her.

"There you go, there you go, missus," Evie murmured, wrapping her tightly in the towel and then leading her back into the bedroom and seating her on the bed, from which the dress and veil had been removed. "Sit you down, missus. There you go. I make you ready for the master."

Ominous words. Drue cringed. *Make you ready . . .*

Evie at her feet, rubbing them, and her legs, and then wrapping them in another towel. At her hair next, briskly drying it.

She felt sapped, suddenly. Bereft.

Make you ready . . .

Evie took her brush and began combing through her tangled hair. Slow, calming strokes, sliding the brush through the thick strands. She was the ideal ladies' maid, properly deferential, experienced in all the ways of handling her mistress.

Just what you would expect from the master of Wildwood . . .

Her breath caught. *Master of Wildwood—master of her . . .*

"We ready now, missus." Evie's soft voice in her ear. "Stand you up now so I can take these wet towels."

She stood, limp as a rag doll, and let Evie remove the towels.

"Master come to you soon, missus."

Evie turned away, leaving her standing naked in the middle of the room.

"Evie—my robe . . ."

Evie turned at the door. "Master give the word, missus. You wait for him there, like so. No robe. No towel. No clothes. Nothing. Nothing to keep you from the master's desire."

And then, before Drue could react, before she could move, Evie exited the room and locked the door emphatically behind her.

Chapter 3

"*Evie?*" She pounded frantically on the door. "*Evie . . . ! Evie . . . !*"

Nothing. No one. She wheeled and darted into the bathing alcove, but Louisa was gone as well, silent as a ghost; the connecting door was bolted.

Locked in! Like an animal confined for mating . . .

She felt murderous, vulnerable. She grabbed the bedspread and wrapped it around her shaking body. She would never be naked for him. *Never!*

She wanted every just impediment to their union.

She wanted Gerard. Furiously, she pulled open the armoire doors.

Empty! But what did she expect; they were *his* servants, they had no loyalty to her, they would do *his* bidding, not hers. And obviously, they had had strict instructions to remove her clothes.

Mistress of Wildwood . . . she thought bitterly, pulling the bedspread tighter around her body as she paced around the room. . . . *In name only. In reality she was nothing more than his slave, as much at his beck and call as anyone else in the house.*

And he had set it up so well she had nowhere to run . . . and no place to hide.

How could her father have let this happen? How could Gerard?

And then—the waiting; how long would he make her wait? And when he came—then what?

He's entitled—to a hundred thousand dollars worth of my body . . . A lifetime of servicing him in the name of filial love and daughterly devotion . . .

A brood mare . . .

She stopped her furious pacing by the satin-draped window and she pulled back the filmy undercurtain. There was peace and beauty outside that window—the bright midday sun softened by the shadows of the oaks that lined the drive, the rolling green lawn stretching to the road, and the levee and the flowing river beyond.

There was no one in sight. In a house like Wildwood, all of the work was done subtly, behind the scenes, so that all a visitor or a passerby saw was a picture of calm and serenity.

But she was neither calm nor serene. A moment from now, or an hour, Court would unlock that door and demand his marital rights.

It was unimaginable. She was so used to Gerard's gentlemanly way of courting her. Of respect and reverence. Of kisses lighter than a soufflé.

She knew already that Court was a man of intensity and passion, and a temper that was underlaid by a very short fuse. He had a low tolerance for fools, and no store of patience at all. When Court wanted something, he got it, and she knew that her body was no exception. He would not have agreed to the bargain if he hadn't, for some reason, wanted *her*.

But no, what he wanted was Oak Bluff, and if he got a reluctant body with it, well, it probably wasn't any different to him than buying a whore in the French Quarter.

Oh, God . . .

A man like Court didn't like to wait. He would be here, soon—she was sure of it.

She dropped the curtain and turned back into the room—the beautiful, luxuriously furnished room that should have been a bridal bower, and a place of transition from her virginal world to one of carnal delights.

It felt like a prison.

What would he ask of her? And how?

Would he even kiss her?

Or would he just throw her down on the thick feather bed and demand that she spread her legs?

He wouldn't be that callous. He couldn't.

But then, he wouldn't know that she loved another, that she had already discovered the pleasure of kisses and caresses in another man's arms . . .

Oh, Gerard . . .

She groaned. The betrayal was almost crippling. She would have given herself to Gerard in an instant, and instead she was waiting for her dark *master* to come and command her as he would any slave.

She shook away the thought. She couldn't keep thinking like that; it would only lead to disaster. She felt resentful enough already.

And scared.

One night, Drue. Just one night and you'll be a virgin no more. He'll just come and sink himself into you, and after that, it will be easy.

Easy for him . . .

Never easy for a woman—

She had never seen a naked man. Not her father. Not Gerard. And she herself had never been naked this long after a bath. Always her maid scrubbed her down, rinsed her off, and trundled her into a towel, robe, and gown within the space of ten or fifteen minutes.

She felt as if she had been exposed for hours. She felt uncomfortable, awkward, stupid, deathly afraid.

Gerard would never have treated her this way . . .

She shuddered. So useless thinking of what might have been . . .

And what was her father doing, this night of the sacrifice of his virgin daughter to the god of saving face?

STOP IT!

She was acting like a frightened child, a victim, when she should be comporting herself like a queen. After all, she *was* the mistress of Wildwood.

For whatever that was worth . . .

. . . for her part, Drue Caledon will act as mistress of Wildwood, including, but not limited to, providing companionship and sexual congress for her husband; attending to all household functions, overseeing the house, gardens and servants; keeping account of and doling out stores, arranging dinners, attending to guests; and other unspecified services as defined by her husband that fall within the purview of her wifely duties . . .

Written up as tightly as any contract executed by a lawyer. Court had known exactly what he wanted and how to get it. She was nothing more than an item on his list to be attended to when he had the time.

And she had willingly signed herself into servitude, goaded on by her father's penitent promises of reform and his visions of a future full of wealth and luxury—for them both.

Did any woman ever have a choice? *Had her mother?*

The silence of the house was disturbing. A house of secrets, she thought despairingly, behind whose walls she was already immured as absolutely as a nun.

And she would know all the secrets of a woman and a man before the day was over.

The ring felt odd on his finger: constricting, eternal, forever *there.*

What a man did in the space of a moment that irrevocably altered his life . . .

He might not have married for years, if it weren't for the lure of Oak Bluffs . . .

And Drue.

He climbed the steps slowly, thoughtfully. It would be so easy—too easy—to just give in to his carnal impulses. He wished he were a creature of the senses, like that blasted Lenoir. Then he'd have no conscience about taking what he wanted and the hell with the consequences.

Lenoir had been so sure that Oak Bluffs would be his. And Drue.

But all that was over now. Victor was contained, for the moment, although he had no illusions about that. Lenoir was gone—Court had made sure of it before they even left the church grounds. And now all that awaited him was the moment of truth with Drue.

He had set up the scenario; the only thing he didn't know was how it was going to play. Without a doubt, she still cared for Lenoir, which was going to make his possession of her that much more difficult.

And his highhandedness had probably made her either scared or furious. He *wanted* her full of spit and sass, like that flash of fire she'd shown at the reception.

For him.

He didn't want a doll that he could prop and pose any way he desired. He could buy that on any street any night in New Orleans.

You couldn't *buy* a lady. Naked. In your bed.

His blood burned at the thought.

You bought Drue.

He quelled the thought and shrugged out of his frock coat, tossing it at one of the console tables, as he reached the landing.

He was no shining knight and he was the first to admit it. His motives were just as base as any man in heat, except that he had gone after one woman, one body, one object he wanted to possess.

But he was not a man of indiscriminate tastes.

His tie went next, draped over a piece of useless porcelain. His boots, kicked across the hallway.

His lust escalated moment by moment.

How often did a man get to set the scene for his seduction? The

thought of Drue beyond that door, naked, quivering, waiting—
waiting for him—made his juices boil.

Even if she didn't want him . . .

He was certain she heard the rasp of the key in the lock, but
she didn't turn from the window as he eased his way into the
room.

He didn't know what he expected, but certainly not Drue
wrapped up like a mummy, staring out the window and looking
impossibly fragile.

He locked the door behind him, slowly, carefully, buying time.
Drue was furious and not a little wary as she slanted an uneasy
glance at him.

He folded his arms across his chest and leaned against the
door, waiting. *Goddamn it, goddamn it. She was thinking about
Lenoir. Saving herself—as if she could—for that jackdandy.*

*Over his dead body. He'd kill the bastard first. And he was
going to destroy every memory of him from Drue's mind, if he
had to kill her, too.*

The silence stretched uncomfortably. She had thought for sure
he would come in making demands, making it easy for her to
resist him, fight him—hurt him so he wouldn't want to touch
her—ever.

But he said nothing. No, that wasn't strictly true. His eyes
spoke. His eyes burned with a message that even she, in her
innocence, could read. He had come to collect on his investment.

And *she* was the payment.

"I want my clothes," she said tightly.

"No clothes." His voice was like iron.

Her heart fell. *No clothes. No mercy.*

*What had she thought? He would come with pearls and poetry,
petting and pleas?*

*He was rough and rude and accustomed to getting what he
wanted.*

So be it.

She turned and climbed stiffly onto the bed, dragging the bedspread behind her. "I'm ready."

He suppressed a flare of annoyance. There was no one less

ready than Drue, with her martyred expression and thick cocoon
of the bedspread swathing her more securely than a chastity belt.

She needed a strong, firm hand. Drue was not stupid. Or
unaware. But what had he expected? The fawn was skittish and
prone to hide from her predator. And his job was to lure her out
and then dominate all her virginal impulses until she begged for
surrender.

"I'm not," he said bluntly. "And this isn't how it's going to
go."

"The only way it has to go is that you get it over with," Drue
snapped, wriggling into an upright position.

That was better: the fawn was showing some teeth.

He didn't change his stance. Not yet. Not yet. This was not
Drue's game, even if she refused to admit it. She had still to learn
who had the power to make demands, and who must submit. But
he *would* have his way. And he would have *her,* even if he had
to discipline her to get her.

"*This* is the first thing we get over with," he said evenly. "Two
conditions, little fawn, and they are *not* negotiable."

Her expression turned mutinous. "You've already dictated the
terms, Court. I won't abide any other considerations on top of
that."

"Two conditions," he said inflexibly, ignoring her. "You never,
ever hide your naked body from me—"

She made an angry motion.

". . . and number two—you will *never* deny me anything I
demand—in our bedroom."

Her heart swooped down to her toes. She closed her eyes and
clenched her fists. She wanted to kill him. He'd bought her and
now he had stripped everything from her, right down to her
clothes.

He owned her, body and soul. There was nothing left of her
now that didn't belong to him. And if she had thought to hold
him off with words or with a puny wall of cotton, she had under-
estimated his determination to get most use of his newest possession.

He was her master and she was nothing more or less than a
body to service him: *his* slave, to his whims, his control, his lust.

For all the days of your life . . . Her breath caught as the impact of those words struck her. Linked to him forever, never to know any other love, any other life.

"Did you hear me?" Court murmured, his voice deceptively, dangerously, low.

Her voice caught. "I . . . heard you."

"Did you? You *heard* me? You *know* what I want—you *heard* what I want and you haven't *yet* complied? Is *that* what I'm to understand, little fawn? That my wishes *aren't* paramount with you? That the two small inconsequential requests I have made are to be disregarded altogether by you?"

"I—" She almost choked. The *master* was speaking, his voice like iron, his eyes cold, his expression impassive. He meant to exert every measure of control, to make her understand that he could do with her whatever he wanted, because he had paid for the right to do so.

Off the auction block and into his bed. What was the difference after all?

"I want you naked—*now!*"

That tone brooked no argument, no resistance. And still, she couldn't bring herself to reveal her body to him. She cowered on the bed, feeling an overwhelming sense of betrayal.

Forgive me, Gerard . . . my love, my love . . .

"Get used to it, little fawn." He started toward her slowly, each step measured by his soft, lustful, dangerous words. "You will be naked for me from now on. There won't be a bolt of material or a piece of clothing in this room that you can use to cover yourself from this moment forward."

Closer he came, and she scrambled across the bed.

"I will dictate what you will wear, when and even *if*, and I will be the one who dresses you—if I ever let you get dressed again for the rest of your life . . ." Implacably, inexorably, he followed her around the bed as she backed away from him.

"I bought your naked body, my fawn, and it is mine, and I *will* have you anytime, anywhere, I want, and nothing you can do will prevent that."

He was within inches of her as she crouched by the locked door. He hunkered down beside her. "What you won't give me willingly, I *will* take. And you'll be confined to this room, naked, until my wishes are clearly understood."

Black devil . . . beast! How could he treat her so? She gathered every reserve of strength she possessed and got to her feet.

"You will *never* have me," she hissed defiantly.

He looked up at her. "Oh, but I will, little fawn. And this will be the hardest lesson you will ever have to learn. The master *always* gets everything he wants."

He rose gracefully to his feet. "I want you naked. Are you still going to resist me, Drue?"

"Someone should," she muttered, pulling the bedspread closer.

"But not the ungrateful drab whose father's life and reputation I saved. You should be naked and on your back, spreading your legs and begging me to stuff myself into you. Any other woman would have kissed my feet and any other part of my body I desired in gratitude for what I did."

He inched closer to her. "But not you. Oh, no, not the princess of Oak Bluffs. All that money and I can't even *look* at your naked body."

He was as close as a breath now, hot and engorged with lust, anger, and pure wanton desire. "You thought you could remain pure for that coxcomb, Lenoir, didn't you, little fawn? You thought I'd just lift your skirts and pump myself into you and that would be the end of it and you still could remain loyal to him. That's what you thought, wasn't it? *Wasn't it?* But that's not nearly how it's going to be."

He closed his hand over the edge of the material that covered her shoulders. "My house. My bedspread. My money. *My* naked wife. Let go of this thing, *now* . . ."

She resisted. She couldn't help herself. She could not willingly submit to him. And to the fury in his voice and the anger in his eyes. And the strength in his hand as he ruthlessly stripped the bedspread away from her body and stepped back.

She clutched the torn, ragged edge of the binding against her breasts, as if that would protect her from him.

He pulled it out of her hands and threw it on the floor, and then she had nothing but the cool gleam of his possessive gaze to cover her, from her burning face, downward to her taut-tipped breasts, downward still to those private places even she didn't know.

She froze as he walked around her to view her from every angle.

"Well, well, well, aren't you the hot-tailed little piece, my fawn. Who would have guessed that under all that virginal muslin and lace there was a naked body that looked like *this*."

And it was all his, his to teach, train, discipline, and do with what he would. No one else would ever have her now.

He was face-to-face with her again, his burning eyes two narrow slits as he gazed his fill of her naked breasts. "I think maybe I didn't pay too much for you." His voice turned steely. "Don't move, Drue. I don't think I can get enough of looking at you."

She could barely stand it—those knowing eyes, the huge obvious bulge between his legs, the feeling of vulnerability, and of being stalked by something more primitive and more powerful than she. He could devour her. He *would,* in ways she didn't even know about.

"Just . . . just get it over with," she ground out.

"No. No . . ." He was circling her again. "You are something to savor, my fawn. Those round, high breasts, those hard, pointed nipples, those hips, those buttocks . . . I want to take my time with you. Days and days, I just want to look at you . . ."

"Court—please . . ."

"No. I want you to live naked in my house from now on, and I will tell you what I want and what to do. And you'll do it, Drue. I promise you. You will do it. And you won't have a moment to think about anyone or anything else. Now, turn and walk away from me. I want to watch the movement of your buttocks when you walk."

"Please don't—"

"Please don't—what? Touch you? I haven't, although I want to, most powerfully. Force you? I haven't. I won't. It's enough for me to have you naked and at my mercy. Now, *walk*."

Oh, yes, at his mercy; precisely. Definitively. And all those references to Gerard . . . they made her blood turn cold.

He knew—

Dear God, how did he know?

And if he knew . . . she had no choice but to do everything he wanted, anything he wanted to protect Gerard and to conceal the fact she loved him.

Her whole body felt like lead. She didn't know how she was going to do this, how she was going to let Court even touch her.

She swallowed, turned, so that for one instant the curve of her breasts and the tight thrust of her nipples were outlined in the light, and then she slowly moved away from him.

Don't think about anything or anyone else. Don't feel his eyes on you or the heat washing all over your body. Don't . . . don't . . . don't—

He watched her through hooded eyes. She was so perfect, flawless, her buttocks soft and rounded and flaring into those swaying hips that were made to be grasped tightly as a man centered himself to penetrate her.

He wanted to grab her right then, right there, and ram himself into her; a thousand fantasies played in his mind as she stopped at the wall and waited for his next command.

Oh? It was going to be like that, was it? A tiny act of defiance that he would squash right now.

"Turn and come back to me," he ordered, and she swiveled around and started pacing toward him.

Her breasts bobbled just a little, her nipples begging that he look at them, marvel at them, lust for them.

He'd never been so hard in his life. He couldn't contain the iron-bar jut of his manhood. He didn't want to. He wanted to do exactly what she desired: throw her on the bed and embed himself in her to the hilt and beyond. He wanted to feel the bones of those hips grinding against him, and the hard-soft play of her breasts and nipples against his naked chest.

He wanted . . . all those things and more, more, more . . .

He itched to slide his fingers between her legs and make her moan with pleasure. She was that close to him, and that far, and not nearly ready for such an assault on her senses.

Her lips were moist from her having tongued them over and over in her nervousness. He wanted to suck them, he wanted her to tongue him all over his body and then root for his manhood and suck him dry.

Instead, she was standing before him, naked, abashed, trembling, virginal, her bosom quivering, her nipples more tempting than fate.

He could not allow himself to feel sympathy for her. She wanted to "get it over with," that was all. She wanted to save her immortal soul for Lenoir. He could see it in her eyes. And that made it easy for him to make the command.

"Get on the bed."

Oh, God, yes, yes . . . She closed her eyes and heaved a sigh of relief. The moment of reckoning was here.

But how did a virgin seduce a libertine, she wondered suddenly, panicked, if she couldn't stand him looking at her naked body with those knowing, ravenous eyes, and the threat of that hard, flexing rod of his sex. There was no way she could escape him, no way she could renege on that contract she had willingly signed.

But she hadn't thought it was going to be like this with him. That he would be so hard, inflexible, cold-blooded.

Just let him stick it into me and have done . . . after that, the rest will be easy . . .

She moved toward the bed, aware with every step of his assessing gaze.

She heard him pull in a hot breath as she climbed onto the bed, and sat on her knees with the curve of her buttocks tucked behind her ankles.

He couldn't believe his response to that one commonplace movement and the tempting picture she made. All he had to do was lift her, straddle her and poke his throbbing ramrod into that hot, *tight* pleasure hole.

But it was too soon for that. She was obedient now because she wanted him out of her room, and because she thought her nakedness would make him instantly come to heel.

Like that upstart, Lenoir.

He would have bet she had the bastard twirled around her little finger. She was probably very used to batting her lashes and putting men off or making them come to heel.

But he was no lapdog.

And that was just one hard lesson the fawn had to learn among many. He was a patient man, in spite of the fact that he ached for the full-bore possession of her sex. Oh, yes, he wanted her; the gnawing was intense, almost unbearable.

Which made it all the better. Because soon, soon, he would teach her how to want him, too.

"On your back, my fawn. Good. Now—hold your breasts up to me, and spread your legs."

She moaned; her body writhed in protest and the movement sent a jolt of pure boiling lust to his throbbing penis.

"Do it, Drue. I want to see everything between your legs."

She turned on her side. "I won't."

Damn the bastard— He had to touch her, much sooner than he had planned, but he had to crush that refusal *now*.

She felt his hot, huge hand on her hip, rolling her ruthlessly onto her back.

"The master always gets what he wants," he growled. "Spread your legs, or I will spread them for you."

"*I won't* ..." It was enough, it was, and he wasn't even undressed, and she didn't know what he wanted or what he planned to do, but she couldn't yield to him in that, not that way, by putting herself in the most vulnerable position for a woman.

But it became clear that her desires held no sway. He ripped off his shirt, and tore off the sleeves with all the anger, lust, and crippling desire to cram himself into her channeled into containing her on the bed.

She couldn't escape him; he was stronger, tougher, relentless in his passion to have her nakedness exposed to the greed of his lust. She couldn't kick him hard enough, scramble fast enough, or roll far enough to elude his hot huge hands.

Mercilessly he wound each sleeve around a bare ankle and tied it to the posts of the bed.

"Bastard!" she spat. "Take me now."

"Oh, no, my naked fawn. No. I won't take you now. That would be too easy." He moved away from the bed to pull a small upholstered chair from the window over to where he could sit and see her perfectly, and he settled himself there.

"I cannot believe you're doing this."

"What am I doing, little fawn? I'm feasting my eyes on my wife's enticing nakedness."

She fell back against the mattress, feeling so exposed, so bare, she thought she would die.

But her body wouldn't let her die. Her body moved incessantly against the bonds that held her legs spread wide, as if the movement itself could loosen the knot instead of escalating the tension and anger she felt.

She arched her back against the restraints. "Damn you, damn you, damn you—" No one had ever treated her like this. *Gerard wouldn't . . .*

His whole body seized up with every undulating movement of her rounded hips. He saw himself between her legs, riding that hot, bucking thrusting body so deep, so hard, that he exploded and drowned in her juices and begged for more.

He couldn't get enough of watching her innocent body finding an erotic rhythm of its own that he matched in his imagination.

This was his domain and he was the master. He had only to drop his trousers and present himself to her and her writhing, grinding body would take him to sweet, hot oblivion.

But denying himself his release only made the pleasure of anticipation that much more intense.

Slowly he rose from the chair and went to the bed.

"I hate you."

"Well, this is your first lesson, little fawn, *I* hate when you refuse me what I want."

"Take what you want," she whispered, "and then just go away."

"No, my wife. You don't yet understand. You are to willingly give me what I want whenever I ask, whatever it is. So—next time I want you to spread your legs for me, you will lie down on that bed and make sure your legs are as wide apart as an ocean. Is that clear?"

"I will *never . . .*"

He clamped his hand over her mouth. "I see. You still need to be taught who is beholden to whom. You'll note that I kindly didn't make a fuss over the fact that you didn't hold your breasts up for my inspection. Well, one must be patient with a sharp-toothed fawn. We have many days, Drue, many lessons to be learned. I didn't think I would have to work you so hard after paying out so much money for you. I thought your overwhelming gratitude would compel your utmost desire to please me. I will tell you, Drue: it will come. You will surrender everything to me. And when you do, you will beg for everything I can give you."

"*Never!*" she spat, pulling at her bonds. "*Never, never, never—!*"

He looked down at her pitilessly. "Evie will untie you in an hour or so. I want you to get used to the feeling of your legs spread wide for me."

"I hate you."

"It doesn't matter, little fawn. All that matters is that you never hide your naked body from me."

He got out of the room not a moment too soon; his sex overpowered him, erupting in spume of frenzied lust for her so intense, he doubled over with it.

Soon, he thought, soon. The fawn was nibbling. Very, very soon, sooner than she thought, she would be ready to feed that dark desire that would drown and consume them both.

Chapter 4

She lay limply on the bed, her legs aching from her struggle with the ties. She was in such turmoil, she could barely move. Didn't want to move. Wanted to just sink through the soft mattress into oblivion.

Court treating her like this!

What could he want from her, if not what every man wanted?

She moved fretfully against the restraints. It was hellish, this . . . this—game of exposing her and humiliating her.

And yet—yet . . . the look in his eyes when he finally got her naked . . . he wanted her; there had been burning, naked desire in his eyes. Even she, innocent as she was, could see that.

And that her nudity had aroused his sleeping giant to the point of explosiveness. It was huge, thick, and hard as iron, and *it* wanted to possess her, even if he did not.

She levered up on her elbows to look at herself, to try to see what *he* saw. A thick, wiry bush of dark hair between her legs, and whatever else was visible beyond that. Her smooth thighs. Her long legs. Her flat belly. Her high, rounded breasts with their ever-erect nipples.

Tentatively, she laid the fingers of her right hand on her bushy mound. The hair between her legs was like a wild woman's; sometimes she felt the wiry strands between her thighs as she walked.

And always she felt her taut nipples pressing tightly against whatever she wore, making her very aware of her body.

She lay back on the bed and cupped her breasts, thumbing one nipple. Her body twinged, impacted by her sprawled legs, her nudity, her touch.

His cruelty.

If she gave in to him, her life, her sex, would never be her own. And she would mourn Gerard forever.

Her only recourse was to seduce him and fight him. Forever. Or to the end. Whichever came first.

Evie came after a while, with a tray. "Master say you eat."

"I can't sit up."

"Master say make restraints prettier." She held up two strips of black satin. "Come. I untie your one leg, and you eat something."

She felt a moment of panic. Court meant it. The bastard meant it, and he was willing to go to these lengths to make her willing to spread her legs.

She could barely eat; she had no idea what it was Evie had on the tray. She watched as the servant untied her one leg, and then, as she nibbled, deftly surrounded her other ankle with the soft, slick satin bonds before she untied the ragged shirtsleeve.

"When you finish, mistress."

But Evie wasn't done. She picked up the shredded bedspread and stripped the bed of its sheets and pillowcases, and pulled down the curtains, while Drue choked down what she could of the food.

Dear God, the curtains, too—

"Mistress cannot refuse the master," Evie said gently, removing the tray at Drue's signal. "Come. I tie your leg and you wait for the master to come."

"I have no choice, do I?" Drue muttered.

"Mistress is beautiful. Master will come to love her," Evie murmured, as she efficiently packed up the bedding and trundled all of it and the tray out of the room.

The door closed.

The ominous door.

Her nipples tightened in anticipation of what was to come. Fear compelled her, closing her throat, making her tremble.

She grasped the edges of the mattress and held on. There was no point to fighting the restraints, to fighting him.

He would do what he wanted, and every slave in the place, including her, would submit to his will.

She waited, feeling every inch of her bare skin against the mattress ticking.

And she waited, her splayed legs accustomed now to the breadth of the extension he had forced on them.

And she waited, trying not to think of Gerard, and the betrayal of his love that this submission to Court's will represented.

There was something about the waiting; there was a cruelty in it and a wisdom. He had wanted her to get used to the feeling of spreading her legs for him, and as she lay there, she became acutely aware of the seductive cleft between her legs that had so entranced him.

And she could feel her nipples, so erect and pointed, becoming tighter and harder.

She felt herself stretching her legs wider apart still, as if her body were arching toward another lover.

"I wish you would take me," she whispered in anguish, and Court's voice answered, "Oh, no, little fawn. I will not take you now. You still have hard lessons to learn and memories I *will* destroy."

Her body jolted, and she heaved up onto her elbows. He stood by the little upholstered chair, dressed in trousers and nothing else, watching her writhe and yearn for another man.

And he was so prime; his shoulders were wide, his bare chest deep and covered with rough springy hair all the way down to the waistband of his trousers.

And below that, his engorged manhood poked out as hard and thick as a tree trunk.

She licked her lips nervously as he sank into the little chair. "What are you doing?"

"I'm admiring the many naked charms of my *wife*," he said, his voice deceptively calm. "I hope the satin bands are more comfortable. There's something about black against a woman's naked skin . . . it's very arousing."

"Are you aroused, Court?"

"Unbelievably."

"Haven't you seen enough?" Daring of her, she thought, licking her lips. But he was like a predator playing with her, a wolf she could never tame. And didn't want to. So why she was taunting him, she had no idea—or did she?

"Not nearly, little fawn. Your naked body fascinates me. I want to luxuriate in it, I want to know every nuance of it . . ."

"And when will I see *your* naked body?" she asked, her voice deliberately coy. It didn't work.

"When I'm ready to show it to you."

"You're ready now, Court. Even I can see that."

"But how hard I am has nothing to do with preparing you for the moment *you* will be ready, my fawn. For now, just looking at you satisfies my lust for you."

"I don't believe that." She couldn't believe that, not with him sitting there and his sex jutting up to the ceiling through his clothing like a flagpole.

"It doesn't matter. *I* am the one who will decide when you are ready. My desire to rut in you can only be enhanced by the lessons I teach you."

"What are you going to do?" she whispered.

He got up from the chair and came to the bed and she could see the hard-boned length of him pokng upward beneath the thin material of his trousers.

"I'm going to tie your wrists to the posts, my fawn, so that just as you are learning the lesson of spreading your legs for me, you will also learn that when I tell you to hold your breasts for me, you *will* remember to do it."

"You didn't tell me—this time."

"These are just today's lessons, little fawn." He grasped her one hand, tied it to the post with black satin, and then the other, and then stepped back to look at her.

"That's better. With your arms over your shoulders, your breasts are lifted toward me, begging for attention. But not tonight, little fawn. I just want to look at those incredible nipples, and maybe next time you will offer them to me of your own volition."

"I will never offer you *anything*," she spat, pulling her arms against the restraints. "You're crazy." But he wasn't crazy; he was her *husband*, for God's sake, her master, and his sole drive was to completely dominate her before he spent himself in her.

He stood right beside her head and she saw that his erection was even harder and more elongated than it had been before.

"Tomorrow, my naked wife, tomorrow we will test you to see what lessons you've learned."

"I know what you want," she whispered.

"You couldn't possibly, little fawn. Not yet."

"Take me."

"*No!*" he growled.

"You want what's between my legs."

"Oh, little fawn, you *do* have so much to learn. Here is a lesson: I want what I want to be mine. And tomorrow, I will see about making sure everyone knows you're mine."

"If you take me—"

"You still won't be mine, my naked wife who still craves another man's sex. So you see—I have many things still to teach you. And what my body wants, what my penis wants—that doesn't matter. All that matters is subjugating you."

She felt a tremor go through her body. Her nipples hardened. She felt a spurt of wetness between her legs as she understood. This was all about Gerard. Dear darling Gerard who never would have used her so cruelly.

He really knew about Gerard. She felt her bones go weak. How long had he known? It didn't matter; nothing mattered. All that mattered was that she couldn't afford one lovely thought about Gerard from now on, not one, or Court would know it.

"Court—"

"Your nipples fascinate me, Drue. And you see how lifting your breasts makes them all the more enticing to a man. I've never seen such pointed nipples on a woman. They beg to be fondled and sucked."

"Do it," she breathed, watching the effect those two words had on his flexing erection. It spurted harder, longer.

He contolled himself with an effort. "But that's not what you want, my naked fawn. Not *who* you want. Not yet."

The threat ... it was a threat—it was why he had chosen to treat her this way. Why why why ...

Damn him, damn him, damn him— She pulled, she raged, she writhed, she moaned ...

He moved away because he felt his iron control slipping. He didn't need to touch her. He didn't need to fuck her. He just needed to get out of that room before she understood the power that *she* wielded.

"Not yet." His voice echoed as he eased out into the hallway, closing the door behind him as an exclamation point to his surrender. "Not yet," he groaned, gasping himself as he gave in to his explosive need and shot his boiling lust down his rock-hard leg.

Not yet ... as he sank, spent, to the floor.

Sometime during the night, a servant untied her; she wasn't aware of the moment, just of the freedom from constriction, and the ability finally to turn and roll onto her stomach.

Finally. Even though it felt as if the satin bonds were still wound around her wrists. In her dreams, Gerard didn't notice them. In her dreams, he held her, coddled her, protected her ...

Sometime in the morning, she became aware of a presence in the room. Not in the bed beside her, but at the foot of the bed, watching her, ever watching her.

Not Gerard ...

She moved her body languidly, knowing he was watching, waiting, wondering of whom she was thinking as she stretched.

"Spread your legs."

She rolled onto her back and extended her long sleek legs outward to show him that this lesson was nothing to her, nothing to learn, nothing to do. But when, during the night of dreamy passion with the evascent Gerard, she had decided this course, she didn't know.

Whatever, it suddenly was easy. So easy.

"Sit up."

Slowly she raised herself upward, sliding down to the foot of the bed so that she could still splay her legs while she cupped her breasts and lifted them toward him, all the while watching the thickening length between his legs.

"Very good, little fawn. It is time for me to claim you as my own naked wife."

Her breath caught. Now, now, he would take her and the thing would be done and he'd leave her to her own devices.

He rose up and came toward her, his spurting erection directly in her line of vision, his extended hand holding what looked like a collar with two very long straps appended from it.

"What is this?"

"This is the first thing you will be permitted to wear, my fawn. Your legs go through the straps so that they are positioned just inside your thighs. You are to wear the collar and thongs at all times whether you are dressed or naked as reminder to you who owns you and who will possess you in good time. Put it on."

She shot him a defiant look and then slowly slipped her legs through the straps, and then stood up, pulling them tightly against her inner thighs, which made her mound more prominent.

"Like that." He could barely say the words; the sight of those leather straps defining her feminine bush and pushing out her high, pointed breasts sent a lightning bolt of desire to his groin. "Put the collar around your neck."

It was a wide, supple leather collar decorated with golden studs and a hook closure. She locked it, and he gestured for her to move away from him so that he could examine her minutely.

It was perfect, the thin leather straps taut against her pale skin, conspicuously outlining her sex and her breasts, and culminating in the symbol of his owning her: the thrall collar.

"Evie!"

Evie slipped into the room.

"Lock it."

Evie came up behind her, and a moment later, Drue heard the almost noiseless click of a lock; she heard him groan, she saw his body convulse before he mastered his sex, and she reached back and touched a tiny padlock, the key to which Evie gave him before she exited the room.

The vision of her collared and strapped to his specification aroused him unbearably: she could see that he was not fully in command of his wayward penis. *It* wanted her. It flexed and stretched and elongated and thickened almost as if it were enticing her as she sashayed around him, letting him view her from every angle.

He particularly liked the way the straps crossed her buttocks and disappeared invitingly into her crease, and then reappeared to tightly confine her femininity.

His penis liked it, too; he couldn't clamp down hard enough on his erection to contain the spurt of juice that stained the material of his trousers.

"On the collar is the seal of the Summervilles, *wife,* so that everyone will know that you are my possession."

"Take me then; everyone thinks you have already."

"Indeed. And only you and I know that I am exerting heroic control in not plowing you until you have been taught *every* lesson."

"I've learned your lessons," she protested. "I wear your thrall collar. I'm ready for your possession."

"No. *I'm* bursting to possess *you,* but you are not nearly ready for me. Come." He rose up from the chair, his erection bone hard in front of him. "We go downstairs for breakfast today."

"I—"

"Naked. Just as you are."

"The servants—" she murmured faintly.

"Naked," he said inflexibly, holding open the door.

"If anyone sees me—" she protested.

"He'll just have to control his lust for you."

"How can he, if you can't?" she retorted.

He looked down at his throbbing manhood. "An aberration. It'll go away."

But it didn't. It never went away all the time they ate breakfast; her mouth went dry every time she looked at his erection, imagining the breadth and thickness, the mystery of him.

But then, her nipples kept reacting to the heat of his gaze. He couldn't take his eyes off them and they kept tightening and tightening and her body felt creamier and creamier just from the touch of his burning eyes.

And he knew it. He made her sit across from him with her legs splayed while they ate, and all of it, her nakedness, his lust, her feeling of being captive and contained, the leather straps on her body, the feral glitter in his eyes, all of it made her body squirm and her juices flow.

Just what she didn't want. She didn't want to succumb to this domination of her. She wanted none of him, except the one moment of possession that would legitimize the marriage.

How could she do that, when every provocation that he had visited on her had not been enough to make him sink himself into her?

How *did* one make a man relinquish that power?

Obviously the dictates of his body were not enough. He was not a man who was led around by his baser nature.

By every standard and what little she knew, he should have succumbed to her charms the moment he ripped away that bedspread.

But then, Court was the kind of man to whom *women* succumbed, and why he had decided that she was to be part of his bargain to obtain Oak Bluffs was beyond her.

And she obviously was not woman enough to entice him.

Except his pulsating body said differently, and he had been in a permanent state of high arousal ever since he'd walked into that bedroom.

And he kept referring to Gerard.

She almost groaned out loud. Gerard would never have forced her to do all the things that Court had. Gerard would have petted and kissed her, and waited on her time for the ultimate moment of possession. He never would have humiliated her like this.

She felt him jerk her arm and haul her to her feet.

"So . . ." he said viciously, "the fawn dreams of rabbits in spite of the fact she has a stallion at her command. Oh, my dear wife, it will give me the greatest pleasure to wipe that milksop from your memory."

"I don't care . . ." she spat. "I *don't* care—he's a gentleman, he would never . . ."

"And I would? I could? This is the first I've touched you in anger, Drue, and you will feel the full force of it. You are *never* to let a thought of that mollycoddle into your mind *ever again* or I will bring him here and let him see you naked and groveling to me. Because, by God, you *will* prostrate yourself and beg for my penis." He was furious, overset by a pure male rage that was frightening in its intensity. "Evie! Louise! Take her upstairs and get her ready."

Instantly, the two servants surrounded her, each taking an arm and pushing her unwilling body up the stairs.

He watched her naked, writhing buttocks in the erotic straps, and he didn't try to control his convulsive release.

Any minute after, he knew, the gnawing desire would take over yet again, stretching and thickening him to rock-hard readiness at the knowledge that the naked mistress of Wildwood would be waiting for him in her room, restrained and restive, and very aware now of his poking, pulsating penis.

Two days was all it had taken. The little fawn was an apt pupil. She couldn't keep her eyes off his towering erection during breakfast, and she'd been eyeing his sex all morning before they left the bedroom.

It was too bad she'd had to spoil it, but—some lessons were hard learned.

He knelt beside the chair in which she had displayed herself as they ate. The scent of her permeated his senses, rising from the minuscule moist blot from her wet. His erection jacked up a notch, his whole body tensed. It took but a moment to strip, to slide himself across the slick satin, to rub against the stain of her sex, to comingle it with his own.

Not enough, not enough. He wanted it all.

He mounted the steps slowly, savoring the sultriness of the morning and the way the heat rose in his loins. He had never wanted a woman's body more. He couldn't get enough as he imagined her laying there, in her collar and straps, her legs wide open in invitation—to him, and only him.

Oh, yes. And when he was certain she wanted only him . . . then—

Evie stood outside the door, guarding it. "Everything ready," she murmured.

Then . . .

He opened the door.

Drue eyed him balefully from where she lay across the bed. "You *monster.*"

She was on her stomach, her buttocks canted up slightly, with her hands in restraints, but not her legs. It wasn't all that unpleasant, especially since she had a first-rate view of his flat belly and the growth of hair that fanned down beneath his belt to his thrusting penis.

It was inches away from her lips, deliberately, she thought angrily, and she wondered what would happen if she pulled it into her mouth, material and all, and sucked it dry.

She turned her head away abruptly. She could not let herself be seduced by a length of muscle and the refusal of the man to do his husbandly duty.

If only he would, she could be faithful to Gerard for the rest of her life.

She felt something probing her sex.

"What's that? What are you doing?"

"I'm just giving you what you want, you vixen. Some*thing* to fill your empty place."

It was perfect. She was all there, and open to him. He sat down beside her wriggling bottom and, propping himself on his elbow, he began to stroke her exposed sex.

She wriggled away from his questing fingers, and he went after her, stroking and dipping, and as she began to push against his fingers, probing and then pushing his three long fingers deep and hard inside her until they met the sweet barrier that proclaimed her innocence and her need.

She shrieked as some*thing* pushed into her most private place as if it were made to be there. But it wasn't his penis or his obvious need.

"You are . . . you are a bastard," she moaned, beating her feet against the mattress.

"And what are you, my naked wife, when your heart is full and yearning for another man? What you have now is all of *me* you can have until you crush *his* memory from your heart." He twisted his hand slightly and her body jolted at the sensation.

"Go away," she hissed, writhing against the sensation of the thickness of his fingers centered within her. "You are unspeakable."

"I am a man whose wife craves another man's sex," he said stonily, "and for that, she can only have *this*—" And he pushed his fingers harder into her, and she gasped as he pushed against her virginity. "And *this* . . ." A merciless twist of his fingers, and the feeling of him expanding her shocked her silent.

She couldn't move. She felt utterly paralyzed by the sensation of his fingers there. It was unspeakable; incredible; unknowable.

And he didn't move. Didn't speak. Just flexed his fingers every few minutes to let her know that he possessed her there, like that, just to that point of pressing her virginal veil; and that he could command those feelings from her whenever he desired.

He felt her every movement; whether she knew it or not, she was rocking against him gently, almost imperceptibly, seeking deeper penetration, enhanced sensation, in spite of the fact he could push no further.

He didn't know how much longer he could last, holding her like that, embedded in the tight heat of her most feminine place. And the straps of the thrall collar crossing over her buttocks almost undid him.

"Here is the lesson, *wife*," he whispered. "Only one man's penis can possess you. Which do you want more? A memory? A substitute?" He wriggled his fingers. "Or your master? Ponder that this morning, Drue, and how would it feel to be filled and fulfilled as my wife."

Never, never, never, never . . .

Her body sagged as he slowly withdrew his fingers. No, no— she didn't expect that—the feeling of emptiness. Not from him. Not that.

She turned her head.

The bulge of his erection told her more plainly than his words what pleasure awaited her when she finally willingly eagerly submitted to him.

If only he would get it over with—

It was in her eyes, and he read it clearly: the fascination with his ever-protruding penis, and her refusal to ever give in to him.

Let her lay there then, he thought furiously. *Let her think about what she had felt, what just his fingers had made her feel. What she could have if she came to him willingly.*

He couldn't take it another moment. He sagged against the door, his breath ragged, his body perspiring and taut with the sheer effort of controlling his lust; he felt like exploding, and shooting his seed all over her naked buttocks.

For one fulminating moment, he didn't care about lessons or love or Gerard Lenoir. All he wanted was that hot, bone-crackling release, and preferably centered deep into her hot, tight, traitorous body.

But then he pictured her nipples, her tight pointy nipples, and he wondered if Gerard had ever seen them, touched them . . . His mind would go no further.

All the sensual games he was playing with her now were still not proof against her having given her body to Lenoir to touch, to play with. And if he ever found out that Lenoir had laid a hand on her . . . Drue Caledon would remain his virgin bride forever.

But he would, finally, regretfully, let her get dressed.

Chapter 5

So . . . all the vixen wanted to do was taunt him and think about another man poking her—

How much should a husband have to take?

Even he didn't know the limits of his control—or his passion. The only thing he knew was she wasn't going to tempt him to take her before he was ready.

And that resolve already required the endurance of a saint.

He lay stretched out on his bed in the room next door to Drue's, and watched idly as every thought of her excited him to a bone-hard erection.

Still a virgin; a beautiful, round bottomed, long legged, hot, wet naked, come-take-me virgin. That at least was some consolation.

You sure are ass-over-end insane for waiting to rut in her trough.

Am I? I should just take her, the way she begs?

Why not?

Why not . . .

That inviting cleft between her splayed legs enfolding him . . . those flaring hips cradling him; and then lunging and plunging and penetrating the final barrier—and spending himself deep in that moist, rich velvet of her . . .

He drew in a sharp, hot breath, every molecule in his body aching to get his hands on her, to thrust his way into her.

Waiting naked for you, primed as a pistol for you, look at how your fingers made her squirm for you . . . she couldn't get enough of your fingers, for God's sake, in her furrow . . .

. . . Hellfire . . .

He had a squirming, naked woman already willing to spread her legs for him, and he sat here having wet dreams about her, instead of *having* her. That sounded a little off-whack to him, too.

But there was a method to this insanity. There was.

It was just at this moment, with his penis throbbing with lust for her, he couldn't quite remember what it was.

He gave her a half hour before he came back to her bedroom.

She lay where he left her, belly down and restrained, her eyes closed, her mouth determined.

Which was how he knew she was not sleeping.

"What now?" she muttered dampingly.

His erection did not die. If anything, the sight of her quiescent body and lush curves aroused him all the more.

"Well, my fawn, you've gotten a taste of what it feels like to have a man's hand inside you. Now I thought I'd like a taste of you."

His words put her in a panic. "No. No. *No!*"

"No—*what*, my wife who is never to refuse me anything . . . ?" His voice was silky, soft. Iron.

"I can't take this, Court." Was she throwing herself on his mercy? Maybe so, but *he* was the torturer, not she. If only, only, only he would do his duty . . . they could dispense with the games and start to live their separate lives.

She could make do with that, she *could* . . .

She shrieked. *"What are you doing?!!"* as he lifted her onto her knees and began rubbing something onto her protruding sex.

"Making myself a tasty treat, my fawn . . ."

She moaned. *Oh, Lord, the feeling of his fingers massaging something thick and sticky into her like that, all around her naked cleft was almost more than she could bear.*

"You like that," he murmured.

She made a guttural sound at the back of her throat. "I don't like anything." Her body contradicted her immediately, undulating seductively against his swirling fingers.

"You'll like this." *No, he* liked *this, the feel of her compressed womanflesh against his fingers as he swirled honey all around it.*

"What are you *doing?!!*"

"I'm coating you with honey before I sip from your cup . . ."

Omigod, omigod, omigod . . . She pulled, she wrenched, she kicked, she writhed and she couldn't get away from him or the inexorable touch of his rubbing fingers.

Bear it . . . just let him get it over with and bear it . . .

But she was doing more than bearing it. She was inviting it, and against every feeling she had about him.

She hated herself. She hated her naked body. She hated him . . .

"Ahhh," he growled. "And now . . ."

"And now?" she whispered fearfully.

". . . I eat my sweet treat . . ."

And she couldn't escape. Where before he had held her middle with his iron-bar arm, now he relinquished her, and straddled her hips, pulling her onto her knees again.

"Now . . ." he groaned, and bent over her. And took her with one long luscious swipe of his tongue against her pulsing, swelling sex.

Omigod . . . omigod . . . was there ever a more relentless mouth . . . She fought him, she enticed him, she couldn't get away from him and his determination to lick and suck every last drop of honey from between her legs.

Her body stretched and pushed and begged; the leather pulled, shaped, contoured her womanflesh to give him the utmost access to her. Again and again, he inserted his tongue into her cleft, seeking the taste of *her.*

For one unsettling moment, she felt as if she were solely connected to him, just there, just like that. Her knees went weak and almost boneless from the sheer insensate pleasure of it.

He took it all and she was helpless to stop him, utterly without control, totally in his power to give her that with his succulent carnal kisses.

There, and there, and there . . .

There was something too decadent, too erotic, and too dark about all those deep tongue-tied kisses.

As if he thought they could make her want him.

No, she could never never want him. But she could learn to live with and yearn for those unspeakable sensations he evoked in her.

She could learn to spread her legs for him whenever he commanded her.

She could learn to be the best whore and wife in the whole of St. Faubonne Parish.

But want him? Love him? No. *Never.*

Never . . .

Her nerve endings quivered and her body quickened as his tongue caught the edge of her shimmering pleasure.

. . . ever . . .

What was he doing? What was he doing?

Her body jolted as he touched some sacred secret part of her she did not know existed—

. . . ever—

—and she slid downward into that dark erotic place and tumbled headlong into a waterfall of silver that broke ever so gently over his tongue.

Ripe . . . ready . . . and resisting him already—

He held her hips tightly as he pushed against her, pulling every nuance of sensation from her body before he let her pull away.

And pull she did. As if she couldn't get away from him fast enough. What more could be said?

That *he* wasn't sated? Not nearly.

That this was her first brush with carnal pleasure? So likely.

That now she would offer herself willingly? Not hardly.

He made a disgusted sound and eased away from her tempting flesh. It was all he could do to keep himself from plunging into her.

She was there for the taking, her bottom tilted at exactly the angle to accommodate his roaring manflesh.

All he had to do . . .

All he had to do—

"Take me," she whispered, hoping against hope as she sensed his agonized indecision and eyed his towering erection.

"I think not, my fawn. I think the taste of you will sate me and prepare me for another day," he murmured, clenching his hands into fists to keep from running them all over her rounded buttocks.

Instead, he forced himself to climb over her and off of the bed.

"Such a pretty sight, my fawn, in the aftermath of your pleasure."

"Is that what it was?" she muttered, unable to keep the thread of sarcasm out of her voice.

"I see," he said stonily, his body flinching at the thought she might have experienced this already, with Lenoir. He hadn't even considered that—that Lenoir might have tutored her in *all* the earthly delights save one—because he had been too caught up in the heady discovery that she was still a virgin.

So there was still much for her to learn—and for him, he could see that now. A man could take nothing for granted, especially when his penis was aching for release and leading him around by the nose.

"What do you see?" she demanded, alerted instantly by that tone in his voice. That tone meant his displeasure. And that he would prolong the inevitable.

She shuddered. She didn't know why she kept taunting him like that. It would only take that one moment of acquiescence to give him what he said he wanted. An actress could do it. A whore.

Surely she, even in her innocence . . .

Not so innocent now—

Her breath caught. *She knew pleasure now.*

She knew the pleasure of feeling something between her legs.

She knew a man's carnal kiss.

She knew the power of a woman's nudity.

Innocent no more . . .

She felt as if he were reading everything in her eyes. "What do you see?" she asked again, keeping her voice as neutral as possible.

"A scared little fawn," he said, his voice deceptively soft. "A fawn who is still hiding from her fate."

She made a sound. She wondered how far she could push him. She wondered if she wanted to try. "And you're a man denying his. Look at you. You'd rather walk around with that pole sticking out than stick it into me. So either you're a coward, you don't want to for some reason, or maybe—maybe your heart and mind are on someone else, too . . ."

She faltered at the expression in his eyes. *Oh, God . . . did I really say that to him? What is* wrong *with me?*

He could feel himself turning stone cold.

Little bitch. Who could have dreamt the fawn's teeth were so sharp? Goddamn whore witch bitch . . .

. . . he felt like showing her. He felt like jamming into her tight, wet cleft just to shut her taunting mouth. He felt like ramrodding his way right to the mouth of her womb and blasting his seed into the very core of her.

But . . . but—

He wanted her prostrate. He wanted her shuddering with need. He wanted her crawling, at his feet, begging him for what he alone could do to her.

Until she learned that lesson, there wasn't a thing in the world she could do to tempt him.

And he'd keep his unruly penis at bay as well; and she would never know what that restraint cost him.

Her body betrayed her. During the night, as she restlessly tossed and turned, she felt herself stretching toward the phantom lover who had pulled such pleasure from her body.

Him!

Never him . . .

How could she forgive him for all he had done?

Done? Done? What have I done, he would say. I've admired you. I've been patient with you. I haven't forced myself on you. And I've given you pleasure. Tell me what I've "done" . . .

She moaned and rolled over again. She could write a litany of what he'd *done,* and none of it would make sense; no one would believe it.

Gerard would believe it . . .

She choked back a groan. *Dear darling Gerard . . . if he knew that monster kept her naked, kept her in restraints when it suited him, made her wear a thrall collar, forced her to display her sex for him, licked honey from her vessel, and made her writhe with pleasure . . . what would he do? What could he do?*

How did it sound?

Insane.

How did she sound?

Ungrateful.

God—WHAT?!! Ungrateful?!

She sat bolt upright, her body covered with a fine sheen of sweat—from the unremitting thick sultry heat, or from her thoughts, desires, dreams?

She didn't want to know, didn't want to think. The collar, the straps, irritated her skin, as she supposed they were meant to do, to remind her of who owned her, and to whom she was beholden.

She swung her legs over the bed and sat for a moment, contemplating the moonlight filtering in through the window.

She could jump out the window and be beholden no more.

. . . ungrateful!! . . .

She wrapped her arms around her midriff.

The heat was suffocating. And there wasn't a window open anywhere except the transom between the bathing room and the hallway.

He trusted her not.

She didn't even trust herself.

. . . ungrateful!!! . . . that he had given her pleasure and made her feel like a trussed-up turkey . . . Oh, no, she wasn't going to give in to that; the pleasure was not going to supersede the indignity.

She wouldn't let it.

No matter how it sounded.

To her.

To Gerard . . .

She fell on her back. *If only he had taken me . . .*

If only he would come now—and get it over with . . .

He couldn't take much more of this. Or maybe he could, if he found a willing body to poke while he waited for his high-and-mighty wife to come around.

Plenty of willing bodies between St. Faubonne and New Orleans—he could just see them, sassy, saucy vixens beckoning in the night, never hesitant to slide a hand up a man's pole to gauge the worth of what they had to sell.

He could settle for that, he could. A little sport, a quick spurt to relieve the tension and the ache, a wink and a kiss and he could be out the door, and nobody hurt.

But nobody with nipples like hers . . . nobody as naked and luscious-tasting as her . . .

. . . nobody—

Hell.

Maybe he'd have her for breakfast, he was that ravenous to possess her.

Maybe not, he thought, as he caught the expression on her face as Evie escorted her into the room.

A man couldn't ease up for a moment.

"Sit there," he ordered, pointing to an upholstered rectangular bench. "Straddle it. Evie—bring over the little table, let her eat something, thank you."

"And coffee, Master Court?"

"Yes, thank you. Stay by for a moment, please."

"I'm not hungry," Drue said. "I want this damned collar off my neck."

"Eat, little fawn, you need your strength."

"I need an open window, a fan, and some clothes," she said in a petulant tone.

"She won't learn, will she," Court muttered, taking a biscuit and slathering it with butter and jam. "Well, I need to keep up my strength, little fawn. You almost sap the life out of me with your stubbornness."

"I hope so," she hissed.

"But not quite. As you can plainly see."

She saw. His whole body had bolted to life the moment she appeared on the threshold. And it just kept getting longer and stronger and harder as she stared at it.

An amazing thing—

She bit into a biscuit with a ferocity that made him quiver.

Interesting . . .

He sipped his coffee and pretended nothing had happened.

They could be any couple sharing breakfast, except that she was naked, wearing a thrall collar, and sat across a bench with her legs spread and her husband's eyes devouring her as greedily as he did his food.

"Evie."

"Master?"

"Do her hands now."

"What . . . ?!" She was holding a cup and a biscuit, but Evie paid no mind; she grasped each wrist, and as the cup and biscuit fell to the floor, Evie firmly pulled her hands behind her and wound a satin tie around them.

"Thank you, Evie."

He watched through hooded eyes as Evie left them, firmly closing the door behind her; and then he turned his attention to Drue.

"Yes . . ." he murmured. "Perfect."

Perfect the way her body arched and her breasts thrust forward because of her bound hands. Perfect how she had to press down against the fabric of the bench to keep her balance and her legs apart the way he liked them.

Perfect because her nipples were tight and hard with suppressed excitement and her eyes alive with curiosity and fury both at what he was going to do.

Maybe she knew.

Maybe she didn't.

He wanted those nipples.

He wanted *her*.

He dipped a finger in the jam pot, and pressed it against her nipple and began swirling it around the hard pleasure point.

She jerked away.

"Oh, no, little fawn. I will have this, too. I thought about it all night. Imagine it: me fantasizing about covering your nipples with jam so I can suck them. *Hold still . . . !*" as she wrenched away from him.

He leapt up and straddled the bench behind her, holding her tightly against his hot hard chest with one hand, and reaching over to the jam pot with the other.

She wanted to stop him; she was desperate to stop him as he rubbed her nipples, first one, then the other pointed peak, with the soft, sticky jam.

She had her hands. She had the weapon, the long bone of an erection sliding up her buttocks. She could . . . she could—squeeze him or pinch him or something—

She groaned involuntarily as his fingers made magic on her breasts.

That wasn't supposed to happen, it wasn't . . . she didn't want to feel them swirling, caressing, squeezing her nipples—the sensation spiraled right down between her legs and there was nothing she could do to stop it.

Her body, her traitorous, pleasure-seeking body, squirmed in delight, and it curved at an impossible angle to demand more of those tantalizing beguiling fingers on her breasts.

Her head lolled against his shoulder, and she moaned over and over, "No, no, no, no . . ."

And he murmured in concert with her protests, "Yes, yes, yes, yes . . ."

And he grew bigger and tighter with every moan, spurting hotter, harder, more insistent with every "no" she uttered.

"I can't, I can't, I can't . . ."

"You can . . ."

"I don't want to—"

"You do . . ."

"Oh, God, Court—*don't* . . ." as the feeling feeding from her nipples swelled and expanded and then streamed and funneled between her legs.

"Yes," he whispered into her ear, "give it to me . . . give me, give me—let it . . . let it . . . come—"

"No-o-o-o-o-o . . ." she groaned as she bent double and ground her hips into the bench. "No-o-o-o-o-o-o . . ." as his relentless fingers kept at her nipples until she could hardly stand the feel of them, and she pulled and pushed at them and undulated her body and grasped at his penis and whimpered in the back of her throat as her body convulsed and pure molten pleasure coursed through her veins and puddled between her legs and then detonated in the writhing heat of her surrender.

"No . . ." she whispered, her fingers flexing against the inflexible length and hardness of him, but it was too late. Too late for her. Too late for him.

He spumed like a geyser beneath his trousers, his manhood so overheated he thought he would die from the pleasure.

It took moments—it felt like hours—to regain some semblance

of sanity, and when he finally did, he gently pulled the satin tie from her wrists where she still grasped him, and slowly, tentatively, he wrapped himself around her.

She held herself stiffly away, still as dazzled and bewildered as he. He was sure of it. It was time to gentle the fawn. He had all the time in the world to wait; and soon, slowly, reluctantly, she settled back into his heat.

It was late afternoon. He had sent Drue upstairs for a long, luxurious bath, and he had had Evie unlock the collar, and he had brushed his lips against her irritated skin.

He liked the fact she had shuddered at his touch. There was nothing about her that didn't arouse him, and now that she had capitulated to him, he was very willing to accede to her demands. A bath. A maid to wield a fan in the suffocating heat. The removal of the collar.

The knowledge in her eyes that he would possess her soon.

She could not, in the throes of that convulsive climax, have been thinking of anyone else but *him.*

She made his blood run hot. She made him boil. She made him hard just at the thought of her.

He was hard for her now, his penis restless, his blood throbbing with the primitive need to claim her in the most elemental way.

Lord Almighty . . . he couldn't keep his mind off her . . . *he never got to suck her nipples* . . .

Tonight . . .

The word thrummed through his blood. No more waiting. No more wanting and aching. He was tired of waiting for what was his; tired of fighting his body, tired of the battle for hers.

Tonight . . .

His penis spurted at the thought; ruthlessly, he got it under control.

A man didn't spend his seed profligately when he had a woman like Drue to service him. He planned to keep her pinned to the bed for a week, a month, a year, naked and begging for his sex between her legs.

Tonight . . .

He liked the fact that there was a factor of time in his decision to finally give her what she wanted. Always, the anticipation made the thought of the act seem even more deeply erotic.

They had so much time . . .

And he would take his time once penetration was complete. And he even looked forward to that moment, when all barriers between them ceased to exist and she could encompass all of him, tight and to the hilt.

He made a hissing sound as he imagined it. His manhood ached for it, tellingly, even now.

He shuddered at the force of his craving for it.

No man should ever be that whipsawed by any woman . . .

Well, damn, he wasn't in love with her; he just wanted her, naked and writhing beneath his body . . .

"Master Court—"

. . . and screaming for more—

"Master Court—"

Damned insistent voice jolting him out of his fantasies.

"What is it, Evie?"

"I got something here you want to see."

"Come in then," he said gruffly, shifting in his chair. "What is it?"

She handed him an envelope. "A man done give that to Louisa, and she come to me."

"I see." He turned it over in his fingers. No identifying marks. No address. "And who was Louisa to give it to?"

"The mistress."

The words fell like stones. "Thank you, Evie. You can go."

He waited until she had exited the room. And waited still longer, turning the missive over and over, as if the blankness of it would tell him something and he wouldn't have to open the envelope at all.

Three days . . . not even a week before the betrayals set in— he was a fool, and she—oh, she . . .

Slowly, he got up and went into his office and closed the door. Slowly, so as not to damage the flap, he slit open the envelope and took out the letter, even knowing what it probably contained.

He had to know. Even though he knew.

My dearest, darling Pet,

I can't stand it anymore. Three days knowing you have been in the arms of that monster and I'm half crazed with anger and jealousy. There must be a way. I cannot bear that he should have you. I cannot bear that I can't.

Remember the things we said to each other? The promises we made? There are other places, other possibilities. You don't have to stay with him. You can come to me. Your father will not suffer, I promise. I swear it. If that is the only reason you consented to this abomination of a marriage, you must believe me. Summerville can never harm your father. On my life I swear it.

Leave him. Marry me, as we had planned from the beginning. Don't stay a moment longer in that hell house. Tell me I may still hope to possess you, my darling love. Tell me you haven't forgotten everything we did, everything we were to each other.

She who delivers this letter to you has promised to be our go-between. Please, please, please answer my prayers, give me hope. Send your lover the one response that will open the gates of heaven—for him and for you.

Your beloved,
Gerard

He read it slowly; he read it again. Three phrases jumped out: *everything we did, everything we were to each other . . . Send your lover . . .*

He felt like smashing something. To his credit, he thought, he did nothing. He just sat there, still as a statue, contemplating the cramped writing on the page.

. . . everything we did . . .

. . . everything we were to each other . . .

. . . send your lover . . .

The lying bastard, he thought violently; the evidence was irrefutable that Lenoir had never been her lover. He felt murderous. Uncontrollable. He wanted to teach the son of a bitch a lesson, to keep his hands, his filthy words, away from his *wife.*

But he couldn't get around *everything they did . . .* He *had* to know. And he didn't want to know. He wanted to kill Lenoir so that one memory of *everything they did* would be obliterated forever.

And he could only think of one sure way to efface it from hers: he was going to pound her body to oblivion and back so that the one thing, the only thing she would remember inside her was *him*.

He would never let her go, never; what was his belonged to *him*, forever. But he had to know.

So now, yes, he would take her so she would never forget to whom she belonged, and because of this betrayal, he would test her.

But he didn't know what he would do if he didn't win.

Chapter 6

She lay on the bed, luxuriating after her bath without the confining collar and straps. Evie was off somewhere else in the house, and there was no sound anywhere but the soft swoosh of the palm fan wielded by Evie's daughter.

She didn't want to think; she tried to make her mind a blank so she didn't have to feel, didn't have to remember the bone-melting excitement of what he had done to her, or her body's sense of still being confined by the straps and collar.

How odd it was, as if that were something so erotic that her senses had derived some pleasure from it even if she had felt as if she were bound and displayed solely for his titillation.

Or had she?

Could she have secretly loved the way those straps defined and outlined her sex and thrust her breasts forward?

No, how could she? This was not an affectionate game between lovers; he had made it a situation of domination and control whereby he meant to teach her fully and completely that she had no control.

So why did she feel as if somehow she secretly wielded some power?

Because he was in a constant state of arousal every time he was around her; that had to mean his sex was responding to *her*. Even if it only meant he wanted to copulate with her, still—he wanted *her*. Her body. Her sex. Her heat.

But so much so, he wouldn't allow himself to have her?

It seemed strange to her. The easiest thing would have been for him to take her. He surely wasn't denying *her* anything. Why would he deny himself?

For control. Always control. To make her give up control.

And hadn't she? She couldn't fight him. She couldn't stop him. He owned her. He hadn't forced himself on her. Not to take her, not really.

All he had done was shatter her resolve and melt her determination.

He had made her forget Gerard and he had made her want to experience that frenzied swamping pleasure again.

Control. He could control her merely by giving her that.

She wondered what it would take to make *him* finally lose control.

Wouldn't that be something to savor? Court Summerville in the throes of mindless passion. Court, helpless in her hands, the way she had been in his.

She squirmed, visualizing it, and a dart of pleasure pierced her straight to her vitals.

No! NO!

What was she thinking?! There could be nothing between her and Court. He had married her to seed a dynasty, nothing more, nothing less.

Why couldn't she remember that? Why did he have to play with her, like a cat with a mouse?

Control.

Always back to that. Control. Power.

She rolled over onto her belly. *She wanted some of that power. Back to that. Back to the games.*

HOW could she make him give in to her?

She turned over again as the rough texture of the mattress ticking irritated her breasts.

What would make Court Summerville capitulate to her . . . ?

"Mistress . . ." Evie's soft voice from the door.

She levered herself up on her elbows as Evie entered the room.

"It is growing late, mistress. Perhaps you did not notice. Master send this for you to wear, and he say you come when you have dressed yourself."

She held out a small porcelain box. "This is for you, mistress."

Drue took it reluctantly. *More games. More control.* She bit her lip as she lifted the gold-rimmed lid.

Inside were two whisper-thin gold loops, the ends of which supported two tiny dangling gold ovals.

She looked up at Evie.

Evie's face was impassive. "Master say you wear his gift."

"Let him put it on me," she muttered, snapping the lid closed. *More games.* Her hands were shaking at the thought of where this gift was meant to be worn.

"I will put," Evie said, taking a step toward her.

She recoiled. "No!"

"You must do." Evie's tone was adamant.

And what could Evie do? She was at Court's mercy as well.

She looked down at her breasts, at her taut nipples that almost seemed to be begging for his gift.

She opened the box again, and lifted one loop and slipped it over the tight peak of her right breast. Her breath caught as she felt it settle, and then, she could barely feel it at all. What she felt was the *knowledge* it was there, encircling, confining, defining, *exciting* her, her body, her imagination, just as he intended, damn him—her nipples hard and tight and dressed in *his* gift of gold . . .

"Yes." Evie nodded. "Mistress is quite beautiful. Just how Master intended. You come now."

Drue swung her legs off the bed. She didn't want to go anywhere, but Evie waited. And Court.

She found herself holding her body straighter, tauter, as she followed Evie into the hall, her back arched to balance the delicate loops on her nipples. She could feel the dangle of the ovals as she walked, saw the flickering candlelight glint off the thin, fragile gold. Understood that those loops bound her as surely and tightly as had the thrall collar.

For one heart-stopping moment, she considered bolting down the steps, naked as she was, to freedom. But then she saw Louisa in the shadows, a step or two below, waiting, watching, her keeper in this house of sensual secrets.

Everywhere, control.

She had to get some control.

Evie knocked on the door of the bedroom next to the one she had been occupying.

"Come." His voice was rough, so rough, as if he couldn't contain himself at the thought of her wearing his gift.

Good.

Now she *had it.*

Power. Control.

Come . . .

"Don't move." There was raw note in the timbre of his voice.

The door closed behind her, the ever-efficient Evie sending her to her fate.

It was in his dark, flaming gaze, and in the heat and emotion that suffused the room. He burned with it, the telling part of his body, clothed as it always was, already erect and stiff as a poker.

She couldn't take her eyes off him. He radiated animal musk and pure male desire. He meant to have her tonight. No more games. No more denial. For whatever reason, he had decided, and with his gift, he had made clear his determination.

And if she hadn't understood by that erotic gesture, she perceived it clearly the moment she entered the room: suspended from the ceiling was an apparatus that was obviously meant to facilitate his full-bore possession of her.

No pretty flourishes. No gentle words. No caresses.

Just a harness suspended from an iron bar from the ceiling: two padded leather nooses joined by a narrow strip that would support her bottom when she thrust her legs through the openings and presented herself to him, open and ready for anything he wanted to do.

As he had been schooling her.

As she'd been begging him.

But not like this—not like this . . .

Still, there was something about the idea of it that was subversively arousing. As if there were a way here for her to exert control. That if she climbed into that apparatus and allowed herself to be displayed and penetrated, she would force him to prostrate himself to her sex.

Because then he would not refuse her.

And he could not deny himself.

Power.

Yesssssss . . .

The lamplight shimmered on the golden loops as she straightened her shoulders. What wouldn't a woman do to gain power? His glittering eyes were transfixed by the loops, and the way they dangled so enticingly from her nipples.

Good.

Power.

She was beginning to understand—a little. His male part flexed insistently. *Yes. That, too—*

She wondered . . . She turned so that her breasts were outlined against the lamplight, and the hard points of her nipples were fully defined. She heard the sharp hiss of his breath. Felt the heat and desire rolling through the room in waves. Felt him restraining himself. Pacing himself, in spite of his savage need. In spite of his ferocious desire.

Felt her body responding to every sensual impulse to use his carnal need to make him crawl to her. No matter what she had to do.

She cupped her breasts as she walked toward him. "Do you like them?" she whispered.

"I can't keep my eyes away from them."

"Which—your gift or my nipples?" she murmured.

"Your nipples."

She felt the shift then, in the hoarseness of his voice and the intensity of his gaze, and she knew instinctively that if she made the first move, he would surrender.

Was she fearless enough? Did she want it enough?

She stopped at the apparatus. There was a bed-step just below it, positioned perfectly for her.

As bold an invitation as anything he had done yet.

And she had to want to do it as badly as he wanted her to.

Did she?

Power. Yesss . . .

She held his glittering gaze as she stepped up and mounted the harness, holding it tightly as she slipped first one leg and then the other into each of the padded nooses, and then shimmied her bottom against the thin leather strip to position herself comfortably; the harness forced her legs apart and her back to arch so that her most erotic self was displayed for him.

And he gave himself up to the pleasure of watching her as she squirmed and writhed, and then, her eyes hot with knowledge that had never been there before, waited for him.

And he deliberately made her wait. Every impulse in him roared to slam himself into her. He couldn't get enough of just looking at her, and lusting for her, and that new, aware look in her eyes that told him she was starting to understand what it meant to wield her sexual power.

But not yet. Not until he had penetrated her and stuffed himself as deep as he could go. Slowly, he stripped away his clothing so that he was finally revealed to her, naked, pulsing, and still in control.

He could tell by her eyes that while she had willingly spread her legs for him, she was not prepared for the size of him, and breadth of him, naked.

He was huge, his rock-hard manhood emerging from a thick thatch of wiry hair between his legs. He was long, lean, and strong, and from the look in his eyes, determined to have her— tonight.

He kicked away the stair-step and poised himself just at her moist center. The sight of her naked and splayed for him, wearing his golden gift on her nipples, was almost too much. Too much for any man.

But not for him. Oh, no, very soon, his wayward *wife* would understand that all the power rested with him, in him, in his sinew and muscle and his ability to conquer her naked body without surrendering his own.

So, even though he was ready to burst, even though just touching her lush, wet flesh could incite his climax, he ruthlessly reined himself in, and just pushed against her, so the very tip of him was kissed by her feminine folds.

She gasped faintly as she felt him there and she looked down from his compelling gaze to see the long hard throbbing length of him just barely enfolded between her legs.

There was so much of him, and he just stood there with the barest nudge of his sex inserted in hers that she instantly felt the surging power of him that he held severely in check.

He wanted her to be utterly aware of him as he claimed her. He wanted her to feel him possess her inch by long, hard inch, and he wanted her to watch as he eased himself purposefully inside her.

He pushed again and breeched her further; she opened wider to take him, and enfold him. He paused there, for several long, breathless minutes, to let her feel the heat of him, the heaviness, the hardness. To let her see how a woman accommodated a man's sex.

And then he pushed again, another throbbing bone-hard inch, and she moaned because there was still so much of him yet to take, and her body felt hot and her nipples were hard, and he— he . . . he was the focus of her world suddenly, and the center from which she could never escape.

She writhed against the inexorable thrust of him, enticing him to come further within her moist heat, examining the rising excitement of feeling his hard heat undulating between her legs, and the sight of them not quite fully joined.

He felt himself pearling up, at the sight, every instinct gathering for the final blasting thrust into her. He had to have her. She was so tight, so wet, so open, so *there* . . . one stroke—he reared back—one tight, high thrust . . . he grasped her thighs, just once . . . he rammed himself into her—

She cried out as he took her with that piercing final lunge— and then he was in, in, in, deep, deep, deeper still, in to the hilt, and finally home.

They were hip to hip now, and she held herself tight against the ebbing pain. She had known it was necessary, but this—oh, this—otherness at one with her—and this unfamiliar feeling of something invading her most secret self—she felt a frenzied urgency to escape.

Who could have known it was so all-encompassing, that she would feel so lost, vanquished, ill-prepared?

"I have to get away, I have to get away . . ." Her voice was a frantic whisper against his hands, which held her immobile.

"You'll never get away, my fawn. I own you now. What is between your legs is *mine*—never forget it. I'm the one who will make you insensate with desire for what only I can do to you . . ."

"No—no . . . go away . . ."

"You'll beg for it . . ." He rocked against her.

"Never," she spat.

"You'll crave it."

"Ever . . ."

"You'll be on your knees, my fawn—"

"Then *do it,*" she hissed.

"Thank you so much for giving me permission. But you never had a say in whether I would do it or not . . ." He ground his hips against her. "Feel that, *wife.*" He pulled back and swooped inside her with a long, hard stroke. "And that—" Pushing deeper into her. "And that . . ." Moving then almost involuntarily into a staccato rhythm because he couldn't take any more— "And . . . tha-a-t—" Because his body demanded that he spend himself now that she was positioned to service him. "And *that . . .*"

She couldn't say a word. She felt as if everything in her were focused on *his* movement, his demands, his need.

He moved like a piston in her; her body stretched to welcome him, to receive him, to feel every hard, surging stroke, to wring from him the sensations that she was feeling, in spite of everything she had said, in spite of herself.

This wasn't supposed to happen—these feelings, this urgency. It was as if it were ordained; his long strong body matched to hers; his hard hot penis rubbing and stroking her in that perfect place where her body craved it, and where nothing mattered but the shattering drive to pleasure.

She felt his fingers dig into her buttocks, pulling her closer, pushing him deeper. She felt his muscles quivering at the effort to contain himself, because if he surrendered control, he surrendered everything.

But even he couldn't outlast his rigidly contained lust. It was too much then even for him; he pounded himself blindly into her, using her as a vessel until his straining body could take it no longer, and then, in one telling thrust, he rammed himself tightly against her, and spent himself convulsively in a long spuming aching release.

"We've barely begun, my fawn," he whispered against her ear and into the silence; he was still hot and hard inside her, his cream thick and seeping around them. And he still wanted her. Was still hot and raring to pin her to whatever surface was handy. "Just barely." He braced his arms around her bottom and lifted her from the harness, somehow still keeping himself joined to her.

"Did you feel me there, *wife?* I swear to God you will never get away from me . . ." He got her on the bed somehow; he laid her down and followed her down, deep down into her where he had shot his seed. "Never . . ."

. . . *never* . . .

He was so hard and so hot and all of his weight was over her now; she had never felt so *naked* and fragile, so much at someone else's mercy. His lust to possess her burned her whole body as he aligned himself against her.

"Just you wait, little fawn. Now that I've slaked my hunger, now that you've gotten a taste . . ."

"A taste of what—your power over me? Isn't that understood?" she muttered.

"I hope so," he growled, and thrust himself more tightly into her. It was as if all the sexual heat had dissipated. She was too cold and he had to stoke her up somehow.

He rocked against her, pushing himself deeper.

She made an incoherent sound in the back of her throat.

"Get used to it, my fawn. I don't know why I waited to have you. I'm going to stuff myself into you every waking moment."

She moaned.

"Just like this: on your back, spreading your legs . . ."

She felt herself sinking, sinking into his scenario of sensual depravity, wondering what there was in it for her. Her feeling of vulnerability intensified. All he had ever made her feel was overpowered, and with his big body and his huge penis deep inside her, she felt even more helpless.

Where was that sense of power that had moved her as she had climbed into the harness?

Like a lamb to the slaughter, she had given him everything he wanted, and lost herself in the process. Stupid to ever think she could bring him to heel.

This would be her life from now on: crushed under his body, a vessel for his mindless lust.

But then, that *was* why men wanted a woman . . .

She felt his body suddenly stiffen with urgency. "What are you *doing?*"

"I want you again."

"You can have anything you want," she muttered, her voice laced with bitterness. "Obviously."

"Ah," he murmured, "the fawn has forgotten the pleasure . . ."

"There is no pleasure. There's just domination and submission. Just . . . do what you want, and let me go."

"But I'll never let you go, my wife. You've only just begun to repay me for everything I've done for you. And I wouldn't call your enticing me to the harness submission, either. Feel how ripe, how wet, you are. Your body is submitting to nothing; your body wants me just where I am."

Yes, she *had* mounted the harness of her own volition; she burned with the knowledge of that, and that she had ever thought she could rule him.

He ruled everything, from what she ate to what she wore to her position beneath him in his bed.

She just hadn't understood about the carnal nature of men.

Or her own.

"And I want to be just where I am. All day, all night." He gathered her tighter against him. "In spite of what *you* want. You want *this*." He undulated against her. "And this—" A long, sleek stroke that took her utterly by surprise. "Yes . . ."

"Noooo . . ." she moaned as he thrust again. And again. And again. And her body began moving in concert with his thrusts. Her traitorous body that had a life of its own, that felt rich and wet and ready for whatever he was going to do to her. "No . . ." her protest feeble now, as a wave of shocking sensation coursed through her and she heaved her body upward to meet his lunges. ". . . n-o . . ."

This wasn't right, this wasn't what *she* wanted. And yet—and yet . . . the sensations became familiar, like those stunning feelings he had pulled from her nakedness with his hands and his mouth. And became insistent, necessary, *there* . . .

She centered on the spangling sensations right between her legs. He was so long, so strong, and he had planted himself exactly where she needed him to be, at the apex of her sensual craving.

Yes, now, with his hard, insistent thrusting, his perfect positioning, she wanted it; she didn't know, how could she have known? He had opened her body and primed her for him. He couldn't go deep enough, far enough, fast enough.

He felt the exact moment she gave in to him, the moment when she understood the pleasure to be had. Her body quickened, she pulled him in tighter, she spread herself still wider, and she found his rhythmic pace.

It crept up on her like the morning heat, with an awareness that it was there, as elusive as fog, and then suddenly it was alive, intense, sharp, fierce, and flaring into something unspeakably erotic.

Her body caved, bearing down with every ounce of her strength on the dark invader centered just at her point of pleasure.

Just there; just there . . . he was hard and hot, and every pointed thrust broke into her, and over her in an incandescent shower of light that cracked and sparked and suddenly, unexpectedly, exploded in the darkness.

And all he had to do was follow her down into the tumult of her climax into the backwash of his release.

She awakened in the morning with a jolt. She was still in his bed, still in his arms, her bottom pressed against his unholy-hard erection, his one arm crossed over her breasts, his other lay over her belly, with his fingers inserted between her legs.

She didn't dare move. He was right there. Right *there* and

she didn't know how it happened that he had trapped her so completely.

Deliberate. Everything with him was deliberate. She hardly dared breathe, let alone move.

And it was so hot, even this early in the morning. It was barely dawn, and the heat already lay over them like a heavy blanket. She felt sticky with the heat, but her body felt rich and sated.

Sated?

From where she lay she could clearly see the harness suspended from the ceiling. The beginning of the end for her. She had surrendered everything, just everything. There was nothing he didn't have now, nothing he couldn't take.

And she would give. It was the consuming failure of women that in order to experience that unspeakable pleasure, they would give everything over and over and over.

And there was no power in that.

There could only be power in withholding it, in making him work, making him beg and grovel for it. Provided that he wanted it badly enough.

Oh, yes, he did, he wanted her—it—now. His fingers flexed involuntarily and her body contracted.

And she wanted *that.*

How far she had come in one night. From virgin to tart, already seduced by the promise of that bone-melting pleasure. Ready to spread her legs at his touch.

What a weapon it was. How unfair. How one-sided.

She would never be strong enough to deny him. Nor would he let her.

Helpless again . . . She moved restively at the thought.

She was a vessel, a body, a servant . . .

Her body contracted again as his fingers moved against her left nipple.

"Good morning, my fawn." His voice was barely a whisper. "You're so wet, so ripe between your legs. I'm going to take you with my fingers."

"I—"

But there was no "I" in the equation. He rolled onto his back so that she was wholly on top of him, her back against his chest and his penis embedded in her buttocks crease.

"Don't be coy, Drue. Drape your legs over my hips—just like that—now I can get to you . . ."

It was like lying on a sun-hot stone, all rough and rounded, and a dangerous slide. He braced her around her midriff, his one hand still free to cup her left breast and play with her hard nipple.

The other hand he had not removed from her body; he slipped his fingers in more deeply, twisting, pumping, and goading her on.

She arched her body involuntarily against each spasm of pleasure. He knew just how to caress her nipple, just how to play her with his magical hands.

She felt him pumping against her buttocks, she felt his sorcerer's fingers rubbing against that one indescribable sweet spot between her legs. She felt her body melting as she pushed down hard on his mesmerizing knowledge of her body, on his knowledgeable fingers that found the pulse of her pleasure and unerringly wrested it from her body until he had pulled her tight as a bow. And then, with perfect timing, he released her—a pitch of arrows piercing her soul, and falling . . . falling . . . and fracturing her convulsing body until she could bear it no more.

That . . .

He rode her buttocks as she lay collapsed against him. She couldn't move. Her whole body felt fragile, explosive. A man ought not know that much about a woman's body.

He . . . he knew—

And every inch of her was his, offered into his hands like the sacrifice she was.

At least there was some reward. At least there was this . . .

He heaved against her, rolling her onto her belly and canting her bottom upward. She felt him probing for her, and then the slick slide of him neatly and tightly into her in this reverse position.

Her body twinged as he covered her, and he lay with her, his penis embedded in her, quiescent, for all the rest of the morning.

Chapter 7

He took her finally as the clock struck noon, riding her to a bone-jarring culmination that left them both panting, and then he left her luxuriating in his bed in the sex-soaked aftermath of their coupling.

He needed a respite. He needed five minutes—a half hour—away from her, away from her naked, seductive body. Away from his urgent erection and his insane need to possess her over and over and over.

Just a little time where maybe he could relax, not think about her, go through some papers that required his attention. Not that he could pay attention.

He was too covered with the scent of her to concentrate. It permeated everything: his head, his mind, his business.

Damn her. It didn't take him a half hour and his sex was driving to get into her again. And why not? The fawn was full of surprises, not least that she was as hot as a poker and tight as a drum, two qualities any man found easy to take. And she was sure as damn easy to take.

Damn it, he had to have her again. Now.

Whipsawed by his unruly penis and a hot-tailed lady. *Damn damn damn damn . . .*

But still, he raced up the steps and burst into his room to find her braced against the headboard, sliding the loops of gold over her protruding nipples.

He almost climaxed then and there. His penis was rigid as a pipe and primed to pop. He stripped off his clothes, climbed into the bed on his knees, and pulled her toward him.

No words, as he lifted her legs to brace them against his chest; no caresses as he poled himself into her as hard and deep as he could go. All he wanted was to climb onto her and ram himself into her. Once. Twice. Three times. He felt himself swelling, his muscles gathering, and not all the willpower in the world could have stopped him. He spewed his seed into her like a geyser, deliberately, purposefully, elementally, and drove himself home.

And it wasn't enough. He collapsed on top of her and he understood: it wasn't enough just to possess her.

It was the other thing he had to know.

He summoned Evie to him later that afternoon and gave her the abominable letter from Lenoir. "You will give this to the mistress."

"Oh, master . . ." Evie murmured.

"Give it to her. Tell me what she does, what she says. Do not stop her if she leaves the house. But I swear, you'd better tell me where she goes . . ."

Drue felt bruised right down to her toes. Court could be rough, unfeeling; that last coupling had been brutal and self-serving.

But that was her *job*, after all. To service the master.

She got up from the bed and paced restively around his room. It was so like him: large and all-encompassing, every wall filled with massive furniture, the linens heavy cotton which did not wick away the ever-hovering heat.

Here, Evie had not been instructed to remove the bedclothes, the curtains. Here, in this chamber of lust, there was hardly any need. There was nothing she could conceal from him anyway.

And the windows were open to catch the faintest breeze.

No thoughts of jumping now. No chance of escape. Her lot was cast. She was Court's wife, Court's whore, and excising every debt every hour for the rest of her life.

Still. It was *not* unpleasant, except for this last coupling. And, truth to tell, even that was full of its own explosive excitement. This time, *he* had been out of control. Utterly. And driven still higher by the sight of his golden gift dangling from her nipples.

Even she felt a frisson of arousal when she wore them. There was something very erotic about the contrast of the whisper-thin gold surrounding and containing one of the most sensual parts of her.

Power. Yes. Where she wasn't looking for it. In her breasts. In her nakedness. Between her legs.

There didn't have to be love or affection. Just her sex and how artfully she could arouse him to the madness of wanting her.

Perhaps it would not be such a displeasing way to live.

She had all the tools, she knew some of the tricks. She walked over to the harness and caressed it. Here was an instrument made to drive a man to the edge of his control.

And hadn't she seen that in his eyes before she let her inhibitions squash her confidence?

Yes. And hadn't she been just a little excited to mount the apparatus, knowing how it displayed her body to him?

Yes, yes, she had been. Yes. And where he had thought to use it to conquer her, she had unwittingly used it to seduce him.

She saw that now clearly.

That, and the gold loops. And probably a dozen other little tricks and ploys that smart women knew—or invented.

He had said it from the beginning. He wanted her naked and willing. He had *made* her willing, but now, she was a partner in this complicity of lust.

Now it would become easier and easier, until he tired of her and left her alone.

But until then . . .

Oh, until then—he would give her all the creamy drenching pleasure she could handle . . .

And she—she would make sure she was the most willing woman in the world, and that Court would never ever desire to plant himself or spend himself in anyone else.

There was a soft knock at the door.

"Mistress . . ." Evie's soft voice. "Mistress—" She entered, carrying a tray of covered dishes. "Mistress must eat, keep up your strength."

Drue climbed on the bed. "I will. I'm ravenous."

Evie put the tray down on the bed. "Got biscuits and eggs and grits for the mistress. And strawberry. Coffee. And something else for Mistress."

But Drue had already seen it. An envelope tucked under one of the plates, just the edge visible and just to her.

"What is this?"

"Man come and give to Louisa for the mistress; she give it to me. Don't dare tell Master. Don't know what to do, mistress. This big trouble if Master finds out."

Drue swallowed, hard. "He won't."

"I didn't see anything," Evie whispered. "If something come for the mistress, I didn't give it to her."

"No. You didn't."

Evie nodded; they understood each other. "You eat, mistress. Got to keep yourself fed for the master. He going to want to be with you again."

Yes, he would. And soon. Oh, damn . . .

She managed a wan smile. "I will." She waited until Evie firmly closed the door before she pulled the envelope out from under the plate.

Ripped it open. Unfolded the letter with shaking fingers.

Read:

My dearest, darling Pet . . .

Her heart sank. Her face flushed as she read his importuning words.

Oh, Gerard . . . Oh, my darling Gerard . . . what have I done? What have I done?

Everything. I've done everything to betray him and our love. Oh, God . . .

There is no way, there is no hope.

Darling Gerard . . . it is too late. You can never want me now that I've given myself to him like this . . .

Oh, God, what am I going to do? What am I going to do?

She crumpled the note violently in her hand, and then smoothed it out again.

Go-between. Louisa would be their go-between. She could answer the letter.

But how—with what?

And what if Court found out?

Oh, but she must, she must. It would be cruel for Gerard to live on any kind of hope. Cruel to her as well.

Evie would help her. Evie would provide the pen and paper,

and she would write the note that would destroy his dreams, the note that would finally send Gerard away.

In the end, she couldn't do it. She couldn't find the words. Impossible to find the words as she sat naked in Court's bed not an hour after coupling with him.

And perhaps no answer was the best response of all. Gerard would have to know that he was putting her in an untenable position. She couldn't leave Court. She couldn't run away with him. Those were the impractical dreams of a different lifetime, before the wolf knocked down the door and demanded restitution.

No. Gerard's love was something she would hold in her heart and take out to savor when things became unbearable. Thinking that she could ever marry Gerard had been unrealistic, and the stuff of fantasy.

And it had taken the hardheaded business deal between her father and Court to make her understand that. That was what made her world go around, not chivalry, or romance. Business. Money. Bushels of rice and cotton and the price per pound. And the mistress of gaming who almost won it all.

She must never forget that. Court must get his money's worth, and his pound of flesh. And she knew she had barely begun to discharge the debt.

Dearest Gerard, forgive me ... because I will lay with him *tonight ... and it will destroy me to even think about you—*

"She answer him nothing," Evie said, as she brought him a goblet of wine. "She have nothing to say."

"I see." Court took the crystal goblet in his hand and held it up to the lamplight. The wine was a deep, rich red, and the light played off the facets cut into the bowl. It was the glassware of a wealthy man, someone who could afford the best and who bought the best.

A man who had purchased his wife without a qualm.

He sipped the wine thoughtfully. Lenoir would not give up. He had lost too much, and he was, perhaps, counting on the fact that he, Court, had not shown much feeling for Drue. For all

Lenoir knew, Court had only wanted to get his hands on Oak Bluffs, and Drue was incidental to the deal.

Perhaps that precipitated his rather desperate letter.

No reprisals . . . Lenoir had written. Her father would not suffer, he'd said. In spite of the fact Victor had been on the verge of killing himself over this humiliation.

And Victor had been very clear about it: once the deal was struck, Drue was never to know that it had been Lenoir to whom her father had owed that disgraceful sum of money.

Nor would Lenoir reveal Victor's secret to Drue: it would kill every vestige of her love for him, and expose both Lenoir and Victor's deceits and lies. Neither of them would risk that.

Of such tenuous secrets were alliances made.

Court wondered if Victor even cared anymore. Since the payoff, and the transfer of the title to Oak Bluffs to include Court's name, Victor had been on his best behavior.

But the time was coming when he would start to get the itch, would feel his confidence coming back, would think that just a little roll of the dice couldn't hurt.

All these things, coming to a head, speared by his own lust for Drue, and Lenoir's determination that he could not lose everything altogether.

Well, there were ways to deal with Lenoir, and he wouldn't hesitate to expose all the dirty secrets, no matter what cost to *him,* if Lenoir kept after his wife.

Which was why a man didn't allow himself to get too tangled between a pair of sleek, naked, feminine legs, no matter how seductive they were.

Drue . . .

Instant erection. But what did he expect?

Goddamn . . . goddamn—she didn't answer the letter . . . and he would have bet Oak Bluffs that she would.

He wanted that body, that hot, tight, traitorous body. He sat in his office, his desire a knife edge to his bulging penis and the faint lingering scent of her sex.

He couldn't go another minute without sinking into her. He was horsewhipped and he knew it and he didn't care. Not tonight.

Tonight. He ordered Evie to bring her to him, and to dress her in a particular way.

When she entered, she was perfect, naked but for her head swathed in a dark veil that covered her face and made her seem even more elusive, and the golden loops glittering around her tight, pointed nipples, and the satin bonds around her wrists.

His erection got tighter than a bone, his excitement—and hers—escalating as Evie brought her into the room. "Just fasten her bonds to the hooks on the wall."

Yes, perfect like that, her arms raised, her breasts thrust forward and quivering so the candlelight shimmered on her gold-encased nipples. And her eyes, glittering beneath the mysterious veiling, as if she knew exactly what had been his purpose and his desire.

He dropped his trousers and kicked them away, and let her glimmering gaze rest on the naked pulsating length of him for a long, long time.

It was almost enough, to have her captive and captivated so intensely by his sex. She squirmed at the sight of him, as if his ramrod manhood aroused her beyond control. Her body undulated against the smooth plaster of the wall, her nipples peaking, her every movement calling attention to them and the shimmery gold that was held in place solely by those tight, hard points.

He didn't think he could get any harder, but with every grind of her hips, he felt himself jutting out still further. She was doing everything she could to entice him to rut in her, he could see it in her eyes behind the seductive veiling, but he intended to deny her that pleasure just yet.

Just . . . yet—

Her body shimmied voluptuously against the wall as if *it* were her lover and could give her what she so desperately craved.

Good—here was a hard lesson learned: let her comprehend that nothing could sate that gnawing desire in her but his cock. That his cock owned her and his was the only cock that would ever possess her. And that it was for him to grant the favor of plowing her and not her need to be plowed that determined whether or not he would rut in her.

But God, his penis was hungry for her. And she was panting for him.

But that was the way of treacherous women. They seduced you with their greedy naked bodies and they dreamt of other men.

He stroked his thunderous erection and the movement of his hand jolted her.

"Not tonight, my naked fawn," he murmured.

She made a sound. "I need it . . ."

"Oh, I know. I know how you need it."

"Then . . ."

"We wait. I want you to know exactly how much you need it, and to whom you will crawl."

She licked her lips, and the movement of her tongue arrested him. Yes. Yes. She bit her lower lip, and locked her gaze on his hot, throbbing member, and then moistened her lips again.

His penis flexed, as if he could feel her lips on him.

Power.

She could have all the power in the world over him, even bound and veiled and writhing with unfulfilled desire.

He liked her in restraints. And he liked thinking he had the power.

But he couldn't pull his eyes away from her quivering nipples. He couldn't escape from the musk of her sex permeating the room.

She had never been so wet in her life. Her body felt like pure cream. All she wanted was for him to sink himself into her and lose himself forever

Her nipples felt hard and tight. She could feel the movement of the golden ovals against the curves of her breasts. She threw her head back in an ecstasy of bliss as she deliberately gyrated and shimmied her hips.

"Oh, no, my naked wife. No. Tonight you don't get my sex."

But he was transfixed by her writhing body and her grinding hips, and she understood that here, at last, was the power: in her voluptuously undulating body, in the visible glistening wet between her legs, in his uncontrollable elongating nakedness, she had found the age-old secret to tantalizing and enticing a man's penis.

She didn't need to speak, to protest the obvious untruth. He started to move toward her unwillingly, led by the ferocious desire that was so hot and hard and heavy, he was swollen with it, he was bursting with it.

"Not tonight, wife. No matter what you do."

Closer still he came, huge, rock hard, aching for possession as she enticed the wall behind her with her wanton movements that she knew would finally tempt him beyond redemption.

"Oh, no. I know these games, Drue. You can't have what you want."

She thrust her hips in a seductive beckoning to his throbbing sex.

He brought himself hard up against her pulsating cleft, and she turned her head away to hide triumph as she pushed herself against him and felt him kiss her feminine fold.

He drew in a sharp breath. He had to stay away from her. There was no middle ground here. He must either take her or send her away. He moved away, oblivious to the spurt of cream coating his ridged tip, and she moaned.

"Yes, you liked that. You'll take anything, won't you, Drue. Any penetration to show you have power over *this*." He grasped it and turned back toward her. "Well, my naked puss, you have no power. And if I choose to take you, it won't be because you seduced me or you tempted me, or because I want you. I brought you here for the sole purpose of ramming your naked body into that wall to gratify my lust."

"Then do it," she goaded him.

"You are a willing piece."

"And you're primed to explode," she taunted. "You can't keep your eyes off my nipples, you love my swaying hips. You want what's between my legs, Court. You can't deny it. You know how tight it is, how wet. How hot . . . how much you want it . . ."

"But I'm not going to take it. That's my strength and my power." But he had come closer to her, jutting erotically toward her as if it had a mind of its own; his words roared in his ears. "I'm not going to take it . . ." Closer. "Not, damn you . . ." His penis nudged her, hard, strong, urgent. *"Not . . ."*

He breeched her and she gasped. "Not . . ." Panting now as he shifted himself and drove into her. "Jesus God . . ." Pumped himself into her in a steady rhythm of short, sharp strokes. Pinned her against that wall with his hard piston length, not letting her move, not letting her feel.

But she felt it anyway, the strength and length and purpose of him. And the strength and power of her body—that she could push him to the limits of his control; that she could encompass every hard, naked inch of him so fully and completely; and that the violence of their coupling blasted them into a rocketing culmination of their erotic game.

She melted all over him; his cream saturated her body, her bones. She didn't want to move. He was still rock hard inside her, his chest rough against her cheek, his heart pounding as thunderously as hers.

Oh, did he not want her . . .

She moved languidly against him, loving the feel of him still rubbing between her legs. Words were superfluous. She wanted more and she knew all she needed to do was wriggle herself more tightly against him to provoke him.

She contemplated doing it for several minutes; even the thought of his explosive reaction was pleasurable, let alone the hard thick thrust of him inside her. And he was all there, thick as a tree and rooting between her legs.

How blatant an invitation did he need to take her again?

"So you think you've won," Court murmured. He eased away from her, and she made a protesting sound at the back of her throat. "You want more." He was still as stiff as a poker. "Who doesn't want more . . . ?" He released her hands. "Everyone wants more . . ." He swooped down and lifted her off the floor. ". . . some of us don't get more . . ."

He awkwardly pulled open the door. "Evie . . . !"

She appeared out of nowhere.

"Take the mistress to her room." He set Drue on her feet. "Bathe her. Make sure she rests."

"I don't want to . . ." Drue started to protest, but he had already turned away from her and retreated into the office.

"You come," Evie said to her. "Master knows best."

Drue shot him a look of pure outrage. He closed the door on her.

Not a minute longer with her, or he'd lose his mind altogether. He'd already surrendered his manhood.

Goddamn. He didn't know where he'd gotten the strength to lift her away and get out of her sight.

One more minute, one more sinuous movement, and she would have had him on his knees and wrung him dry.

She'd gotten enough out of him today. More than he'd wanted to give, today.

Goddamn ... goddamn—he could have rutted in her all night—

A glint of light on the floor caught his eye. He bent and picked up one of the thin golden loops she'd worn around her nipple.

He rubbed it between his fingers, feeling himself swelling and thickening still more.

And he was in real trouble if just the thought of her breasts could jack him up like this.

Damn her, damn her, damn her ...

Damn her.

"Master ..."

He pulled himself up groggily. It was morning and he was in his bedroom, but he remembered very little of how he got there.

He thought he had had a glass of wine—or two, or three to quell the gnawing desire, to calm his rampant body.

He shielded his eyes against the incandescent sun. "What is it, Evie?"

"Another note, master. From Louisa, who give it to me."

Shit ... He bolted out of bed and grabbed for his clothes.

"Maybe she find a way to write to him in secret."

He didn't choose to comment on that. "Where's the note?"

"I have it here." She gave him the envelope, but he waited until she'd left the room to open it.

He didn't want to open it.

Who in his house had betrayed him?

He picked up the envelope and removed the note.

My dearest, darling Pet,

Your words do not console me. I must see you. I must hear from your own beautiful lips that you have willingly chosen this course, and you mean to honor your vows to a man who isn't worthy to kiss your feet.

Please, please, please, I beg you—come to me tonight; I will await you in the arbor by the light of the moon. No one will know. She who has delivered this is devoutly to be trusted.

If you come to me tonight, if you tell me face-to-face with your own sweet mouth that we must part, I swear on my life I will bother you no more.

But give me the chance to see you, to hear your lovely voice, to look at you one last time, to claim one last meaningful kiss if that is truly your final, irrevocable decision.

Your beloved,
Gerard

He slammed his fist against the wall.

So—the bastard wants to see her now . . . It's not enough that he makes love to her with his hot-blooded words. It's not enough that he covets another man's wife. No, he must ask for an audience with her as well—

So be it. It is in my power to grant his fondest desire.

And I will finally put an end to his obsession . . .

Chapter 8

He couldn't help himself. He wanted her. In spite of common sense, cool head, male determination, and his fury over her feelings for Gerard, Court wanted her.

And she wasn't so sure about her feelings for Gerard now. Not after these explosively erotic couplings with him.

What was happening to her?

She rolled over in her bed and stared at the morning sun pouring in through the window. The window was open now. The bed had been covered with a crisp cotton sheet. There were curtains on the windows suddenly.

Changes that she hadn't even perceived—or expected. Changes in herself, changes in him. Changes in her wants, her needs, her desires. Her power.

She wanted Court. *He* had changed her, by teaching her to understand the depths of her power.

Thank God she hadn't answered Gerard's letter. What would she have said to him? What *could* she say after yesterday's shamelessly carnal mating with Court?

Her body twinged. Already she wanted more, she was ready for more And to think, this ravenous electric joining with Court would now be the tenor of her life with him.

She shivered with anticipation. *How could she have known?*

She stretched languidly, reveling in the freedom and safety of her naked body. If he came right now, this minute, she would spread her legs for him willingly.

She drew a deep hissing breath. *Let him come.* Now.

She reached across the bed for the veiling that had shrouded her head and draped it across her breasts. Her nipples protruded, erotic and mesmerizing against the black veil.

And bare. She bolted upright. The golden loops! They were gone—oh, Lord . . . they were gone!

Noooo . . . She scrambled around on the bed frantically. *Not on the bed.*

But had she even been wearing them when she came upstairs last night? *Oh, God, I can't remember . . .*

She'd worn them last night. Yes . . . she remembered exactly the feel of them on her nipples as she'd done her erotic little dance to entice him.

So then . . . when? That thrilling moment when he had picked her up? The unbelievably disappointing moment when he set her down?

She got down on the floor and crawled around. Nothing, nothing, nothing. Not even dust, a testament to Evie's housekeeping skills.

... where? ... She *needed* those loops, she loved them ...
... wait—there by the door ...
... only one—

She picked it up and held it to the light. It was so light, so thin, malleable ... *malleable*—

Could be squeezed and tightened ...

The way her body was squeezing and tightening at the thought of it.

What an unbelievably voluptuous little thing.

And even more erotic just adorning one nipple.

She stared at herself in the mirror, cupping the one breast, trying to see what *he* saw, to imagine the carnal impulse *he* felt looking at her.

The bedroom door opened behind her.

Oh, yes—my fantasy—

But it wasn't fantasy: he was there, bare-chested, his trousers just barely hanging on his hips, the bulge of his sex contained ... for the moment.

She held her breath as he cat-footed his way behind her, close, hot, a breath away, his arm coming around her, his fingers dangling the missing golden loop.

She dropped her hand. She couldn't breathe. She felt him taking her hands and loosely binding them. She didn't care.

She arched her back against him as he began caressing her bare nipple. As he dropped the golden loop over the hard point and then gently squeezed.

A thousand darts of pleasure assaulted her body, enhanced by her sense of being held captive. She caved against him as his fingers kept up the inexorable pressure and he took the other nipple in his hand.

Both now, both tender, hard points compressed by his fingers until she was squirming for mercy. Her buttocks writhed against the hard ridge of his penis, as if she were both trying to elude his relentless touch and begging for more.

He wouldn't let her go; her nipples were so hard, so pliable, so lusciously erotic, two voluptuous pleasure points that were his to do with as he desired. His to adorn, to play with, to stroke, to squeeze, to drive her to the explosive edge of frenzy.

Never to stop; always his: his wife, his pleasure, his power, as he kept up a consistent erotic pressure on her nipples.

She had to get away. She would crack wide open if he didn't let her go. She kept backing against his hips, pressing and seeking the throbbing rock-hard bulge of him, wanting to settle herself against it and crash to the shore.

She was breathless with the sensation of it. It was unspeakable, indescribable, and heightened by the reality of the image of her watching him, watching the unrelenting press of his fingers on her nipples, watching her body's voluptuous undulations, and the way she arched herself forward and mutely begged for more.

She was an utter wanton in his hands. She could not stop him; she didn't want to. She could have loosened the bonds in a moment, and she didn't.

She was, in her fantasy, a slave to the inescapable pressure of his fingers on her nipples. And she would not plead for mercy until he had wrung the last drop of pleasure from her rippling body.

She craved more and still more of his ruthless touch. She felt it swelling up in her, billowing, gathering, comingling with the twisty feeling spiraling from her breasts.

She was breathless with it; she felt the sensations collide, implode, and shoot between her legs like a rocket.

She bent double with it as it burst all over her body, and he followed her down, down, down, his fingers unyielding on her nipples, and her hands grasping his penis convulsively as she slipped to the floor.

"No, no, no . . ." she moaned. "No more, no . . . oh, God— oh . . . oh—no more, please, no more—"

He couldn't stand to let her go, but he heard the raw edge in her voice, and reluctantly, slowly, he removed his fingers from her breasts and pulled her roughly against him.

She felt his fingers fumbling with the restraint, and then a gentle caress as he removed the golden loops from her breasts as well.

She felt mindless, floating—maybe she was: he lifted her easily to the bed and then he placed the golden loops on the bedside table; and without saying a word, he left her.

Evie was waiting outside the door, a tray in her hand.

"She is mine," he said roughly. "Serve her. *I'll* see where she goes."

The second note came with her breakfast not minutes after Court exited the room.

Dear God—she hadn't any time to luxuriate, to think, to plan . . .

My dearest, darling Pet . . .

Oh, God, how could he? Why couldn't he have just understood by her not responding to his previous note that they could never have a future together?

And now—oh, now—he wanted her to *meet* him?

Of course he didn't know that she had no clothes, that Court was keeping her a sexual captive, that today she had totally become his carnal slave.

This was impossible!

Court should see him; Court should be the one to tell him . . .

Tell him what? Tell him about all the games they had played? About the thrall collar and the harness and the restraints. And how willing, how wanton she was—*really?*

And how all thoughts of Gerard had evaporated once she had experienced the voluptuous satiation of his masterful coupling with her?

And to top it off, she thought mordantly, Court could reveal the secret of her lusty nipples, and how she exploded with pleasure when he squeezed them while she watched him play with her in the mirror.

Yes, Gerard would love knowing about all these things he could never have. She had been a fool to encourage him in the first place. Ever—when she had known that her father's folly would be the deciding factor of who she would marry.

What am I going to do? What? How could he do this to me? Why couldn't he have just gone away?

Why? Why! Because four days ago, you still loved him. Four days ago, Court had not adorned your nipples with gold. Four days ago, you knew nothing about the whims, the power, and the carnality of men.

And now you know . . . and you've chosen, and you must be fair and tell Gerard face-to-face, just as he entreats you to.

How? Wearing what? My thrall collar . . . ? My golden loops around my nipples . . . ?

She couldn't bear to sit still. She paced around the room agitatedly, trying to make some sense of things, trying to figure out a way to avoid it altogether.

Gerard wanted to meet with her tonight. He wanted to hear from her own lips that she wanted him no more—*tonight.*

Which meant that somehow she had to find a wrapper or dress to cover her nakedness and sneak down to the arbor after the moon rose.

Elude Court—at night—when every carnal impulse was in play . . . including her own . . . ?

The gods were crazy; there was no way she could accomplish it.

Even if Evie were to help her.

She had to get rid of Gerard. He was perfectly capable of continuing his onslaught of notes and pleas. And always in his gentle, but determined way. He'd never stop, if *she* did not put a stop to it.

And, in fact, it was entirely possible that he would continue to hang around, hoping against hope that she would leave Court.

But that was impossible now. Not after tonight. Not after the ferocious pleasure she had experienced at his hands.

She would meet Gerard—somehow—

She pulled open the armoire door and almost fell forward in her astonishment. *Changes.* There were dresses hanging in the armoire.

She didn't even know if she remembered how to wear one.

She would wear one tonight. Just for a few short moments, tonight. And then she'd never have to get dressed ever again.

Midnight. The house was quiet, too quiet, she thought; Court had been gone all day, conferring with his overseer at Oak Bluffs.

It was time to get back to business, he'd said, and maybe she was glad, at least today, that he felt that way.

He'd be staying overnight, Evie told her. And maybe that was a good thing, because she needed that time; she had to make Gerard understand: she belonged to Court, and she wanted everything Court chose to give her.

She wondered to what extreme she would have to go to convince Gerard of that. He was not a man who was easily brushed off. He had been very persistent in his wooing of her, and now, in his pursuit, in spite of the fact that she was married.

She might well have to use every weapon at hand: the way she dressed, what she said, and how much she would admit about how far she had gone . . .

How far . . .

The thrall collar hung on a hook in the armoire. She took it down thoughtfully. *Too far?*

She stepped through the straps and pulled them up slowly. Under the right dress, it wouldn't show. And it would keep her on course, reminding her that Court owned her body, and that she was his *willing* sexual slave.

She fastened the collar around her throat, her heart pounding with a kind of heady fusion of fear and arousal.

She found a muslin dress with a high pleated collar and short, puffed sleeves that she could wear with one crinoline. The skirt looked deflated, and the hem dragged on the ground, but that was of small consequence to the purpose. It concealed the collar and her rising excitement. She wore nothing else beneath the dress but a pair of kid boots that would do for a moonlight walk, and she was ready.

And she was hot, suffocating with the brazenness of what she was about to do. Thank God Court wasn't home.

This was so risky. Court would kill her if he found out. He'd kill Gerard.

Stupid. She shouldn't even go.

Let Gerard hang. If she didn't show up, he would have to understand that this was the end of their . . . friendship.

Or maybe he wouldn't. He didn't read her lack of response correctly the first time.

Oh, damn, oh, damn. She didn't want to ever see Gerard Lenoir again.

What would it take? An investment of twenty minutes, perhaps, to tell him clearly that he could not entertain any fantasy that she would leave Court and come to him.

Twenty minutes, maybe less, to impart her message to Gerard and get back to the house. Court would never have to know. *But only . . . if . . . she left . . .*

. . . now . . .

The moon, so bright it was as though she were carrying a torch, lighted her way through the trees, down the rear carriage drive, past the *garçonnière,* the smokehouse, the kitchen, and the vegetable gardens, every path carefully laid out as if someone had planned for lovers to trod this way.

No, not lovers. They'd never been lovers, she and Gerard. They'd been dreamers. And every conversation, every plan they formulated had been the insupportable fantasy of two lonely souls looking for escape.

That was the unpalatable reality she had to tell him, along with the fact that she reveled in her death-do-us-part coupling with the domineering and possessive Court Summerville.

Hard truths he would not want to hear.

But he had promised, if she met him, he would go away.

Her heart started pounding as she skirted the vegetable gardens and paused at the entrance to the arbor. It was laid out between the gardens and the stables and there were a half dozen paths to enter it on three sides, and it was so dark within, the moonlight just filtering through the vines.

Somewhere in there, Gerard waited.

She called to him softly; there was only a thick silence and the hoot of an owl in response.

This is too stupid. He's not here. He's playing a stupid game. He didn't come. I hope he didn't come. I pray he didn't come . . .

Something grabbed her and she shrieked; a hand clamped over her mouth and a hard male body pulled her under the cover and fecund smell of the leaves and vines.

"Shhh . . ."

Gerard . . . ! Damn! Her heart was pounding so hard, she thought she would die.

He spoke in a whisper, hissing in her ear, "Can I let you go?" She nodded, and he relinquished his grip on her mouth.

"You came."

"Let go of me."

"I can't. I *can't,* God help me," he breathed, and she felt, in the weight of his arm around her midriff, the weight of his suppressed passion. And she didn't know how she was going to manage him.

"You have to," she hissed. "I belong to Court now. It's irrevocable. I can't change it. And listen to me, Gerard—*I don't want to.*"

He ignored her. She couldn't believe it. He just chose not to hear the words with which she committed herself to Court.

"My darling, you can change it. You can change anything. Remember what we said, what we promised. It's not too late—"

"But it is. It's too late, Gerard."

He stiffened. "What do you mean?"

"I mean what you think I mean."

His arm loosened. "No. No. You promised he would never lay a hand on you."

Time for the lies. "I didn't know how little choice a woman had."

"He forced you." Gerard moved away from her. "I'll kill him." *Now for the truth.* "He didn't."

He wheeled on her, and she was glad she couldn't see his face. "I'll kill you. I won't let him have you."

"It's too late." She moved closer to him, in a combative stance.

He didn't want to hear her. He took a step back. "All right, all right."

"He took me," she said inexorably. "He took away my clothes; he forced me to be naked. And then he did things to my naked body that I liked. That I begged him to do . . ."

"No!" She could feel the force of his fury. He had lost her, lost control. Gerard did not like anything to be out of his control, especially her.

So much like Court. She'd never considered the similarities before.

"No. No. No." As if his denial would make it true. "You didn't. You . . . didn't—you couldn't . . . Let's say . . . let's . . . just say there were circumstances over which you had no control. Let's say his baser nature got the better of him—"

Push him to the edge . . . "Or mine," she whispered.

Explosive now; he radiated pure volcanic rage as he grasped her with a violence he could barely contain and shook her.

"Or yours . . ." he ground out. "You could have been *mine . . .*"

"I belong to him. He bought me, remember? He paid for anything he did to me . . ."

"Noooooo . . . o-o-o-o-o . . ." he moaned, and she went on relentlessly, "And I let him, Gerard. After the first penetration, I begged him to. I spread my legs for him willingly. I wear his thrall collar. I let him restrain me so he can do whatever he wants to me."

"You bitch, you bitch, you bitch . . . You swore you'd save it for me . . ."

"I didn't," she said brutally. "It wasn't real, what we said, what we thought we had. But he's a *real* man. And I want what he has between *his* legs."

"Bitchbitchbitchbitch . . . I could have taken you at any time . . . I could have forced you . . . I could take you now . . ."

"Keep your promise, Gerard . . . kiss me good-bye and leave me, as you swore in your note."

"Ohhho, I'll kiss you, you bitch. I'll kill you before I let him fuck you again . . ."

He grabbed her and forced his mouth on hers, his body against hers.

He was wet, hard, furious, powerful.

He was not Court.

She went limp in his arms and prepared for the worst.

In the shadows just beyond the arbor, he stood and watched. He heard the voices, heated with passion, though he could not make out distinctly what they said.

It didn't matter. What mattered was what he knew: that all

the sexual heat and pleasure in the world could not keep his wife from her former lover.

He didn't think she would want to leave him, even for Lenoir. She had it too good. He'd made a huge mistake there, giving in to her body, giving her all the sex she could handle.

Hell. She could probably do them both: Lenoir at midnight in the arbor, and him whenever he wanted during the day.

Those voices were so passionate. They were arguing about the circumstances. Lenoir probably still wanted her to go. She wanted him to stay. She wanted them both and she was probably trying to reason with him, to tell him she had enough juice for them both. All Lenoir had to do was agree to her terms.

By God . . . nobody knew better than *he* what a bitch in bed she was: hadn't he already fucked her nipples to a paralyzing orgasm, and here she was, not eight hours later, in heat for another man?

Over his dead body.

Over Lenoir's.

If that bastard touched her . . . if he tried to penetrate her—

He watched as Lenoir grabbed her and she came willingly into his arms and reached for his hot kisses . . . watched her body undulate against Lenoir's, seeking his heat, his hardness . . .

Goddamned trollop . . . he should have known the minute she'd agreed to the marriage. She could be bought. She knew what she had: virginity and the hottest naked body in Louisiana— and he would bet Lenoir had known that all along.

Damn her to hell . . . the bitch . . . damn her to goddamned hell—

He wheeled away from the ugly scene and lifted his arm.

It was time to end the farce.

She couldn't stand him, his touch, his kisses, the feel of his body pressing against her.

His rage made him strong, his passion drove him. He grasped the collar of her dress and ripped it away from her neck and down to her breasts. "You bitch, you bitch—"

He reached for her throat. "Jesus shit . . . what's this?"

"I have to wear it, every day, everywhere," she whispered. "He made me, but now. . . now I revel in it. He owns me . . ."

He howled—it was the only word for it, and he wrenched the material of her dress all the way down to the hem . . .

And a shot rang out.

He froze. "I could kill you . . ."

"Don't move . . ."

A new voice—her *father's* voice.

"Pull up your dress, you little tart."

Drue hurriedly gathered the folds of material to her breast as her father appeared at the opposite end of the arbor.

"How cozy," he said. "You and Lenoir forever, eh, Drue."

"No," she protested. "No."

"Looks like it to me. Court's home, by the way. Got done with business *real* early."

Drue's heart dropped to her stomach. "What are *you* doing here?"

"I want to get rid of a pestilence that could ruin my garden."

"Go to hell," Gerard growled.

"I think you're there already," Victor said. "You got your money. Get the hell out of town. Drue . . ."

That registered. "What do you mean, he got his money?" she asked, turning toward Victor.

"Let me have the pleasure of telling her, Victor. Seeing as how we're airing all our dirty secrets tonight," Gerard said nastily. "Or do you still not want her to know?"

Oh, God . . . no . . . what? She waited. But her father didn't seem discommoded. Whatever Gerard was talking about, it couldn't hurt Victor anymore.

Or her.

"Tell her," Victor said.

"I was the one to whom your father owed all that money," Gerard said maliciously. "Me. *Not* Summerville."

"WHAT!!!????" Her whole world tilted. Everything went crazy, spun upside down.

"Not Court," Victor amplified. *"This* piece of dung, who planned the whole scheme: get me in enough debt and I would turn you and Oak Bluffs over to him."

"No! No . . ." She shook her head as she backed away—from her father and his perfidious lies, from Gerard and his heinous plans.

"Summerville saved your ass," Gerard said.

"And kicked yours all to hell," Victor interpolated smugly. "Killed your plans. Destroyed everything you worked for. Got the girl and the plantation, too. Couldn't have asked for a happier ending."

"Until you get your hands on the cards again," Gerard spat. "Until the idea of fast money lures you out of hiding and Lady Luck seduces you all over again. And she will, because you, my friend, are a goddamned sucker."

Omigod, omigod, omigod . . . Gerard her father's debtor. Not Court. Not Court. Court didn't buy her. Court saved her. Saved her father, saved Oak Bluffs . . .

Omigod . . .

She backed out of the arbor blindly. *Omigod . . .*

And what if Court had been listening—had been watching . . . ?
Omigod . . .

She couldn't get away fast enough. And she couldn't get out of earshot, either.

Her father was determined to enrage him; crazy, when Gerard had lost everything. Gerard would kill him.

She didn't care. She didn't care. Her father had just lost her, too.

"No," Victor taunted. "You're the dupe, believing I would let you come within inches of Drue, would let you step one foot on . Oak Bluffs. You gull. You butt. You goat."

"You son of a bitch—!" Gerard roared.

"You bastard—" Victor goaded, his voice taut, controlled.

She heard a scuffling, a thump, as if Gerard catapulted himself at her father. And then a shot into the echoing silence that reverberated all over Wildwood.

All inside her.

Father— Tears streamed down her face. She didn't care, she didn't. The betrayals were too crippling.

She didn't want to see. She didn't want to know.

She hoped they'd killed each other.

Father . . .

Pulling the shreds of her dress around her, she turned and ran.

Chapter 9

Court had removed himself from her completely. She hadn't seen him for days after the incident in the arbor and she was feeling very irritable.

At first, she hadn't wanted to see him, not after that night. Not after her father had wounded Gerard so seriously. He lay recuperating even now in the surgery of a Dr. Boulois of St. Faubonne, and according to her father, he and Court had exacted a promise from Gerard that he would leave St. Faubonne Parish and relinquish any idea of contacting *her* again.

"Oh, he will run his little businesses in New Orleans," her father told her a week later, coming to visit when he was certain her anger had died and that she would forgive him. "And he will find eventually another wealthy dupe, another innocent girl, you can be sure of that."

She wasn't quite in the mood to forgive. She felt ill-used, as if she had been nothing more than a puppet, caught between her father's cupidity and Court's avarice.

Nor did she like her father's assessment that reduced her feelings for Gerard to those of a raw, simple-minded, green girl.

"You *knew* how much I cared for him . . ." she said testily.

"Exactly," Victor said. "I owed him so much money; I was sure you would marry him just to cancel the debt, but I could *not* have that upstart *parvenu* in possession of property that has been in my family for generations."

"So you sold me to Court," Drue interpolated, unable to keep the bitterness out of her voice. "He's probably the only one in the whole of St. Faubonne who could afford you—*and* me."

"It's an excellent match, my dear. I knew what I was doing," Victor said breezily.

"I wish you had told me," Drue grumbled, but in point of fact he had: *She'd be taken care of, he'd said of one of the advantages of her marriage to Court, and he had been so right. He had no idea how right.*

"You were in love with that bastard," Victor went on. "You would have defended him to the death—*and* married him to spite me."

She clenched her fists. She probably would have. She probably wouldn't have seen the vast, eager scheme behind Gerard's sensual seduction of her. She certainly wouldn't have believed her father's interpretation of it.

And so Court became the villain.

And Gerard had been so enraged, he probably would have done anything to dishonor Court—if *she* had been willing.

Willing. The key, the prime word. Willing. There had never been a woman so willing as she, once she comprehended the depths of her body as an instrument of pleasure.

The real point was, Court had read *both* of Gerard's notes. Court had been in the arbor, listening, watching. Assuming.

"And that beast did try to kiss you—" Victor added somewhat righteously.

And then getting her father to do his dirty work. "So you tried to kill *him*—thus the code of honor has been satisfied," Drue finished caustically. "And it doesn't give you one moment of pain that you allowed Gerard to get such a hold over you?"

"Oh, no . . . never think that. I was in absolute turmoil before Court agreed to marry you. It was the most humiliating thing, the deepest secret. And I let Gerard believe until the very last that a deal for Oak Bluffs was possible. I thought that was clever, actually. That way, Gerard had good reason not to expose my depravity. And after it was over, he still didn't want to lose you. Of course, down the line, he might well have used the fact that he had held my notes to hurt you and Court, but to what harm, after he had been paid off? The marriage was irrevocable, and the best he could hope for was that you still loved him and might consider running away.

"But I never thought you'd do that. Too much was at stake.

So it was just a matter of time until it was completely over, and it happened sooner than I ever thought, I'll tell you."

He was as smooth as glass, her father: everything slipped off him. Gerard was right, she thought. The cards *would* get him again, and nothing, not even the possible loss of Oak Bluffs, would stop him because he had the ability to slough off what was distasteful, and focus on the pleasurable.

And what was more pleasurable than seeing his daughter married, a dynasty created, his enemy vanquished, his coffers full of money and his plantation out of debt?

For the moment.

"So you see, my dear, everything worked out just fine," he said, as he took his leave of her.

For you, she thought. *Always for him. Even when he lost, he won. And he always had someone to clean up after him.*

Her. Court.

But what had Court gained? A reluctant wife whom he'd taken on at the cost of doing business with her father, even knowing that her heart belonged to another man.

And who believed it still, in spite of all evidence to the contrary. He might never again come to her, and she felt the thought of that as keenly as the cut of a blade.

No. She wasn't going to let that happen.

How did her father do it? *Even when he lost, he won.*

Was she not her father's daughter?

She hadn't lost yet—she was going to be married to Court forever.

She had all the time in the world.

But Court didn't make it easy. He spent all of the succeeding week at Oak Bluffs, and the nights at the St. Faubonne planter's hotel, and she knew immediately that winning him was going to take some drastic measures.

Besides, she was getting more than a little annoyed that he was avoiding her.

She needed a plan. She couldn't just continue to walk around Wildwood naked when he was already exercising that monumental control of his to shut her out.

Her nudity would not seduce him now. He was too angry to allow himself to want her.

She had to conquer *him*.

And she liked that idea. It all came down to the power and control that seesawed between them.

But she was going to win now. She was going to go after him aggressively. She would be mysterious and elusive—forget all that business about his conditions and his rules. She wasn't going to do anything he wanted her to do.

Irresistible.

Scary.

What if—? But she wouldn't think about that.

Very soon he would start spending his nights at home, and then the games could begin . . .

Slowly, at first . . .

He didn't give an inch.

One had to have the patience of a saint—

Until the night, five days later, she heard him climbing wearily up the steps.

It was late, late, late, surely well past midnight. The heat was, as usual, oppressive, the darkness formidable.

She had been waiting so long. She had prepared so well. But she had to be sure he was sound asleep.

She waited. A half hour later, dressed in a thin muslin nightgown and carrying a candlestick, she slipped into the hallway and listened at his bedroom door.

No sound. No motion.

She eased open the door and, shielding the candle, she crept inside.

He lay sprawled on the massive bed, as if he had just dropped his clothes and fell onto the mattress naked. His breathing was deep, regular, the sleep of someone who was exhausted.

The heavy sleep of someone who might have an involuntary erotic dream. Especially someone who didn't hesitate to employ a sexual apparatus that was still suspended in the shadows.

That was a good sign, that he hadn't yet taken it down.

She set the candlestick down in the fireplace cavity so that its glow was muted, and approached the bed, unsure just yet what she would do.

She wanted to touch him everywhere. His body was so smooth in some places, and yet so rough with hair elsewhere, she just wanted to slide her hands all over him and feel the heat and texture of him.

She wanted to wake him, and mount the harness, and entice him to copulate with her. Her body swelled with anticipation. She wondered how she could wait.

She had worn a satin sash around her nightgown. She untied it and wound it around her hand. There—six inches of silk to stimulate his insensate body. Beginning at his feet, working her way up his thighs, his tight buttocks, the intriguing crease, across his narrow waist, up his spine, tantalizing his neck, his ear, his mouth; watching him writhe as his body responded, shifting slightly to get away from the insistent tickling movement of the silk.

Lovely, lovely to have him in her control, to see his hips press mightily into the mattress as he began to become aroused.

Elusive . . . She trailed the silk over his buttocks again, swirling it all around, and then down his legs and finally, regretfully, away as he began stirring, dousing the candle quickly, and slithering from the room, leaving him groggy, erect, and just barely aware of the faint scent of smoke and sin.

That was the first step. The second night was even trickier. She wore an old corset that she had refurbished. She had dyed it black and hand-sewn jet beads all over the bosom. It was cut just low enough so that she could bare her breasts if she wished, and it cinched her midriff so tightly it made her hips seem more rounded and voluptuous.

Not that she was planning for him to *see* her.

No, her plans were bound up in something different. Like immobilizing him.

Tricky.

She waited until there was the deepest silence permeating the house. Until the clock in the parlor struck one-thirty.

Again, she took the candle and placed it in the fireplace so that the light was diffused.

He was stretched out naked, this time on his back.

Perfect. She spent a full five minutes just looking at him. God, he was beautiful, even in repose.

But she had no time to waste looking at him.

The next part was the tricky part: lifting each of his arms and placing a satin restraint under it; then lightly forming the knot on each; and finally, pulling one so that she could tie the ends around his bedpost—at which point he would stir, which meant she had to be quick and clever to get to his other arm before he fully awakened.

She was so gentle. Her fingers were like a whisper against his skin. She pulled slowly and finely on his left arm with all the finesse she could manage, until she got it up over his head; and then she tied the satin bonds to the post.

And indeed, as she surmised, he started to stir; she darted to the other side of the bed and grabbed the second satin tie quickly and yanked it and his arm toward the bedpost and knotted it.

"What the hell—!" He pulled against the restraints, and then heaved his body upward in a massive effort to loosen the knots.

Drue stood at the foot of the bed, enjoying the sight of his bucking body. She wanted to ride those hips. She wanted to slide her hands around his secret places and explore them all.

She climbed onto the bed and straddled his legs.

Instantly he stiffened—all of him. Every inch of him as he felt her press her feminine pelt tightly against his thighs.

"Get off me."

She had decided beforehand that actions were more potent than words. His body was hers now to do with as she pleased, since he wasn't willing to take hers.

"Bitch."

She stroked his belly.

"Don't *touch* me—" He bucked again, and she tumbled off him.

Maybe that was a good thing. There was a wealth of male secrets to be explored around his root and between his legs.

She inserted her fingers there purposefully, and he recoiled.

He liked that.

Good.

She probed further, and found a particularly interesting fleshy place beneath his scrotum; a dark, hidden *male* place. She stroked it purposefully and his body jerked involuntarily.

"Don't do that—!"

She cupped the taut sacs in her palm and continued the rhythmic stroking of her fingers against that hairy, fleshy patch of skin. His penis rose majestically before her.

Some part of him just adored what she was doing.

"Shit . . . !!!" He pulled and twisted at his bonds, his body jolting again as she kept up her insistent examination of that most private place.

"Damn you, damn you, damn you—"

"Ummm . . ." She pushed him onto his knees. This was an intractable man who needed to be shown who was his master.

She reached for his jutting penis with her free hand. Her breath caught: she had never touched him there before. Had never contained him with her hands. Had never felt the heat and length of him, never understood before that the power of him was pure flesh and blood and muscle.

"Just what I want," she growled, and surrounded him, and it seemed as natural as light for her to hold him, and instinctive as air that she begin to pump him firmly, tightly, purposefully.

"No. No. No . . . *NO!*"

"Yessss," she breathed. He was amazing, all length and strength and heat and muscle and pure pounding erotic fury. He couldn't stop her; she knew he saw she was that determined, so he was going to use her. She could feel all that rage concentrated in her hand, could feel the moment he turned himself over to her and challenged her to wring him dry.

"Ahhh . . ."

That monstrous power of his will—that was his strength: that he would not give in to her easily. That she would have to work for her triumph, and his culmination, and from the most awkward position.

But she didn't care; she still held him in that hidden male place that drove him so wild, and now, in her hand, she held the focus of all that fulminating male power.

It was heady, luscious, erotic. He could only hold on for so long, and then she would have him utterly in her power and she would squeeze every drop of his cream from his body and revel in his torment.

She felt his every muscle flex and tense with his determination not to cave in.

But a man's penis could only take so much; this she was to learn. And that if she concentrated her efforts on the sensitive ridge, she could bring him to the edge. How far was it, then, to pull him over?

He resisted. She pushed harder; she wanted nothing less than Court's utter capitulation to her. And she would fracture herself trying.

She felt the very moment the power shifted into her hand; it was in the way his body tensed, shifted, braced—little subtle signs—over and above something about the way he felt in her hand: stiff and pliant and ready to blow.

And then, with one involuntary heave of his hips, he erupted, spewing like a volcano, covering everything with the thick cream of his release until he collapsed mindlessly into her power, into her hand.

She held him. She watched him. He wouldn't look at her.

The hell with him. No one else could give him such an explosive completion. She knew it in her soul.

He had better stop ignoring her . . . or she would keep him in restraints forever.

Lovely idea . . .

She wriggled her fingers between his legs. Yes, he reacted, and tried to hide it as well.

"You don't understand, Court. This is my will, my game. You do what I want."

"Not a chance in hell."

"Well then—I guess we'll see," she purred. "The night is young. Your body's hot. I can go as long as you can."

"I'm going nowhere with you."

She smiled that knowing smile he was beginning to dislike. "I think your penis disagrees with you." She stroked it gently. "I think I'm going to tease it for a while. Make it hungry. Make it hard for me."

"It gets hard for any naked woman," he retorted.

"I think I'll tie it up and make it mine," she murmured, ignoring his nasty tone. She had come prepared for this too, concealing in the corset between her breasts both her golden loops and the satin sash.

She fished out the sash and pulled it meaningfully around and under his thighs and between his legs, and then she looped it purposefully around his scrotum and wound it back up around his penis.

"You wouldn't—"

"Yes, I would . . ." She tied the ends together so that his scrotum was lightly bound against his root. "Oh, that's good. And look at how much you want it . . . you're stiff as a poker already."

And feisty as a boxer, wrestling with his bonds, cursing her under his breath, transfixed by the coil of satin she wound around him. The bigger he got, the tighter the sash pulled against his scrotum, and the hotter and more aroused he got.

"I like that," she sighed. "All tied up. All mine. Now. One more thing." She pulled out the golden loops as she eyed the nubs of his male nipples in their wiry nest of chest hair. Always hard, always there. The loops would fit over them perfectly, she thought.

Everything perfect: everything in her control.

Not that he liked the idea of it. He bucked and heaved as he realized her intention, and he tried hard to twist away from her as she bent over him and she stroked his nipples.

Another secret male place . . . lovely—just . . . deliciously lovely . . .

"Hold still now," she murmured, and slipped the golden loops first over one nipple and then the other. "Made for you, Court."

"Goddamn it—!" He felt trussed and tied and decked out like some top-over-tail turkey; but if he were uncomfortable, his penis wasn't: it poked up, a towering wall of granite flesh, waiting for her to humiliate and excite him still more, and he hated the fact that all her tender mercies could whip him up to such a peak of arousal.

"Bitch. When I get my hands on you . . ." he muttered, jerking his arms this way and that, his throbbing sex always in his line of sight, and the awareness of the whisper-soft loops surrounding his nipples ever present in his imagination. "Goddamn . . . god-damn . . . goddamn—"

"No talking," she commanded, running her hands up his thighs, around his scrotum, and between his legs. "Oh, this is nice. Very nice . . . Why don't you just spread your legs . . . ?"

"The hell I will—"

"—or—I'll spread them for you," she finished sweetly. "You do understand . . . it's *always* better to give me what I want. There—" She caressed him. "And there . . . I like that spot—and look . . . your scrotum is so tight—"

He made a growling noise in the back of his throat.

"Oh, yes, I can see you're ready for me, Court. But I'm not nearly ready for you." But she knew she was; she knew her body was so wet for him that she could just sink herself onto his shaft and swallow him whole.

But the anticipation was sweet. And all the control in her hands. And his trussed-up body. And his bound-up penis begging for release. All hers, waiting on her need, her desire. Her time.

That was power.

The next thing she wanted to exact from him was the promise.

She moved away from him and contemplated the harness. Such a lovely piece of equipment, perfectly pitched to present a woman's body for penetration.

She quivered, remembering it, visualizing how he probed her and pushed her, slowly, carefully, inch by sensual inch.

What would it be like for a man to be splayed between those hoops?

She shuddered, an image of him positioned just so flashing through her mind. She wanted it. She wanted everything, and there was so much to be explored, so many answers she didn't yet know.

She turned back to him and caught him off guard, his gaze transfixed by the cushion of her bare buttocks.

He wasn't nearly that furious with her, she thought. Not nearly. He wanted what she wanted: the edgy arousal, the erotic games, and the explosive coupling of their naked bodies for the utmost pleasure.

And if it meant wearing his thrall collar, she was willing. If it meant complete submission to his whims, his desires, she was willing. If it meant living naked with him and spreading her legs for him at his demand, she was willing.

But only, only, only if she could have these luscious, powerful moments with him when she could be completely in command.

She started unhooking her corset as she walked slowly to the bed. She draped it over his penis as she climbed on top of him.

"I always wanted to do this," she sighed as she bent over him and brushed his hard right nipple with hers.

His reaction was swift and hard—he jammed himself up as sensation spiraled down toward his groin.

"*Jesus . . .*"

"Ummm." She rubbed his other nipple with hers, and she, too, felt it again, that curling sensation of pleasure that flowed like silk through her veins and precipitated that galvanic reaction in him.

He pulled frantically at his restraints. "Untie me, Drue."

"I don't think so. This is too much fun."

"I'll give you what you want."

"Ha." She brushed her nipples against his hairy chest, and moved downward and downward until she butted up against his satin-robed penis. "That's what you say today."

Carefully, she turned herself around so that she could envelop his penis with her breasts and all he could see of her was her rounded bottom.

But he could feel the heat and softness of her breasts surrounding his length even through the thin satin. Her nipples pressing into his thighs. Her hands, stroking him purposefully between his legs.

She liked that secret place just a little too much, he thought, his nerve endings tight with frustration.

Too much power in her hands, he thought, and his body convulsed.

This is the last time . . . he swore. *The last time she'd ever get the upper hand. He'd keep that bitch naked and contained from now on. He'd teach her what her place was and he'd make her stay there, even if he had to . . .*

What was *he thinking? He was thinking like a man who was besotted with a woman. Damn her . . . He didn't give a good goddamn about her. She was part of a business deal, there for his convenience, his use, his possession.*

Shit—

. . . what was she doing?!!

She'd wriggled her way down onto him so that her body was stretched flat and her feminine vee was almost within tonguing distance of his mouth.

And she was playing with him.

She'd unsheathed the satin hood from the tip of his member and she was twirling her finger lightly around the ridge at the tip.

Never again, he thought, gritting his teeth and girding his hips against the swirling sensations. *I'll tie her to the bed before she ever gets me in a position like this again. If I have to stay awake for the rest of my life, I'll teach this bitch who is her master and just what she's good for—*

But she knew that already; she had his body knotted up with lust, surging toward culmination.

"Let me give you what you want, Drue."

"No," she said dreamily, "that's too easy."

"Anything you want, any way you want it."

"Oh, promises . . ." she murmured, caressing him at the very tip with her very hot wet tongue. "You say one thing today, and tomorrow—it's gone . . . This is nice, though . . ." She folded that tip between her lips and pressed on it gently, meaningfully.

He rocketed off the bed. She could have him now—she knew it and he knew it; he was tight as a drum and ready to explode.

"You win, damn it. What are your terms?" he demanded hoarsely.

"Oh?" she cooed. "Oh. The terms. The conditions. Those." She compressed her lips again and he shuddered. It was too much, and she knew it, and that he did not want to blow. He was about ten seconds away from it, and using every ounce of control to keep himself contained while he waited to hear her everlasting *conditions.*

"Ummmm . . . Oh, let me see, my rutting stag. Conditions. You will never, *ever* hide your naked body from me . . . *ever* . . ." she cautioned throatily. "And—you will never deny me anything I demand—in our bedroom."

She swirled her tongue around him again. "You are a body to service *me,* my stag. Do you think you're up to it?"

"Untie me, and you'll find out."

"Delicious idea," she sighed and covered him with her mouth again.

"Now, Drue."

"Oh—there was one thing about those conditions . . ."

"Why . . ."—his body jolted as she sucked him—"why"—his voice dropped precipitously as he got hotter and harder—"did I know that . . . ?"

"Listen, my lusty stag—those terms hold for all the days of our lives together. And if you don't agree to those conditions"— she pulled on him again, knowing exactly what power she wielded with her mouth and tongue—"you will never, ever have me again."

Did he have to say it? "Untie me."

"Not enough, Court."

"Damn you, how much more do you need?"

"But there were days and days that you weren't available to me." She squeezed him mercilessly. "Days and days. How do I know it won't happen again?"

"If you stay put, it won't happen. Again."

"If I . . . ? If *I* . . . I see—" She levered herself off of him. *"Your* terms, Court." She swung her legs over the bed. "I don't think so."

She reached over and flicked the golden loops on his nipples and he shuddered. "Not if you want my body, my nipples. Not if you want to couple with *me."*

"All right, damn it, all right—"

"All right, what?"

"I agree to your conditions. For all the days we are together."

She smiled, that faint, knowing smile of feminine power.

But not for long . . .

"Untie me, Drue. Let me rut in you."

"Oh, I *like* that idea . . ." she murmured as she sashayed around the bedpost. A minute later, his one arm was free. And then the other.

And then he grabbed her, ignoring the tingling, ignoring the ache, he grabbed her and pulled her onto the bed, onto his lap, and he pushed her on her belly, and he held her with a grip of iron and he paddled her bottom once, twice, three times with the impatience of a man who has been too long out of control and too long in heat. And then he released her abruptly and she tumbled to the floor.

"Don't you ever do that to me again."

"No promises, you bastard. Since you don't know how to keep them."

"Test me, my fawn. The slate is blank as of today. See if I don't keep my promises . . ."

She curled up onto her feet and stood looking down at him. *Maybe—maybe not . . . but what she knew was, in spite of his discipline, and despite his fury, she wanted what was between his legs.*

She turned slowly and walked to the harness. "This is what I want."

"Then make yourself ready for me." He stood up, still enshrouded in the satin as she pulled the stair-step under the harness and climbed up and mounted it.

And she knew, as soon as she positioned her legs, that he could see how wet she was for him, because he had started toward her before she was even settled and was nudging against her almost immediately.

"This has nothing to do with love," he whispered as they both watched him press against her cleft and his tip penetrate her welcoming fold.

He held himself there for a long erotic moment, really aware for the first time of the nature of this erotic joining between them. That part of him needed *her,* wanted *her.* Every emotion in him surrendered to her power. He wanted nothing more than to claim her. Nothing less than to love her.

He reached out to her breasts, the golden loops dangling from his fingers.

"I hereby claim you," he said huskily, slipping the loops over her nipples once again as the mark of his possession.

And I will love you, he thought. *For all the days we are together, I will. It was a promise, it was a dream.*

And then, with all the mastery at his command, and the need and desire for her growing deeper within him by the moment, he claimed her willing body, he claimed her trembling lips, and for the first time, he claimed her heart.

A Lady's Pleasure

by Robin Schone

Chapter 1

Rage.

It filled the storm, pounding and striking the night sky.

It filled the stranger, fueling and stoking a burning lust.

For a woman.

A woman who knew more of life than surviving one day at a time.

A woman with kindness and passion.

A woman who would share with him her soul as well as her body.

A woman who, perhaps, could give him back his own soul.

The man raised his face to the sky and cursed the icy rain. He cursed the wind that drove it into every pore of his body. He cursed the African Boer who had used his left leg for target practice, thus necessitating convalescence in the cold, drafty country that was England. He cursed the horse that had thrown him in such a godforsaken, isolated area. But most of all he cursed the need that had driven him from the warmth and comfort of his seaside cottage.

Need that a man like him, born on the streets of London, could not afford.

Need that, in a man like him, haunted by the nameless dead, could never be appeased.

A fork of jagged lightning split the sky; a warning shot of thunder echoed through the night.

The storm promised death, lost as he was with neither horse nor shelter.

The storm promised life, the dawning of a new day in the aftermath of pain and desire.

The stranger lowered his head.

And saw the light.

"My desires were excited to the highest pitch. I depicted to her the pleasure she would experience when, after arriving at the chateau, I should deflower her of her virginity, and triumphantly carry off her maidenhead on the head of this, 'dear Laura,' I said, as I took one of her hands and—"

Exploded.

A raging black wall of wind and rain turned candlelight into night, swallowing whole the illicit, newspaper-type print that was in that second the sum total of Abigail's existence.

Blindly, instinctively, she scooped up the forbidden journal she had been reading. Beside her, frenzied fingers rifled through the earlier installment of erotic literature, whipped it through the air. Behind her, china clicked and clattered in the cupboard. And before her—

A dark silhouette, darker than the storm outside, filled the space where the cottage door should be. Where it *had* been but a moment before.

Abigail's heart slammed against her ribs as she made the mental transition from the fictional Laura who was being initiated into the pleasures of sex to the flesh-and-blood spinster that was herself.

Another explosion resounded through the one-room cottage— the door slamming shut. Barring the buffeting wind and the drumming rain. Barring what light the night provided.

Barring Abigail inside the cottage with an intruder.

An intruder who, judging by the height and breadth of the silhouette that had filled the doorway, could only be a man.

A very large man.

Lingering desire pulsed through her body—and dawning horror.

She was all alone and *she had forgotten to bolt the door.*

Abigail surged to her feet—naked feet, defenseless feet, *where had she put her shoes?* "Who are you?"

Her voice was loud—too loud in the sudden quiet. Certainly it did not belong to the placid spinster everyone took her to be.

No more than it belonged to the wanton woman she had been but a moment before.

Hair rose on the back of her neck as she strained to see through the black abyss that was all that separated her and certain theft—or death. "What do you want?"

Droplets of water pelted her in the face—as if some great animal shook itself dry.

"What do you think I want?" The low, masculine growl came from the vicinity of the door. "Lady, in case you haven't noticed, there's a storm outside. I want shelter."

Abigail's breath escaped in surprise at the blistering censure in the intruder's voice. His accent proclaimed that he was no local boy, but an educated man.

"I am fully aware that there is a storm outside, Mr. . . ."

"Coally. Robert. Colonel," the disembodied voice curtly supplied.

White dots pricked the blackness in front of Abigail's eyes. "I am fully aware that there is a storm outside, Colonel Coally, but you can not possibly stay here. There is a"—warmth flooded her cheeks at mentioning the unmentionable—"a little house out back. You will find shelter there."

"Lady, I am soaked; I am cold; I am hungry. I am *not* going to spend a night in a privy. Light that candle before one of us does ourselves an injury."

The order was abrupt, imperious and rude. As if Abigail was a soldier—a rather dim-witted soldier at that—derelict in her duties.

A tide of shock washed over her; it was followed by rage.

She forgot that the colonel was an intruder. She forgot that gently bred ladies such as herself fainted in the face of danger and submitted to the voice of masculine authority. She forgot everything but the fact that *she was not going to take orders, here,* in this seaside cottage that she had rented far away from the dictates of society so that she could enjoy one precious month of freedom before she gave up *everything,* and how *dare*—

A dull clunk of boots on wood ripped through Abigail's fury—the colonel was bridging the darkness that separated them. The clunk was interspersed by a dragging sound, as if he limped—or staggered.

Military men were notorious for their drinking habits.

Abigail hastily stepped back.

Only to collide with the chair she had just vacated. It skidded across the floor.

"Please stay where you are while I light the candle." Her voice in the darkness was just as sharp as the colonel's. "Are you injured?"

A grunt was her answer. And a flare of light.

Abigail stared at the intruder alias colonel—from across the scarred wooden table instead of from across the room where he should be.

Her first thought was of how dark was his skin—as dark as the gentlemen of her acquaintance were fair.

Her second thought was how ridiculously long his eyelashes were. They created jagged shadows on his cheeks as he concentrated on touching the head of the match to the wick of the candle.

Then he was entirely visible, illuminated in a widening circle of light.

Droplets of water trickled down off pitch-black hair. His face was lean, shaved clean of the sideburns or mustache that fashion dictated. The hand holding the match was as brown as his face. His fingers were long, strong, with square, blunt tips.

Far, far too large to fit inside a woman other than one at a time, surely, was her third and totally incongruous thought.

Shaking his hand to extinguish the match, the colonel abruptly straightened.

Unwittingly, Abigail's gaze followed his movements.

Standing five feet nine inches tall, there were few men Abigail did not top, but she had to tilt her head back to look at this man. Eyes the color of pewter locked with hers.

The one-room cottage shrank to the size of a closet.

She had never seen such stark eyes. There was nothing soft about them. And yet they were beautiful in their uncompromising masculinity.

The dark lashes flickered; she could feel the touch of the cold gray gaze on her lips, her throat, her breasts—

Breasts, she suddenly remembered, that were confined by neither corset nor chemise.

Her fingers involuntarily clenched—about damp, curling paper.

A hurried glance downward confirmed her suspicion.

The colonel wasn't staring at her breasts; he was staring at *The Pearl, A Journal of Facetiae and Voluptuous Reading*, NO. 12 June 1880. Which she clutched to her chest with the cover outward.

She whipped the journal behind her back.

Simultaneously, the colonel pivoted toward the iron bed against the right wall.

The covers were turned back in ready invitation.

Alarm leapt up her spine. "What are you doing?"

He bypassed the bed and limped to the smaller of the three trunks that sat at the foot of it.

Scalding blood filled Abigail's face. Just as quickly it drained.

For the first time in her life she thought she would faint.

She darted after the colonel. "Now, you wait just one minute—"

Too late. He thrust open the trunk.

To reveal a jumbled collection of leather and paper. Books with unmistakable titles: *Adventures of a Bedstead; The Story of a Dildoe; Tales of Twilight, or the Amorous Adventures of a company of Ladies before Marriage.* And more copies of *The Pearl.*

No one had ever seen her collection of erotica.

Anger that this man, *this colonel* had barged into her private retreat and discovered her secret vice overrode fear and shame.

"I asked you a question, sirrah, and I expect to be answered! What are you doing?"

The colonel stared at the contents of the trunk for a long moment before he lifted his gaze to hers.

For a second there flared inside the gray eyes something that caused Abigail's nipples to harden. Then the eyes became cold and flat, like his voice. "I am looking for a towel. And a blanket."

"Well, you will *not* find them there." Abigail threw the journal inside the trunk and slammed shut the lid. She glared up at him, daring him to comment on the literature that no lady was supposed to know about, let alone possess. "There is a towel by the pump in the corner near the stove. Why do you want a blanket?"

She must have been mistaken at the brief flare of heat in those eyes. They were as hard as the pewter they took their color from. "My clothes are soaked, Mrs.—?"

"Miss." Abigail hesitated. She was not about to give this autocratic colonel her last name lest he know someone in society who was acquainted with her family. "Miss Abigail."

"My clothes are soaked, Miss Abigail. I want a blanket so that when I strip down I can cover my nakedness."

Abigail stared. The words *strip* and *nakedness* momentarily drowned out the pelting rain and the relentless wind.

"Colonel Coally." She drew herself up to her full height. "I will give you shelter from the storm, but I will not allow you to—to—"

The gray eyes were implacable. "Miss Abigail, there is nothing you can do to stop me."

Abigail bristled, fully prepared to fight—or flee.

A crack of thunder shook the cottage.

A warning that she had nowhere to run.

A reminder that she was behaving more like the juvenile Laura in *The Pearl* than a mature spinster dressed in a faded green shirtwaist and who, furthermore, was already sprouting a few strands of gray in pale-brown hair that was straggling free of its bun.

Clothed or buck-naked, there was little likelihood of a man like him forcing his attentions on a woman like her. Especially chilled through and through as he no doubt was.

Dripping water formed a dark circle about his boots.

"I asked if you are injured."

The coldness in the gray eyes intensified. "No."

"Good," she said curtly. "Then you will have no trouble walking to the table and taking a chair. I shall procure you a towel—and a blanket. But first let me stir up the fire in the stove—"

"That won't be necessary."

"Colonel Coally—"

"Miss Abigail, there is a full-fledged storm going on outside your door. You have a thatch roof. If the wind should remove your chimney, it will, if the stove is blazing, quite probably cause a fire. I would as soon suffer from a slight chill as roast to death."

Abigail took a calming breath. Even her elder brother, the Earl of Melford, was not as overbearing as the colonel.

"Very well." Tight-lipped with anger, she retrieved a towel. While he briskly dried off, she flounced toward the bed and yanked off the top blanket.

When she returned to the table, he had dried his hair and slicked it back from his forehead. It was not black as she had earlier thought it to be, but the color of burnt umber. The water, she noted, did not bead on it, which meant he did not pomade his hair like his contemporaries in London.

Abigail could not recall the last time she had seen a man who did not pomade his hair. His cleanly shaven skin, tanned from the sun, was extremely—virile.

She dropped the blanket onto the table.

"I will wait over by the bed. Pray tell me when you have changed and I will hang your clothes up to dry."

The wailing of the storm did not hide the creak of the chair as he struggled to remove his boots, or the thunk they made when they dropped to the plank floor. Cloth, too, made a sound, she discovered. It whispered, the outer clothes a harsh one, the inner clothes softer, more beguiling.

She suddenly wondered if all of his body was as brown as his face. And fought the flare of heat the thought engendered.

"You may turn around."

He sat at the table with the blanket wrapped like a toga about his body. The stark gray gaze snared hers as he held out a wet bundle of clothing.

Quickly averting her eyes—the naked brown arm and shoulder sticking out of the gray blanket were indeed as brown as was his face—Abigail accepted the sodden mass of clothes.

They smelled of rain and damp wool and something indefinable. Spice. Or musk. Something strictly male.

Bending down, she grabbed the mud-caked boots.

Only to have a cat's-eye view of a pair of long, narrow feet. He had shapely, muscular ankles.

They were brown, too. And liberally sprinkled with fine dark hair.

Abigail had never before seen so much man—naked.

Cheeks burning, she straightened.

The gray eyes were waiting for hers.

"In the future, draw your curtains, Miss Abigail. Few men can resist a free peep show. And bolt your door. Some men might take more than you are willing to offer."

For a second Abigail thought she would burst with rage at the insinuation that she might welcome such attentions. Humiliation immediately followed, at the thought that perhaps unconsciously she had. Hostility was born, that the intruder should guess at her secret desires that were not at all ladylike.

"Colonel Coally, I have been at this cottage for an entire week and the only man I have encountered who was unable to resist a 'peep' is yourself. Furthermore, how dare you castigate me for not bolting my door when it is you, sir, who are the intruder—"

The violence of her feelings erupted in a shatter of glass.

Pivoting, she stared in astonishment at the tree branch retreating through the window closest to the bed. Wind and rain tunneled into the jagged hole it left behind.

The candle flickered and flamed, creating a wild jig of shadow and light.

"Stay where you are!" The colonel's command was pistol sharp. "The floor is covered with broken glass. We need something to bar the window—the cupboard will do. Hand me my boots, then douse the light."

Abigail gritted her teeth. The colonel had issued one too many orders.

Turning, she took deliberate aim and dropped the heavy, mud-caked boots.

Brown toes curled back in the nick of time.

"Do you move cupboards best in the dark, Colonel Coally?" she asked politely.

"Not at all, Miss Abigail." The gray eyes staring up at her were narrowed. "I thought only to spare your blushes."

He stood up and dropped the blanket.

Abigail dropped the sodden mass of clothes that was the only thing between them and dove for the candle.

The cottage plunged into swirling darkness. At the same time, something brushed against her hip.

She instinctively put out her hand—and grabbed naked flesh.

Hot, hard, naked flesh. It was shaped rather like a thick pump handle, half-cocked, with skin as smooth as silk. Underneath it was a throbbing vein—

She jerked her hand back. "Colonel Coally—you surprised me."

"Miss Abigail." The voice in the dark was colder than the wind shrilling through the broken window. "If you insist upon grabbing what you cannot see, you will someday suffer from more than surprise. Edge your way over to the bed and stay there. I don't want to have to worry about surprising you again."

Abigail stood her ground. "Nonsense, Colonel Coally. This is my cottage. I am quite capable of assisting you."

"Let me put it another way, Miss Abigail. I am not so much worried about surprising you as I am of being surprised myself. Use your wits, lady: You have no shoes on. I have no desire to minister to both a broken window *and* bleeding feet."

Speechless with fury, Abigail stared up into the blackness.

Surely he could not have thought that she had grabbed him on purpose. It was *he* who had brushed against her!

And then, how dare he comment about her wits—or her person! A gentleman *did not* mention a lady's feet.

"Very well, Colonel Coally."

She stalked to the bed, skirting wide the area in front of the broken window.

The mattress sagged beneath her weight. Planting her bare feet firmly together on the cool plank floor, she wondered where the colonel planned to spend the night. Then she wondered what it would be like to sleep with a man. Naked. With his warm flesh curved around hers.

The grate of wood on wood interrupted thoughts that she had no business thinking. The colonel was pushing the cupboard across the floor, steadily, heavily. The gale whistling through the cottage abated to a dull moan.

"There. That should hold it."

Suddenly a hand weighted down the top of her head, slid down to her ear, her cheek. The fingers were cool, slightly damp from the rain. They rasped against the softness of her skin, against her breast—

Fire shot through her body. "What do you think—"

Her hand that reached up to push his away was clasped in a firm grasp.

A hard, calloused grasp.

He forcibly curled her fingers around—dog-eared paper.

"This was lying on top of the cupboard."

So that was where the wind had whipped the other journal.

She held her spine ramrod straight. "Thank you, Colonel Coally."

He released her hand. "My pleasure, Miss Abigail."

Heat dispersed the cold of the darkness—his body was mere inches away from her face.

She wondered if he had donned the blanket again. A particularly intriguing scene from *The Pearl* flashed before her eyes.

If she leaned forward, would she kiss wool or—

"Are you all right?" he asked abruptly.

"Perfectly, thank you." She jerked her head back, wondering if she was losing her mind. "And you?"

The end of the mattress dipped. "I'm an old warhorse—moving a cupboard is hardly dangerous work."

Abigail rolled up the damp journal. The colonel was far from decrepit—as he must very well know. There was not a single strand of gray in his hair. "Fishing, Colonel Coally?"

"Merely stating a truth." She jumped at the shock of a heavy thud—a boot dropping onto the floor. Another thud followed. Then the entire bed shook. She sensed rather than saw him scoot across the mattress to sit with his back against the wall. "I am thirty-five years old. The last twenty-two years have been spent in the Army. What are you doing out here all by yourself?"

Abigail refused to be cheated of her anger. "What are *you* doing here, Colonel Coally?"

There was a brief silence. "Convalescing."

She craned her head back in the direction where she knew he

was sitting. All she could see was darkness. "There is another cottage near here?"

"No. Not nearby."

Straightening, she listened to the tempest outside the cabin for long seconds. "Twenty-two years ago you would have been thirteen, Colonel Coally. The age of consent for a noncombative position is fifteen."

"You are correct, Miss Abigail." The voice in the darkness was dismissive. "I lied."

Lied? Twenty-two years ago or now?

"What are you convalescing for?"

Again that silence, followed by a reluctant, "A bullet wound."

She remembered his limp. And the sight of a well-shaped muscular ankle sprinkled with fine black hair. "In the left leg."

"Yes."

Abigail followed the war movement through the newspapers. "By a Boer?"

"Yes."

The seaside cottage was miles away from the nearest thoroughfare. She had deliberately chosen it for its isolation. "That still does not explain why you are *here,* Colonel Coally."

The silence was longer this time. She concentrated on the cool damp of the journal rolled in her hands and not the throbbing warmth that came from the end of the bed where his legs stretched out.

"My horse threw me. I walked for a while, but there was no shelter to be found. Then I saw your light . . . and here I am."

"But why were you out in the storm?"

"Why do you read erotic literature?"

Abigail prepared to defend her choice of reading material—it was educational; it was amusing; *it was none of his business.* She surprised herself by baldly stating, "Because it is the only way a woman can learn about sex."

A current of electricity passed through the darkness, as if lightning had struck nearby.

"I could be mistaken, of course," the colonel's voice was gravelly, "but I believe there exists another method that a woman may discharge her curiosity."

"I never met a man who I was interested in 'discharging' my curiosity with, Colonel Coally," she said repressively.

Outside the cottage, the force of the storm rose. The wind howled around the cupboard. Waves pounded on the beach below. Thunder roared in the skies above.

It occurred to Abigail that a very real danger existed. The wind *could* take the thatch roof off. Waves *could* swell up out of the ocean and swallow the tiny cottage. Lightning *could*—

"I wanted a woman."

The unexpected words jarred Abigail back to reality. "I beg your pardon?"

"You wanted to know what I was doing out here in the storm. I rode out, hoping to find a village. Or a tavern. And a willing woman."

The confession was abrupt.

Colonel Coally begrudged the need that had driven him out into the night. As Abigail begrudged the conventions that did not allow a lady the same privilege.

She should have felt shock at the admission no gentleman made to a lady; instead, she felt the lingering remnants of rancor evaporate. It was replaced by a strange sense of camaraderie.

This man had seen her trunk filled with erotica and he had not judged her. It was the height of hypocrisy to judge him now, when he obviously had his own needs.

"I envy you, Colonel Coally. Were I a man, I, too, would have ridden out in search of companionship."

"It wasn't companionship I rode out for, Miss Abigail."

"I know very well what you rode out for, Colonel Coally."

"Do you, Miss Abigail?" The voice in the dark was curiously passionless. "Do you know what it is like for your body to burn and throb until you want to throw aside everything you have ever believed in for just one moment of oblivion?"

Abigail closed her eyes against a lifetime of wanting things that could never be, gently reared as she was. Things she would never have, spinster that she now was. "Yes, Colonel Coally. I do."

The bed shifted. "Do you have fantasies, Miss Abigail?"

Unbidden images danced behind her eyelids. Forbidden images

of a man's naked desire filling a woman's body. Sexual images of things she had never done. Things she had never seen. Things she had never even read about.

Yearnings that in the next three weeks she must somehow put aside.

"Yes." She opened her eyes and stared into the darkness. "I have fantasies."

"Tell me." The abrupt command was harsh.

"I . . ." How could she tell this man who was a virtual stranger what she had privately dreamed about for years? But the darkness provided a certain anonymity. It almost seemed as if she talked to herself . . . or a fantasy.

"I fantasize about what it is like to kiss. Not the small peck that I give and receive from my family and friends. But a real kiss . . . like they do in my books. With their . . . tongues." Before she could lose her courage, she blurted, "Do men and women really kiss that way, Colonel Coally?"

"Sometimes. What else do you fantasize about, Miss Abigail?"

Abigail transferred the journal to her left hand and scooted sideways across the mattress so that her back rested against the iron headboard. The sole of her right foot brushed against wool—and a muscular leg.

Heat shot up her calf.

She curled her foot underneath her skirt. "I . . . fantasize about what a man looks like. I mean . . . I have little nephews and I . . . have changed their nappies. They are . . . not really very impressive. Yet in the books they describe a man as being . . . much larger. *There.* Are men as large in real life as they are in books?"

It could have been the intake of his breath that she heard. Or perhaps it was hers. Because suddenly she realized exactly what it was that she had grabbed in the darkness, all silky sinew with pulsing veins.

And yes, it had been very large indeed.

"Some men are large, some men are small." The voice in the dark deepened. "Just as some women have large breasts, and some have small. Is it important to you?"

"Yes," she said softly, wondering what or even *if* he had thought about her breasts during that fleeting touch, wondering how large were his measurements, wondering if all men were his size. Then she laughed self-consciously, embarrassed yet strangely exhilarated at discussing a man's anatomy. "I mean—I suppose it would not matter as long as a man can give a woman satisfaction. Is it possible, Colonel Coally? Can a man give a woman satisfaction?"

"Do you doubt it, Miss Abigail?"

"Oh, yes, Colonel Coally. Every time I look at one of my pomaded, bewhiskered brothers-in-law I doubt it. I try to imagine them kissing with their tongue or—or touching a woman's breast or—or kissing a woman between her legs, and, quite frankly, I cannot. I cannot imagine them doing any of the things I read about. I cannot even imagine them begetting their own children. They have fat bottoms, Colonel Coally. I simply cannot imagine those fat bottoms pistoning up and down."

Fat bottoms pistoning up and down rang out over the muted frenzy of the storm.

Abigail clasped her right hand over her mouth in horror at the words that had come from it. At the same time, a shout of laughter burst from the other side of the bed. The mattress shook and shimmied.

"I am glad that you find my speech amusing, Colonel Coally," Abigail said stiffly.

The masculine laughter subsided. "I suddenly find this whole conversation amusing. Here you are, telling me your darkest fantasies, yet you address me as 'Colonel Coally.' And here am I, equally reprehensible, calling you 'Miss Abigail.' Let's call a truce, shall we? For the duration of the storm, let us be simply Abigail and Robert."

It was absurd, of course, but calling the intruder by his first name seemed more intimate than telling him her "darkest" fantasies. As long as he remained a colonel instead of a man, then he was a part of the storm and she remained a spinster lady merely engaged in safe, however illicit, conversation. But cross that barrier and—

"Very well." Abigail took a deep breath to still the rapid acceleration of her heartbeat. "I find that I am sharing my fantasies, but you are withholding yours. What do you fantasize about . . . Robert?"

"A woman, Abigail. I fantasize about all the things I would like to do to a woman."

Abigail's breath caught in her throat. She envisioned his tanned hands caressing the pale skin of a woman's body. And wondered what they would feel like touching *her* body.

Liquid desire pooled between her thighs.

"What about . . . size? Do you fantasize about the size of a woman's breasts?"

"No."

The short answer did not encourage further questioning. But this was the first man—indeed, he was the first person—who had ever discussed sex other than in terms of polite platitudes and *Abigail wanted to know more.*

When she returned to London in three weeks' time she would have this memory, at least, to chase away the lonely nights.

"Well, then. What sort of things would you like to do . . . to a woman?" she asked casually, almost flippantly, while inside her chest her heart thudded against her ribs.

"Everything." The disembodied voice was a dark rasp. "Everything she has ever dreamed of. I want to ram my body into a woman until I lose myself inside *her* body, until her pleasure is my pleasure. I want to make her scream and beg for more. I want her to make me forget that I have spent the last twenty-two years of my life killing."

Abigail felt as if the air had been sucked out of her lungs.

Death was a part of war. The newspapers were filled with the tallies. Abigail read the accounts, mourned the victims, and had never once thought about the survivors, those soldiers who fought in the name of Her Majesty. Men who were not born to kill, but who did so nevertheless. Men who would suffer their actions for the rest of their lives.

As the autocratic colonel was obviously suffering.

For long seconds she clutched the cool, damp journal in her left hand, riveted by the raw need that radiated from the man at the foot of the bed.

As a soldier he had faced death; the only danger Abigail had ever experienced was that of exposure, should her erotica be discovered. As a man, he had endured physical pain; the only pain Abigail had ever borne was loneliness, pretending to be what she was not. Yet she felt the colonel's desire as keenly as she felt her own—he forced to seek forgetfulness in the midst of a storm, she forced to bury her frustration between the pages of illicit books and journals.

She wondered what it would be like to forget the future—in the arms of this man. Just as he sought to forget the past—in the arms of a woman.

She was a woman, she thought on a leap of reckless desire. In the darkness she did not feel like an aging spinster. Surely her body would not feel old, either.

Suddenly a voice came from a long distance away, surely not hers, any more than the ache in her breasts and the throb between her thighs belonged to her, a spinster who should be beyond the desires of her youth, a lady who should never experience such desires no matter what her age. "I will help you forget, Robert, if you will help me forget."

Chapter 2

"You're a virgin." The gravelly voice was flat.

Abigail's face flamed in the darkness. "Yes."

"And a lady."

No lady did the things Abigail did . . . or proposed to do. "No."

"What do you need to forget, Abigail?"

"In three weeks time I turn thirty years old."

And would forever leave behind her the vestiges of her youth.

"Turning thirty isn't the end of the world. You'll find that you won't feel any differently three weeks from now than you do tonight."

She stared into the bleakness that was her future. *"That* is what I am afraid of, Robert."

"I haven't had a woman in over a year."

Abigail's heart thudded against her ribs. It sounded, incredibly, as if he was on the verge of accepting her offer. "All I ask is that you be gentle."

"And what if I can't?"

"Then I will no longer be a virgin," she said with a practicality she was far from feeling.

And she would at last know if there was anything beyond sleepless nights and endless frustration.

"Sex isn't fastidious." The disembodied voice was crude. "It's dirty and noisy and sweaty. Pain can become pleasure and pleasure can be painful. Once I start, I won't be able to stop. And I won't stop until I make you beg and cry for it."

A shaft of unadulterated desire stabbed through Abigail's stomach. It was chased by fear. And a blazing hope that what he said was true, that he could take her outside the realms of propriety and show her what her body cried out for.

She squeezed the rolled-up journal. "I sincerely hope not."

"Why?" he barked.

Abigail jumped at the sudden violence in his voice. And replied with quaint, totally incongruous logic. "Because you do not pomade your hair. And because I cannot imagine you insisting that a woman clothe a piano for fear the sight of its legs will overly excite her sensibilities."

She could sense his shock. Could feel the blood pumping through her veins and her heart pounding in her breast.

A shout of laughter cut through the darkness of desire. Beneath her, the bed shook and shimmied.

Suddenly all Abigail wanted to do was stop that laughter.

"Shall I disrobe?" she asked curtly.

The laughter abruptly died. There was a flurry of motion—the mattress dipping, the bed creaking. She flung out her right hand to retain her balance, contacted hot, hard flesh. It was covered with wiry hair; there was bone underneath muscle, and a tiny, beaded nipple—

She jerked her hand back just as long fingers closed over her hip. And held herself perfectly still as they skimmed her waist, her abdomen, a breast—her heart gave a lurch beneath the touch—then curved around her neck. Calloused fingers forced her chin upward to the darkness.

"If I take your virginity—if I touch your breasts—if I kiss you between your legs—what will you give me, Abigail?"

"What do you want?" She was paralyzed by the starkness of his words and the closeness of his body—a body that was not wrapped up inside a blanket.

"*Everything.* You have to give me everything. Your body. Your needs. Your fantasies. Everything that you have."

Abigail sucked in scorching air—his breath. Then her lips were sucked inside liquid, velvet heat, and his tongue was inside her and Abigail's first fantasy was made into a reality.

Only to find that a French kiss had no bearing whatsoever to the anemic thing experienced in literature and fantasy.

Books did not describe the incredible intimacy of a man's breath fanning a woman's cheek while his tongue filled her mouth and his fingers cradled her chin as if she were infinitely desirable.

Fantasy did not conjure taste.

But Robert did. He tasted like brandy. And man. And hot, wet desire.

The journal slipped out from between her fingers the same time his tongue slipped out of her mouth.

"Let me be your fantasy man, Abigail." Hard skin whispered across her cheek—a finger. "While the storm lasts, give me everything you give to him."

Abigail's breath caught in her chest.

He was accepting her offer.

His pain must indeed be great to bury it inside a thirty-year-old spinster.

She squared her shoulders.

The reason that he took her did not matter.

She *wanted* him to be her fantasy man.

She *wanted* to make him forget.

She wanted to forget . . . and for one night be the woman who he had made her feel like while he kissed her. Beautiful. Desirable. Young and full of hope.

She tilted her chin at a lifetime of denial. "My fantasy man undresses me."

"Think very carefully before you embark on this journey, Abigail. Because once we start, there is no turning back."

Abigail inhaled, breathing in the faint odor of brandy—his breath; breathing in the smell of rain and spicy musk—his body.

Tangible reality instead of bloodless fantasy.

"I have no desire to turn back, Robert."

The mattress dipped, shot up, leaving her alone on the bed. Then suddenly she was standing on the floor and the entire length of her body was bombarded by heat while intent fingers worked the row of buttons that lined the front of her dress.

She grabbed the invisible hands—hands that were nearly twice the size of hers. "But you have to live up to what you said, Robert."

The fingers stilled underneath hers.

"You have to make me beg and cry for it."

Burning fire enveloped her body: Embarrassment at her boldness—and a wave of incinerating lust that radiated from the man in front of her.

His hands slid out from underneath Abigail's. Her face was cupped between calloused palms, lifted upward.

"I will live up to what I said." Brandy-scented breath caressed her lips. "But remember this: As long as the storm lasts, your body, your needs, your fantasies—everything that you have—is mine. And *I* will hold you to that, Abigail."

Abigail's heart skipped a beat. "Then I would say we have struck a bargain, Robert."

The voice in the darkness rang with finality. "Then let me undress you."

Chill air caressed her skin as one by one the buttons on her dress popped open. Instantly the chill of the night was replaced by heat—hard, hot hands slid inside her dress and peeled the faded cotton away from her breasts.

"You're not wearing a corset."

His breath was ragged—as ragged as hers.

"No." It was inside a trunk, where she had packed it along

with her chemise and petticoats immediately upon arriving at the isolated cottage.

The dress slid down over her shoulders, off her arms, a whisper of cool air and warm skin, to bunch around her feet. Then the hard, hot hands settled on her hips and gently pulled her forward. Equally hot, hard flesh prodded her stomach. "Do you always wear silk drawers?"

She hesitantly raised her hands and gripped his shoulders. The muscles were hard—everything about him was hard—and hot. "Yes. I enjoy the feel of them."

"So do I." His voice was a husky murmur inside her right ear. Agile fingers sifted through the seamless vent in the back. He touched her in a place that made her knees buckle. "You're soft here."

Involuntarily she arched into his fingers as he repeated the caress, there at the top of her buttocks.

"And here . . ." He pushed deeper into the crevice, a tantalizing inch. "I never had time to learn a woman's body. But tonight, with you, Abigail, I am going to take that time. When the storm is over, I am going to know what every inch of your skin feels like."

She tensed underneath the unexpected invasion, his fingertips raspy hot against the tender flesh there. And determinedly smoothed her hands down the sleek, muscled flesh of his back to locate hair-roughened cheeks that were taut where hers were soft, concave where hers were plump.

She hovered over the place where his spine flowed into the crevice between his buttocks—"When the storm is over, Robert, I am going to know what every inch of *your* body feels like, too"—and lightly stroked him.

The flesh pulsing against her stomach jerked while the flesh beneath her hands stiffened.

"I do not need a woman to know my body, Abigail."

She had gone too far to back down now. "But *I* need to know your body, Robert."

"Do you often fantasize about fondling a man's butt, Abigail?" The voice in the dark was caustic.

"Do you, Robert?" she asked tartly.

"I can assure you, I have *never* thought about fondling a man's ass."

It took Abigail a second to realize that Robert was jesting—to hide his embarrassment.

It emboldened her, to think that he was as new to this kind of intimacy as she was. And equally vulnerable.

She continued to stroke the soft vee of skin at the base of his spine. "Is that what men think about during battle, then, fondling the posterior of a woman?"

His entire body stiffened. Black tension filled the air. "Men in battle are too tired to think. Or too scared. It's before the battle that men think. Or while they lie dying."

Abigail bit her bottom lip, momentarily diverted by the cold hostility in his voice. And the pain that it hid. "Before battle—what do *you* think about?"

The calloused fingertip lightly strummed up the small of her back, down into the crevice between her buttocks another breathtaking inch. A hard weight pressed down on her forehead—his forehead.

"I think about how to keep my men alive. If you are asking if I will kill again, Abigail, the answer is yes."

"Only in battle, Robert," she said firmly. "And you are supposed to forget about that now."

Suddenly the deliciously erotic finger was gone and her silk drawers slid down over her hips—he had untied the tapes. He stepped back and she was enveloped in darkness and cold air. "Then make me forget, Abigail. Tell me what your fantasy man does after he undresses you."

Uncertainty warred with desire, urgent little voices telling her to turn back: She was too old, too small, too plump, a thousand and one reasons why he would not find her attractive. Bringing her arms to her sides, she straightened her shoulders. "He touches my breasts."

Heat grazed the tips of her nipples. She locked her knees to keep from falling.

"You're hard." The relentless friction was part caress, part prod. "I can feel where you are made to discharge milk—little puckered indentations on the very tips—here. Does your fantasy man suckle you?"

The flesh between Abigail's thighs involuntarily clenched at the evocative words. "Do you fantasize about suckling a woman?"

"Yes. I fantasize about suckling her until I make her drip with cream. Give me sustenance, Abigail."

Suddenly the insistent rasp of his fingers against her left nipple was replaced by a hot, wet, voracious mouth.

For a second Abigail was frozen with shock. Then the breath was sucked out of her lungs as the intense pulling, tugging sensation caused her entire body to contract.

Without volition, her hands came up and sank into silky thick, damp hair. Seemingly in response to her touch, Robert cupped her bottom in his left hand and pressed hard on her stomach with the palm of his right hand, as if to feel the rhythmical drawing inside her womb that his suckling mouth was producing.

And perhaps he did. Abigail felt closer to Robert, cradling his head while he hungrily fed at her breast, than she had ever felt toward any other person.

Just when she thought that milk would indeed drip from her nipple, the black world of passion tilted. She was swung up into his arms—her right breast caught between their bodies—and then she was lying on the bed with her head sinking into a soft pillow and the cold knotting of the quilt pricking her back.

"Cream, Abigail." Hard, hot fingers delved between her thighs. "You're dripping with it. Do you ever put your fingers inside of you when you fantasize?"

Lightning shot up through Abigail's body. "Of course not!"

"Our agreement, lady." Slowly, gently, he mapped out the soft folds of flesh between her legs, overruling modesty, overcoming resistance. "I want to know every erotic thought, every touch."

Abigail held herself rigidly.

Everything, he had said. And she had agreed. But Robert was taking control—and she did not know if she liked that. It was what her fantasy man did—but this was *not* fantasy.

She felt wet and exposed and there was nothing to do but . . . enjoy it.

And add to her bank of memories.

"No," she reaffirmed on a soft intake of air. "I do not."

"Does your fantasy man?"

"Yes."

Oh, yes . . .

"How many fingers does he put inside you?"

She closed her eyes, blocking out the black silhouette that was more than fantasy. "Three. Do you fantasize about putting your fingers inside a woman?"

"Yes." His fingers swirled and swirled, there at the entrance to her body, gathering moisture, creating heat.

She could hear the wet play over the staccato sounds of the storm—or was it her breathing that was so uneven? "How many fingers do you fantasize about putting inside of a woman?"

"Five. I fantasize about sticking my whole fist inside her."

Abigail's eyelids snapped open. She remembered the length of his fingers in the circle of candlelight. Remembered the size of his hands, clasped between hers. "That . . . Surely that is not possible."

"Perhaps. Certainly not with a virgin. Perhaps after a woman has had a child or two . . . You're so small here." Abigail involuntarily squirmed at the deepening pressure. "Hold still. I can feel your maidenhead; you're taut as a drum. It hardly seems possible that you could accept— Take my finger, Abigail."

Abigail took the entire burning length. And gasped into the fury of the rain and the wind.

It was raw invasion. It was his body becoming a part of hers.

It was the substance that books and fantasy lacked.

The foot of the bed dipped; she drew her legs up to counteract the motion, opening herself wider, forcing the finger more deeply inside her. A gust of heat seared her stomach. "Talk to me. Tell me what it feels like to have a man's finger inside you."

Abigail threw her head back, concentrating on the sensations serrating her body instead of the dark silhouette poised over her. "Your finger feels—hot. And rough. It burns. I feel open. And stretched."

"Not stretched enough. Is this what you feel like when your fantasy man puts his finger inside you?"

"No."

Oh, no . . .

The reality of having a man's finger inside her bore no resemblance at all to the fantasy.

This was heat and cold and bone and muscles with the knotting of the quilt underneath her and the knot of his knuckle inside her.

"Take another finger, Abigail."

The burning fullness that was more than fantasy abruptly turned to painful intrusion as one finger became two. "Stop—"

"Lie still. Relax. You are a virgin, there's bound to be some pain. It will pass—let it become pleasure."

Abigail forced herself to lie still. She felt uncertain and vulnerable and stretched beyond endurance. This was *not* fantasy. Yet . . . Yet her body pulsed and throbbed around the invading digits, telling Abigail there was indeed pleasure beyond pain. Telling her—

"I think my fantasy man has smaller hands, Robert."

A feather-light kiss ruffled the damp hair at the apex of her thighs. "I think my hands are exactly the same size as those of your fantasy man. What does it feel like having two fingers inside you?"

"I feel—invaded."

"You are. What do you feel like when your fantasy man has two fingers inside you?"

"I feel—like I want more."

Hot breath fanned her nether regions. "And you are going to get more, Abigail."

An electric surge of awareness overcame the burning discomfort between her legs. He could smell her, with his head down there like that, he could—

"I'm going to kiss you between your legs now. Then I'm going to give you three fingers."

Abigail sucked in air to tell him that she could not possibly take three of his fingers. At the same time he sucked her inside his mouth and all thoughts of protest died. His lips and tongue were every bit as hot in this most intimate of kisses as they had been when he had French-kissed her.

She grabbed two handfuls of silky thick, damp hair and hung

on to him as she had held on to the mane of a runaway pony when she was ten years old.

It had been frightening, plummeting across the countryside, and it had been uncomfortable with her bottom wildly bouncing on the saddle. But it had been exciting, too, with the world a blur of color and the wind whipping her cheeks.

Now the world was a blur of blackness and she had never before experienced such heat or an unrelenting drive for something to happen. His tongue circled her on the outside; inside her, there was more pressure, a stinging, popping sensation, and Abigail knew that he had added another finger, yet suddenly it did not matter because he was stabbing her with his tongue in such a rapid motion that she could not catch her breath. And then she did not need to, her body rose to catch it for her, bowing perfectly with the three fingers lodged impossibly deep inside her.

Abigail convulsed in a blinding spasm of raw, burning pleasure, lungs laboring, breasts heaving.

"What does it feel like now, Abigail?" Scorching breath—there on her nether lips that were wet and pulsing and still swollen. The fingers deep inside her wriggled.

Abigail's breath caught in her throat. Hot blood rushed down from her cheeks and up from where his fingers gently agitated. It met in the center of her stomach and spread out over the rest of her body. She could not help bearing down on a fluttering contraction, opening herself wider.

A liquid trail of desire trickled from her body. "It feels"—she gulped air, released his hair to clutch the more secure anchor of the quilt—"like I have three fingers inside me."

"Shall I take them out?"

"Please do not."

"What does your fantasy man do next?"

"He comes into my body."

His fingers continued a silky flutter. "I do not have anything to protect you with."

The words rang a discordant bell of reason. Something was wrong—but then thought gave way to the sensation of her flesh pulsing around those three fingers.

They had gone beyond fantasy, beyond reality. This man had

promised her everything, and for the first time in her life she was not worrying about breaking a code of etiquette or failing to make the prescribed marriage of money and title. *Nothing* was going to destroy this stormy interlude. Mentally she reviewed every erotic manuscript she had ever read.

"I have—there is a sponge by the sink."

The fingers made another gentle flutter before slowly easing out of her. She winced. With pain. With loss. Then she grabbed the bedcovers to keep from catapulting out of bed.

He soundlessly maneuvered through the darkness. The pulsations inside her body counted the seconds he was gone, gently contracting, relaxing, contracting . . . Harsh liquor fumes intruded on the delicious ripples of anticipation.

Abigail lifted herself up onto her elbows. "What are you doing?"

"I had a flask of brandy in my jacket. A sponge is more effective if soaked in something, usually vinegar, though this will do. But it's going to burn a little. Lie back and lift your knees up."

The mattress dipped, forcing her body downward. Something icy cold and wet brushed her most private parts. She instinctively closed her legs, but an arm was there, wedged between her knees, holding them wide.

Danger.

Desire.

For a second, Abigail could not differentiate between the two.

This man had killed.

This man was about to take her virginity.

She would never be the same after this.

"Have you ever done this before, Robert?" She gulped calming air, feeling old, feeling gauche, feeling terribly, terribly frightened. "Put a sponge inside a woman?"

"No. Does your fantasy man do this for you?"

"Of course not. Women do *not* get pregnant by fan—"

The words caught in her throat as the sponge breached her opening. Then it was in and his fingers were gently prodding the unaccustomed fullness inside her and somewhere in the process the stinging discomfort blossomed into abject need.

She stared at the dark silhouette that knelt between her knees and clung to the self-control that was fast slipping away. "Robert."

"Abigail."

"You said you rode out into the storm looking for a woman."

The fingers prodding the sponge inside her stilled.

"I find it hard to believe you would make such a journey without bringing along certain . . . necessities."

"I have French letters." His voice in the darkness was flat again, emotionless, as if he had not just given her the most intimate pleasure a man can give a woman, as if he did not now have his fingers inside her.

"Why did you say you had nothing to protect me with?"

There was a harsh intake of air. "Because for once in my life I wanted to feel a woman's flesh wrapped around mine without benefit of a rubber galosh."

Her heart fluttered inside her breast. "What would you have done if I had not possessed a sponge?"

"Then I would have introduced you to a brandy douche."

Abigail winced—the brandy *had* burned. "I think I would prefer the rubber galosh, Robert."

"Shall I get one?"

The stillness and the darkness were absolute. Outside, the storm itself seemed to wait for her answer.

She was a substitute for another woman, a younger woman, the woman whom he had rode out into the storm to find. And yet . . .

He wanted to feel *her* flesh . . . *as she wanted to feel his,* every vein, every pulse, everything that he was.

For a second, she was overcome by the thought that perhaps he wanted her as much as she wanted him.

But of course that was impossible.

The storm would end and this was all she would ever have and *she was going to take everything he could give her.*

"No. Will you come inside me now, please? I feel—quite prepared, thank you."

"Quite prepared isn't good enough." The dark voice throbbed. "I want you wide open. I want you so wet that when I thrust inside you, there won't be anything you can do to stop me. Starting now. When I pull my fingers out of you—like this—squeeze as hard as you can."

There came a soft slurp as he slid from her body. Abigail squeezed, first to contain the long, calloused fingers, then to restrain them, there were too many, surely—

"Relax, Abigail. Three fingers, you had them before—there, just the tips—now bear down." Warm lips nibbled her knee, an unexpected caress, her body opened with a will of its own, swallowing the three fingers in their entirety, first knuckles, second knuckles. "The first time was to stretch your maidenhead, but this is to stretch you. Now squeeze again . . . relax, bear down. I'm your fantasy man, Abigail. Don't fight it, open up, I will be far larger than this—*there*. Squeeze . . . relax. It's a rhythm, a dance. Let me open you up, Abigail, let me make you so wet I'll drown inside of you."

It felt as if *she* was drowning, she was so wet, so stretched, squeezing as he instructed, opening for more.

It was unbearably intimate, what men and women did together. Better than fantasy, better than literature. The burning, churning sensation inside her and the harsh rasp of Robert's voice drew Abigail out of her pristine Victorian world into the place of forbidden sensuality that she had always dreamed of.

Throwing her head back, she let his fingers drive her, open her, become her, faster, harder, deeper, until she was gasping for air and—

"How does your fantasy man take your virginity, Abigail?"

Robert's voice was a harsh intrusion. She dug her fingernails into the quilt to gain enough composure to speak. "He . . . He takes me while I lie on my back."

"Do my fingers still hurt you?"

"No." She lifted her hips to take him more deeply.

"What do you want, Abigail?"

Her response was one of mindless pleasure. "More!"

Suddenly his fingers were gone and the pillow on either side of her head sank down while hard, hairy legs pushed wide her thighs and she could feel him between her legs where his fingers had been, huge as a stump and hot as a poker and pulsing with life.

"Like this?" The voice above her was feral. "Is this how your fantasy man takes your virginity, Abigail? With his legs holding you open so he can get to you?"

"Yes." Abigail clutched at his shoulders; they were slick with sweat. Muscles rippled underneath her palms—real, not fantasy. Hungrily she smoothed her hands over his back, tested muscles that women did not have, sank her fingernails into those small, taut buttocks—memorizing him for all the empty months and years ahead. And all the while, that male part of him pulsed and throbbed against the feminine part of her and she was wide open and completely accessible *and things were progressing far too fast.* "You feel very large, Robert," she gasped. "Are you? In comparison to other men, I mean."

Moist breath fanned her cheeks, her lips. Callused fingertips soothed aside the tangled, damp hair that had escaped her bun— they trembled against her skin, as if it was he who was about to lose his virginity and not her. Then his right hand slid down between their bodies. "You be the judge, Abigail."

Without warning, his mouth swallowed her breath and his tongue was inside her and *oh*, he was plunging inside her down there, too, and yes, he was large, far, far larger than his three fingers and there was nothing she could do to stop him as he plowed through the open, liquid heat that he had made of her body. Deeper and deeper he slid, stretching her wider and wider until he could not possibly go any deeper or stretch her any wider but he did and she had never imagined anything like it.

It felt as if he touched her soul.

She tore her mouth away from his. "You said sex was dirty."

"I lied."

She arched her back, momentarily overwhelmed by the heavy weight of his body pressing down on her. "Robert—"

Instantly the hand between their bodies slid over and under her hip. He supported her there in the middle of her back where she arched. "Hmm?"

Tears pricked the backs of her eyes. "Nothing. I just . . . I feel . . . so *full.*"

Whisper-soft lips brushed her mouth. Again. And again. And

again. "You are. Relax, Abigail. Hook your legs around my waist."

Abigail tried. She really did. But every movement made him slide deeper and deeper and he was bigger than a fence rail inside her and—

"Robert, the limbs of a woman are *not* made to—"

He nipped her lip. "But *you* are not just any woman, Abigail. For the duration of the storm you are *my* woman."

Suddenly her legs were locked around his hips and they were no longer two bodies but one.

"Stay open for me, Abigail."

Abigail strove to catch her breath. "I do not believe I have a choice, Robert."

She could feel a fleeting smile, there against her forehead; it was followed by a fleeting kiss, on the tip of her nose. "Then come for me."

"But you have yet to fulfill your part of the bargain."

That stillness again. "What is that?"

"You have yet to make me beg and cry."

Without warning, the body pinning her to the bed shifted. The thick shaft that filled her to capacity drew out and up, so that it sawed between her swollen nether lips. The angle stretched her unbearably as he slowly thrust back inside her, and again withdrew, thrust harder, withdrew, sawing back and forth, taunting and teasing the engorged bud at the top until suddenly—

Raw heat replaced all traces of discomfort.

"Robert, please!" She dug her fingernails into his back.

"Please what, Abigail? Tell me. Shall I do it harder? Faster?" Robert matched words with action. "Slower? Deeper?"

Gritting her teeth in frustration, she churned her hips in a most unladylike manner. "No, no, *do not slow down,* harder, Robert, please, do it harder! Faster! Harder, Robert, *harder!*"

The breath whooshed from her lungs as he plunged inside her—hard, fast, deep; harder, faster, deeper, a fantasy more compelling than any she had ever imagined.

"There! There!" She clawed at his slippery back and pumping buttocks to keep the necessary friction, the necessary speed, even as she wondered if she would ever be able to walk again. "Do not stop, Robert, *please don't stop!*"

"Open wider, Abigail. Beg me some more, cry for it. *Make me forget that I have killed, damn you.* Give me *more.* Let me know you want more. Come for me—now—now—*now!*"

Rage. Pain. Desire.

Abigail should have been frightened—she could not tell if the man inside her was the colonel who commanded obedience or the lover who wanted forgetfulness or the soldier who killed out of duty. Nor did she think that Robert could tell who he was in that second. But suddenly the black rage of the storm split apart under the pistoning pressure and Abigail screamed Robert's name as he demonstrated that a man can indeed give a woman pleasure.

Robert! carried through the night.

Just as she fell back inside her body, he ground his pelvis into hers. As if to become a part of her. Or perhaps he was trying to bury his past inside her. Then a scalding jet of liquid spurted into her and a strangled cry erupted from Robert's throat.

Her books mentioned a man's ejaculation; they failed utterly at describing the feel of it filling a woman's body.

A fantasy man did not drip with sweat or fall bonelessly atop a woman's body in the aftermath of passion while his breath gusted inside her ear like a bellows and his satisfaction echoed in the wind.

A fantasy man did not take away loneliness as well as give pleasure.

Abigail rubbed her hands down his slippery spine. "Thank you, Robert."

Chapter 3

Before Robert had joined the Army he had been Robbie; once in the Army he had been Coally. Private Coally; Corporal Coally; Sergeant Coally; Lieutenant Coally; Captain Coally; *sir.* After a lifetime of doing other people's killing he had become Colonel Coally. Outside of battle with the occasional whore or even during battle with the occasional camp follower, he had remained anonymous. No one save Abigail had ever used his christened name.

No woman had ever screamed for him when reaching her pleasure.

No woman had ever thanked him for fucking her.

Small, firm breasts heaved against his chest. Tiny little contractions continued to ripple about his spent manhood.

Abigail's pleasure.

She was a lady—there was no doubting her accent or her mannerisms.

She was a twenty-nine-year-old spinster—who had willingly sacrificed her virginity.

She had accepted his pain and his passion and given him the gift of her body.

Without her he would not have survived the storm.

And he knew, just as surely as he knew that he should get up and spend the rest of the night in the privy, that he would hold her to her promise. By the end of the storm there would be nothing that he did not know about her.

Including the reason she lied about her genteel status and hid herself in an isolated cabin with nothing but erotic literature for companionship.

Carefully levering himself onto his elbows to take the brunt of his weight off her, he pressed his mouth to her ear.

A bittersweet surge of pleasure washed over him.

It was such an innocent thing—a woman's ear.

He suddenly wanted to know that ear, to taste each nook and cranny, to make it a part of himself.

He wanted to make Abigail a part of himself.

Her ear was shell-shaped—deceptively cool and delicate on the outside, like Abigail herself. He mapped the interior, slowly thrust the tip of his tongue into the hot, narrow channel.

The ripples in her vagina increased.

Shifting his weight onto one elbow, he swept his right hand down the length of her side, then burrowed between her and the quilt to grasp a soft cheek. The motion pushed him deeper inside her. "Did I hurt you?"

"A little." Her voice was husky in the night, the prickly formality mellowed by passion. "I think you hurt me more with your fingers than you did with the . . . other."

"That's because I used my fingers to stretch your maidenhead." He found her lips, swollen lips, sensitive lips that instinctively softened against the pressure of his. Lips that only he had kissed.

Gently he circled inside her, his tongue and his manhood.

Then, "What does your fantasy man do after he takes your virginity?"

"He . . . shares his body with me."

Impossibly, Robert felt his manhood stirring to life. Deliberately he flexed inside her. "How does he share his body with you?"

Her breath escaped in a small gasp. Short nails carved half-moons into his back. "He lets me touch him. And kiss him. And taste him. Everything you did to me."

Whores had kissed Robert and whores had taken him into their mouths, all for money. No woman had ever expressed a desire to do so out of pure pleasure.

Gently he disengaged his body from hers and rolled over onto his back.

He wasn't prepared for a woman like Abigail. His fantasy woman took his passion and his body and gave him only her pleasure. She did not seek to know his body as he did hers.

The mattress dipped. Cool fingers tentatively rested on his stomach, trailed up his chest. "Do men have feelings in their . . ." She lightly swept his chest in a searching motion, found him, and was instantly distracted. "You are smaller than I am."

He stared up into the darkness. "I am a man."

"But just as hard. When you touched my nipple, I felt it deep inside my womb. What does it feel like when I touch yours?"

She ran the pad of her thumb over his nipple. Again. And again. And again.

White fire shot straight to his groin. He grabbed her hand and held it flat against his chest, breathing in the scent of her body, of his body, of sex.

And wondered why a woman like Abigail, a woman who was filled with clean, innocent passion would take into herself a man like him, a man who had killed and confessed he would kill again.

"Does your fantasy woman suckle you, Robert?"

"All I need, Abigail, is a woman to give herself to me." His voice was even, remote. "I don't fantasize about giving myself to a woman."

"But you would?"

Not before tonight, he thought bleakly.

"Your fantasies, Abigail. Whatever you want."

"Then I want to suckle you, Robert."

Robert's chest swelled at the feel of her hot, wet mouth rooting through the coarse mat of his hair for his nipple. He was inexplicably overcome by a surge of vulnerability.

Women gave their breasts into the care of a man that he might nurture off her gentleness.

Men who killed did not nurture.

Men who killed had nothing to offer a lady.

Closing his eyes, he curved his hands around her head.

And realized that her hair was still caught up in the ugly bun that told the world she was a staid spinster, while inside her burned the same needs and wants that burned inside him, she caught up in a society that denied her womanhood, he caught up in a career that he had chosen when he was too young to know better.

He found a hairpin—pulled it out.

The wet heat nuzzling his chest was abruptly replaced by cool air. A hand reached up—grabbed his that was searching for another pin.

"What are you doing?"

"Unveiling you."

Without warning Abigail scrambled up, mattress dipping, bed creaking. She gasped with dismay.

He opened his eyes, instantly alert, a soldier prepared for action.

"What is it?" he asked sharply.

"Nothing."

He reached out—found her knee. She was kneeling on the bed.

"Our bargain, Abigail." He tightened his grip. "Talk to me."

"It is just . . ." He could see her, a dark silhouette, head thrown back toward the black ceiling. "Oh, for heaven's sake, it is nothing, really. When I sat up, something . . . *you* . . . came out of me."

Robert's manhood leapt to full life.

Sitting up, he followed the line of Abigail's knee, soft and slender, growing softer, softer . . . Their fingers met on her thigh.

A cool, viscous fluid was smeared on it. Her fingertips rested on the outer parameters.

"My sperm." His voice was flat in the darkness.

"I know." Her voice sounded more like she was nine going on ten instead of twenty-nine going on thirty.

"There's still some inside you." He linked his fingers between hers and guided their hands between her legs. "Feel. Me. And you."

She gasped when he brought their joined fingers up to her hot, swollen lips.

There was more of him. And her.

The essence of a man and a woman.

He had never felt himself on a woman before. Had never felt himself inside her.

The combined sensation of the slick viscous fluids warmed by her body struck him with the force of a bullet.

When she would have jerked her hand away, he forced their fingers between her swollen, passion-slick lips, pushed upward until two fingers slid inside her flesh, one his and one hers.

"I never knew two people could be this close." Her voice was a sough of breath.

"Neither did I," he murmured hoarsely. "Why did you pull away from me when I started taking down your hair?"

"It gets tangled."

Robert recognized a lie when he heard one.

Another secret to unravel, another obstacle to overcome.

"I'll brush it for you tomorrow. Spread your legs wider."

Clumsily she acceded; her body dipped lower to the mattress, forcing their fingers further up inside her.

The muscles inside her vagina rippled. "Robert."

"What?"

"Did you really peep through the window?"

"You didn't open the door when I knocked."

She clenched her body, forcibly trapping their fingers inside her. "I was reading."

He wondered what sex act she had been reading about to put the sublime expression on her face that he had witnessed when looking through the window. "So I saw."

"What did you think I was reading?"

"Devotional literature."

He waited for her next question, could feel it trembling on the air.

When it didn't come, he answered her anyway. "I did not take you because I thought you were wanton, Abigail. I took you because I needed you. And you were right. What we shared tonight is not dirty."

The huskiness in her voice deepened. "Robert."

"What?"

"Lean forward."

"Why?"

"Because I want to kiss you."

Heart lurching inside his chest—he who killed without blinking an eye—he leaned forward, made her lean forward, too, for the pleasure of feeling her body adjust around their fingers.

Her lips missed his at first. She raised a cool hand and found his jaw, aligned her lips accordingly.

It was a virgin kiss.

A first kiss.

He let her learn his lips while inside her he could feel the myriad little convulsions the two of their fingers were causing. And then, suddenly, the wet heat that inundated his fingers covered his lips.

Abigail learned quickly. She rimmed the seam of his mouth with her tongue. Immediately he opened for her, allowed her to enter him as he entered her.

But he wanted more.

More of the storm.

More of Abigail.

He sucked her tongue more deeply inside him, then he suckled it as he had her clitoris and her nipple, suckled until the tiny ripples around their fingers became one large contraction, and with a little gasp she came into his mouth.

Gently he released her tongue and her hand. And found the remaining hairpins in her hair. They fell to the plank floor like a rain of firing pins. Carefully searching for more, but finding none, he plunged both hands into her hair and worked it loose until it hung wild and free down her back, a curtain of living silk.

He felt his penis grow another inch.

"Lie down."

"Why?"

"So I can crawl over your body."

"Not into it?"

"Later." Robert's lips twitched—his prim and proper lady was game to the end. "First we need to get you cleaned up."

"I am quite capable of washing myself, Robert."

"That's not the bargain, Abigail. You agreed to *everything*."

He ended the conflict by the simple expediency of scooping her up and lying her down. And ruefully wished that skirmishes were as easily won on the battlefield.

"If you wash me, I will wash you." Abigail's dignified threat was meant as a warning.

Robert grinned. In the next second it felt as if the wind had been knocked out of his lungs.

He had not been washed since he was a child—a lifetime ago, before the killing had started and overnight he had grown into a man. "I'll hold you to that, Abigail."

The bucket was underneath the sink—he primed the pump. Icy water splashed into the worn metal. He pumped twice more before grabbing the washcloth on the rack beside the sink.

Setting the bucket onto the floor by the bed, he dipped the washcloth into the water and wrung it dry before easing down onto the edge of the bed. He warmed the cloth inside his hands. "Doesn't your fantasy man ever do this for you, Abigail?"

"There is no need to wash after a fantasy man," she replied tartly.

Robert found himself smiling in the darkness.

He had smiled and laughed more with Abigail in the last few hours than he had in the last twenty-two years.

The two should not go together—laughter and passion. Then again, a man like him and a lady like her should not fit together, either.

But they did.

He was not going to let a belated sense of modesty interfere with their union.

She held perfectly still for his ministrations, as if she derived as much enjoyment from being touched by him as he did in touching her. He memorized her face through the rough, damp cloth, discovered a high, smooth forehead, a slender nose, a rounded jaw—and regretted only that he had not thought to light the candle so that he could see her as well as feel her.

She had brown eyes, he suddenly remembered. They had widened in outrage when he had opened the trunk and revealed her erotica. Then they had flamed with amber when she had glimpsed his unchecked passion.

Abigail arched her neck. She had a fragile neck, long and slender like those of the Egyptian busts he had seen when stationed in Egypt. Her right breast filled the palm of his hand—her nipple was hard. Slowly, so slowly, he eased the cloth over her stomach, a soft little mound that had rippled beneath his hand when he had suckled her, and then there was slick wetness that owed nothing to water.

With single-minded intensity he explored the changes he had wrought in her body. With heart-stopping trust, she allowed him.

Her flesh was swollen where he had entered her, the opening stretched, so that now he could easily penetrate her with one finger, two, not as easily with three, hampered by the cloth. Gently he swirled away the evidence of their passion.

Working down to her thighs, he cleansed away the stickiness there, unerringly returned to the mystery between her legs.

He washed Abigail slowly, thoroughly, lost in her heat and softness, here the skin crinkly with hair, there plump and smooth. Reaching further back, he found the top of the soft crevice and swirled the washcloth round and round, down and down, in tight little circular motions.

The washcloth was plucked out of his hand.

Robert's muscles coiled. "I said *everything*, Abigail."

"You said *my* fantasies, Robert." The mattress dipped, then the bed was empty. "Lie down."

Robert found himself smiling—again. She knew him for what he was, yet she dared give him orders as if he was a normal man who had never experienced the horrors of war. He lay down.

Abigail rinsed and rinsed the cloth out.

He wondered what thoughts were going through her head. If she thought about what he had done to her. If she thought about what she was going to do to him. Or if she thought about what she had been reading before he had barged into the cottage.

Erotic acts she wanted to engage in but didn't dare.

Sexual acts her fantasy lover dared.

Sexual acts perhaps Robert was unaware of, steeped in war and death instead of erotica.

Sexual acts he would dare . . . before the storm was over.

Suddenly the cloth was on his face, cold, with the heat of her fingers penetrating underneath. Robert could feel the anger and despair of his past draining out of him, as if underneath his skin there still existed the innocent youth he had once been.

"Kiss me." His voice grated in the dark.

"Only if you tell me what you do to your fantasy woman."

He stared up at the dark silhouette hovering over him. And closed his eyes to the truth.

Abigail *was* his fantasy woman.

"I kiss her."

"Like this, you mean?" Her lips teased him, more confident now, more taunting. She gently rubbed them against his. Until he felt like his lips would burst into flame. Then she tasted them, delicately, her tongue swirling into the corners of his lips, along the seam, before her mouth opened and covered his, gradually learning the art, sucking slightly to adhere their flesh, her tongue touching his, then mapping out his mouth, the roof of his mouth— he exhaled sharply at the stab of desire that shot through his groin—underneath his tongue. Her breath fanned his cheek in little warm puffs while she smoothed his hair back from his forehead.

Robert had never realized how deeply a woman's tongue could penetrate a man's defenses. He fisted his hand in the warm curtain of her hair and took control of the kiss.

Only to find that when he dueled her tongue back into her mouth, she sucked on his like he had earlier sucked on hers until she wrung from him a groan.

"What else, Robert?" Her breath was a whisper of heat on his lips. "What else do you fantasize about?"

Bloodied faces flashed before his eyes. Men he had killed. Men he had sent out on missions to be killed. Innocent women and children caught in the crossfire of war.

And with the images came the need that had kept him alive.

But Abigail wanted fantasies, not a battle-scarred soldier's needs.

Before he could think of a lie, the cold, damp cloth trailed down his neck, his chest.

He groaned, knowing what was in store for him. And found that it was a fantasy of his. A fantasy that he had never known he possessed.

"You never answered my question, earlier," she said, the cloth circling and circling a hardened nipple. "Is it as sensitive for a man here as it is for a woman?"

"Yes," he growled.

"Good." The cool cloth lifted. Only to be replaced by a scalding mouth.

He could feel the pull of her lips and tongue all the way down to his testicles. My God, he had *never* felt like this. Had never known that the male body was capable of this much sensation.

He grabbed the back of her head when she freed his nipple. "Don't stop."

"I read that a woman can orgasm from a man suckling her breast. Do you think a man can orgasm from a woman suckling his?"

Robert almost orgasmed at the mere thought. "I don't know."

He gritted his teeth, prepared for Abigail's next move. Only to find out that he was not prepared at all.

He had just spent himself not more than thirty minutes earlier. He should not even be hard, let alone on the verge of coming.

She ran the now-warm cloth past his straining manhood and cupped his testicles.

"Abigail . . ."

She ignored his growl of warning.

He could sense her hesitance, could have told her the second that she made up her mind. The cloth slipped lower still, pressed into his perineum. Silky warm hair covered his groin at the same time that her mouth daintily gulped his manhood.

A jolt of heat flashed through his body.

Shame.

That he could not control himself.

Awe.

That she had brought him to this point.

"Jesus Christ. *Abigail!*" With a groan he jerked aside.

She grabbed on to him and swallowed him as deeply as she could while his flesh exploded inside her mouth.

When he could breathe again, he reached down and caressed her head, needing her close, needing to hold her. Needing her to hold him. "Come here."

She sat up. "Did I do it . . . properly?"

She was trembling. With desire? Disgust?

"No one, Abigail, has ever done it more properly. Did you enjoy yourself?" he asked warily.

"Yes, thank you. I have always wondered what a man tastes like."

"And what does a man taste like?"

Robert should have been warned by the hair that suddenly spilled around his face. But he wasn't.

"Taste for yourself."

He was momentarily paralyzed by shock, allowing her mouth to cover his and her tongue to thrust inside him. It was coated with his sperm.

He blindly grabbed her upper arms and hauled her back. *"Jesus."*

"Have you ever done that before?"

He plunged his hands into the silky heat of her hair. "What? Tasted myself? *Never.*"

"No. I mean . . . Have you ever kissed a woman between her legs before tonight?"

Her hair clung to his fingers; it was as soft as butterfly wings. He hesitated, "No."

"Why not?"

"Whores are not always the cleanest of people."

"Do you do it to your fantasy woman?"

Robert picked her up and sat her sideways across his stomach. Abigail squealed.

Children squealed like that when they were shot. As did some women. And men.

Grabbing her right leg, he pulled it up and over his body so that she straddled his hips.

Her hands smacked against his chest. "What are you doing?"

He reached up and cupped her breasts. "Guess."

"But—can you do it again?"

"Perhaps. If not, I can satisfy you in other ways."

Her nipples were rock hard. He rolled them between his thumbs and forefingers until she was squirming and pressing her hands over his.

Incredibly, he felt himself stir underneath her seductively soft bottom.

"Robert. Robert. Not there. Touch me somewhere else."

He continued rolling her nipples, wanting to push her to the limit. Wanting to push himself to the limit. Wanting to end once and for all the darkness of death. "Where, Abigail?"

"You know where, Robert."

"But I want to hear you say it, Abigail. I know you know the words."

"Robert—"

"I won't stop teasing your nipples until you say it."

"I want you to touch my—to touch my—*my pearl!*"

There was no question about what was or was not stirring underneath her bottom. Abigail, too, noticed the phenomenon. She ceased attempting to pry his fingers away from her nipples and reached behind her to grab his manhood.

Without guidance, she lifted up. Holding him tightly in her fist, she brought him to her vaginal lips, a wet, hot kiss of intimate desire. Only to tease him with herself. Or perhaps she teased herself with him.

"Do you mind?" she gasped.

Robert gasped when she slid him past her opening and up to the top of her clinging, swollen lips. He could feel the hard bud of her clitoris, could feel it throbbing. She rubbed the crown of his manhood against her there, round and round, slid it back down to tease her opening. Again. And again. On the forth pass he couldn't hold back a reflexive arch of his hips.

It wasn't going to take much for Abigail to gain satisfaction. Suddenly Robert minded very much that she should orgasm alone.

When next she brought the crown of him down to moisten it at her opening, his hand was there, too, holding his manhood steady while, with his left hand, he pulled her right thigh wider, forcibly bringing her body down closer.

This time the gasp belonged to her.

"Easy. Are you sore?"

"A little."

He pulled her thigh out further—and sank further up inside her.

Her muscles clenched and tightened around him as if they could force him out.

He gripped her more tightly.

He *would not* let her reject him.

"Bear down, Abigail. Once I'm in, I won't hurt you anymore, I promise. Open up. Relax." Having breached her body, he slid his right hand down to her left thigh; using both hands, he steadily, relentlessly, pulled her thighs wider and wider apart until she had no choice but to— "Take it. Take all of me, Abigail."

She did.

He knew he was causing her pain. He also knew how to take that pain away.

Lightly he soothed the taut muscles in her thighs. "Relax, sweetheart. Relax, Abigail." When her muscles eased, he slid his left hand up and rubbed her nipple. Bringing up his right hand, he touched her clitoris.

A pearl, she had called it.

From *The Pearl*, no doubt.

Below her swollen bud was a taut ring of wet, pulsing flesh—
her surrounding him.

Robert had never realized before how thin feminine skin
stretched to hold a penis . . . or how fragile was the bonding of
a man and a woman.

She quivered as he rimmed her clitoris with the pad of his
thumb. Her inner muscles told him all that he needed to know.
They told him how hard to press, how fast, until suddenly the
taut band of flesh surrounding him relaxed utterly. In the next
instant it clutched him so tightly it was almost painful.

Abigail cried out.

Robert cried out.

But he didn't move. He had promised her he would not bring
her any more pain, only pleasure, and he meant to keep that
promise.

Before she had time to catch her breath, he rubbed her swollen
bud again. Until her inner muscles again gripped and milked him
in climax.

He used her pleasure to bring about his own peak. It took six
orgasms in all. When he arched up into her, she collapsed over
him in a blanket of soft hair and damp flesh.

Mustering up energy he had never known he possessed, he
jerked the bedcovers out from underneath his body and pulled
them up around her.

Holding her tightly in his arms, his flesh snugly encased in
hers, he prayed that the storm would last another night.

Chapter 4

Rain was a steady drum of sensation; it pounded against the walls
and the ceiling, impaling Abigail's body on a shaft of raw heat.

She shifted to find a more comfortable position—her pillow
was fuzzy and the bed bone-hard.

The feeling of being impaled grew. As did the raw heat inside her lower body.

Her eyes flew open.

A mat of wiry black hair greeted her gaze. It covered a very broad, naked chest.

Stifling a cry of alarm, Abigail lifted her head.

She stared into pewter-gray eyes framed by ridiculously thick, long black lashes.

Every muscle in her body clenched in recognition at what filled her to capacity.

She had taken a stranger into her bed. She had taken him into her mouth. And she had taken him into her body.

Where he was still lodged.

Pale-gray light illuminated the dark stubble lining the oddly tensed face of the man underneath her. "Good morning."

In the dark heat of night Abigail had been a woman; in the cold light of day she was once again an aging spinster.

An aging spinster who had propositioned a stranger—and then had begged and cried for him not to stop.

Abigail stiffened her spine. "Good morning."

He folded down the covers from around her shoulders and eased her upright so that she sat across his hips. "Do you mind?"

Do you mind ricocheted inside her head—the words she had asked before using his manhood to rub against her engorged flesh.

Flesh she had named.

I want you to touch my—to touch my—my pearl!

Her muscles tightened in protest; she felt as if she sat on a fence post. His shoulders were brown against the white of the sheet and pillow—tight little brown nipples peeped through black chest curls.

Which meant that her breasts were equally visible.

Breasts he had suckled like a starving infant.

She slapped her arms across her chest.

His hips surged upward with unmistakable intent.

Abigail gasped. At the sensation of him prodding the very depths of her body. At the realization that the intolerable pressure had nothing to do with what was inside her vagina and everything to do with what was inside her bladder.

Freeing her right arm, she braced her hand on the mat of wiry chest hair—chest hair that *she* had rooted around in like a starving infant. "Actually, yes, I do mind. You see, I need to—to—"

Words failed her.

She closed her eyes at the loss of whatever dignity she still possessed.

There simply did not exist a polite formula for informing a man buried deep inside a woman that the dictates of nature preceded the urges of the flesh.

A boisterous laugh penetrated her mortification. The motion of his body combined with that of the bed caused her to jiggle up and down on the extremely solid flesh planted between her legs.

Opening her eyes in pained outrage, she anchored herself to his chest with both hands; her freed breasts swayed unimpeded. Hard, calloused fingers dug into her hips while pewter-gray glinted up at her.

"A lesson for the both of us. Men wake up with a hard-on. Whereas women, I take it, wake up merely needing to relieve themselves."

Gritting her teeth, Abigail attempted to scramble off him, only to find that her legs refused to move—they were numb from lack of circulation. "I beg your pardon, but I seem to require assistance in getting—down—up—"

The tanned skin around his eyes crinkled. "My pleasure, but you reversed the order. First we lift you up—" Strong hands circled her waist. "Then we help you down."

Robert jackknifed up in bed and onto his knees in one fluid motion. Abigail hardly had time to gasp before he was out of her body and she lay sprawled on the bed. He loomed over her with his manhood jutting in front of her face.

It was every bit as impressive in the pale light of day as it had been in the murky dark of night.

Grabbing the gray blanket at the foot of the bed, she pulled it around her naked body. "Thank you."

His grin widened. "It's still storming outside."

She was all too aware of the weather. "Yes."

"I take it you have a chamberpot."

She did. Under the bed.

Supremely unself-conscious in his nakedness, Robert climbed off the bed and leaned down. The monotonous patter of rain was interrupted by the drag of smooth porcelain over hard wood.

Robert straightened. "Shall I help you?"

The heat blazing in Abigail's face felt like it would burst into flame. "I think not."

"Abigail, there is no place for modesty inside a one-room cottage. Men and women share the same bodily functions. I have to make use of it, too. What is the difference, for God's sake?"

She refused to look away from him. "The difference, Colonel Coally, is that women squat and men do not."

His gray eyes widened momentarily; then he threw back his head and roared with laughter.

He had very white teeth.

The laughter stopped when Abigail scooted out of bed—slowly, carefully; the flesh between her thighs stung as though she had been impaled on a shaft of nettles. Her legs were like two slabs of wood, with no feeling in them whatsoever. Standing, bracing herself so she would not fall flat on her face, she reached for the faded green dress that lay heaped on the floor.

"Don't be ridiculous, Abigail." It was the colonel's voice of last night, sharp and autocratic. "It's pouring down rain outside."

Firmly clasping the blanket across her breasts, she threw the dress over her head—and got totally lost inside it. Her stilted reply was muffled. "You may dictate to your men, Colonel Coally. I, however, am not ruled by military law."

Long, hard fingers reached inside the dress, grabbed her left hand, thrust it into a sleeve. "You did not object last night, Miss Abigail."

They both knew they were not discussing military dictatorship.

"Last night, Colonel Coally, was an anomaly."

"It is not necessary to go outside." The muted voice was suddenly flat. Her right hand was forced into a sleeve. "I give you my word as an officer that I will not intrude on your privacy."

"Thank you, but no." Her head cleared the dress. "I am in need of fresh air."

"Very well." He whirled her around.

Abigail stared past his dark head—his hair was hardly mussed, while hers felt full of live rats. "I can button up my own dress, Colonel Coally."

"Can you, Miss Abigail?" he asked enigmatically. Reaching inside the open placket of her dress, he grabbed hold of the blanket and yanked it up and out. Before she could voice her objection, he pulled her dress together and commenced fastening the tiny buttons.

Abigail silently endured his ministrations. The colonel just as silently retrieved her drawers.

She grabbed the silk from his hands and turned her back to wriggle inside the flimsy underwear.

"Where are your shoes? Or do you make a habit of running about barefoot?"

Blushing, back ramrod straight—where *had* she put her shoes? *ah, yes*—she marched to the door and crammed her feet inside the half-boots there. She contemplated putting her hair up, but knew there was no time to waste.

The wind almost knocked her back inside the door. It was accompanied by a blast of memories.

I want a woman to make me forget that I have spent the last twenty-two years of my life killing.

He had thought she was reading devotional literature when he had peeped through the window. Matrons and spinsters read devotional literature, not a woman who a man would choose to help make him forget.

What a shock he must have experienced, seeing *The Pearl* clutched to her chest.

What a whore he must have thought her when she had propositioned him.

How pitifully desperate she had been, an old maid unable to accept her virgin status.

I did not take you because I thought you were wanton, Abigail. I took you because I needed you.

The rain was icy.

For a second Abigail's intent wavered.

He knew everything else about her body, what was so shameful about this aspect of it? But then reason prevailed.

The colonel knew the wanton she had been in the night; not the spinster she was in the day.

Bowing her head, she fought the wind to close the door, then fought the wind and the rain and the mud all the way to the backyard privy. Only to fight it all the way back again on the return trip.

The colonel met her at the door; a towel was wrapped around his lean hips. After one look at Abigail's sodden clothes and dripping hair, he unbuttoned her dress and peeled it and the silk drawers off her. Wrapping the blanket around her, then, he picked her up as if she weighed no more than a child and sat her down on the wooden chair at the table where the air was unaccountably warm.

Abigail should have been outraged at such cavalier treatment. Instead, she felt chastised . . . and oddly comforted.

Hunkering down in front of her, he matter-of-factly removed her shoes. "I fired the stove and put a bucket of water on to heat. All I could find in the cupboard was a tin of tea, half a loaf of bread, and a jar of strawberry jam. Would you like some toast now or would you rather wait for the water to heat up and have it with your tea?"

Abigail turned her head to look at the wood box behind the stove. It was missing a hefty portion of wood. The other chair was pulled up to the far side of the stove; it was draped with his clothes that she had dropped last night. Turning her head in the opposite direction, she surveyed the floor in front of the cupboard. There was no broken glass littered about—a broom leaned against the wall.

The Pearl, where she had dropped it by the bed last night, was gone, too. As were the hairpins he had taken from her hair.

She faced the man who waited at her feet. "I will wait for tea, thank you."

"You're a stubborn woman, Miss Abigail."

Abigail stared into the stark gray eyes that were on a level with her own and felt her heart skip a beat.

He looked—vulnerable. And intensely masculine.

Last night *had* been an anomaly.

It must have been.

He had gone out into the storm—and had come upon her cottage. Once past the initial heat of lust, a man like him would not want a woman like her.

But you are not just any woman, Abigail. For the duration of the storm you are my *woman.*

It still stormed.

Abigail braced herself against the rejection that was certain to come. "You lied, Colonel Coally."

The dark face grew shuttered. "In what, Miss Abigail?"

"You said you wanted everything."

"*You* said last night was an anomaly."

"Then *I* lied."

For one endless second the steady rhythm of the rain ceased. Then tiny lines radiated out from the corners of Robert's gray eyes, and they were no longer stark but warm pewter.

"How does the sponge feel?"

Blushing, Abigail tilted her chin. "It feels—there."

"I'll take it out for you."

The blush grew hotter.

"After I soak you in hot water to relieve the soreness."

She refused to look away from the pewter gaze. "And what then, Colonel Coally?"

"Then I'm going to put it back in."

Suddenly the damp, dreary rain was more pleasant than a sunny day.

"Perhaps I will have that toast now, Colonel Coally."

"We made a bargain, Abigail. Until the storm ends we call each other by our first names and you are free to indulge in any sexual urges that you wish."

The redhot stove hissed as water boiled over onto it. Grabbing a towel, Robert picked up the handle of the bucket and poured the hot water into the little hip bath beside the sink. Steam roiled up to the ceiling. The remainder of the water he poured into a tea pot. Then he refilled the bucket and set it back on the stove.

"Are we on bread-and-water rations?"

"Only until Mrs. Thomas makes it through the storm. She and Mr. Thomas look after the cottage. For a few extra shillings a week she cooks and cleans and does my laundry."

"I doubt she'll make it today."

"No." A warm glow of anticipation grew inside Abigail's stomach. Another night with this man was well worth a little starvation.

Robert toasted bread to a fine turn. And spread strawberry jam lavishly.

She waved her cup toward the cupboard. "There's butter inside—not much, so unless you want to save it for later . . ."

His gray eyes darkened. He met her gaze, a half-brooding, half-searching look. "Why did you pull away last night?"

She squared her shoulders, fully prepared to lie. If he had not discovered her faults, who was she to point them out? Instead, she said, "You were taking my hair down."

"You have beautiful hair, Abigail."

"I have gray in my hair, Robert."

She did not expect evidence of her rapidly approaching old age to inspire laughter. But it did.

She tilted her chin and held up her cup of tea with her little finger sticking out at the required degree. "I am glad you find my age amusing, Robert."

"Abigail, I am five years older than you are. And if you had any gray hairs, I would not be laughing."

"But I do," she stubbornly insisted.

"Then I don't see them."

"A woman my age should not let her hair down."

"Perhaps that is why there are men like me, to take it down for them."

She lowered her eyelashes to block those pewter eyes before she started believing in the impossible.

"Is your leg well?"

"Which one?"

Abigail's gaze rose to the bait. "Your left one—"

Only to be stopped by the glint in his eyes.

"You have a wicked sense of humor, Colonel—Robert."

"And you have a sore bum to look after, Miss—Abigail."

"It is not my bum that is sore."

"I know what is sore. And I know how to make it better."

The bucket of water on the stove hissed. He added it to the hip bath—and disappeared behind a fog of steam. Vigorous pumping sounds penetrated the gray mist; they were followed by the cascade of water pouring into water. The writhing steam thinned, revealing Robert leaning over the tub, checking the temperature with a seductive swish of liquid.

He straightened. "Your bath, madam."

Abigail approached the tub and boldly dropped the blanket. Robert just as boldly picked her up.

He kissed her.

His tongue was scalding hot. It was flavored with strawberry jam.

The bathwater was just as scalding hot, with none of the sweetness.

Disregarding dignity, Abigail threw a leg over each side of the tub and heaved herself up. Robert was equally determined to hold her down. And far more successful.

"Let me up! This is scalding!"

"Hold still, Abigail. The water is not going to do you any good unless it is hot."

"Only a lobster would benefit from water this hot!" Closing her eyes in pain and frustration, she tried a more civilized approach. "Please let me up."

"Did I tell you how beautiful you are?"

Abigail knew perfectly well that she wasn't beautiful. Her eyes snapped open. "You are fond of the color red, I take it?"

A low, masculine laugh filled the hot steam. "Abigail, you get much redder when you blush. I promise that after you've soaked for a while, you will feel much, much better."

"You mean that after I have soaked for a while, I will be well done."

"Done enough to eat."

The blistering heat that flooded her body had nothing to do with the water.

With a little sigh, Robert sat down on the floor at the head of the tub. "Lean back, Abigail."

With an answering sigh, Abigail leaned back. The hair on his chest made a wiry pillow. A sure hand came up and brushed the damp hair off her forehead. It repeated the soothing motion until

the water and the caress became one and Abigail felt as if her
bones were dissolving. She tilted her head back.

His head tilted forward to meet her gaze.

She felt her heart skip a beat.

He looked so alone.

No man, regardless of what he had done, deserved to bear
that much pain.

"Tell me," she softly commanded.

The gray eyes grew opaque. Bending his head down, he rubbed
his nose against hers. "Tell you what?"

"Tell me why you entered the Army at the age of thirteen."

"But you said that was illegal."

"And then tell me what you did in the Army."

He raised his head. Thick black lashes veiled his eyes.

"I enlisted in the Army because I was ambitious and I wanted
to see the world. I was a big strapping boy—no one questioned
my age. No sooner did I sign on as a drummer boy than my
dream came true—I was shipped to India."

Steam collected on his lashes, pearled on the black stubble
covering his face.

"India is a diverse country," Abigail prodded. "What section
were you stationed in?"

The thick black lashes lifted. He looked so terribly remote,
staring at her out of eyes that were looking back twenty-two
years. "Have you been there?"

"No."

"You are correct, India *is* a diverse country. It has jungles. It
has deserts. And it has mountains. When the morning sun rises
over the mountains, it turns the sand blood red."

"It sounds beautiful," Abigail said quietly, cautiously, wondering what could possibly have happened there to put that kind
of expression on a man's face. "Were you there for the Sepoy
Rebellion?"

The pewter-gray eyes filled with cynicism. "It's ironic, actually.
The Sepoy Rebellion started because the Muslims and the Hindus
objected to the British use of rifle cartridges greased with pig
and cow fat—whereas the British infantrymen would have been
perfectly happy to have some of that fat on their hardtack."

He shrugged, a fleeting scratch of hair and muscle against her back. "No, the rebellion was over by the time I arrived in India. My regiment was stationed at the foot of the mountains. I sneaked away to practice my drumming one morning—it's easier to drum than to sew and cook, which were the duties assigned to me until I learned how to properly drum a march."

Robert paused, lifted his right arm. Long fingers gently stroked her throat.

She arched her neck, giving him access to her body, the only comfort, she suspected, that he would accept. "So that morning— did you learn how to drum?"

"No. A *sepoy*—a Bengal army man—came upon me where I was playing in the ravine. The rebellion wasn't over for him. He thought it sport to kill a drummer boy—one less British soldier to deal with in the future. Not worth a bullet, but certainly I was worth the effort of skewering on a bayonet."

Abigail writhed—inside. Outside, she calmly held his bleak gaze and accepted the gentleness of his touch while she tried to imagine her eldest nephew—thirteen now, still playing with hoops—in the Army facing death.

"What happened?"

"Do you really want to know?"

"Yes." Her voice was firm.

"The *sepoy* taunted me, rushing me with the bayonet, drawing blood, pulling back. After a while he got overconfident, thinking that the English boy with blood and sweat and snot and tears running down his face was no threat. He forgot about the drumsticks. They're tapered, you know, and made out of good, solid wood. I drove the first one into the soft part of his belly."

Abigail's breath caught in her chest, seeing the bloodred sand, seeing the *sepoy*, seeing the child Robert had once been.

"Did it kill him?" she asked evenly.

"No. But it took him off guard."

The fingers thrumming her skin pressed down at the base of her neck where her pulse wildly drummed. "I drove the second drumstick into his throat. The moment I did it I wanted to take it back. I will never forget the look in his eyes. He pulled the stick out and stood there staring at it while blood and air gushed out of his throat and I thought, *he's not going to die*. But it was too late, there was no stopping it, the blood, it kept coming even when the wheezing breath stopped."

Hot, salty steam ran down Abigail's cheeks.

"When my commander saw what I had done, he gave me a rifle. The rebellion hadn't really ended; wars never do. We weren't there to establish peace, but to establish British rule. I killed my first man three months to the day of my enlistment, Abigail, and I have been killing ever since."

"You had no choice, Robert." The words that were meant to be a practical condolence were curiously thick.

Something flickered in his gray eyes. His chest moved against her head—his left arm came up. He cupped her face in both hands, thumbs smoothing her cheeks.

Abigail tensely waited, willing him to say it all.

"When my enlistment was over, I went back to England, quite prepared to take whatever work I could find. But it wasn't the same England. I wasn't the same man. I couldn't tell my family the horrors I had committed, fighting for their beloved country. I couldn't take the same pleasures they did in their simple day-to-day lives, knowing what so-called God-fearing men were capable of doing. So I reenlisted."

He bent his head. A whisper of a kiss closed Abigail's eyes; hot breath caressed her lashes.

"In hand-to-hand combat there is a certain closeness; you almost feel an affinity with the enemy. Black man, white man, brown man, yellow man, it makes no difference. When a man is stabbed, or shot, his eyes open wide in surprise. Surprise that the impossible is indeed possible—that they should die while the enemy lives."

Tears—Abigail distantly recognized the hot, salty substance that spilled down her face as tears, not steam. She was crying the tears that he was unable to.

"Four months ago, I didn't shoot—so I got shot." His thumbs continued smoothing her slippery cheeks. "They shipped me back to England. The leg healed and I knew I would go back to the Army. And I knew that the next time I looked into the eyes of a man, that the surprise would be in mine. And I found out something about myself while I was laid up, convalescing."

She had to strain to make out the rest of his words, feeling them rather than hearing them. "I found out that I did not want to die without knowing what it is like to lose myself inside a woman."

He raised his head and rested his chin on her forehead, a soft prick of stubbly beard. "I am not indulging you, Abigail. You are indulging me."

Dear God, she had wanted to know, and now she knew.

Abigail swallowed the lump in her throat. "Robert."

"Hmm?" His response was a low rumble in his chest.

"I think the sponge is growing."

The rumble grew, until it erupted full force into a shout of laughter.

Her head fell back from loss of support.

Robert leaned over the tub and extended long, brown fingers.

Without a moment's hesitation, she placed her hand in his. And was hauled up in a cascade of water.

"No. Don't stand. Squat down."

She stiffened, tears forgotten.

"Trust me."

The stark gray eyes were warm pewter.

She squatted.

"Spread your legs."

"In case you have failed to notice, Robert, this is a hip bath. There is no room to spread my legs."

Before she could divine his intentions, he bodily picked her up and faced her sideways in the tub.

"There is now. Lean back against me and spread wide, sweetheart."

Sweetheart. No man had ever called her by an endearment. Five-foot-nine-inch-tall women were not endearing. Yet this was the second time he had used the word. Once in the dark of night, and now in the light of day.

Excitement coiled in her stomach—and spine-melting vulnerability. Spreading wide her legs, she pressed her back against his chest, trapping her hair between them. The small pain seemed insignificant in comparison to what was going to happen.

Very firmly, very gently, he reached between her legs.

"Relax," he whispered. He nuzzled aside a strand of damp hair and rimmed the tip of her ear with his tongue. "Bear down."

His tongue stabbed into her ear. At the same time, his fingers delved inside her, creating pain, giving pleasure. And then he had it, the sponge, and he was pulling it out and holding it up for her inspection.

It was engorged, as big and swollen as—as if she had washed dishes with it.

Amusement was rife in Robert's voice. "A far better fate than to be scrubbing the back side of a pan, I would say."

Abigail threw her head back and laughed. And laughed. And laughed.

It was so totally ridiculous, that a common household item could be used for sexual protection.

It was so totally unexpected, that a man like Robert Coally would have a sense of humor.

He nipped her ear. "Still sore?"

"How can I tell?" she asked tartly. "My whole body is boiled."

"English meat, Abigail. Time to eat."

Chapter 5

Abigail opened her body willingly when Robert pushed the brandy-soaked sponge inside her. And tangled her fingers into his hair—unbelievably soft and warm—when he commenced "eating."

The orgasms she had experienced last night faded in comparison with the sensations that spiraled higher and higher inside her body. Last night she had not known what to expect—today she did.

She lifted her head up from the pillow and glanced down. The sight of his tanned fingers digging into her pale hips and his dark brown hair buried between her flexed thighs plummeted her over the edge.

When she opened her lashes he was there, leaning over her with pewter-gray eyes narrowed intently.

She smiled, equally intent. "My turn."

"I don't believe in waste. The sponge is ready."

"But you have the advantage over me."

Two hard, hot, hairy legs settled between hers. "In what respect?"

"You have seen my all, whereas I . . ."

"You saw my all before you decided to trek outside."

"But not like this." Abigail lifted her hand and touched his cheek. It was prickly with dark stubble. She wanted more than anything to examine this man, to record every inch of his body, every texture of his skin. She wanted to make herself as much a part of him as he had made himself a part of her. "In my books it says that a man changes color when he orgasms. I want to know, Robert. I want to know everything there is to know about you."

His gray eyes grew shuttered. Rolling off her, he lay down on his back and threw an arm over his eyes. "Then know me, Abigail . . . and let me know if I change color. The knowledge might come in useful on the battlefield. I could, armed with the information, astound and confound the enemy. Like a chameleon."

A reluctant laugh escaped Abigail. "You are mocking me, sir."

He lifted his arm and slanted a look at her. "Not at all. You will forgive a sudden sense of vulnerability on my part. It's not every day that a man bears his all for a lady's private schooling."

A twinge of reality intruded on her pleasure. "I am not a lady, Robert."

He reached out a long, tanned finger and flicked her nose. "You are a lady, Abigail, from the top of your head to the tips of your toes. And I am here to give you pleasure."

"What about your pleasure?" She trailed a hand down his chest, a muscled, contoured belly, and grabbed the root of their discussion.

"Get on with your studies, Miss Abigail, else you lose a student."

Abigail scooted down the bed. And was distracted by the sight of the angry red scar on his thigh. She lightly touched it with her left hand.

"Does it still hurt?"

His gray eyes were unreadable. "That's not part of the lesson plan, Miss Abigail."

"You were limping last night."

"Because I fell on it when the bloody horse threw me. Continue with your studies."

Abigail obligingly studied the swollen shaft that sprang out from a bed of black, curly hair. It seemed impossible that he had fit inside her. "Have you ever measured yourself?"

"You're putting me to blush."

"The head is purple." She ignored his sally. "It is very large, like a small fist. It has an eye." She captured the single drop of moisture that glistened on the tip and smeared it over the swollen glans. "And it weeps. Is it sad, Colonel Coally?"

"Very, Miss Abigail." Robert's voice was strained. "Why don't you kiss it and make it better?"

Abigail leaned down and touched her tongue to the purple-hued bulb. "You taste—salty, sir."

"You cannot judge the flavor by a single taste. Take it between your lips."

Robert knew exactly what he tasted like—just as Abigail did. Yet he was as entranced by this play between a man and a woman as was she.

Grasping the stalk of his penis in both hands, she pulled it taut so that she could take the crown of him fully in her mouth. And retasted him for flavor.

"You still taste salty, sir."

Robert's breathing quickened. "Perhaps you are mistaken—you should try again. Taste made in haste is not a good method by which to judge."

"Perhaps. But only if you tell me if you have ever measured yourself."

"Never."

"Then I shall do so." She spanned the length of his manhood with her fingers. They fell short of the purple-hued crown. "My fingers spread six inches—here. If I take my other hand and spread it out, so, then I span—nine inches, Colonel Coally. When next you go into battle, you can not only astound your enemy with your chameleon properties, but you can also intimidate him with the size of your great lance."

The mattress shook with Robert's laughter.

"But you have yet to determine whether it does indeed change color, Miss Abigail."

"How do you suggest I test that, Colonel Coally?"

His laughter stopped.

"By suckling me, Abigail. As hard and as deep as you can take me."

Abigail cradled him between her hands—the purple-hued crown throbbed. "But I did that last night, Colonel Coally. Today I want to do something else."

A half-smile formed on his lips. "Your fantasies, Miss Abigail."

She gently rubbed the thick shaft between her palms—and imagined him all alone on the eve of battle. "Do you ever touch yourself?"

"Do you?"

The rain echoed softly inside the cabin.

Abigail swallowed her fear and uncertainty at confessing what no respectable person did, let alone admit. "Yes."

"I think we all do. The only problem in the field is finding privacy—but sometimes even that doesn't matter."

"Show me how you touch yourself."

It could have been a blush on Robert's cheeks—the light was too dim and his skin too dark to be certain. The thought that he could still be rendered as vulnerable as she warmed her—and fired her determination. "You said everything, Robert."

Closing those dark eyelashes, he reached down and cupped his hands over hers. "Rub me between your hands—like this."

Abigail's hands were sandwiched between heat and friction. She quickly learned the motion, varied the motion, until he took his hands away and he was all hers.

She could feel his readiness through his body, drawn as tautly as a pulley. See it in the stomach that corded and strained for release.

Suddenly the bulbous head grew a deep burgundy. Even as she watched, marveling at the change that was occurring, it throbbed and shot up a geyser of white fluid. At the same time, a groan worked its way past Robert's throat.

The sound drew Abigail's attention. Robert's eyelids were squeezed shut and his lips pulled back from his teeth as if he were in the throes of agony. Slowly his features relaxed into an expression of utter peace.

His black lashes lifted.

Abigail stared into the depths of those stark gray eyes that had seen too much death and pain and wanted to give this man . . . *everything.*

Reaching out a finger toward his stomach, she touched the mound of warm, white fluid there.

His essence.

Last night it had shot up inside her.

"So, do I change color, Miss Abigail?"

Abigail thought of him, inside her, doing all of the wonderful things she had just witnessed. And felt tears clog her sinuses.

"Oh, yes, Colonel Coally."

His gray eyes were too intense. Just when she thought she would laugh or cry or do something else entirely uncalled for if he continued to stare at her so, the skin around his eyes crinkled.

"*Lance,* Abigail?"

"Do you prefer a different name, Robert?"

"Prick."

Hot color flooded Abigail's face at the explicit word that she had only ever been exposed to in print. "Battering ram."

"Cock."

"Jacob staff."

Robert threw his head back and laughed in that purely masculine, uninhibited way of his. "Wherever did you learn such phrases? Never mind. Your erotica. You were quite enraptured when I peeked through the window last night. What were you reading about?"

Before Abigail could reply, Robert crawled over her and stood up on the floor.

She watched the sway of his testicles with interest as he leaned over the foot of the bed. They were rather hairy—and oddly touching; man at his most vulnerable. And exposed.

He was all too aware of her interest—his gray eyes, when he turned around, glinted. He held up a copy of *The Pearl*.

"Is this the one you were reading?"

"What number is it?"

"Twelve. Do you have them all?"

She flipped the quilt over her naked body. "Yes."

He flipped the quilt away from her. "Come over to the window."

She gazed at the front of him. He had gone from limp to hard. "Why?"

"I want you to read to me."

Abigail's mouth dropped open. "Absolutely not."

"Ashamed, Abigail?"

She closed her eyes against the truth. She *was* ashamed. That she had desires. And pursued those desires.

She opened her eyes. "No, I am not ashamed. Merely feeling very vulnerable. It's not every day that a woman shares her secret life."

Robert's dark face hardened—she could imagine that look on his face before he killed. Without warning, he reached down and grasped her hand in his, his skin hard where hers was soft, calloused where hers was smooth.

For a second she felt trapped. And knew that he, too, was trapped by the desires that, for however long the storm lasted, were neither his nor hers, but theirs.

He pulled her across the bed and up to her feet.

"Go stand by the window— No, the other window."

Abigail skirted the cupboard and stood uncertainly in front of the surviving window on the opposite side of the door. The open curtains offered neither warmth nor concealment.

Robert deposited a chair in front of the window. "Sit down."

Abigail primly sat down with her back toward the light. The

wood was cold and hard against skin that was flaming hot and achingly sensitive.

Robert dropped a pillow onto the floor, then dropped down on his knees in front of the chair. He held out the journal.

"Turn to the page you were reading when I walked in on you last night."

She flipped through the pages. The murky light penetrating the window blurred the print, as if the only thing real in the room was her . . . and him.

"Have you found it?"

"Yes."

"Start reading exactly where you left off. But first tell me what happened before, so I can follow the story."

She cleared her throat. "The story is called 'La Rose D'Amour; Or the Adventures of a Gentleman in search of Pleasure. Translated from the French.' The man, Louis, is forming a—a harem of women, and he has kidnapped Laura, a virgin. When I stopped reading, he was in the process of persuading Laura of the pleasures to be had if she travels with him and allows him to deflower her."

Robert leaned closer, cocooning her in his body heat. A single drop of desire bridged her knee and his manhood. "How was Louis persuading Laura?"

Abigail inhaled—smelling him, smelling her. And stared into his stark gray eyes mere inches away from her own. "He had his finger in her cream jug."

The expected laughter did not appear, only a blazing heat that took her breath away. Holding her gaze, he grabbed her hips and pulled her forward in the chair until her buttocks were draped over the edge of the seat.

Gasping in surprise, she dropped the journal and grabbed the sides of the wooden seat.

He promptly picked up the journal. Prying her right hand free of the chair, he clasped her fingers around it. "Read, Abigail."

It was one thing for Robert to be aware of her collection of erotica; it was an entirely different thing to read it aloud.

"Robert. I really think I would prefer *you* to read."

"Not part of the bargain, Abigail." His voice was as intractable as his expression. "I want to hear *you*."

"Is that all you want?" she asked tartly.

"No, Abigail, I want far more than that—I want you to share your secret life with me. Tell me when you end a paragraph."

Licking lips that were suddenly as dry as the paper she was holding, she found the appropriate page and raised the journal to best catch the light. Her breasts bobbed up and down on her stomach with each breath she took. She had a curious feeling of déjà vu, looking at the black print.

"My desires were excited to the highest pitch. I depicted to her the pleasure she would experience when, after arriving at the chateau, I should deflower her of her virginity, and triumphantly carry off her maidenhead on the head of this, 'dear Laura,' I said, as I took one of her hands and clasped it round my"—Abigail took a deep breath, uttered the forbidden word—"prick. 'Then,' said I, 'you will know all the joys and pleasures of a real,' " she took another deep breath, " 'fuck.' "

Hard, hot, calloused thumbs dug into the tops of her thighs.

Abigail peered over the top of the journal. He was waiting for her.

"I finished the paragraph."

"Read on." His voice was dark and low and gravelly.

The fluttering inside her stomach traveled to her heart.

" 'You will then,' I continued," Abigail read on in a ragged voice that bore little resemblance to her own, " 'experience all the sweet confusion, far different from what you now feel, of stretching wide apart your thighs to receive man between them, to feel his warm, naked body joined to yours, the delicious preparatory toying with your breasts, the hot kisses lavished on them and on your lips, his roving tongue to force its way between your rosy lips in search of yours, the delicious meeting of them, their rolling about and tickling each other as mine now does yours,' at the same time thrusting my tongue to meet hers."

Abigail's voice died away on a moan of wind. Heat flooded her body: A mingling of embarrassment and desire.

Without warning, Robert stretched wide her thighs. Cold air invaded her most private parts. It was immediately replaced by heat—the touch of a finger.

"You're wet, Abigail. Is this what happens when you read to yourself?"

She shivered, feeling more exposed than she ever had in her life. "Yes."

The hard, naked strength of his body pressed into the vee of her thighs. "Move the journal."

She lowered *The Pearl.*

His mouth swooped down on her right breast, scorching hot and wet. It felt as though he was trying to swallow her whole. Hard, hot fingers closed around the soft mound, squeezed it to fit more deeply inside his mouth, while his other hand found her left nipple, a raspy touch of pure fire.

Pain was a sharp intrusion.

Even as Abigail opened her mouth to protest the not quite gentle biting of her nipple, the teeth were gone and his mouth covered hers, still scorching hot, flavored with strawberry jam, brandy, and her.

She inhaled sharply, in response to the gentle twisting of her nipples; in response to the stroke of his tongue against the roof of her mouth.

She forget about *The Pearl.* She forgot about shame. She wrapped her arms around Robert's neck and pulled him closer, *closer . . .*

He kissed her and pinched her nipples until she panted and squirmed, on fire for more. When she reached between their bodies to take more, he pulled back.

His lips were shiny wet. "Read."

Abigail suddenly realized that whatever Louis said or did to Laura, Robert was going to do to Abigail.

She rapidly scanned the page, found where she had left off.

" 'And then to feel him take his prick, and with the tips of his fingers part the lips of the flesh sheath into which he intends to shove it, putting the head of it between the lips, and gently shoving it in at first, stretching the poor little thing to its utmost extent, till, not without some pain to you, the head is effectually lodged in it. Then, after laying a kiss on your lips, he commences the attack by gently but firmly and steadily shoving into you, increasing his shoves harder and harder, till he thrusts with all his force, causing you to sigh and cry out, he thrusts hard, he gains a little at every move, he forces the barriers, he tears and roots up all your virginal defenses, you cry out for mercy but receive none. His passions are aroused into madness, fire flashes from his eyes, concentrating all his energies for one tremendous thrust, he lunges forward, carries everything before him, and enters the fort by storm, reeking with the blood of his fair enemy, who with a scream of agony yields up her maidenhead to the conqueror, who, having put his victim *hor de combat,* proceeds to reap the reward of his hard fought and bloody battle.' "

The journal was plucked out of Abigail's nerveless fingers. Eyes wide, she stared down between their bodies.

Robert held his swollen manhood in his right hand. He leaned forward, until she couldn't see it at all, could only feel his calloused fingertips delicately parting her nether lips. Then it was there, the bulbous head, as smooth as a plum and burning hot. Slowly, gently, he rocked forward, prodding her, stretching her, drawing back just before he breached the opening and gained admission. Again. And again. He teased and taunted, prodded and retreated until Abigail could feel her wetness leaking out of her body onto the wooden seat beneath her.

Just when she decided that the game had gone far enough, that he was not Louis and she most decidedly was not Laura, there was a popping sensation and he was inside her, just the head. It felt as big as the fist she had compared it to earlier.

He leaned down and dropped a hard, openmouthed kiss on her lips. Then his lips were gone and he was no deeper inside her than he had been a moment before.

"Robert—"

He smiled, a crooked smile. "You can sigh, Abigail. Or you can cry."

He slowly sank into her, another inch, not enough, two inches, still not enough, three inches, not nearly enough. Then he pulled all the way out, teased and prodded her with the engorged head, never quite entering her, never quite leaving her.

Just when she thought she would scream with frustration, he smiled that crooked smile again.

"Or you can scream."

And lunged forward.

Abigail screamed.

She could feel their pubic hair meshing, he was so deep inside her, *and it still was not enough.*

A wall of paper blocked Robert's face. She blinked at the black print.

"Read."

The outspread journal shook and shimmied in her hands—she was trembling. Or perhaps it was he who trembled, buried inside her body so deeply that she could not tell where he ended and she began.

She took a calming breath and read.

" 'Now he again draws himself out to the head, and slowly enters again. Again he draws out, and again enters, till the friction caused by the luscious tightness of the rich flesh which clasps tightly his foaming pego causes such delicious sensations that he is no longer master of himself.' "

It was Abigail who lowered the journal at the end of the paragraph. He would finish this, or by God, she would.

His gaze locked with hers. Still wearing that crooked smile, he dug his fingers into her hips and drew himself out, slowly, so slowly she could count the inches. And then he was easing back inside her, an inch at a time. Nine inches, all the way in. Nine inches, all the way out. Smoothly, rhythmically, until she was so wet and open it did indeed feel as if he was foaming inside her and she was coming, coming, *coming*—

Sweat beaded on Robert's forehead, trickled down his temple. He threw his head back toward the rafters while his body thrust into hers, almost hard enough, almost fast enough. The muscles in his neck and shoulders bulged as he fought to keep the self-imposed rhythm.

A pace that he would keep, Abigail suddenly realized, until one of them died or she finished the literary sequence of events.

She pushed up the journal.

" 'He lunges with fierceness into her,' " she panted, body contracting, opening and closing, seeking its own release even as she forced out the words that would gain it for her, " 'the crisis of pleasure approaches; he feels it coming, he drives it home to her—deeper, deeper. At last it comes—' "

Abigail closed her eyes and cried out as her body arched under its own volition.

The journal flew out of her hands. She could not have heard what she thought she heard—it sounded like the snarl of an animal tormented beyond endurance. Blindly she grabbed at a muscular arm, a shoulder, a neck—and knew that, like the description in "La Rose D'Amour," the man pumping and grinding himself into her body was no longer the master of himself.

The wooden chair rocked and creaked in time to his lunges. Dimly she wondered if she would get a splinter in her behind. No sooner did the thought enter her head than her entire world exploded and Robert exploded with her, his flesh inside her spasming while it spurted liquid fire and she was falling, falling—

Onto the cold plank floor. Pulled there by Robert. He locked his arms about her as they labored for air.

A rumble started up inside his chest. Abigail dazedly wondered how he could laugh when she was dying.

He plunged his hands into her hair and held her face up to his. Hot breath filled her nose, her mouth. "That's one hell of a secret life you live, Miss Abigail."

Abigail suddenly felt renewed. The shame that had tainted her entire adult life dissipated.

She opened her eyes and stared at his naked chest that continued to heave up and down for air. "Let's walk on the beach."

"In a storm?"

"I love storms. I want to walk naked on the beach. I want to feel the rain kiss my breasts. I want to see what color your pego turns when it's immersed in the ocean."

No sooner were the words out of her mouth than she was on her feet and, together, they opened the door to the rented cottage and walked naked into the storm.

The rain was no colder than the showers she had been routinely subjected to when growing up. Waves washed the shore. Distant thunder rumbled in the sky.

The storm was wet and beautiful and wild—the way Robert made her feel.

Breasts bobbing, giggling like one of her small nieces, Abigail raced down the path to the beach, enjoying the mud squishing between her toes and the rain pelting her naked skin. Robert sped after her, a not-so-little boy with a blue, pitifully shriveled manhood.

She triumphantly reached the foaming froth that was the English Channel. It was too much to resist. Bending over, she plunged her hands into the water that curled around her knees—

"That's one *hell* of a mighty lance you have there, Colonel Coally. It is blue—and must be all of two inches long. You might be able to spear a minnow, but I do not think you will be parting any seas with it."

—and splashed him.

Robert leapt after her into the roiling ocean—

"I have always fantasized about giving a woman a saltwater douche, Abigail."

—and proceeded to wrestle her down into the waves.

It was a game—had Robert exerted himself, Abigail would have been flat on her back at the edge of the ocean in one second flat—and they both knew it. Instead, their water-slickened bodies slipped and rubbed together until suddenly it did not matter what he put inside her. Just when she reached for him as a lover instead of a playmate, he put a leg behind hers and tripped her. Only to catch her and arch her backward over the water.

"You were saying something about parting seas, Abigail?" he growled playfully.

It was ridiculous. It was exciting. It was as if twenty-two years of Robert's life had been erased and they were two not-so-innocent children frolicking on the beach.

Her laughter rang out over the crests of the waves and the spray of the surf and the steady patter of the rain. It almost drowned out the sound of a neighing horse and a frantic shout.

"Miss Abigail! Miss Abigail! Where are ye? Miss Abigail!"

Abigail covered her mouth with her hands. Then she wriggled free and covered more prestigious spots.

"Robert! It is Mr. Thomas! Robert! Our clothes are in the cottage. Robert, *we are naked!*"

Chapter 6

Abigail's left arm shielded her breasts while her right hand cupped her womanhood. She looked as tempting as a sea nymph. And as frigid as a virgin debutante.

Robert wanted to strike down the man called Mr. Thomas for turning the wildly sensuous woman who had shared with him her body and her fantasies into this woman who looked as if she had never needed or desired a man in her life.

It was too soon. He needed more time. He needed more—

"Miss Abigail!" The man started down the path leading from the cottage to the beach—an elderly man, judging by his stooped shoulders and halting gait. "Be that ye down there? Miss Abigail—"

Robert caught Abigail as she turned to run into the dangerous waves behind them. "Stay. I'll take care of him."

Quickly, before she did something silly like drown herself in the name of modesty, he maneuvered the muddy path to block the landlord's descent.

"Ho, there. You've caught my missus and I in a rather embarrassing situation. Abigail—"

"How do I know that be Miss Abigail?" Small, birdlike eyes stared suspiciously past Robert's shoulder. "Ye could ha' done her a danger, ye and yer doxy down there."

Anger blazed a trail down Robert's spine at hearing Abigail referred to as a doxy.

He forgot about the rain pelting his body.

He forgot that he was standing naked in front of a man old enough to be his grandfather.

He forgot everything but the insult this man had issued.

"I have said it is Miss Abigail," Robert snapped icily, "and it will be the worse for you if you do not level your eyes elsewhere."

The aged caretaker guiltily hunched his head between his shoulders. Water streamed down his slicker. "Miss Abigail didn' mention no man."

"I am on leave from the Army; my . . . wife did not expect me. You are interrupting our reunion, so make sharp, man!"

"She didn' say nothin' 'bout no husband, neither." Thomas glanced at the stormy sky over Robert's left shoulder, then over his right, anywhere but at his naked body. "Said it be just her—"

"I have explained the circumstances. We will reimburse you for your efforts, if that is what troubles you."

"M' wife only agreed to cook an' clean fer one." The small eyes glinted in greed at the mention of payment. "I put a basket of victuals in the cabin. She didn' make no food fer two—"

"Give my regards to your wife. I am sure whatever she prepared is enough for the two of us. Now I bid you good day, sir!"

The old man took the hint. Robert breathed a sigh of relief when Mr. Thomas jumped into his trap and set off. Turning around, Robert caught sight of Abigail.

And felt as if he had been kicked in the gut.

Her hair adhered to her back like the skin of an otter. Below it he could make out the white globes of her buttocks.

The storm still lasted—nothing was going to deprive him of the coming night.

Purposefully he stalked her. When he cupped her buttocks in his hands, she yelped and jumped around. When he cupped her face and lifted it up to his, she sighed and wrapped her arms around his neck.

Slowly, softly, he savored the cool slickness of her rain-washed lips and the eagerness with which they parted. Her mouth on the inside was as hot as the rain beating down on them was cold.

"Cold?" he murmured, nuzzling her cheek, smelling the fresh rain on her skin mixed with the salt of the ocean and the lingering traces of sweat and sex.

"Hmm," she returned.

He pressed the hardening length of his manhood into her stomach and murmured, "Ride me."

She jerked her head back, brown eyes wide with shock. "What?"

Robert silently cursed Mr. Thomas again. There would have been no shock at his suggestion had the old man not appeared.

"To the cabin." Turning, he bent his legs and offered her his back. "Hop on."

He waited with bated breath—this was the deciding moment. Reality had intruded—would she choose it over the fantasy world they had created together?

A tentative hand rested on his shoulder—followed by the hitch of a soft, warm leg.

His heart skipped a beat—swelled with exultation. Before she had time to think about just how awkward and vulnerable the position rendered her, he grasped her underneath her knee and hoisted her higher onto his back.

Surprisingly strong arms clasped him about the neck while her left leg tried to gain purchase. Reaching back with his left hand, he grabbed it, spread her wide so that both knees were locked against his hips.

The soft flesh between her thighs pressed into his buttocks. She was hot and slick against his rain-drenched skin, from her, from him.

For a second, he thought he would orgasm right there on the spot. Then he thought about dropping her and taking her on the beach in the mud and the rain.

A smart smack on his hip brought him round. She was shivering with cold—not desire. "My ride, sir."

Digging her heels into the tops of his thighs, she hitched herself higher—*Jesus*, her open vulva ground into the small of his back— and shouted, "Tally ho!"

Then the gray sky rang with her laughter, and Abigail was once again the little girl who had given back to him his childhood.

He didn't remember the climb to the cabin, only the feel of her rubbing and grinding into his back, his buttocks, the sudden thrust of a heel against his "lance" when she brought both legs around him and tried to lock her feet over his groin.

When she wriggled down his back, he groaned in pure agony and collapsed against the safety that the cabin door represented, eyes squeezed shut, his manhood so hard, it thrust straight out from his body.

A soft, cool hand touched the bunched muscles in his forearm. "Robert? Are you all right? Did you hurt your leg?"

Robert didn't know whether to laugh or cry at the concern in her voice. He needed her passion now, not her kindness that had taken away the agony of his first kill.

"Abigail, look down and tell me what you see."

"A basket of food," was the too innocent reply. "Are you hungry?"

He opened his eyes in pained amusement. "Did the stroll on the beach meet up to your expectations?"

"I will never forget it, Robert."

His lips twitched. "Neither will Mr. Thomas."

The brown eyes staring up at him were solemn—too solemn. Her eyelashes were spiked from the rain. "What did you tell him?"

"I told him we were man and wife."

"But I specifically stated in the lease—"

"And that you were not anticipating my arrival because my leave of absence from the Army came unexpectedly."

"You did not have to say that we were married, Robert."

"But we are. Joined at the hip."

Laughter glimmered in her brown eyes, a spark of amber where before there had been none. "It was not my hip that was joined to you, Colonel Coally."

"I know very well what was joined to me, Miss Abigail."

Her spiked lashes lowered. "Your feet are muddy. You need a bath."

"Only if you wash me."

"But I am hungry, Robert." She raised her eyelashes; behind the amber laughter was warm desire. "If I wash you we will not eat. And I have a particular fantasy that I want to act out."

The water in the small tub was as cold as the rain outside. Robert experienced a strange contentment, watching Abigail's small, plump breasts elongate when she leaned over to clean the floor. When she turned around and scrubbed her way backward toward the tub, Robert thought his heart would stop.

"You have a round bottom, Miss Abigail. And between your legs you have dainty pink lips surrounded by wet brown curls."

That got her attention.

Straightening, she turned and stepped around the tub. Her face, before she swirled around, was as pink as the lips he had mentioned. "You have a concave bottom, Colonel Coally. And hairy—ballocks."

"Shall we compare tit for tat, Miss Abigail?"

Turning, she offered him a towel. "Not at all, Colonel Coally. You have a tit and I have a twat."

Eyes glinting with laughter, he took the towel that she offered, stepped one foot at a time out of the tub as he dried off. Then he blotted dry her hair, her shoulders, her breasts, her hips, worked his way down to a pair of elegant, narrow feet.

"Time to eat," he murmured into the jointure of her thighs, deliberately breathing into the soft nest of damp brown curls there.

Her legs quivered.

Grinning, he jumped up. "Real food this time, Miss Abigail. If I am to satisfy more fantasies, I have to keep up my strength."

Used as he was to field rations, the basket contained a veritable feast. Cold mutton. Cheese. Hard-boiled eggs. A loaf of bread still warm from the oven.

There was more than enough for two.

Abigail ate daintily but with a definite appetite. When her eyelids drooped, he repacked the food and carried her to bed.

He had never before slept with a woman until Abigail. Had never before experienced the simple joy of having a woman's spine curve to fit his abdomen and her butt snuggle into the flatness of his groin. Had never imagined this closeness that had nothing to do with sex and everything to do with the woman in his arms.

The reality of Abigail far surpassed his fantasies.

Sighing, he buried his face into her damp hair.

A blast of cannon fire woke him.

Jesus God, he had fallen asleep during battle. Boneless flesh curved to fit his body—a corpse, already stripped by the natives, body still warm.

Heart pounding, his fingers tightened around the butt of his rifle—only to sink into giving flesh.

And he remembered.

The storm. The burning need that had driven him out into it. The light in the cottage and the woman named Abigail.

He gently soothed the breast he had abused.

Abigail stirred. "Robert?"

"Why are you here, Abigail?"

The boneless spine stiffened.

He refused to let her go, pressing her more firmly into the curve of his body while he braced his chin on the top of her head. "Tell me."

"I told you." Her heart pounded against the palm of his hand. "In three weeks I turn thirty."

"Every second—somewhere in the world—a woman turns thirty."

"But not every woman is a spinster."

"By your choice, Abigail."

"But I *don't* want to be a spinster, Robert." He strained to hear her over the steady drum of rain. "I *don't* want to be passed between my brother and sisters. I *don't* want to be—alone."

Robert braced himself against the pain in her voice.

"So why are you here, then, with only your books for company?" he persisted, determined to solve the mystery that was Abigail.

For long seconds he didn't think she was going to reply, then—

She sighed. "I came to say good-bye."

Fear pumped though his veins. Along with images of death—her death now instead of his. Immediately he thrust the images away. "Who did you come to say good-bye to?"

"My dreams, Robert. I got tired of wanting things that could never be. I brought my books and journals with me here because I planned on leaving them behind. In the hope that without them, perhaps I could find . . . a little peace."

Peace.

Hardened soldiers like himself sought peace, not gently bred ladies who had never faced death and chosen life. But the same loneliness was there, the utter aloneness that was the price paid for stepping outside the rules that bind societies together. Robert had killed—in duty; Abigail had indulged her desires with forbidden erotica—in secrecy. And had been passed from brother to sister—

"What about your parents?"

"Dead. I have one brother and three sisters of whom I am very fond. But I am still the spinster sister. And I am the youngest, so of course they know what is best for me."

He rubbed her nipple in gentle consolation. "Not this."

"No." A hint of laughter lightened her voice. "I think William would die of an apoplectic fit if he ever discovered my chest of books."

"Tell me about your brother and sisters."

Abigail cupped her hand over his. "My brother and sisters have kindly provided me with twenty-one nieces and nephews. They are convinced that a woman's happiness lies in marriage. Or I should say, in having a family—the husband, or wife, which- ever the case may be, is a trial one must endure in order to have children. And you are correct—I *am* a spinster by choice. But I found myself wondering if my brother and sisters do not have the right of it. That perhaps life with one of the eminently eligible but dreadfully boring men they are constantly surprising me with might just possibly be preferable to—being alone."

Robert had no reason to be jealous. But he was—furiously.

"You'd marry a fat-bottomed man with side-whiskers?" he growled. "A man who would have you dress a piano for fear he would excite"—he pinched her nipple—"*this?*"

She caught his fingers and laughed softly. "Cease, Colonel Coally, you have convinced me of the error of my thoughts. What about you? Do you have a family?"

Perhaps it was relief that prompted Robert's response. Perhaps it was the way her body bonelessly melded to his and her laughter chased away the darkness. Or perhaps it was merely that he did not mind sharing his past with this woman who was so willing to share her body.

"Four brothers and five sisters."

"Are your brothers in the Army?"

"No." He cautioned himself to stop—she was a lady, it was one thing to accept the fact that he killed in the name of duty. She would not want to know that her fantasy man came from low origins. But the words came unbidden. "They followed in the footsteps of my father."

"Is he still alive?"

"Very much so."

"Why did he not stop you from enlisting in the Army?"

Robert smiled at the indignation in her voice. "One less mouth to feed. But your blame is misplaced. Very few people can stop me when I make up my mind."

"What does he do, this father of yours?"

Robert tensed, but knew he had come too far to lie now. "He's a street vendor. He sells ices."

Abigail's response at learning his pedigree was as unpredictable as her response to his lovemaking.

"Oh, I love ices!" she enthused, as if she was still the little girl who had played in the ocean. "Strawberry is my favorite."

"Take my advice, Abigail. Eat lemon ice or cream ices. But stay away from strawberry."

"Why?"

"There are no strawberries in strawberry ice."

"Yes, there are." Her voice in the darkness was endearingly earnest. "Not whole ones, of course. They are all mixed up in little pieces."

"They're not strawberries, Abigail," he murmured wryly.

"Then what are they, pray?" she asked tartly.

"Cochineals."

"You mean . . . *bugs?*"

"I mean—bugs."

He could feel her coming to terms with the fact that she had eaten bugs—the initial stiffening of her body, the slow relaxation when she realized there was not going to occur some sort of delayed reaction. Finally, "Is that why you joined the Army when you were thirteen?"

He smiled in cynical amusement. "Eating insects is hardly the worst thing that happens on London streets. Aside from the constant threat of being killed or robbed of your profits, making and selling ices is hard labor. You work from four in the morning until seven at night. *That* is why I joined the Army."

And had ended up working far longer days surrounded by far more danger than that met on a London street.

"Would you do it over if you could?"

And miss Abigail and the storm?

"I don't know."

"Are you going to go back?"

He gently squeezed her breast. "I don't know."

The rain was a comforting play of sound and motion. He had never thought to have a throbbing erection and be content to merely hold a woman. No more than he had ever thought that there would come a day when he prayed that the rain not stop. On the battlefield the cold wet and the slippery mud was a harbinger of death. Here, in England, it had brought him Abigail—and life.

"Robert."

"Hmm?"

"I want to fulfill a fantasy of yours."

He inhaled the warmth of her hair. "You already have."

"Nonsense."

"You allowed me to fulfill *your* fantasies."

"But I want to be *your* fantasy woman, Robert." She delved behind her and grabbed his turgid flesh. "I want you to give me everything you give her."

Robert grabbed her hand, deliberately curt. "I told you—I don't fantasize about what a woman does to me."

Abigail was not to be denied. "Then what do you do to her? You said that you fantasized about doing everything. What is everything, Robert?"

Robert closed his eyes as the old need came over him. "You'd be shocked, Abigail."

"No, I would not. *How could I?* Tell me . . . Tell me what you want, Robert. Let me be your fantasy woman. Tell me what we do before a battle."

Robert desperately resisted. "You said, before we ate, that you had another fantasy, Abigail."

"This *is* that fantasy, Robert. To be your fantasy."

God help him, it was his fantasy, too.

Heart suddenly pounding, he molded his body more firmly against hers, chest against her back, her rounded buttocks pressed against the flatness of his stomach, and cupped the silky nest of hair at the apex of her thighs. "I do this."

Her body tensed expectantly. "What else?"

He sifted through the silky hair, found the indescribably soft flesh hidden inside. "Open up your legs."

Robert smiled in pained satisfaction against her hair, noting how quickly she complied with his request, and worked his finger between the seam of her lips. Inside the tight little valley she was hot and wet. Her soft lips curled around him as he gently slid back and forth, lingering at the head of her clitoris, sliding back down, pausing infinitesimally at the small opening there that he had created, then sliding back up again to her clitoral hood.

"When I am alone at night, exhausted by death and dying," he murmured gruffly into her hair, "I fantasize that I have a woman who feels what I feel. And that I can feel what she feels."

He slid his hand back up, over her moist mound, through the triangle of soft hair there and across her stomach.

Abigail wriggled in disappointment. "Robert, I assure you, *you were feeling her.*"

He laughed shortly, gaining confidence at her ready acceptance. Nipping her shoulder, he slid his hand over her hip, between their bodies, down her buttocks, between her plump cheeks.

Her legs clamped down.

He fluttered his fingertips against the wet heat of her. "I want to feel her again, Abigail. Open your legs—wide. Put your right foot flat on the bed—" He followed the line of her thigh, arranged her leg. "There. Now you are wide open for me."

"Is that what you fantasize about, Robert? That a woman is wide open for you?"

"Yes." He petted and stroked her wet, clinging lips, preparing her. "Wide open. Give me your hand."

"Why?"

"I told you—I want my fantasy woman to feel what I feel. Give me your hand."

But she did not give him her hand. So he took it.

She struggled feebly when he guided it down between her thighs.

Her ribs rose and fell underneath his arm. "We did this last night, Robert."

"Not like tonight, Abigail." God help them both, *not like tonight,* he thought. "You wanted to know what my fantasy woman and I do before battle—this is part of it. Be her. Feel yourself as I feel you. The silky wetness here—" He rubbed their joined hands against her petal-soft lips until they were slick with her essence. "The tight sheath of flesh inside."

Gently he parted her slick lips with their intertwined fingers. Slowly, so slowly, her flesh stretched to accommodate them.

Her breath caught. "Robert—"

"What do you feel, Abigail?"

"I feel you—your fingers—"

"Your fingers, too." He tamped down the mounting desire. "Our fingers. Your skin is soft inside, like wet silk. I have never touched another woman like I am now touching you. Feel that? That is your sheath contracting around us. Further back—there—you can feel the sponge—behind that is the entrance to your womb."

He prodded the sponge, soft and springy, forced her to prod it, too, knowing that the minute movements were rubbing her wrist against her clitoris. Her sheath sucked and nipped at their fingers.

"That is what you feel like when I am inside you. When I push our fingers into you, like this, relax your muscles and bear down, just as if my manhood filled you. Now when we pull out, grip our fingers, tighter, as tight as you can . . ." He sucked in silky strands of hair, feeling the safety of the cottage and the warmth of the bed dissolving into a muddy field and a wet, dirty sleeping roll. "I need you to feel what I feel, Abigail. I need you to feel how hot and wet and tight you are."

I need you to feel my pain.

I need to share it with someone, else I don't think I can live with it.

Abigail's hair tangled around his chin. "What about the other part of your fantasy, Robert? I feel what *you* feel, but how can you feel what *I* feel?"

Robert protectively curled his body around her. "Promise me that if what I am about to do is repugnant you will say so."

"You said that once we embarked on this journey there would be no turning back. I want you to feel what I feel, Robert . . . If it is possible."

"More than possible, Abigail."

"But how—"

Robert released her fingers, gently withdrew from her body. Planting a kiss on the nape of her neck, he turned over and slid out of bed.

"Where are you going?" The husky arousal in her voice was laced with impatience.

Robert took a deep breath. "To get the butter."

The silence was electrifying.

Robert waited for the rejection that must surely come, of him, of this fantasy, of the life he had lived, dreaming about this moment. He could sense her shock, her uncertainty, and then, finally—

"It's in the cupboard."

For a second he thought his knees would collapse from the unadulterated surge of relief. It was followed by the primitive need to possess.

No man would ever do to her what he was about to do.

He grabbed the damp washcloth draped over the sink, then found the small crock of butter in the cupboard.

She was sitting up in bed, a dark silhouette against a slash of pale linen. "What should I do?"

"Lie down on your stomach. Then lift yourself up onto your knees and put your head down on the pillow."

"Have you . . . ever done this before?"

He reached out, found her nose, her chin, smoothed tangled hair back from her face.

His hands—hands that aimed a rifle with deadly precision—were trembling.

"Never. You don't have to do this, you know."

"But I want to. I want you to feel what I feel. I want to be your fantasy woman, Robert. *I want you to give me everything you give to her.*"

Robert threw his head back to study the darkness.

If he did this, he didn't know if he could ever go back to a life of killing.

If he did this, he didn't know if he could die, knowing what he was leaving behind.

If he did this, he didn't know if he could let go of Abigail when the storm ended.

The sound of the mattress shifting told him she had positioned herself.

He looked down at the dark silhouette, buttocks arched in the air, and knew that it didn't matter what the repercussions were— he was going to have her.

The bargain had been everything, and everything was what he was going to take.

Leaning over the dark silhouette that was Abigail, he found the iron headboard, draped the wet washcloth over it. Then, reaching into the crock, he scooped up butter and smeared it along the length of his penis. Nine inches, she had said during her mock measurement—he felt like he was twelve inches long going on twenty, hard and powerful and never more aware of his masculinity. Scooping up more butter, he set the crock down onto the floor and knelt on the bed behind her.

He touched her lightly, reverently.

Abigail tensed.

"Relax, Abigail. This is part of the fantasy. To touch you everywhere." Gently he worked the butter around and around her tight opening, rimming it over and over and over until unwittingly she thrust back toward him.

His middle finger slipped inside her.

She gasped.

He gasped.

She was unbelievably tight.

And hot.

Everything and more that he had imagined a woman to be.

Deep inside her the flesh ballooned out. He wriggled his finger. "Does that hurt?"

"No."

His voice was hoarse with desire. "Do you take me, Abigail?"

Her voice, when she responded, was equally hoarse. "I take you, Robert."

Leaning down, he planted a kiss onto her upraised buttocks, her skin taut and cool on the outside, soft and hot on the inside, then slowly withdrew his finger. Carefully he cleansed it with the wet washcloth.

"I'll try not to hurt you." Kneeling on the bed between her legs, he rubbed himself round and round her tightly puckered flesh, pressing inward, harder and harder with each circle until he felt it blossoming open, and then suddenly he was inside her and Abigail was crying out in the darkness.

He sucked in a deep breath and held still. Her flesh nipped and milked him. The soft mounds of her buttocks quivered against his groin.

Robert felt an emotion so strong that for a moment he thought he would be unmanned.

Lust. Tenderness.

He wanted to ram her so hard and deep that she screamed. He wanted to hold her until the tears passed and she never felt loneliness again.

Reaching out, he followed the trail of her spine until it merged into the nape of her neck, then reversed the trail, bringing his fingers back to the place where he was buried to the hilt.

She arched her back, drawing him deeper inside her.

Leaning over her, he cupped her breast with his left hand while, with his other hand, he found her right fist balling the pillow. "Feel the two of us, Abigail."

Threading her fingers with his, he relentlessly brought their joined hands to the apex of her thighs. "Spread your legs."

The motion brought him even deeper inside her. "No, don't pull back. Here." He found her slick, pouting nether lips, nudged them apart, rubbed their joined fingers back and forth until they were slick with her essence, until her body opened and accepted the first tentative thrust.

"Robert—Robert—I can feel you—"

"Jesus." He could feel himself, through the thin membrane separating the two channels. He could feel her flesh milking his fingers, her fingers, feel her other flesh milking his manhood.

Carefully, inexorably, he pushed their middle and forefingers more deeply inside her, prodding the sponge, wanting to feel her womb, wanting her to feel him inside her womb. And all the while that he pushed and pulled inside her vagina, he gently pushed and pulled in that other place, too, until finally they established a rhythm, their fingers pushing in, passing the hard ridge of his penis pulling out, then the fingers pulling out, rubbing the engorged bulb of his crown as he thrust into her other opening.

The pleasure of having her like this, of feeling her body at the same time that he felt his own body, was more than he could have imagined. Thoughts and images flashed before his eyes as if he was a dying man.

The Indian sun rising over the mountain and turning the sand bloodred. Crimson-stained drumsticks quivering inside the *sepoy's* body. Abigail's tears as he recounted to her the twenty-two-year-old story. His own voice, *I found out that I did not want to die without knowing what it is like to lose myself inside a woman.* Abigail's voice, *I came to say good-bye.*

Who did you come to say good-bye to?

My dreams, Robert.

Without warning, Abigail's body tightened, locking fingers and manhood inside her. "Oh, God, Robert. Robert, I can't stand it." Her voice was agonized. "Robert, please, God, take it out, do something, more, Robert, *Robert*—"

"Promise me, Abigail." Robert barely recognized his voice in the darkness—it was a savage snarl punctuated with labored gasps and the slap of his skin against hers while the *sepoy's* whistling breath echoed in the ravine.

"Robert, please—"

"Without your fantasies and your erotica you will be just like any other lady. And we would never have had last night and today. We would not be doing this, now. Would you give that up, too?"

"No, never!" she gasped, with pain, with pleasure, it no longer mattered, she was his and she was here to give up everything that had made his life bearable and he *was not going to let her do it.*

"Promise me you won't give up your dreams!"

"Oh, God, God, *I promise*, Robert—"

"Then let go." Robert gritted his teeth. "This is what kept me alive, Abigail, *this* dream. Come for me. I want you to feel what I feel when you come for me. I want you to take the pain and turn it into pleasure. I want you to come *now*."

In a quick motion he reversed the synchronization of their fingers and his penis, filling her simultaneously, faster, harder, deeper until there was no Abigail or Robert, only one body, one heartbeat, and it all centered there where their flesh was joined. Suddenly Abigail's entire body opened, taking their fingers and his manhood inside her more deeply than he would have thought humanly possible before clamping down in orgasm. Her muscles contracted around them, around him, until, with a muffled groan, he buried his face into the nape of her neck and came and came and came.

And knew that the storm had irrevocably changed his life.

Abigail had taken his pain and turned it into heart-rending pleasure.

Abigail had given back to him his soul.

Chapter 7

Abigail awoke to a warm flood of memories.

Robert kissing her between her legs. Robert buried so deeply inside her that they were one body. The taste of Robert on her tongue; the sound of his shock when she had shared that taste with him. Robert kneeling before her while she read to him from *The Pearl*. Robert's manhood pulsing against their entwined fingers while all around them her own flesh pulsed with the same aching need.

They should invoke shame, those memories. After all, she was a modern nineteenth-century woman raised to have a healthy aversion to human sexuality. At the very least, those memories should invoke embarrassment.

But they did not.

They reminded her that, whether she be a staid spinster or a genteel lady or a wanton seductress, she was first and foremost a woman.

Do you take me, Abigail?

I take you, Robert.

For the first time in her life she was thankful for her erotica. She would need every bit of knowledge she could gain if she was going to spend the rest of her life making Robert forget.

Smiling, she reached out a hand.

Only to encounter cold sheets, slightly rumpled where Robert had lain beside her.

Abigail's eyelids shot open . . . to sunshine. And the shriek of a gull.

The storm was over.

Reality was sharp, invasive, words Robert had said in passion, words he had said in passing.

For the duration of the storm, let us simply be Abigail and Robert.

As long as the storm lasts, your body, your needs, your fantasies—everything you have—is mine.

For the duration of the storm you are my *woman.*

She scrambled up in bed, ridiculously hoping that perhaps Robert was in the hip bath or kneeling in front of the stove, putting wood into it, anything, *but please, God, don't let him be gone.*

But there was no place to hide—the cottage was empty. His clothes, which had been draped over the chair by the stove, were gone. In their place hung her faded green cotton dress and white silk drawers.

Abigail closed her eyes against the sunshine filling the cottage.

Like the storm, Robert was gone.

Suddenly Abigail could not bear the sheets that smelled of him and of her. She scrambled out of bed, wincing at the feel of the engorged sponge inside her and the greasy traces of butter between her buttocks.

She hurt. Between the legs. Her bottom. Her breasts. Her lips. Everywhere he had touched her, she hurt.

Yet everywhere she looked, the cabin carried a part of him.

The fire in the stove. The hip bath on the floor by the sink. The cupboard barring the window. *The Pearl,* lying on the floor.

How could he leave her?

She had promised him! Promised him that she would not give up—

Her dreams.

Outside the cabin, a horse neighed; it was accompanied by the jingle of reins.

Robert.

Abigail raced to the door, heart pounding.

It did not matter that her hair hung wild and tangled down her back. It did not matter that she was two weeks and five days shy of turning thirty.

The only thing that mattered was that Robert had not left.

His horse had thrown him, he had said yesterday. Duty-bound soldier that he was, he had left the cottage to find his horse, and having found it—

"Be ye decent, Miss Abigail? I've come to clean fer ye. And I've brought more food fer ye and yer mister."

Abigail felt as if she had been shot by a bullet.

Or stabbed by a pair of drumsticks.

Robert said he had killed. That he would kill again.

And he had.

He just had not stayed around this time to see the look of surprise in the victim's eyes.

Through the door she could hear the ocean waves gently washing the beach. The lonely sea gull shrilled in the sky above.

Straightening her shoulders, she called out, "Give me a few minutes, Mrs. Thomas. I need to—"

She closed her eyes against the truth.

She had had her two nights of passion and she would have no more.

I need to cleanse from myself the old life and step into the new.

Hurriedly she laid out the clothes she had arrived in—bustle, corset, chemise, petticoats, stockings, garters, dress. *Tears.*

They dripped onto the bed like fat droplets of rain.

She wiped her cheeks—there would be no tears; one did not

mourn stormy fantasies—then she pumped a bucket full of cold water and set about removing the remains of Robert Coally.

Only to end up in the ignoble position of squatting and desperately reaching into tender flesh for a sponge that would not come out.

It struck her how ridiculous she must look, perched on her toes with her tangled hair—hair that he had promised to brush—flowing between her outstretched thighs. The absurdity of it was the final straw, somehow.

Once the tears started, Abigail thought she would drown in them, fishing around where a lady's fingers should never be while silently bawling as if she had a right to.

As if he had promised her more than a stormy union.

A union that *she* had proposed.

To make him forget his past. To make her forget the future.

But now the storm was over and it was time for him to rejoin his regiment.

And it was time for her to put aside fanciful fantasies.

The cottage door opened just as her fingers gained purchase. The sponge came out in the same moment that Abigail came up.

Mrs. Thomas stood framed in the door in a spill of sunlight and dancing dust motes. "It be all right, dearie. Men be forever takin' advantage of us women. I tol' my mister he shouldn' 'ave left you alone in the storm. We'll watch o'er ye now, me an' Mr. Thomas."

Ignoring the sponge in her hand and the tears that refused to stop, Abigail grabbed the towel by the sink and wrapped it about her as if nothing more untoward had occurred than a maid inadvertently walking in on her bathing mistress. "Thank you, Mrs. Thomas. There is no need to worry. I have decided to return to London. My family needs me, you see. I would appreciate it if you would assist me with packing, however. You may then drive me to the train station."

"There's a train that leaves in two 'ours time." Mrs. Thomas's face was full of pity—a far, far more devastating emotion than the shock or disapproval that a spinster lady who strays from the straight and narrow path would expect to see in the eyes of a virtuous married woman. She retrieved Abigail's chemise from the rumpled bed. "Plenty of time, we got. I got a nice pan of Cross buns, just baked 'em, and a fresh crock of butter—"

"I am not hungry," Abigail interrupted abruptly, wondering if she would ever be able to eat butter again. Or tolerate the odor of brandy. "But thank you."

She accepted the chemise with quaint dignity. Mrs. Thomas turned her back when Abigail had to perforce drop the towel.

"Of course I will pay you for your trouble." Abigail's head cleared the neck of the chemise. "No!" Her voice whipped the dust motes surrounding Mrs. Thomas. "Leave it!"

Mrs. Thomas looked up from where she bent over the journal that Robert in his passion had ripped out of Abigail's hands and flung across the room.

"It is merely something that I purchased for my vacation." She hurriedly spanned the distance that separated them. "Here, let me have it."

Abigail grabbed the journal from the befuddled woman. Walking across the room to the foot of the bed, she lifted the lid of the smallest trunk and tossed inside it *The Pearl,* edition number twelve. The brandy-soaked sponge followed. Opening the largest trunk, she retrieved her reticule, rummaged inside it until she located the small key she stored there for safekeeping. Then she locked the small trunk, returned the key to her reticule and wiped her cheeks before turning to Mrs. Thomas with a formal smile. "Would you help me with my corset, please?"

Mrs. Thomas was as good as her word. Abigail was dressed and packed in plenty of time to catch the train. While Abigail laced up her half-boots, Mrs. Thomas took care of the chamberpot and stripped the linen off the bed. Together they emptied the hip bath, then together they lifted up two trunks onto the back of the worn gig. Dusting her fingers with a handkerchief, Abigail lifted her skirts and stepped high to reach the metal step. There was pain between her legs when she settled onto the worn leather seat, yet it was strangely distant, as if it did not belong to her but to someone else.

Mrs. Thomas stood by the side of the gig. "Ye be forgettin' a trunk, miss."

"No." Abigail stared at the rhythmical swishing of the horse's tail—it was not bobbed, as were those of the horses her brother kept. A brutal operation, she had always thought, involving as it did the removal of several vertebrae. "There is nothing more for me in the cottage."

"But—"

Abigail pulled out a gold sovereign from her reticule. She looked down into Mrs. Thomas's wrinkled, worried face. "I would consider it a favor, Mrs. Thomas, if you and your husband would destroy the trunk. Its contents are no longer of any value to me."

"Of course, miss."

Mrs. Thomas turned and entered the cottage. She returned just minutes later carrying the basket Mr. Thomas had left yesterday.

Fleetingly she wondered what Robert had done to the crock of butter—if he had put it back into the cupboard or if he had stuck it inside the basket. Just as fleetingly she wondered if Mr. Thomas had told his wife of finding Miss Abigail and her "mister" frolicking naked in the rain.

But of course Mr. Thomas would have told her.

The mortification that Abigail should feel would not come.

The road to the station meandered around the ocean. At one spot a slip of the carriage wheel would plummet the vehicle over the cliff and into the water below.

"Stop!"

Mrs. Thomas nervously sawed on the reigns to stop the horse. Abigail reached into her reticule and grabbed the key to the trunk that carried her every fantasy.

How ironical that it should be dreams that had kept Robert alive these last twenty-two years.

They had given Abigail nothing but pain, isolating her from those she should emulate.

Before she could think about what she was doing, about what she was leaving behind, she stood up in the carriage and threw the key as far as she could.

It sparkled for a second, arcing over the water, then it disappeared. Into the air. Into the ocean.

It mattered not.

From this day forward Abigail had no dreams.

It was, after all, why she had chosen the isolated cottage, to say good-bye to the erotica that fueled impossible desires.

She closed her eyes against the sparkling clarity of the sea and made the decision she had been unable to make a week ago.

When she returned to London, she would accept the hand of the first man who her meddling siblings presented her with.

"You bloody horse, I should sell you to the glue factory."

Softly whickering, the horse looked over its shoulder.

And allowed Robert to grab its halter.

After a two-hour chase—and a three-hour hunt.

Robert stared into the horse's soft brown eyes and felt a melting sensation all the way down to his toes.

Toes that now sported a set of blisters, thanks to this great beast.

He had indeed lost his mind if every pair of brown eyes reminded him of Abigail, he thought in disgust.

Grabbing the pommel, he swung up into the saddle.

The sun was brilliant, the sky a cloudless blue as it can only be in the aftermath of a storm.

The melting sensation flowed from Robert's spine to his testicles at the thought of the storm . . . and Abigail. And of how they would spend the rest of the day.

She would read from her erotica while he soaked his feet. Afterward, he would brush her hair as he had earlier promised. Then he would lick her and suckle her until she begged for mercy. And then . . .

Then he would propose to her. She wouldn't dare refuse him, hanging on to the edge of release.

It was well after noon by the time Robert returned to the cottage.

He should have been warned by the lack of smoke trailing out of the chimney pipe in the thatched roof. He should have known that a cottage that appeared so utterly alone and desolate was just that. Being a military man, he should have noticed the fresh wagon tracks outside the cottage.

And he did. He merely attributed the lack of smoke coming out of the chimney to Abigail's exhaustion. And the wagon tracks only incited his hunger—for food. He had had nothing to eat since yesterday evening.

Stomach roiling, he burst inside the cottage.

Only to find emptiness.

The bedding had been ripped off the mattress. The floor near the sink was bereft of the hip bath.

For a second he wondered if he had gotten the wrong cottage.

One coastal cottage looked much like another. He could have gotten the wrong one . . .

But of course there was the cupboard barring the window. And the small trunk at the foot of the bed.

Abigail was gone.

Pain filled his chest; it took his breath away. For a second he wondered if he had caught pneumonia from the storm.

But then the pain was washed away in a flood of rage.

Damn her. She had planned it this way, from the moment he had introduced himself. While he had told her his full name, she had said her name was merely "Miss Abigail." *She had known then that with the end of the storm she would be gone.*

How could she walk away from him after what they had shared last night?

He had felt her pleasure.

She had felt *his* pleasure.

Damn her to hell, she had accepted him, *all of him,* his body, his past, his fantasy.

She had taken his pain and turned it into pleasure.

For the first time since Robert had killed the *sepoy* with a pair of drumsticks twenty-two years earlier, he felt like crying. Bawling like the gullible thirteen-year-old boy he had once been, forever searching for an easier way to live.

Fool that he was, he had allowed Abigail to become more than his fantasy woman. She had become a part of his soul.

While *he* had given her the weapon that she needed to sever the union. Ladies might dally with men raised on the streets of London, but they did *not* marry them.

No wonder she had fled. Last night he had asked her if she accepted him—and she had said yes. No doubt when she had awakened alone, she had expected him to return with a preacher.

Angrily he jerked at the lid of the trunk.

It was locked.

He kicked it.

Only to burst a blister on his toe.

He hopped up and down.

Damn, damn, damn!

His hopping led him to the sink.

The hip tub was empty, propped up against the wall beside it. The water bucket sat in the sink. And the sponge . . .

Was gone.

He distinctly recalled placing that sponge inside Abigail. Either she wore it still . . . or she had taken it with her.

And with the incongruous thought came reason.

He had left her at the crack of dawn to hunt down the cursed horse that had thrown him two nights ago. She had been curled against him, soft and replete.

He had thought to find the damned horse by the time she was awake. Instead, it had taken half the day.

The bargain had been *everything*—for as long as the storm lasted.

If he had been Abigail, what would he have thought if he had awakened, alone, in a cold bed with sunshine pouring through the window?

Damn. Why hadn't he asked for her last name? Or even more importantly, where she lived?

But the old caretakers would know.

It took Robert three hours to locate the Thomases. He was met with stoic silence.

"Her didn' leave no address." Mrs. Thomas's weathered eyes were full of hostility. "I drove 'er to the train station an' that be that."

Robert clung to his patience. "Then give me her family name. You must have that information."

"It 'pears to me, ye bein' 'er mister, ye should know that yerself," Mr. Thomas said craftily.

Short of beating the information out of the old man and

woman, there was nothing Robert could do. Except try the train station.

Which was closed.

He returned to the cottage by the sea.

There were candles in the cupboard—but no butter; Mrs. Thomas's doing, clearing out the perishables. Lighting a candle, he contemplated the stripped bed and the trunk at the foot of it. Then, calmly, methodically, he retrieved the pistol from his saddlebag and blew the lock off.

The sponge lay on top of *The Pearl,* edition number twelve.

Blistering pain enveloped Robert's chest.

Grimly he picked up the sponge. It still smelled of brandy and hot, wet woman.

How does the sponge feel?

It feels—there.

I'll take it out for you ... After I soak you in hot water to relieve the soreness.

Bottomless brown eyes alight with amber fires stared out of the sponge. *And what then, Colonel Coally?*

Then I'll put it back in for you.

A wave of exhaustion rolled over him.

It was immediately followed by a rush of rage.

By leaving behind the trunk and the sponge Abigail had made clear her decision.

He should let her walk away. He should let her have her cold, passionless reality.

But he wasn't going to allow that.

Abigail would not get away from him that easily. He was a soldier—a damned good one—used to tracking down far more wily quarry than a genteel lady.

He would find her. If not tomorrow, then the next day. Or the next.

Robert picked up the journal. It was marked by a dark wet circle.

And when he found her ... he would know every sexual act that she had ever read about. That she had ever fantasized about.

*   *   *

The next morning found Robert a thoroughly educated man. Acting on impulse, he packed the twelve copies of *The Pearl* into his saddlebag.

Old man Thomas was tending a pig and a dozen squealing piglets when Robert reined in his horse.

"Miss Abigail left a trunk inside the cottage. Store it—I'll arrange to send it to her later. Meanwhile, I will give you a sovereign if you will take me to the train station and feed and care for my horse until I return."

Old man Thomas upturned a bucket of slops into the sty. "Miss Abigail said we wus to throw that trunk away. Ain't no need to store it. 'Less you care to buy it, of course . . ."

Robert grimly dug out another sovereign.

"I don't suppose Mrs. Thomas remembers what town Miss Abigail was getting off at?"

The birdlike eyes fastened onto the gold. "We don't keep track of renters. In an' out like flies, they are."

"And of course you don't know the name or address of the owner of the cottage," Robert remarked cynically.

Thomas licked his lips. "We just does what we're told."

The old man stuck to his story all the way to the station.

The ticket seller was more helpful. He remembered selling a ticket to a lady—"going to London Station. She didn't look too happy going there, neither. Her eyes were all red—like she'd been crying. You her husband?"

Robert hardened his heart at the image the ticket seller painted.

Abigail had given him everything—and had left him with nothing. Tears seemed a cheap price for the pain she had caused.

He purchased a ticket without answering.

In London a cab drove Robert to an affordable hotel on a quiet street like the ones on which he used to work when helping his father sell ices. After visiting a tailor, he commenced his search.

The thought of Abigail turning thirty without him there to celebrate with her spurred him on.

Unfortunately, he was not of the upper ten thousand. Nor had he ever made friends with commissioned officers who belonged to that prestigious club.

After three weeks in London, Robert was no closer to finding Abigail than he had been when questioning the Thomases. Until he picked up a newspaper.

There was her face, in the society section.

Underneath it hailed the news that Lady Abigail Wynfred, sister of the Earl of Melford, was marrying Sir Andrew Tymes, eldest son of Baron Charles Tymes and Lady Clarisse Denby-Tymes.

The wedding was to be a small family affair, the article went on, that would take place on the twenty-seventh of June at the Earl of Melford's London town house.

Robert could feel the color draining out of his face.

Abigail was the sister of an earl—the *William* who would die of an apoplectic fit should her trunk of erotica be discovered.

No wonder she had not offered Robert her last name—a liaison with a common colonel would rock society.

Had she been simply a woman born into gentility, Robert could afford the simple luxuries due to her station in life. But she was of the aristocracy.

There was nothing a man like him could offer a woman like her.

He studied the picture of her fiancé.

Sir Andrew Tymes had side-whiskers framing plump, round cheeks.

No doubt he and Abigail would own several pianos.

And every one of them would be draped with ruffles.

I killed my first man three months to the day of my enlistment, Abigail, and I have been killing ever since.

You had no choice, Robert.

He crumpled the paper between his fingers.

Perhaps he *had* had no choice twenty-two years ago. But he did now.

Abigail did not deserve ruffled pianos.

Today was the twenty-fifth of June.

Robert hoped the earl's town house could accommodate one more guest.

Chapter 8

Abigail stared into the full-length mirror and knew that she had accomplished her goal.

The pale, brown-eyed lady with her hair pulled back in an elaborate French bun did not read erotic literature. She did not have forbidden fantasies.

She had no dreams other than to be what she was—the daughter—and now the sister—of an earl who was aligning the House of Melford monies to the House of Tymes money.

For the first time in her life she was content.

There was no pain in that pale, expressionless face. No lust. No loneliness.

Abigail liked that.

It was everything and more she had ever wanted to be.

A sharp knock interrupted her complacent perusal. There was a genteel fuss—her sisters. Elizabeth, the middle one, twitched Abigail's heavy, dove-gray skirt over a fashionably full bustle; Mary, the youngest next to Abigail, daintily wiped a tear out of the corner of her eye with a lace handkerchief. Victoria, the eldest, waited by the door to give Abigail into the hands of their brother, who would then give Abigail into the hands of the man who was waiting to become her husband.

Abigail liked the fact that there were no raw emotions intruding on the serenity of the occasion.

It was a beautiful day, a perfect day.

One of those rare London mornings where all the soot had settled with the morning dew and the sun shone out of a blue sky with picturesque clouds that a less pristine lady might mistake for a face with stark gray eyes or a cottage with a thatch roof or some other silly pipe dream, when really clouds were merely particles of dust and moisture marring the horizon.

Victoria opened the door and shooed out Mary and Elizabeth. Faint piano chords drifted into the bedchamber.

Abigail smiled at her sister's whispered instruction to lie back and think of England when her husband did his duty. Then her brother stepped through the doorway and took her gloved hand.

"This is an extremely important day for you, Abigail. Sir Tymes is a fine man; you will want for nothing. We trust that you will not do anything to disgrace our family name."

Abigail smiled.

Of course she would not do anything to disgrace the family name.

She was happy in her new life.

She wanted this marriage.

She wanted to be the Lady Abigail Tymes.

Abigail Wynfred had died three weeks and two days ago; it was time that she be buried.

Robert waited long minutes after the last carriage pulled away from the tall, narrow town house before mounting the cobblestone steps. Faint music penetrated the closed double doors.

He gained entrance by the simple maneuver of elbowing aside the butler when he opened the door in response to a brisk knock. Robert's scarlet dress uniform complete with a sword that was not ornamental prevented retaliation.

The butler clearly knew his duty; it was equally clear he was reluctant to carry it through. "May I help you, sir?"

"I am a friend of the groom's," Robert said grimly.

"I am afraid the wedding is for family members only, sir." The butler stared warily at Robert's dark-brown hair that was overlong and not pomaded, then at his tanned face that was shaved clean and spoke of climates and practices more barbaric than those belonging to England. "If you will give me the package, you can be assured that I will—"

Robert hoisted high the silk-and-ribbon-wrapped box. "I will deliver the package personally, thank you. Carry on with your duties. There's no need to show me the way."

His heels clicked along the length of the elegant black-and-white marble floor. He followed piano music and the low murmur of voices to a dark salon filled with vases of flowers and a ruffled grand piano. Rows of chairs were positioned so that an aisle led to a white marble fireplace. The chairs were occupied by overbustled women in subdued colors and too tightly collared men in funeral black with slicked-back hair tamed with grease and side-whiskers that bristled like wire brushes. A crow of a minister and a plump cherub of a man, both with the same pomaded hair and bushy side-whiskers, flanked the marble fireplace.

Robert had timed it perfectly. No sooner did he enter the room than a hush fell over the crowd of politely expectant faces and the pianist ended the recital in a soft crash of chords. He stepped aside at the sound of rustling silk.

Abigail.

She wore a dove-gray dress with a tent-size bustle and she had never looked worse, he was sure, he thought with a stab of vicious satisfaction. Her face was chalk white with dark circles underneath her eyes. The man leading her—her brother, the earl, no doubt—was the same height but at least fifty pounds heavier. He, too, had pomaded hair and side-whiskers.

Abigail's back was ramrod straight as she faced the minister to take her vows. The groom, Robert noted, had a fat bottom. And he was two inches shorter than the bride.

The minister's voice was a pompous drone. "Dearly beloved, we are gathered together here in the sight of God . . ."

Robert leaned against the wall and waited for his cue.

". . . Therefore if any man can shew any just cause, why they may not lawfully be joined together, let him now speak, or else hereafter forever hold his peace."

Robert stepped away from the wall into the aisle. "I have just cause."

The slender back underneath the dove-gray silk grew even more stiff; suddenly Abigail pivoted, caught on the train of her gown. She floundered for a second before catching her balance.

Brown eyes were snared by pewter gray.

If it was possible, she turned even paler. Then bright crimson flooded her cheeks.

Shocked murmurs filled the dark room.

374 / *Robin Schone*

The minister lowered his spectacles. "I beg your pardon?"

"I said I have just cause to stop this wedding." He held up the beribboned silk package. "Twelve reasons, to be exact."

Abigail knew what was inside the pretty white-and-silver box. She had left behind her twelve issues of *The Pearl*.

The bright red color drained from her face. "Robert—"

It had been three weeks since he had heard her voice. Not one single person had used his christened name since she had left him.

He didn't want to hear her say *Robert* with that cold, polite ring of command. As if they had never been as close as it was possible for two people to be.

He wanted to hear his name husky with her passion. Or on a scream when she found release.

"Twelve reasons," he repeated. "If you can accept this gift, Abigail, and marry that man, then I will accept the fact that what meant more to me than life itself was nothing more to you than an *anomaly* caused by a storm. And I will heartily beg your pardon for this intrusion."

"Who is this man?" The groom raised a monocle and stared at Robert from an eye the size of a saucer.

Robert ignored him.

"On the other hand, Abigail, I have in my pocket two other gifts. One goes on the ring finger. The other gift is a favorite device of Lady Pokingham."

Shocked masculine gasps carried on the tide of feminine whispers—so-called respectable gentlemen who recognized the name taken from *The Pearl*. Robert could feel the male attention swivel from him toward Abigail, cold eyes no doubt filled with hot speculation.

Crimson color flared anew in Abigail's cheeks. Her head jerked back as if she had received a slap in the face.

"Sir." It was the butler's voice. "Sir, if you will follow me, please."

Robert's gaze did not waver. "And last but not least, Abigail, I have edition number thirteen."

Three footmen joined the butler. The silk-wrapped package slithered to the floor as Robert struggled to free himself.

Abigail silently watched.

Damn her. She wasn't going to accept either him . . . or his gift.

She stood there, pristine and remote like the lady she had confessed she wanted to become.

He should be content that he had accomplished one goal, at least.

Her secret was out.

Sir Andrew Tymes would not marry a woman whose name was whispered in the same breath as the name of a heroine out of *The Pearl*.

But Robert did not feel relief at saving Abigail from a lifetime of ruffled pianos.

For a searing second he hated her.

Hated her with all the passion in the soul that she had given back to him.

She had given him everything; *she was his.*

He had resigned from active duty . . . so that he might live. *With her.*

Fury gave Robert the strength of two men . . . but not the strength of three.

He refused to look away from Abigail's eyes, losing the battle, both with her and the footmen. He struggled to look back at her over his shoulder as they hustled him out of the funeral-dark salon. Then he struggled to stand up on the cobblestoned sidewalk as pain arched along the entire left side of his body and the sharp closure of the town house doors echoed through the street.

Damn.

He *would* land on his bum leg.

"Ye need 'elp, guv'nor? Cost ye a ha'pence."

Robert stared down at the three-foot-tall street urchin whose age could range anywhere from five to fifteen. A kaleidoscope of activity burst around him—horses trotting, carriage wheels rolling, a man hawking his wares—the vivid awareness that only comes before death.

"No," Robert said shortly. He pulled out a shilling and tossed it to the boy.

Hell, it didn't matter if he gave out all of his money.

Dead men didn't need it.

He dug into his pocket and pulled out everything he had on him.

The boy's too-old face lit up with greedy life. Before the military mort with the scary gray eyes could change his mind, the street urchin grabbed the money and ran.

Without warning, the door to the town house slammed open. As if in slow motion, Robert turned.

Abigail raced down the steps in a jiggle of silk and bustle. She carried in gloved hands the silk-wrapped package, her dreams, his life.

She was breathless. "You forgot your package, Colonel Coally."

Death did not harbor so much pain.

Neither should life, Robert thought bleakly.

"The package is for you, Lady Wynfred."

"That cannot be, Colonel Coally," she said briskly. "You offered me three gifts, not one."

"I am afraid I am at a loss, Lady Wynfred," he said stonily, imagining her with Sir Andrew Tymes, imagining him pistoning up and down—inside Abigail. "Does this mean you are rejecting or accepting the package?"

"It means, Colonel Coally, that I am accepting . . . all three gifts."

For the first time that day, Robert noticed how very warm the sunshine was and how clear the sky was when free of fog and soot.

"I take it you know what Lady Pokingham's favorite toy is."

Face flooding with bright color, Abigail reached out, lightly touched the front of his scarlet trousers with white-gloved fingers before hurriedly withdrawing her hand. "Oh, yes, Colonel Coally. I know what Lady Pokingham's favorite toy is."

"I am not a gentleman," he warned her stiffly. "Nor am I wealthy. Though I have enough to live in comfort."

"Colonel Coally." The brown eyes staring up at him glowed with amber. "What you have is far more important than wealth or a title."

"And what is that, Lady Wynfred?"

Robert held his breath, not daring to hope, afraid he could not bear the pain if she rejected him now.

A curse rang out on the street—a coachman soothed the lead horse that a lady's parasol had frightened.

Abigail smiled, the smile he had come to love, wild and free as the storm. *"The Pearl,* Colonel Coally."

"Do you take me, Abigail?" The sound issuing from his throat was stark and raw.

"I take you, Robert."

Suddenly the streets of London disappeared and there were only the two of them, a man and a woman.

Laughing, oblivious of the curious, shocked stares, Robert picked Abigail up and swung her over his head. "You are quite wrong, Miss Abigail. Lady Pokingham has another favorite toy, one that can be gift-wrapped without requiring amputation. But you can only have it after we are married. And if I insert it."